Ghosts in the Attic

She looked into his dark, intense eyes, wanting to resist him . . . yet taste him again . . . Tiny pearls of heat seemed to roll through her veins at the expert touch of his full, soft lips. Her entire body tingled with fire and life at his nearness . . .

Yes, it seemed magical . . . But Tori realized that there was something else extraordinary here: the air. It had been still and warm . . . though now, as Bruce kissed her, Tori felt a draft . . .

He turned to her with a finger to his lips. "Listen."

Sure, plodding feet were pacing above them, the boards creaking with each step . . .

Someone was in the attic. Or some*thing* . . .

ETERNAL
VOWS

ALICE ALFONSI

J

JOVE BOOKS, NEW YORK

ETERNAL VOWS

A Jove Book/ published by arrangement with
the author

PRINTING HISTORY
Jove edition / January 1997

The Putnam Berkley World Wide Web site address is
http://www.berkley.com/berkley

ISBN: 0-515-12002-2

A JOVE BOOK®
Jove Books are published by The Berkley Publishing Group,
200 Madison Avenue, New York, New York 10016.
JOVE and the "J" design are trademarks
belonging to Jove Publications, Inc.

PRINTED IN THE UNITED STATES OF AMERICA

10 9 8 7 6 5 4 3 2 1

For my mother,
Rose Capaccio Alfonsi,
I know you're up there watching, Mom.
I just know you are.

Acknowledgments

My heartfelt thanks to a wonderful agent, Alice Orr, for believing in me, and a brilliant editor, Gail Fortune, for believing in this book—and coming up with its great title!

There are plenty of ghosts in New Orleans, but the city's true spirit is maintained by a great deal of special people. They should be commended for their hard work in preserving the history of one of America's most unique cities. My sincerest appreciation for assistance in research goes out to the kind folks at Friends of the Cabildo, Vieux Carré Commission, Historic New Orleans Collection, and New Orleans Historic Voodoo Museum. If there are any errors in this book, they are entirely my own.

Finally a big thank you to my family for their unfailing support, and a big kiss to Marc Cerasini, a writer whose excellent advice has made him my muse as well as my love.

—and if God choose,
I shall but love thee better after death.

—Elizabeth Barrett Browning
Sonnets from the Portuguese

Prologue

It was midnight, and the drums were beating near Congo Square. As the incessant, driving rhythms filled the sultry Louisiana air with primal yearnings, a beautiful young bride restlessly awaited her groom's return.

In the master bedroom of a newly built Victorian mansion, the young woman closeted her silk and lace gown, her thick veil, and her pearl-encrusted headpiece. As she removed her stockings, she found herself entranced by the pulsing sounds in the nearby park.

Marina wondered how many other lovers were out there this night, entwined upon feather mattresses, lured beneath the gauzy cloud of mosquito netting by the seductive primal call of the *Vo-du* drums.

A flash of glimmering green caught her eye, and she paused to admire the exquisite emerald-encrusted band on her finger. She slanted her left hand, charmed by the sparkle of the faceted jewels in the candlelight.

"Your magnificent eyes," her love had whispered at the altar only a few hours ago, "they were my inspiration. . . ."

He had designed the ring, just as he'd designed this large splendid house. She laughed as she began pulling off the rest of her underthings. What joy she felt this night. Her Robert, as gifted an artisan as he was a lover, had at long last become her bridegroom.

Passing by the full-length mirror on the door of the bedroom's mahogany and rosewood armoire, Marina glimpsed her reflection and stopped. For a long moment, she observed her naked form.

Outside, the beat continued. The primitive rhythm seeped into her body, and throbbed in her veins. Slowly she lifted her hands to shamelessly cup her bare breasts. With a restless sigh she closed her eyes, happy in the knowledge that her strong, handsome husband would soon be here to take whatever pleasure he desired from them.

A smile graced her wide mouth and very full lips—the only hint of her true heritage, the only sign that her blood was not all lily-white, but mixed with the inheritance of a darker lineage and the ancestry of a great spiritual people. Perhaps that was why the beating drums in the nearby park did not frighten her as they did so many others. It often amazed her how residents and new visitors to this bustling port would grow pale merely at the strangeness of another people's ways.

By the light of ten flickering candles, Marina reached up and unpinned her hair. Curling tresses cascaded past her shoulders and waist, blanketing her soft skin in deep auburn color. *Yes,* she thought, her gaze taking in the reflection of ivory skin and flaring hips, perhaps she *was* of value—something worth bartering.

Despite that rich bastard's ugly scene at her wedding celebration, despite his terrible insults and threatening words, Marina gloried in the knowledge that the "bargain" her late father had made with that vile man no longer mattered.

No one can take me from my love now. No one.

Too restless to lie on the intricately carved four-poster bed, the bride paced the room. Pushing open the French doors, she stepped barefoot onto the master bedroom's gallery. The night air was cloying, drenched with the thick, sweet scent of magnolia blossoms and her favorite flower—white roses. She inhaled deeply, recalling the day her love had planted them. Dozens of white rosebushes now graced the garden of this newly built house—now *their* garden and house.

No. Their *home*, she corrected.

It would be a *home*, filled with great love, as well as great passion.

Leaning against the gallery rail, she found herself wondering how many times in the past weeks she had stood on this very spot. How many times had she crept from her late father's house on Esplanade Avenue to come here? How many times had she searched this shadowy street in the Quarter, waiting for her love to turn the corner and look up, his intense expression filled with barely contained need.

She wished he had not left her, even for this short half hour. But he'd insisted that she open his wedding gift to her. It was a surprise. All she knew was that he'd commissioned an artisan friend to make it for their new home.

She looked down now toward the street corner, but dense fog had enveloped the port of New Orleans, and nothing but the faint, yellow halos of the city's streetlamps could burn through it.

No matter. Marina welcomed the dark, ethereal blanket. Welcomed it as a misty curtain of privacy.

Her late father may have bartered her to another man. Bartered her like a horse, or a sack of grain, or a *slave*, she thought with controlled fury. But the days of slavery in this country were done and over. Now no one could deny her and her love what they had rightfully claimed.

Tonight, behind this thick curtain of mist, inside this pounding circle of drums, they would consummate their marital vows and protect the power of their love forever.

Suddenly a noise came from inside, and Marina turned to see the master bedroom's door opening. *Finally* he was here.

Robert stood stock-still, clearly taking pleasure in the sight of his young bride. In the candlelight her rich auburn curls seemed to shimmer like gold. Her curving, naked figure was framed by the balcony doorway, and against the backdrop of the dark fog, she appeared to be the breathing embodiment of a great painter's finest work.

But she was more than a mere artist's image. Tonight, with each step closer to the edge of that frame, this woman became more and more real to him.

Marina, in turn, surveyed the awe in Robert's expression—the reverence and love. She watched as it quickly turned to desire and need; watched as he set the large wrapped wedding gift upon a nearby silk-covered chair, flung the hat from his blond head, and slipped off his black cutaway. With quick, efficient movements, he pulled off his white bow tie and removed his trim waistcoat. As he unbuttoned his shirt, he began to walk toward her in measured, determined steps, the wedding gift momentarily forgotten.

With the sculpted, smooth muscles of his chest bared, he flung away his shirt and the rest of his clothing. Then he stood by the bed, magnificent and proud in his nakedness—and more aroused than she had ever seen him.

"My bride," he whispered, "let me touch you . . ."

Marina's breathing became labored as her bare toes moved forward. She felt the roughness of the balcony's planks give away to the polished cypress of the bedroom's floor.

Robert watched as she moved beyond the door's wooden border, with each step confirming to him finally that *yes*, she was more than the semblance of a work of art.

She was real. She was here. And she was his.

She had stepped beyond the frame to become a warm, breathing reality in his life.

As Marina moved toward Robert, she found herself poignantly aware of the many moments that they had already shared. The many moments of their past. She was more than ready for the countless moments of their future. Enjoying love, raising children, growing old—the future's promise stretched out before them like a long, soft carpet. All she had to do now was take the first step.

With the sound of the pounding *Vo-du* drums echoing in the distance, Marina took it—and found herself in Robert's arms. Immediately she felt his strength and love completely envelop her, like the thick mist blanketing the city.

"You're home now...." Marina whispered.

"*Our* home now," Robert answered, his eyes shining with pleasure. Then his head lowered, and his mouth claimed hers in a kiss that promised a lifetime and beyond. Past, present, and future—they were three points of a circle that surrounded them now, a circle of love that could never be broken.

This was a vow.

They knew it more than in their minds or flesh, but in their spirits. And as she returned his kiss in kind, they barely noticed the smashing, violent noises from one floor below, the voices and the heavy footsteps on the stairs.

"In here!"

They barely heard the growing sounds of disaster, the crash of the master bedroom door, the cocking of a weapon.

They barely comprehended the glare of a gas lantern flame, the long gray barrels of the shotgun, or the shards of jagged metal exploding toward them, ripping into their bodies.

It was in that instant that a shattering scream of blood and terror ascended through the night fog, a terrible testimony to the violent act that would brutally slaughter a destiny.

The cry traveled into the night and up to the heavens,

and for a long, full minute—as if the beating drums had heard their heartrending wail—all sounds stopped.

Across the shadows and fog of the port city, thousands of listening lovers suddenly stopped with them, chilled to the bone by the deadly silence.

Until the drums began again.

Chapter
One

NEW ORLEANS, FRENCH QUARTER
ONE HUNDRED YEARS LATER

Tori Avalon slammed the door of her compact blue rental car and started toward the old mansion. After plucking at the peach silk blouse that clung annoyingly to her damp, sticky skin, her slender, manicured fingers moved to push the auburn bangs off her forehead.

Tori swore she'd sell her soul in a minute for a good stiff breeze off the Mississippi. She had come here straight from the airport, leaving a temperate New York May for the heart of this sweltering hothouse. It had been a long time since she'd been in Louisiana, and Tori had simply forgotten how oppressive the Delta's humidity could be.

Licking her dry lips, she could almost taste a sip of that cool, mint iced tea—the kind Aunt Hestia used to brew in a jar on the porch of this very house. Tori smiled at the memory of those days years ago when her aunt took a young niece by the hand and showed her how to step with care through the herb garden to pick the tender sprigs of fresh mint.

It seemed to Tori that Aunt Hesti would be around forever, growing fresh herbs in her garden and conjuring up Creole gumbo, pecan pralines, and café au lait for guests. But Hesti herself hadn't even resided here for ten years, and now Tori's aunt was gone from this life, leaving Tori the fourteen-room guest house before her—a large Victorian relic that had once seemed like a grand palace to a shy little Northern girl.

Tori's smile at past memories soon disappeared with the onset of the gloomy realities that faced her now. Weeds and tangled vines obscured the stone path as she approached the mansion. Thorns scratched at her legs, pricking her silk stockings and deflating her spirits. Even the scent of lilacs in full bloom could not soften the sight of the unkempt and overgrown state of the house's surrounding grounds.

She stopped at the old cast-iron fence—the very feature that had supplied this house's name. The clever pattern in the grill gave the impression of budding roses on the vine, but it was now far from the beautiful ornament she recalled.

Streaked with ugly grime, the filigreed fence was in need of repair in many places, starting with the gate, which now hung by a single twisted hinge. Tori stared at it glumly, deciding it compared with her own life—unstable and precariously dangling on a tenuous prop. The metal groaned as she pushed it out of her way and stepped gingerly over the thorns of an overgrown bush, unhappily barren of a single flower.

Finally she could get a better look at the house itself. But it didn't help. Like a stone vanishing under the waves of the muddy Mississippi, Tori's heart sank with the realization of what sat before her. It was Blanche Dubois in the last act of *Streetcar*—a grand belle tragically reduced to an old woman, her once-prized beauty ravaged by the hardships of years passing, her haughty dignity cruelly stripped from her by careless handling.

There was no getting around it. The once-elegant Rosegate Mansion Guest House bore the scars of too many years of conscious neglect.

Aunt Hestia had hired a management company to run the guest house for the last decade. Clearly they'd done a terrible job with the upkeep, but on top of that, the house had been completely empty for over a year.

Still, like Blanche, there was some fleeting shadow of grandeur left in her, the notion of how truly majestic she once had been . . . and perhaps, still could be again.

Tori's gaze scanned the exterior, evaluating the damage. Someone had haphazardly painted over the carefully conceived gingerbread color scheme that Hesti had always scrupulously maintained. In place of the distinctive hues that highlighted the elaborate brackets, balustrades, and moldings, the beautifully carved woodwork had been unceremoniously washed with a single unimaginative shade of an already chipped and peeling yellow paint.

The spacious, wraparound porch was sagging, several shutters hung as precariously as the cast-iron fence's gate, and some of the gutters were broken. The turret still stood erect, though one of its windows was shattered and a dirty-white lace curtain hung limply within its frame. She could only imagine the state of the flower and herb garden in back.

Overwhelmed by it all, Tori turned toward the street to look for any sign of Aunt Zoe. She definitely needed some moral support.

But there was no sign of her. Except for one passing sedan, the only other vehicle in sight on this quiet block, besides her rental, was a parked car she didn't recognize—one of those flashy red sports jobs, the kind some men drove because they'd decided somewhere along the line that it would impress the opposite sex. A supposed "woman trap" on wheels, thought Tori with mild disdain as she anxiously patted the back of her French twist. It had been neat earlier in the day, but now she could feel locks of hair loosening, and it bothered her.

Perhaps Aunt Zoe had run into some last-minute business at the restaurant. Tori dug through her purse for the keys to the front door, but paused the moment her fingers touched the metal. If the exterior was any indication, the house's interior was going to be a horror show. She just couldn't face that alone.

Securing her tan leather Coach bag on her shoulder, she took a fortifying breath of damp, lilac-scented air and moved briskly toward the rear of the property. But after she turned the corner of the house, Tori found herself stopping dead in her tracks. The condition of the garden was suddenly forgotten with the sight that now met her eyes.

A man was here . . . just off her back porch.

His skimpy white tank shirt revealed layers of well-defined arm and shoulder muscles as he crouched near the basement window of Aunt Hesti's house. As the man reached down to pull back some weeds, Tori was reminded of a series of pen-and-inks she'd seen at a New York gallery, a simple study of the male form.

But this was no drawing. These sculpted muscles moving fluidly across a sun-bronzed back were very much alive, and Tori Avalon was forced to admit she'd actually paused to appreciate a living man's body.

In another few moments Tori would ask herself what this man was doing here. But for now her usual internal litany of queries and concerns was silenced, and something else within her was observing and absorbing. Something else had taken control of her very being.

Since her one, disastrous experience with the opposite sex, Tori had avoided letting any man get closer than an occasional lunch date. And she hadn't missed it . . .

Until now.

She watched the sun glimmer off the damp moisture on this man's powerful bare shoulders as he struggled to pull a particularly stubborn clump of onion grass away from the small window's edge.

She tried to blink away her body's immediate response. Tried to tell herself that her time among the pale executives and tailored business suits of New York City had clouded her memory of a working man's body. Even tried to pretend it was the heat, or the humidity, or the jet lag . . .

She tried . . . but failed.

It had been so long—too long. And the natural attraction of woman to man echoed through her like a cry into an empty canyon.

Taking another deep breath, Tori finally forced her left brain to come up with some logical questions, like . . . *Who is this man?* and *Why is he here?*

From his worn olive-green pants and tan work boots, she judged that he was some sort of manual laborer. But the house was clearly abandoned, so it was likely that he was here scavenging for fixtures, or even valuable antiques.

Could he be dangerous?

That thought made sudden sense to Tori. She decided that she should just turn quietly, go back to her car, and wait for Aunt Zoe. After all, she was alone, and within walking distance of the seamier parts of this town.

Others might think the heart of the French Quarter quaint—a place filled with colorful characters and the sound of jazz—but Tori knew that it harbored a darker side as well. She was not comfortable with the crowds, the decadence, and the crime that frequented the Quarter. This man could be a thief, her left brain counseled. *Or worse.*

Immediately Tori turned to go. But after a few steps she stopped herself. Her right brain seemed to have something to say in this matter, too, as anger began to replace the dull fear. After all, this was *her* house now, and if anyone should leave, *he* should.

Wheeling on the heel of her tasteful leather pump, Tori strode purposefully toward the stranger and addressed him in a tone she prayed sounded commanding.

"Excuse me . . ."

Those two words were the only sound for two long minutes. Once they were said, the man did not rise right away from his stooped position. Instead, he merely turned his head. His sun-streaked, dark blond hair shaded his brow, and when Tori tried to meet his eyes, her own doubled reflection greeted her in the mirrored surfaces of his sunglasses.

For a long moment the man's head moved slowly up Tori's form as he clearly took his time surveying the object in front of him. She in turn tried to remain coolly aloof, a state that quickly left her when he finally rose from his crouched position to reveal his full height and breadth.

As the broad back revolved to reveal a powerful chest, its layers of hard-earned muscles clearly defined under the thin material of his white tank, Tori knew this was not the kind of artificially sculpted body produced by an upscale city health club. This man's form gave the impression of being built through strenuous labor—and, for some reason, that fact made him all the more intimidating.

Leaning back, the intruder studied Tori's face. With painstaking economy of motion, he folded his strong forearms across his chest.

Tori sighed. *Obviously, this guy is used to taking all the time in the world to do anything.* Then her eyes caught sight of a small blue anchor tattooed to his well-defined bicep, and she suddenly decided that he was standing much too close.

She considered backing up a step or two, but stopped herself. With this one, Tori got the idea that she should most definitely stand her ground.

"May I ask what you are doing here?" she finally asked again, impatient with his silent stare-off. She was still trying to sound commanding, but she feared her tone came off as nothing more than curt.

An arrogant smile slashed across the stranger's full lips. "*May* you ask?" he said in a low Cajun drawl. "Well, now, I can't t'ink of a reason why not, me. Go on right ahead."

Wit? Tori was taken aback. Wit was *not* what she expected from a man like this. Clinging tightly to the shoulderstrap of her expensive handbag, she spoke again, a bit more bluntly this time.

"*What* are you doing here?"

"S'pposin' I might ask you dat same quest-ion."

Tori wiped her damp palm on her white linen skirt, immediately regretting the move. His attention was obviously drawn to her long legs, clad in the sheerest peach silk, and she tried again to keep the mounting nervousness out of her voice.

"I have business here," she said.

"Dat so? Well, now, so do I."

"You don't understand—" She stopped herself, annoyance at his aloof attitude slowly overtaking her apprehension. She wasn't about to explain herself to this trespasser. On the other hand, she couldn't quite bring herself to demand he leave her property. After all, what was she going to do about it? Eject him bodily from the premises? Another glance at his powerful frame ruled the very idea ludicrous.

Maybe, just maybe, counseled her left brain, she should just *ask nicely.* "Sir, I think you should leave at once."

"Do ya now?" He paused a moment. "And do y'know, *chère,* what I t'ink?"

Tori glared at him in response, but he stood unaffected, remaining as cool as dew frost, even on this sweltering day.

"I t'ink," he drawled, "you in ovah your *joli* red head."

"Do you want me to call the police?"

"*Bon Dieu*—" Vianney Bruce Gautreau smiled weakly at this Northern princess. She gave off as icy a blast as he'd ever felt in his navy days, sailing the North Atlantic. On the other hand, those long legs, and that sweetly curving form, now *they* were enough to warm a man. Bruce figured it was worth the trade-off.

"*Chère*, I s-u-u-re do hope you got a sell-you-lore phone in your auto, 'cause you won't be finding no working line in dis old girl." He tilted his head toward the house, his smile widening.

Bruce knew he could put the princess at ease with a short

explanation, but the devil inside him thought otherwise. Her Highness had simply assumed him to be some kind of French Quarter riffraff, and it rankled him. He figured he'd put her on a bit—exaggerate his Cajun drawl and his old bayou manner.

It just wan't in Bruce's nature to let anyone get off easily. Besides, he figured he could teach this Yankee princess a thing or two about the way folks did things down here.

Tori glared at the stranger. The man had turned her threat of police involvement into a joke. It made Tori's blood steam, and every bit of her nervous anxiety was quickly dissolving in the heat of her anger. *Who does this cocky bayou bonehead think he is, anyway?!*

Bruce read the thought loud and clear, and his ire flared a beat behind hers. Then he saw that she was beginning to speak again, but it was simply another threat, so he ignored her. Instead he turned sharply and continued to walk toward the house's back porch.

His special ability—"the talent," as his French Creole *maman* had called it—was sometimes a curse, sometimes a blessing, and it wasn't always there for him. Right now, Bruce liked the fact that he could read this attractive woman like a builder's blueprint. It gave him the advantage in this little game.

"Excuse me!" she fairly shouted.

He turned toward her. "*Quoi?* You still here?" he drawled, trying to suppress his satisfaction at Her Highness's indignation.

"Yes!" she pronounced. "And I'm not leaving. *You* are. This is *my* property, and you have no business being on it."

He stopped at that. *Her* property. That wasn't what he'd read in her; he'd read that it belonged to her aunt. It seemed the little lady had some tricks in her bag after all.

Tori stood her ground as the stranger closely surveyed her once more. She still could not see his eyes through his mirrored sunglass lenses, yet she felt like the house itself: She was being looked up and down in a frank appraisal.

Suddenly Tori felt vulnerable, as if her peach blouse was

too sheer and her white skirt too short. She certainly wasn't comfortable with the intense interest now evident on his features.

"Me, I t'ink you lost, *non?*" he said, throwing out some bait. The tone of his low drawl now carried a threatening edge. "De woman who own dis house—I know her. And she not you."

"You knew Hestia Arnaud?"

"Who?"

"That's what I thought," snapped Tori. "You're lying. I don't know why, and I don't know what you want here, but I've inherited this house, and my aunt, Zoe Duchamp, is due here any minute, so you better leave. *Now.*"

Tori watched the man survey her a moment. His eyebrow rose in thought, or maybe at the mention of Zoe's name, decided Tori. After all, Duchamp's was now recognized as one of New Orleans' top restaurants.

Now he'll leave, assured Tori's left brain.

But he didn't.

Uncrossing his large forearms, Bruce turned from Tori and again started for the house.

"Hey! Didn't you hear me?"

"I hear you, *chère*," he drawled, the rickety wooden steps groaning as he climbed them, "but I t'ink you in need of something tall, cool, and sweetly alcoholic to cool your *chaud* head."

"*Where* are you going *now?*" she asked, following close behind him. She was so intent on preventing him from entering the house that she nearly crashed into him when he stopped suddenly on the spacious wooden porch.

He'd paused to examine something on the floor. Following the path of his gaze, Tori saw a weird assortment of items. They sat collected inside a crude chalk circle drawn onto the porch floorboards.

Three pink candles had been burnt down, their pastel wax already settled into hard puddles. Beside them sat a few ornate perfume bottles, a box of sugar lumps—which a family of ants had already laid claim to—and a crosshatch marking of some sort.

Tori watched the stranger take off his sunglasses, and for the first time she noticed the details of his face. His jaw was strong and square, his lips full, and his features were rugged, yet still held a boyish appeal. Though she hated to admit it, this was an exceedingly handsome man.

"*Vo-du,*" murmured Bruce, the sight of it bringing back the memories of his childhood.

"What?" she asked, noticing his eyes as he turned more fully toward her.

The man's hair was golden, so Tori expected his eyes to be light colored—a shade of blue or green. But this man's eyes were dark brown, the color of the richest earth or the most splendid mahogany. Though she was still trying to resist such observations, Tori had to admit that the shining depth of obvious intelligence in his gaze was perilously attractive to her.

She took a half-step backward with that thought, her eyes dragging themselves away from his handsome face and fixing on the strange tableaux before them. When he spoke again, his voice almost made her jump.

"*Vo-du,*" Bruce repeated. He folded his sunglasses and casually hooked one leg of the frame over the neck of his white tank undershirt. He could read in this woman that she did not readily recognize—or wish to recognize—the idea of Voodoo. He could also quite strongly feel her impressions of him. *She wants me,* thought Bruce. *Well, well, well. I guess Her Highness isn't beyond slumming when it comes to primal urges.*

Bending low, Bruce reached one callused hand down and rubbed away some of the crudely drawn chalk circle.

"*Vo-du,*" he said. "Just another way o' sayin' Voodoo." His dark eyes met her green ones.

"What? I don't understand . . ." Her voice trailed off as she recalled her days as a girl growing up in the care of Aunt Hestia and Uncle Richard. Tori remembered furtive conversations between her aunt and uncle; talk of charms and spells and . . . Voodoo. A shiver ran through her, despite the day's oppressive heat.

Tori knew that Voodoo practices were a historical part of New Orleans, but the whole idea seemed far away from the quiet, ordered life in the Arnaud household.

"I know you a stranger to New Or-lee-anh," drawled Bruce, "but you got to heard of Voodoo."

"Of course I've *heard* of it, but what I don't understand is *this*," she said, pointing to the floorboards.

Picking up one of the small bottles, Bruce rose and moved a few steps closer. He watched as the woman's gaze again surveyed his powerfully sculpted torso and the rugged contours of his handsome features. Bruce felt the waves of physical attraction flowing from her, and he drank it in like an intoxicating beverage.

Tori didn't know what was happening—other than this man had stepped much too close, and she could not seem to step away. Whether it was her own curiosity about this Voodoo on her porch, or the dark eyes that suddenly caught and held hers, she honestly couldn't say.

Reaching up, the man held the elaborate glass container under Tori's nose, and she detected the faint yet unmistakable scent of citrus.

"Orange blossom water . . ." he said. His voice was low, smooth, and provocative, and Tori felt the air around them growing as thick with seduction as with the heavy Louisiana humidity.

"Mix it up with some of dat rosewater and a *petite* spoon o'honey," he continued, moving yet closer. Tori inhaled to clear her head, but a mixture of dizzying scents assailed her. The orange blossom water and the garden's cloying bouquet of lilac and azaleas had mingled with the earthy scent of the man's skin.

His right arm rose casually above her head as he leaned against a tall corner post, trapping her close to the faded wooden porch rail.

"Why would someone want to do that?" she asked, her voice a bit shaky.

"Dat where de sugah come in. Dis a love conjure. You write de name of de person you desire on lumps of sugah, den you burn de sugah with pink candles in de scented mix for nine days. De man use it to draw de woman he desire into his bed."

"You mean like . . . a spell?"

"Mmmm. It work both ways, too. A woman might use it for de same *raison*. Say, if she saw a man she wanted . . . " Tori noticed that he had quieted his deep voice, using a lazy drawl to cast his own spell of subtle intimacy between them.

She watched the edges of his mouth twitch into a slight smile. He was leaning so close that she could feel the heat of his breath near her cheek; and, for a fleeting moment, Tori felt part of her wonder what his lips would feel like.

Tori, what in the hell are you doing?! sounded a voice within her. *Get a hold of yourself!*

Quickly Tori slipped around the man to stand on the far side of the porch.

"So, ah, you're telling me that people have been, ah, casting *love* spells . . . on this porch?" Tori managed, trying to clear her head and get hold of her senses. "On *my* porch?"

Bruce tried not to laugh out loud. He was certainly winning this game, and he was enjoying it. Why, he'd reeled her in so far, she'd almost let him kiss her. But there was all the time in the world for that, he decided, a confident smile touching his lips. *No need to rush things.*

Fingering the ornate bottle, Bruce casually raised it to his nose. His eyes returned to the young woman again, gently scanning her figure, and then caressing her face.

"*Oui, chère*, Voodoo on *your* porch," drawled Bruce. "Love spells've been cast and likely many others. You see dat crosshatch marking?"

Tori's gaze found the strange black marking near the circle.

"Dat's likely de specialized mark of a certain pract'-

tioner. Dis house look abandoned. Me, I 'spect many a conjure been practiced here for some time."

Tori's eyes widened. "You mean someone set up some
sort of Voodoo *clinic*? On *my* porch?"

Tori watched the stranger shrug. Then she shook her
head in despair. "I remember talk of Voodoo when I was a
little girl, but it was nowhere near this house—"

"One t'ing you can count on in life, *chère*. T'ings always
change—"

Tori heard something in the distance, like thunder. It was
then she realized the sky was growing a bit overcast and the
air's thick humidity was starting to smell of oncoming rain.

"—and dey always stay de same," he continued. "We not
far from Louis Armstrong Park. Dey called it Congo
Square years back. Open Voodoo went on for years. Folks
danced to drums, performed dair rit'als—it was even outlawed for a time. But it never did stop dem believers, *non*.
Folks carry it on today, sometime at night. You'll be hearing drums on occasion. But maybe you better stay clear o'
dem—"

"It's *that* dangerous?" Tori's gaze fell. She had wanted
to return this place to its former glory and open it as a
Guest House again. But she hadn't imagined how much
work it would need. And *now* she was being told the area
was some kind of a ritualistic danger zone.

"Oh, now, sweet, I didn't say it was *dangerous*. I just
meant dat people ought to stay away from t'ings dey don't
understand. It unnerves dem. Don't bring harm, just fear."

Another low rumble of thunder sounded in the distance.

"But you're not scared of it," stated Tori.

"Oh, n-o-o-o. Listen here, people of New Or-lee-anh
have a kind of fill-oz-o-free: Live and let live. You see a
lotta t'ings in de Quarter, not just Voodoo. Visitors come
here to let off steam, *compris?*, let some of their primitive
side loose. Don't hurt anythin'. Of course, some folks don't
understand dat." Bruce shrugged his wide shoulders, looking off into the rear grounds. "Same with Voodoo."

"But I intend to live here," explained Tori.

The man nodded his head. "And once you do, the Voodoo folks'll go elsewhere. They'll find another place. 'Course, no telling what manner of spirits been released here already."

"Spirits?"

A hot breeze wafted across the porch, kissing Tori's cheek. Again she sensed the heaviness in the air shifting, the pressure change, the smell of rain.

"African animism," said the stranger, waiting again for her comprehension.

At Tori's wrinkled brow, he sighed. "*Vo-du* has roots in African animism. Pract'tioners believe dat spirits live in de trees, de rocks, in everyt'ing, even dis here house."

The man slowly wiped the back of his hand across his damp brow and tilted his face toward another current of warm air. "Dey believe we share spirit space with de ghosts of ancestors dearly departed. Some spells release spirits, some spells trap dem . . . "

"Who *are* you?"

He smiled broadly. "Why, Vianney Bruce Gautreau, *chère.*"

Tori's eyebrows rose. Although Tori didn't recognize the name, she couldn't believe how easily he had volunteered it to her after being so cagey about what he was doing here. Thunder again rolled in from the river, this time bringing with it a sheet of warm, heavy rain.

"Why wouldn't you tell me your name before?" asked Tori.

"You never did ask my name . . . did you now?"

A gust of strong wind suddenly whipped through the porch, a spray of water riding in with it. Tori felt the warm moisture sweep across her legs as heavy drops hit her silk blouse. Bruce moved toward her. His large calloused hand grabbed her soft, slender one, and he tugged gently. Moving to the back door, he tried the knob.

"You got a key in dat bag."

Tori thought it was strange that he'd stated this to her as if he *absolutely* knew that she possessed one.

"Only for the front door," she replied hesitantly.

He quickly stepped to the left of the locked door and tried to open the large, head-high window. But it was boarded up from the inside.

He took her hand again and pulled her down a few more windows, where he found one that was not blocked. He put both hands underneath the lower panel's frame and pushed, grunting with the effort. There was a sharp scrape of wood against wood as the protesting panel slid upward.

Another roll of thunder shook the clouds, and they released the storm's full fury. Rain lashed the porch, soaking them as they quickly crossed the threshold.

Then together, they entered the murky darkness of the century-old Victorian house.

Chapter Two

Energy.

Life energy.

It was like air to her—that is, when she had needed air.

Marina remembered breathing it. Vaguely remembered. It was coming back to her now, gradually.

Breathing had been a part of life. But not just any part. It had been an intricate part. A vital and necessary act, magically performed by the body in sleep, without thought or effort. It was slow and steady at peaceful rest. It was labored and rapid in fright . . . or arousal. And it was a part of life that Marina had never given a moment's thought to.

Oh, perhaps, she had considered it fleetingly—when it had been abruptly stopped by a sip of wine down the wrong pipe. But Marina had never really been aware of how distinctly and precisely breathing had been a part of being alive.

Yes. *Being* alive.

The concept of it came back to her spottily, like the words to a poem once securely fixed in memory, then somehow . . . lost.

From the floor below Marina, small wisps of precious energy began to waft upward, and she felt them slowly seeping into her.

Yes, she decided, whatever this energy provided for her, it *was* like breathing—that sense of being filled, nourished with something she needed desperately.

Still, Marina knew that what she had needed desperately in her life had not so much been air as . . . well, as something else . . .

Robert.

The name came to her with a hundred images and ideas, a thousand sensations and thoughts.

Robert.

She had loved him in life. And she loved him still. Even in this strange state of being . . . whatever it was. Not alive, she supposed. She did know that much.

Marina reached out with her awareness. She stretched it as far as she could—which wasn't very far in her weakened state—but she could not sense her Robert. She tried to remember something, anything, that would tell her where he was. But she had no idea.

For that matter, Marina wasn't entirely certain where *she* was. She could only be certain of one thing now. That precious life energy, crackling with warmth and strength.

It was moving somewhere below her, and she felt the powerful pull toward it, even as she began to become more aware of her surroundings.

The room she was in seemed to fade in and out, but gradually she was able to focus the precious little energy she had and make herself begin to materialize.

The sight that finally greeted her efforts to survey her surroundings made her cringe in repulsion. She recognized the *vague* appearance of the lovely new bedroom Robert had built and furnished for her. But this was clearly not it. This bedroom was a dingy, tattered wreck!

Upset and saddened, Marina stomped hard on the floor.

"Robert!" she tried to cry out in frustration. But she no longer had a voice.

Not knowing what else to do, Marina allowed herself to flicker back into the atmosphere and be pulled by the energy one floor below.

Fluidly she moved along, gliding through air molecules that appeared to her as billions of small colorful dots. It was as if she'd entered the landscape of that interesting painting of Robert's—the one he'd inherited from his father. Now what did he call that style? she asked herself. Impress-something or other . . . ?

Impressionism, she suddenly recalled. *Yes, that's right.* Marina remembered suggesting that he hang it in their bedroom.

Slowly more memories of life and being alive were coming back to Marina. All of them were the brightest and happiest moments, which meant that most of them included Robert, along with the splendid home he'd built for her.

Yet as Marina flowed through the rooms of what she recognized as Robert's house, she wanted to cry. Fading in and out were glimpses of the dingy walls, the broken furniture, the dull woodwork.

This is no longer the home that Robert built for our life together, thought Marina in despair.

What has happened to Robert's lovely home?

Marina would not, could not rest until she found out. . . .

"Looks like we're in de dining room," said Bruce Gautreau. The tall windows were covered with heavy drapes, making the room very dark in the overcast afternoon.

For the moment Tori was more concerned with peeling her wet silk blouse from her skin and brushing the raindrops from her damp white skirt than with her immediate surroundings.

While Bruce stepped farther inside the room, Tori's hand automatically went to the back of her French twist. It felt like chaos. Too many auburn strands had finally escaped their pins, so she reached back with a sigh and let her hair come down all the way. She shook loose the long, wavy locks, and it tumbled well past her shoulders. Her hair was thick, and she preferred to keep it neatly up off her neck, but there was little she could do about it now.

She looked up to find Bruce's eyes on her, once more seeming to appraise her. Yet again, she was too aware of his close and unnerving proximity. She noticed that he had shed his wet tank top and was now wringing the moisture out of it. When he finished, he draped the garment over a nearby chair and stepped closer.

There was nowhere for Tori to look now but at the expanse of bare, powerful muscles across the wide chest before her. The damp, curling chest hair, a shade darker than the sun-streaked blondish brown of his head, clung to his skin like ivy to a sturdy oak.

Tori's mouth was suddenly dry and she licked the few raindrops that had beaded on her upper lip. Sheets of water pelted the roof, pounding down in a strong, steady rhythm. It sounded to Tori like the pulsing beat of a drum, and she thought of the Voodoo drums Bruce had just spoken of.

Suddenly an ice-cold shiver slipped over her skin. It seemed to come out of nowhere on this hot day.

Tori chalked it up to her nerves—after all she was now supposedly entering a house with allegedly Voodoo-loosed "spirits." She'd much rather attribute the odd shiver to that than the idea that she was actually affected by the stranger's hard naked chest.

"Did ya hear dat?" asked Bruce, his gaze staring up at the ceiling and then off into the darkness of the house. He'd heard a sharp thud, as if someone had stomped on the floor above them.

"What? The rain?"

"*Non.*" Bruce held up a hand for quiet as he continued to stare and listen. But after a few moments, he seemed to relax and returned his attention to Tori.

She sighed. "If you're trying to scare me, you can rest

assured I'm no believer in . . . what you said. That *anim* thing."

"Animism," supplied Bruce, an eyebrow rising as he studied her with contained amusement. "No spirits for you den, *chère*? Just de concrete. De solid. De t'ing in front of you?"

It occurred to Tori that what was "in front" of her now was this man's bare chest. He must be making some sort of joke at her expense, thought Tori, swallowing uneasily. Then again, she *had* been looking.

Feeling her cheeks warm slightly, Tori forced herself to turn her head away. She focused her attention on the window they had come through.

The rain continued to beat down, and Tori glanced at the overgrown rear grounds, thirstily soaking up the afternoon shower. "I remember these downpours when I was growing up," murmured Tori, trying to change the subject. "As I recall, they don't last very long."

"No. It'll be clear in a quarter hour at de outside."

The man dug into the pocket of his olive work pants and pulled out an expensive gold lighter. He flicked it. The small flame helped dispel enough of the gloom for Tori to see that they were standing in the house's dining room.

He pointed to a fat old candle on the heavy, ornate sideboard. Tori brought it to him, and he touched his lighter against the aged wick. After a few moments, it finally sputtered and flared to life.

"T'anks," he said with a slight smile.

Tori nodded, her eyes shyly avoiding his. She was about to move to some of the tall windows and pull back the heavy drapes when the man's hand reached toward her to finger a soft auburn curl.

"*Belle femme*," he murmured.

Tori looked up and saw in the light of the single candle the raw attraction shining in his deep brown eyes. Like the flash of lightning that suddenly lit up the dark room, it startled her. She didn't know this man who'd just called her beautiful in the raw sound of Cajun French. She hadn't even known his name until a few minutes ago. Unease took over again, and she stepped away from him.

She retreated toward a window and quickly pulled back the drapes, hoping to flood more light into the room. But she had forgotten that heavy boards covered the glass, preventing even the dull light from the overcast sky to dispel the room's gloom.

Worriedly, she looked toward the open window they had come through and wondered whether or not to bolt—

"Don't panic, *chère*," said the man flatly. "Zoe Duchamp is a good friend. I'm not about to harm her niece."

Tori noticed immediately that the man's raw Cajun drawl was now lessened considerably. She rounded on him. The desire in his eyes was banked, but his gaze remained intense. "Zoe didn't say anything about a man being here."

"Don't know 'bout that. I just know she asked me to stop by and take a look at this ol' beauty."

"Why?"

"For an estimate on restoring her," he said. "Naturally I figured the place was hers."

"Why didn't you tell me this before?"

Suddenly he began to chuckle. Crossing his arms over his bare chest, he leaned back against the mantel of the fireplace. "*Chère*, how long's it been since you been south o' the Mason-Dixon line?"

Tori shook her head. "Except for a few trips to Florida, a long time, I suppose."

"Probably Disney World, huh? Well, it don't count. You came at me like a Yankee freight train. I didn't much like it, so I figured I'd tease you a bit. Besides, sweet, like I said, I didn't expect *you*, either—"

Suddenly Bruce stopped talking. Tori watched as his relaxed posture tensed and his eyes seemed to glaze over as if he were listening for something.

"What?" asked Tori.

For a silent moment Bruce waited for signs. There was an odd vibration in the air of the room—a strange unsettled feeling. It was similar to feelings that he'd pick up while working to restore other very old houses. And yet . . .

This feeling in *this* particular house was more powerful than any he'd ever known before. It was a bit unnerving—even for him.

"What is it?" Tori spoke again.

Bruce tilted his head, cocked an ear. "I'm not sure."

Here.
Here is the life energy, thought Marina.

After floating from room to room, she had finally found it.

She was hovering above it now, taking it in. Like food to a famished infant, it strengthened her. Like an inn fire to a chilled traveler, it warmed her.

Gradually Marina grew strong enough to begin focusing on the center of the energy.

There were *two* separate sources, she realized.

Marina could just make out two life-forms moving and, she deduced, speaking, though she could not "hear" as she had in life.

Perhaps it would take more strength for that to happen.

Perhaps I can find a way to communicate with them, she thought. *Perhaps they can help me find my Robert.*

"Well, what is it? Did you hear something?" asked Tori.

"No," said Bruce. "It was nothing."

"Fine. Getting back to our discussion, I'd just like to point out that regardless of whether you were expecting me to show up here or not, I don't think it was fair of you to play games with me that way. No, it wasn't fair at all. And another thing—"

"My-oh-my," interrupted Bruce with a mild smile. "You sure like to use a lot o' words."

Tori glared at him.

"Don't take this the wrong way now, but I never met a lady who was more in need of—"

"Don't you dare—"

"—a drink," he finished, flashing a lazy smile. "Listen, you wanna know what *else* I think?"

"Not if you paid me a million—"

"*I* think you forgot the first rule of the Southern belle, something that I'd expect, knowing and admiring your good Aunt Zoe the way I do, that she would have certainly taught you."

"I hardly think you're in a position to—"

"Don't you *know* the rule?"

"What rule?" snapped Tori.

"Flirtation, *chère*, is the means by which many ends are achieved."

Tori scoffed. "That's about *the* most ridiculous, outdated—"

"And a little bit o' charm will get you a long way."

Suddenly a sharp thump sounded in the next room.

"What the—" Tori's gaze quickly went toward the sound, but she could see nothing in the gloomy darkness.

"Shhhh," murmured Bruce, freezing in place.

Tori watched him and felt uneasy. His eyes again glazed over and his head was cocked.

Suddenly the candle flame began to flicker and then rise in intensity as an odd shiver brushed Tori's skin. But this time Tori recognized the chilly feeling as being *outside* of her body. It wasn't her own nervousness creating the sensation, as she'd thought before. It was actually a cold thin stream of air flowing through the room.

But what was a cold thin draft doing in a hot stuffy house? It made no sense to her.

In another few moments it was gone, and Tori noticed Bruce's body relax in the same instant.

"Is anyone there?" whispered Tori.

"No," said Bruce, not meeting her eyes.

"How can you be so sure?"

"I can."

Tori shrugged, assuming he knew something she didn't about old houses settling. "Well, anyway, Mr. Gau—?"

"Gautreau."

"Mr. Gautreau, that's right. As I said, I do apologize for being rude. But you should know at the outset that I cannot afford a professional. I'll be fixing up this place myself. And that's the way I want it."

Bruce pushed off the mantel and stepped closer to her, stopping within inches, then sliding his hands casually into his pockets. "You need me."

Tori was speechless for a moment. "I'm sure you *think* I do, but really, I'm determined to do the work on the house, and —"

"Have dinner with me tonight."

"What?"

"A man don't come across a *belle femme* like you without he try, at least, to buy her dinner." His Cajun drawl had suddenly thickened, along with the seductive charm in his eyes, which were now sparkling with mischievous amusement.

But Tori didn't care for his cocksure flirtation. And she was determined to show him that, despite the Southern "rule" he'd spouted, it was certainly *not* the means to an end where she was concerned. "Mr. Gautreau, I hardly know you. In fact, I *don't* know you."

Abruptly he turned from her, pulling a small silver cylinder from his pocket. She heard a click and a beam of light shot across the room. He ran it up the wall's corner and across the ceiling.

Tori nearly gasped when she saw the terrible state of the wallpaper and the cracks in the plaster above. She remembered the beautiful carved and stained woodwork of the doorframes and the chair rail around the room's perimeter. But someone had washed over the beautiful details with yet another unimaginative shade of yellow paint—just like the outside.

"You ever hear o' the *Vieux Carré* Commission?"

"No," said Tori cautiously, guessing that he was probably getting at something she probably wouldn't want to hear.

"The commission controls all the renovation in the Quar-

ter. All work on the exterior of the buildings has got to con-
form to the architectural style of the period they were built
in. I'd say this here ol' beauty, an unmistakable Queen
Anne style, was erected 'round about the turn of the century. The previous century, of course."

"What do you mean the commission *controls* all the
renovation?"

The cocky smile was back, at Tori's annoyance. "Well,
now, I'd be happy to tell you all about it. Over *dinner*."

"I don't look kindly on blackmail."

"Oh, now, *chère*, I wouldn't call it blackmail," teased
Bruce. "I prefer the term *extortion*. It's so much more . . .
sophisticated."

Suddenly the beam of his flashlight crossed something in
the room very familiar to Tori, and she cried out. "Look!"

"What?"

Tori moved toward Bruce. "May I borrow that?"

He presented the flashlight to her with a flourish, and she
immediately fixed the beam on a tall piece of furniture at
the other end of the room. She walked toward the heavy
built-in china case, almost mesmerized.

On top of the scarred and barren shelves, she could see
the edges of a small painted wooden horse. It was *Champlain,* the little horse her late mother had given her when
she was just a small child. Oh, how she'd loved that horse.
She hadn't realized it was still around.

Could it be the same one, after all these years and all the
different occupants renting the place? hoped Tori as she
stood before the heavy case.

She could see it was pushed too far back for her to reach.
But all she had to do was step on the lower shelf, then she
could surely pull it forward. She didn't even hear the sound
of Bruce Gautreau's warnings.

"*Chère*, get away from that—"

But it was too late. She'd barely put half her weight on
the lower shelf when the entire heavy case of shelves somehow pulled away from the wall and began to descend on
top of her. Suddenly she felt a rushing blow to her middle,

and then she was flying through the air and landing on the floor, just before she heard the terrible sound of the case's crashing down.

It was all over in a split second. Bruce had wrapped a powerful arm around her middle and pulled her to safety. But the sudden movement had thrown them both off balance and to the floor.

Now a heavy weight was pinning her down, but it wasn't the weight of the heavy shelves, which lay inches beside her. They could have crushed her and killed her, she realized with a moment of cold paralysis. What had her trapped was the sweet warm weight of life, and the body of the man who had saved hers.

Bruce moved, his arms shifting some of his weight from her, but not all of it.

"You okay?" he asked in a worried tone, his dark eyes studying her expression for evidence of pain.

"Y-y-yes . . ." she responded. "I'm fine."

"I'm glad," he whispered low, a wisp of his breath warming her cheek.

She watched in the flickering light of the single candle as the expression in his rich, brown eyes changed from concern to relief and then . . . to something else.

Tori was acutely aware of the press of his strong, bare chest against her soft, round breasts—her damp peach blouse and thin lace bra were a slim barrier between them.

Tori's left brain decided that his muscles were every bit as rock-hard as they had looked, but her right brain didn't much care. It simply basked in the feel of his body pressed against hers.

"You sure like doin' things your way," teased Bruce, his lips barely an inch from hers. He could see that she was nearly breathless with the closeness, and he had to admit, his own body was reacting to the softness underneath him.

"That's true, I do," whispered Tori.

"But it's not always the best way," he pointed out.

The energy.

It was glorious!

Marina had been hovering around and above the two life-forms below her, patiently attempting to sort out the puzzle of how to enter their world.

And then something had happened.

Like two small candle flames joining to inexplicably become a roaring inferno, the humans touched each other and created a dazzling source of shimmering, golden energy.

The radiance poured from the two humans, like a stream of liquid fire, and soon the entire room was filled. Everything was glowing. It was all so brilliant and clear! And that's when she knew he was there . . .

Robert.

He, too, was basking in the glowing light of the warm life fire, and she reached out to him. . . .

Robert sensed Marina's presence, but he could not connect with her. He tried, with every bit of what little energy he had. But he was trapped somehow. Helplessly isolated.

Marina too reached out, but she also found it impossible to connect with her love. She was just as trapped, just as helplessly isolated.

Was there no way to touch him? thought Marina, beginning to panic. Was there no way to kiss him, to hold him again?

Even in the joy of this roaring fire of life energy, Marina felt a terrible anguish.

"The lovers . . . "

Marina heard the words. Although she no longer had ears, she recognized it as Robert's voice. *"The lovers,"* he communicated to her again.

Marina realized that Robert was referring to the two humans below them. She watched as he used his gradually strengthening energy to move fluidly downward, toward the center of the glorious life fire and into one of the forms.

Marina understood now. Focusing on the woman below, Marina allowed her essence to dissolve into the molecules of the second human's energy.

This is the way, Marina realized. *This is the way I will be with my love again.*

Tori could feel that Bruce Gautreau was about to shift his weight and rise from his position on top of her. Then suddenly he stopped.

"Mr. Gautreau?"

Bruce stared into Tori Avalon's face a long moment and then his head tilted back.

"Mr. Gautreau, are you all right?"

"Yes," he said. "I just . . . there's a strange chill racing through my—"

With a sharp intake of breath, Tori, too, felt a chill streak through her body. In a few seconds, whatever it was seemed to warm again, and she felt herself return to normal.

Except it wasn't normal.

All of a sudden Tori felt a bit unsteady, as if she'd drunk one too many aperitifs.

When her attention finally returned to the man *still* lying on top of her, she realized that his expression had changed. It was no longer absently pensive. It had become blatantly sexual . . . twice the look of hunger and desire that had earlier made her consider fleeing back into the downpour.

Though the beat of the rain on the roof was softer now, it was every bit as steady. It seemed to echo the loud, rapid beating of her heart, and the beating seemed to further confuse the already-woozy Tori. She recalled Bruce Gautreau's mention of the Voodoo drums, and suddenly the pounding of the rain and of her heart became transformed into the pounding of drums.

The rhythm was hypnotic to her, and she didn't even think to protest when Bruce's head slowly lowered so that his lips could slightly brush across hers.

Tori closed her eyes. In her slightly stunned state it seemed a natural response to the feel of the soft, tender caress. Part of her, the sane, rational part, knew she had to stop him, but she wasn't listening to her left brain at the moment; she was listening instead to the beat of the rain, and the yearning pulse of warm blood through her veins.

It was the rhythm of life, she realized, and suddenly she wanted to join with it.

She began to return Bruce's kisses, her own tongue sampling the salty flavor of his upper lip and the sweet, warm taste of his mouth. His hand moved to her hair, stroking her soft auburn curls and cupping her head as the kiss deepened.

Tori barely knew what was happening when a faint voice nudged at the edges of her consciousness.

"Victoria! Tori, where are you, sugar?"

Aunt Zoe's voice was calling her back to reality. And Tori's eyes flew open with a sudden realization of where she was and what she was doing.

Before Tori knew it, the familiar face of her aunt was smiling at the open window. The pink paisley pattern of a large umbrella fluttered closed as it preceded the stylishly attractive older woman through the tall window's doorlike frame.

Tori's palms pushed at the bare chest of the man on top of her, but he didn't get the hint.

As he looked down at her, he seemed a bit stunned, but nonetheless pleased, and not the slightest bit embarrassed to be caught in such a position. One of those annoyingly cocky grins was now spreading across his face.

"So," he said finally, "your name's Victoria?"

"Tori," she supplied.

A slow smile touched his lips. *"Enchanté."*

"Uh . . . thanks, but would you mind . . . getting off me now?"

"Well, well, well," said Zoe, stepping closer with a raised eyebrow and an amused smile in her eyes, "I see you two have met."

Chapter
Three

"Why won't you just have dinner with him?"

Tori sighed in exasperation at her aunt's words. She absently fingered the leaded-crystal stem of her nearly empty wineglass. Lifting the glass, her green eyes followed the swirls of the intoxicating vintage as she tried not to think of Bruce's kiss only hours before. It was embarrassing that her aunt found them in such a compromising position. That never should have happened, Tori decided, and it never would again.

"Aunt Zoe, you know I love you dearly, but please let's *drop* the subject of Bruce Gautreau and talk about the house."

Zoe ate the last of her poached oysters—a delicacy prepared in a seasoned cream sauce and served with Oregon caviar. When Duchamp's had opened a little over a year ago, this dish, along with the turtle soup and pecan-crusted trout, had put the Garden District restaurant in the same league as such famous, four-star New Orleans kitchens as Commander's Palace and Brennan's.

Duchamp's had become a great success for Zoe. Both natives and tourists alike flocked to the place, and the older woman was in her glory—whether she was commanding the dining room staff, cajoling Pierre, the temperamental French chef, or sharing bawdy stories with her many regular customers.

Sitting now with Zoe at a small, linen-covered table in a quiet corner of Duchamp's, Tori couldn't help but feel very proud of her aunt. Zoe had made her business a success with hard work and the risk of her lifelong savings.

Tori knew she had the determination to do the same—if only she could find the resources.

"My dear," Zoe asserted, dabbing a bit of cream sauce from her lips, "Bruce Gautreau and the house *are* the same subject."

Tori tried to swallow her frustration with a sip of her Chateau Haut-Brion Blanc.

"Look around you," her aunt continued with a theatrical flourish. "This place was in a terrible state when I bought it. And just look what Bruce did with it."

Tori's eyebrows rose with surprise. She couldn't deny that the ambiance at Duchamp's was splendid. The Italianate mansion had been converted into a beautiful, stylish showplace. Huge mirrors were evenly spaced along the walls, reflecting the gold of the ornate trim and the soft glow of the overhead gas-powered crystal chandeliers that illuminated the spacious dining area. Duchamp's was renowned as much for its authentic decor as for its world-class cuisine.

"Gautreau did all this?"

"Yes, and a few others around the city. But Duchamp's was his calling card."

"What do you mean?"

"I hired him out of San Francisco a few years back. He's been featured in *Restoration Quarterly, The Victorian House,* and a few other magazines."

"San Francisco? But he sounds like a native!"

"He is . . . but, you see, sugar, you should be asking *him* all of this. Why don't you have dinner with him?"

Tori could see her aunt was going to keep her on a perpetual merry-go-round with this issue.

"Please, let's drop it," repeated Tori gently, adding, "*for now*," at the determined look of her aunt's.

Their conversation halted when a tuxedo-clad waiter deftly cleared the table. Tori noticed the slight nervous tension on the young man's face as he finished the job. The boy's anxiety was not lost on her aunt.

"Fine work, Orin," she said with a smile and a wink at Tori.

He blushed faintly as he turned to go. "Thank you, ma'am."

Tori smiled. At sixty Zoe's aristocratic features, still-red hair, and slender, always fashionably clad figure made for a very attractive presence. But one brief encounter would tell anyone that Zoe Duchamp was no wilting magnolia. Her sweetly Southern yet unquestionably formidable personality often revealed the iron fist in her velvet tongue. Her employees both understood and respected their boss.

"I want to do the work myself," said Tori.

Aunt Zoe shook her head. "My dear, I'm sure you're quite determined, but this is beyond your capabilities."

Tori's gaze drifted across the room. She knew in her heart that her aunt was right. "How could Rosegate have gotten this bad? Did Hestia know?"

"I think it was the loss of her husband. After Richard died, you know what happened. Hesti left for Florida retirement and never looked back. The memories were too much for her to face."

"But what about the management company? Didn't she know they weren't maintaining it properly?"

"They sent her the rent money every month, and that's all that mattered to her. I tried to tell her, but she didn't want to think about it. She was done with it."

Tori sighed. "I've *got* to do the work myself. I can't afford—"

"She left you money, didn't she?"

"Yes, but not enough to hire . . ." Tori's hands swept the room. "Not enough for a man who does this kind of work."

"Bruce is reasonable, Tori. He's independent, you see. Besides, he owes me a favor. No one knew him 'round here till he came in for this job."

"But you said he was mentioned in those magazines."

"But *not* for work in the city. 'Round here, people like to hire folks they *know*. Duchamp's and I helped *introduce* Bruce to New Orleans, if you see what I mean."

"Yes, Aunt Zoe, I see. And I thank you for wanting to guide me, but I simply do not want any favors from that man."

"Which man would that be?" a deep, familiar voice broke in.

Tori didn't have to look up to know whose voice it was. She saw the answer in the delighted expression on her aunt's face.

Reluctantly Tori turned her head and looked up at Bruce Gautreau, who had moved to her side. The workman's attire was gone, replaced by an expertly tailored charcoal-gray suit, a crisp white shirt, and a conservative blue and silver tie. His square-jaw was cleanly shaven and his dark blond hair neatly brushed back off his brow.

Well, well, thought Tori, the gumbo handyman with the bayou-boy leer had transformed himself in a few short hours. Now he looked as though he were very much at home in the elegant dining room of Duchamp's.

Tori watched with surprise as Gautreau took her aunt's hand and brought it to his lips. She had always considered Zoe to be a discerning judge of character, but now she wondered if her aunt had somehow been taken in by this man's obvious good looks, obnoxious confidence, and completely *faux* charm.

You're being too hard on him, said a voice in the back of Tori's mind, and she knew she was. But then again, she knew what happened when she let her guard down with this man. *Passion*, supplied that little voice, reminding her of their kiss a few hours ago. *Sweet, hot . . . and dangerous.*

"Well!" Zoe exclaimed. "Speak of the devil, and he doth arrive."

Devil is right, Tori thought in agitation.

"Just be sure to give the devil his due, Victoria," Bruce said pointedly as his dark brown eyes flashed and the edges of his full lips curled into a wicked half-smile.

Tori blushed slightly—he acted as though she'd said those words out loud, but she was certain that she hadn't.

"My dear Bruce," said Zoe, "are you here for business or pleasure?"

"A little of both, I hope," Bruce replied smoothly. "I was in the neighborhood on business, but seeing you is always a pleasure. . . ." Tori nearly blanched at his slick reply, though her aunt's expression displayed pure delight at his flirtations.

Tori also noted that Bruce Gautreau's earlier Cajun drawl had magically vanished. His speech was now tempered into educated Southern tones, and she wondered what the grand switch was all about. *Will the real Bruce Gautreau please stand up?*

"May I join you both for coffee?" he asked sweetly, his gaze straying toward Tori.

"Splendid idea! But I must attend to some duties in the kitchen," said Zoe, rising from the table. "Pierre's a perfectionist. And he's a grizzly to the staff at this time of night unless I'm around to handle him. Bruce, perhaps you could escort Tori though the Quarter and get coffee there. It's a beautiful night, and she hasn't seen N'Awlins in years. . . ."

Before Tori could protest, Zoe was turning to go. "I'll see you back at my apartment, sugar. Have fun, now!"

And then she was gone.

"As I said, the devil wants his due," said Bruce. "If we can't have dinner, dessert will have to do." With polished ease, Bruce stepped behind Tori and held her chair as she rose.

"You rhyme, too?" Tori quipped.

"I'm a man of many talents," he whispered from behind, his warm breath tickling her ear. "You've only seen a few. . . ."

Ignoring her body's automatic reaction to him, Tori quickly began to stride through the crowded dining room, not stopping until she'd pushed through the restaurant's outer doors. She immediately took a breath of fresh air, hoping it would calm her.

The brief rainstorm hadn't dispelled the humidity, but the heat of the day was gone. A cool, thin fog now enveloped the city in a dreamlike mist. Tori enjoyed the caress of fresh night air around her bare arms and legs.

"You look beautiful tonight," Bruce's low voice murmured, his eyes taking in the curve of her figure in the fitted bodice of her green silk dress. He admired how the thin shoulder straps set off the creamy skin of her long, slender neck.

"Look, Mr. Gautreau—" Tori began.

"Bruce."

"You obviously do wonderful work, *Mr.* Gautreau, and I'm sure you are a very nice man, but—"

"Nice?" Bruce arched his brow as he cut her off. He could feel the rejection coming a mile away. "You may be sure I'm a lot o' things, but 'nice' isn't one o' them. Nice is for puppies, or those accountants you likely dated way up there in New York."

He stepped closer to Tori, backing her against an ornate wrought-iron lamppost. "What I am," he said in a low voice, "is dangerous, Miss Avalon. I'm a risky proposition, and it's clear enough to me that you haven't taken a chance in a long time."

"That may be so, but risks are—"

"Dangerous. I know, but life is short. It begs some risk-taking now and again; otherwise, why bother living at all? So, before you tell me to disappear, why don't you consider how interesting it might be to try a roll of the dice?"

Tori thought of a dozen retorts. But instead, she found herself intrigued, yet again, by this man. Her green eyes searched his face and settled on his soft lips, recalling the feel of them against her own.

Yes, she could stop it right now, tell him to take a hike back to the bayou, but instead she stared at him a long moment.

"How did you know I came from New York?"

"I asked Zoe about you this afternoon after you sped off in your little blue rental car."

Tori wondered what else her aunt may have told him, but she didn't dare ask now. Instead, her eyes searched his.

"Okay," she finally said. "I'll 'roll the dice,' as you put it. But only for a few hours."

"Good. Shall we go?" Bruce asked.

Bowing to the inevitable, Tori nodded, allowing Bruce to lead her toward a vaguely familiar red sports car. Tori realized as he held open her door and handed her into the two-seater that this was the same car she'd seen near Hesti's Victorian. The very car she'd labeled a "woman trap."

Tori now felt strangely penitent, realizing that she *was* impressed with the Porsche's sleek lines, leather interior, and convertible top. And when he slammed the door, she did feel as if she'd been trapped . . . but not so much by the car.

They sped smoothly down St. Charles Avenue, winding through traffic and around the crowded trolleys that crawled along the center of the street. In no time Tori recognized the familiar wrought-iron lace that graced the balconies of many French Quarter buildings.

"The streets are narrowing," murmured Tori absently.

"Ah, a design observation about our fair city. And do you know why the streets narrow?"

"No," she admitted, "I don't. I assumed it was a historical feature."

"It is. The French Quarter is the oldest part of the city. Back in the eighteenth century an engineer named de Pauger designed the basic grid pattern of streets. Imagine that," mused Bruce, "being given the job of designing a whole town."

Tori glanced at Bruce, who was shifting the car from fourth down to third. She got the distinct impression he'd have had the nerve to bid on that particular job in a second.

"Of course, back then the streets were really nothing more than open gutters," Bruce continued.

"In some ways they still are," Tori retorted as they passed the garish red lights of a topless bar.

"*Bon Dieu*," murmured Bruce. "You're a cynic, Miss Avalon. What a surprise!"

"It's the truth, isn't it?"

"Only partly. The city's got a two-hundred-million-dollar revitalization project going on along the river. And in the Quarter there are plenty of historic buildings that've been carefully restored. You've got pedestrian malls on Bourbon and Royal streets, a smaller red-light area, and whole sections of the Quarter that've become gentrified. Look over there—" Bruce pulled the car up to the curb and let it idle.

Tori's gaze followed his gesture, and she saw a three-story Spanish structure with intricate balconies and a visible central courtyard, set back from the street.

"A year ago that building was empty, except for a run-down, seedy bar," Bruce continued. "Now, as you can see, it houses beautiful apartments."

"Yes, it is beautiful," Tori acknowledged.

"It's mine."

"You own it?"

"No," he said with a laugh, "I restored it."

Tori took note of Gautreau's overtly possessive phrasing. But then, she figured, this man seemed exactly the type to be possessive—until he grew tired of a project . . . and another captured his attention.

"N'Awlins has been a crazy quilt. First French, then Spanish, then French again." His dark gaze shifted back to Tori. "Historically, you might say the Big Easy's a city of many contradictions. But it's always retained its peculiar individuality."

Funny, thought Tori, she could use those same sentiments to describe Gautreau himself. With a back bayou accent in the afternoon and a polished professional image after sundown, the man was a bundle of intriguing, and unsettling, contradictions.

"I find this city and its structures endlessly fascinating"—Gautreau paused a moment, casting a final loving look back to his restored structure— "like a beautiful woman."

Somehow Tori figured Gautreau would compare just about *anything* to "a beautiful woman."

"Not anything," he said sharply, then turned to meet her eyes. "And not *any* woman."

Tori was taken aback. "What is it with you, are you psychic or something?"

"Or something," said Gautreau cryptically as he abruptly turned back to the Porsche's wheel. Shifting gears with more force than necessary, he pulled away from the curb and started down the narrow streets again.

Tori could see Gautreau was agitated. She considered delving further into his mind-reading tricks, but decided instead to leave the subject alone. The last thing she wanted was to cross into some sort of touchy terrain with this man.

In another few minutes Bruce slid his sleek car into a space near Jackson Square. He opened her door and handed her out of her seat.

When they started down the sidewalk, Tori felt Bruce take hold of her hand and deftly slip it through the crook of his arm. Her eyebrow rose at the gallant gesture. Other than his obvious gift for restoration, Tori could see why her aunt had been completely taken in. She stiffened a bit with that thought, and reminded herself that she'd been taken in before by a man.

"You don't have to trust me," whispered Bruce as he led her across St. Ann Street. "In fact, I would advise you not to, except when it comes to my work."

"It's your price I'm worried about, Mr. Gautreau, not my virtue."

Bruce's unexpected laughter resounded. It joined the many night sounds of the French Quarter: the blaring horns of nearby jazz bands, the clop of mule hooves pulling tourist-filled carriages, and the shouts of nearby revelers.

Tori had to admit that the Quarter wore night well. As

they walked down the narrow street beside Jackson Square, the glowing lanterns of gaslights burned through the fog like yellow beacons magically joining present and past.

They crossed the busy thoroughfare of Decatur Street. Just beyond were the levee and the night-dark water of the Mississippi. The air, still thick with fog, was cooler here and tinged with the many scents carried by the big river.

They arrived at the green-and-white-striped canopy of Café Du Monde. Bruce led them to a table under the awning of the crowded outdoor patio.

After ordering a heaping plate of beignets and two café au laits, Bruce removed his jacket and draped it over the back of his seat, then settled back. Of its own accord, Tori's gaze followed his fluid movements. Her mind automatically pictured the powerful muscles that she knew lay beneath the thin material of the starched white dress shirt.

She wished she could wipe out the picture he made standing before her in the candlelit dining room of Aunt Hesti's house, his powerful bare muscles slick with rain, his dark eyes seducing her with their devouring hunger.

When his gaze met her face, Tori flushed, realizing that he'd caught her looking. It seemed to give him unspoken permission to return the favor. His dark eyes boldly surveyed her form.

He started with the curve of her full breasts, lingered on her long bare neck, and finished with her wide green eyes. Tori could almost feel him touching her where his gaze wandered, and a warmth suffused her body. She could not deny that she'd looked him over, too, but she hadn't been so blatantly *obvious* about it.

Bruce Gautreau was agitating Tori yet again, and she began to wonder why in heaven's name a woman who'd never thrown dice in her life had allowed herself to enter a game with an obvious expert.

Taking a deep breath of night air, she could only advise herself one thing: *You had better set some rules down—fast.*

Chapter
Four

"I think we should get down to business, Mr. Gautreau," stated Tori, hoping that her cool, rational tone would help direct the conversation back onto less *distracting* ground. "What's your estimate?"

Bruce paused a moment. "A classic work."

"I agree."

He leaned forward, his dark gaze capturing her green one. "A beauty."

"What's your estimate?"

"It may last a few months. Possibly more, but I can't ga-ron-tee a t'ing."

Tori sighed, hearing the Cajun coming back to haunt her. "I'm not talking time. I want to know about money."

"It's not a question of money."

"Of course it is."

Bruce let a devilish grin overtake his face. "You're talking about the house, aren't you?"

"Of course. Aren't you?"

The busy waiter interrupted. After a swift placement of beignets and coffees, he gathered his payment, then sped off to another table.

She watched as Bruce casually sipped his café au lait. She suspected he was playing her for a fool. Closing her eyes a moment to compose herself, she picked up her own cup. The taste of the rich, delicious mixture of strong chicory-laced coffee and hot milk immediately calmed Tori's nerves.

Memories of her childhood years assailed her. Café au lait and beignets at Café Du Monde had been a Sunday tradition when she'd lived with Aunt Hestia and Uncle Richard. It had been the happy break between morning mass and a session of shopping for fresh produce at the French Market.

Tori knew that same Sunday tradition had been passed down by countless French Creoles, part of the old line of European aristocrats who'd ruled the city for nearly two centuries. It reminded Tori of just how much Rosegate meant to her—which in turn made her consider the man sitting across from her now.

Leaning back in her chair, Tori judged the situation. She knew the Cajun was still trying his best to get her to flirt, and she bristled at his obvious teasing at her expense, but she also had to admit that she needed his help—or at least his expert advice.

"Mr. Gautreau . . . *Bruce*," she began, trying a less defensive tone. "I want you to know how much that house means to me. Some of the happiest days of my life were spent in that house, and—"

"I know. . . ."

She looked into the uncomfortably penetrating gaze of his dark brown eyes and shifted in her seat. How could he *know*?

"What I mean is," put in Bruce, "I did watch you risk your life for that little horse—the one we found in ten pieces under that old china closet. It obviously meant something to you."

Tori sat in silence. She reached for a beignet, shook the excess powdered sugar off the small, square French doughnut, then took a bite. Slowly she savored the warm, sweet piece of fried pastry.

"I know it was pretty stupid, what I did," she admitted softly. "But, you see, my mother gave that horse to me . . . I was very young when she died, and so . . ." Tori just shrugged.

Bruce nodded. "I'm sorry we weren't able to save it."

Tori shook her head. "You saved me, and, believe me, I'm thankful for that . . . thankful to you."

Bruce shook off the compliment, absently fiddling with his cuffs instead. He watched Tori slowly dip a torn piece of beignet into her cup, and he noticed a smudge of powdered sugar clinging to the edge of her perfect mouth.

For the first time Bruce could begin to see just how vulnerable this tightly wound woman was, and he could begin to sense the layers of pain just under the icy surface. Tremendous pain, in fact—and not all of it from the past.

Bruce had a bit of weakness for women like Tori. They were the kind who lasted beyond a few hot weeks of sex, often allowing him months of something deeper.

That's about as long as it would ever last, though, Bruce well knew. A few precious months. He supposed that if he took this restoration job, he would complete it and be done helping Tori get over her pain in about the same block of time.

A weak feeling of irony touched him, as he considered the sign he could hang from his third-floor apartment's gallery: "Restorer of historic homes and female hearts."

Reaching for his coffee, Bruce sipped as he thought about the job, then looked directly into Tori's distracted face. "Tori, the house's structure is sound," he began, his voice sincere, almost earnest as he got down to business. "You're lucky it is, too. Some idiot let the shrubs and weeds grow right up against the foundation. Plants hold moisture, and in this climate, it could have done plenty of damage.

"You have a bit of a termite problem on the front porch, but other than a bad case of mildew and some roof repairs, that's about it for the exterior problems. The bulk of the work will be restoration, not major structural repairs."

Tori nodded. "I want to remodel it a bit and open up the attic. Right now it's just a storage area."

"Zoe tells me you want to reopen the place as a guest house? You realize the *Vieux Carré* Commission has instituted a crackdown on hotel expansion in the Quarter."

Tori blinked. "What?"

"Rosegate *was* a guest house for years though, right?"

"Yes, of course."

"Then we can make a case to the Commission that it's not 'expansion' per se."

Tori could see this was already becoming much more complicated than she'd ever imagined, sitting alone in her New York apartment. She didn't like admitting how badly she needed Gautreau's help. But it was obvious she did.

"Do you think it will work?"

Bruce smiled. "The commission has been happy with me and my work so far, and I believe I can convince them . . . *if* you hire me, of course."

Tori eyed the man. "Well, it's already late May, and I was planning to get the place up and running for fall. What do you think?"

"Four months and sixty thousand dollars should cover the interior and exterior."

Tori nearly choked on her café au lait. "I knew it," she said. "That's way beyond my budget. That's why I want to do the bulk of the work myself."

"Without a large crew, I can save you some, but it'll take longer."

Tori's eyes met his in question.

"Six, seven months, but we're still talking real money."

"What can you do for nine thousand six hundred and fifty dollars?"

Tori expected him to laugh her out of the café, but instead he sat back in thought, crossing his forearms over his chest. For a full minute he stared off into the night fog. Then he began to think aloud.

"Well, somebody put in a new hot water heater at the most, five years ago; and, as I said, the roof and structure are basically sound. A bit of the wiring has to be upgraded—and a lot of the plumbing, unfortunately—and I'll have to secure the proper permits from the commission.

"You'll also need some new windows, and there'll be stripping, painting, staining, and the best materials—the right materials—aren't cheap. With the *Vieux Carré* Commission looking over our shoulders, we can't take shortcuts."

Tori was a bit overwhelmed with Bruce's retention of details, not to mention the amount of work the house would need. Now all she had to hear was his answer. She watched him sit quietly for another minute, then reach for his coffee and take a long sip. Leaning forward, his face betrayed the most serious expression she'd seen it wear that evening.

"You have three floors, plus the attic. For the amount you mentioned, I could give you the wrap-around porch, ground floor, and master bedroom on the second floor restored. I won't touch the kitchen for that amount, but I'll get the rewiring done and make sure your fireplaces and baths are in working order."

"I intend to help, Mr. Gautreau . . . Bruce. I know how to paint, I can strip and sand and stain the woodwork—"

"How many Victorians have you restored?"

"None, but I've read a few books and—"

"Look, let me make something clear. If you hire me, it's *my* job." Tori was about to jump in, but he cut her off. "I know it's *your* house. I also know you're a very headstrong lady. But my work is the best, and if you hire me, you'll do it *my* way or not at all."

"What about my taste? I have certain color schemes I—"

Bruce shook his head. "Restoring a house and keeping its historic integrity intact requires expertise. The colors applied to any building must be selected from those that were available and considered appropriate for the date, type, and style of the building at the time of its design and construction. And those colors should be applied to enhance the design in the manner intended by the original builder."

"You sound like a professor."

"I'm not some cheap contractor, Miss Avalon. Historic restoration isn't grunt work. It's a discipline and an art."

"You hardly looked like an artist this afternoon—" The words were out of Tori's mouth before she could stop them.

Bruce's eyebrow rose. "Don't you think Michelangelo perspired after ten hours of painting the Sistine Chapel?"

"Quite a comparison," Tori retorted. "You clearly think well of yourself."

"*Chère*," he said with a laugh, "my *work* is what I think well of."

Tori nodded, sorry that she'd needled him.

"And what about *your* work?" asked Bruce, leaning forward.

"Well, well, if it isn't Vianney Gautreau. Havin' a nice evenin', Vianney?"

The low voice startled Tori. Looking up, she saw that two men had approached their table. Both had dark hair, yellowish hazel eyes, and thick, blunt features. Tori guessed they were brothers, although one looked at least ten years older than the other.

The older man was short, with thinning hair and a small scar on his neck. He was well dressed in a tailored blue suit.

The younger one was attractive, in a rough way, but his expression looked hard for his years. He wore his dark hair in a short buzz cut. A gold chain shimmered against the black T-shirt under his shiny gray silk suit jacket, and when he glanced briefly at Tori, she felt uneasy.

The two stood close to Bruce. Although their postures appeared casual, Tori could see the hostility evident just under the surface. Neither looked very friendly, and even though the one who spoke—the older one—wore a mild saccharine smile, it didn't reach his eyes. In fact, Tori could swear she saw pure malice there when he looked at Bruce.

Tori looked across the small table. Bruce hadn't moved. He sat completely still, unblinking.

"Gentleman?" he asked, looking stiffly up at them. Bruce didn't like interruptions. Not when he was working. Nor when he was intimately conversing with a woman as attractive as Tori Avalon. But Bruce knew this visit from the Vonderant brothers went way beyond an interruption; it was an intimidation. Plain and simple.

"We'd just like to speak ta ya, Vianney," said Gilbert Vonderant, the older brother.

"We've already talked." Bruce reached for his cup, and looked at Tori, throwing her a wink.

She guessed that the gesture was meant to reassure her.

It didn't.

"Well, we didn't t'ink yo' words was wise," said René Phillipe, the younger Vonderant.

Tori noticed the younger man turn toward her, then boldly look her up and down. Unlike the intense feelings she experienced with the touch of Bruce's gaze, Tori felt her skin crawl at this man's ogling. Automatically her arms crossed protectively in front of her.

Bruce saw where the young man's attention had strayed, and Tori nearly gasped at the ferocity of his immediate response. His eyes narrowed menacingly and his expression suddenly took on the fierceness of a wild animal barely kept in its cage.

Slowly he put down his cup and rose to his full height. Bruce was no taller than the younger brother, yet in a mere moment, he had solidly fixed himself in a powerful and immovable stance.

"Gentlemen," Bruce said, his Cajun drawl returning. "As you can see, I'm wit' a *lady*, right here an' now. This is not the time or place." Though the words themselves were polite, the dangerous edge beneath them made them sound more like a deadly threat. *"Fout ton camp, compris?"*

Tori watched in confusion and curiosity, trying to guess what this was all about. The younger brother inhaled with agitation, his hands clenched into fists. His tense body began to push forward toward Bruce when the older brother's arm shot out to block him.

"*Oui*, Gautreau. We goin'. 'Nother day then. *Vien nous voir*," said the older brother.

"Yeah, I'll come see you, but de answer isn't gonna change," warned Bruce.

"We'll jus' see, yeah?" said the younger brother.

Then the older man tipped his head toward Tori. "Sorry to trouble you, miss. Evenin'."

Tori watched as both men turned to leave. The younger brother made a show of turning to check her out one more time before the older brother placed an insistent grip on the young one's upper arm, forcefully guiding him from the café's patio and into the night's fog.

Not until they were out of sight did Bruce's muscles appear to relax. He turned back to her and sat down.

"I'm truly sorry about that," he said smoothly, his gaze searching hers.

Bruce's sudden transformation from Southern gentlemen into rough bayou boy and back again was unnerving for Tori. She considered asking what the men wanted, but part of her really didn't want to know. Maybe the dispute was over a woman or a bet or something.

She sighed to herself. Her better judgment had already advised her not to get involved with Gautreau; this incident simply confirmed it.

Yes, her first impression of the man had been the *correct* one—Bruce Gautreau was dangerous.

"Now, where were we?" he asked.

"Ah . . . I don't remember."

"Oh, yes," he said, reaching for his coffee and taking a sip. "We were discussing what *you* do for a living?"

"I'm between jobs right now," Tori answered, her gaze turning to the fog where those men had disappeared. "Actually, I hated my New York job, if you really want to know.

I studied French literature in college but ended up making a living writing a corporate newsletter."

"French?"

"Yes, and after I move down here, I'll be teaching French at a small girls' academy. It's part-time and doesn't pay much, but it's work I'll truly enjoy."

"Mmm . . . *la langue d'amour*."

She nodded. "More than the 'language of love,' as you put it. Around here it was the language of the people—as I see you obviously know. By the way, I've been meaning to ask you what happened to your Cajun accent? Was that the real you, or is it this genteel business-speak?"

Bruce smiled mildly, aware that the Northern wind had returned at full gale. "Is it your New York years that make you phrase things so rudely, or is it just your reaction to me?"

Tori's gaze left Bruce's handsome face and searched the foggy outline of tourists in the nearby sidewalk. "I don't mean to be rude, but I don't trust you." *Especially after that visit from thugland,* thought Tori. "And, if you recall, you did warn me not to."

"That's true. But this isn't an issue of trusting *me*, Tori." She eyed him.

"Take fire, for example."

"What?"

Bruce leaned forward. "You trust fire to cook your meals, to provide the beautiful gaslit streets, warm you on a cold winter night . . . but that's because you found a way to control it."

Tori reached for another sip of coffee. "I still don't see what—"

"Fire can be very helpful, pleasant—if you control it. It can also be very dangerous, it can have a mind of its own; and if you're not careful, it can consume you." Slowly Bruce's dark eyes penetrated hers with an intense exploration, and Tori felt her heartbeat quicken. "It's not that you don't trust *me*, Miss Avalon. You don't trust yourself."

Bruce rose and slipped on his jacket. Tossing a bill onto

the table, he stepped close to her, and offered his hand. Tori tried not to be overtly rude, but she did not take up his offer. She rose from the table and started toward the exit. Bruce followed, and they silently left the café.

Driving back to the Garden District, the two mutually avoided conversation. Instead, they listened to a jazz station on the Porsche's sound system until they reached Duchamp's. Bruce pulled up to the back entrance, where an ornate spiral staircase led to the third-floor gallery of Zoe's apartment. For a moment they sat quietly in the car. Then Tori broke the silence.

"I don't want to strain my aunt's hospitality. . . . If I hire you, can you have at least one room livable in four weeks? I'd like to occupy the house and work with you on the restoration."

Bruce looked hard at Tori. "You understand that I'm in charge."

"Yes . . ."

"Well, then. I suppose I can call in some favors to get the building permits in time to start work immediately. But what are you going to do when you've spent your nine thousand six hundred and fifty dollars?"

Tori sighed and leaned back into the plush leather car seat. "I don't know. But I'm not giving up. I'm determined to think of something."

A long silence ensued, and when Tori glanced at Bruce, she found him gazing at her with an odd expression, one of newfound interest and—oddly—respect.

With a questioning gaze, she met his dark eyes. She could see that they had softened considerably since their last exchange at the restaurant.

"Fine, then," said Bruce, unable to help but admire Tori for not running from the battle before she'd even seen the enemy. He'd been involved with enough women who would have done just that. "I'll see you to the door."

Bruce exited the car and came around to the passenger side. He took Tori's hand in his, and they walked together to the bottom of the wrought-iron staircase. The fog had gotten heavier, the night cooler. The dampness touched Tori's skin, causing her green silk dress to cling to her body.

As she turned to say good night, she could not help but notice the appreciation in Bruce's eyes. Suddenly his strong arms were encircling her waist and pulling her against him. Once more she felt the power and hard strength of his muscular form. Tori's eyes widened and before she could even utter a sound of protest, his full, sensuous lips touched hers, first tentatively, then more forcefully.

Her senses spun as the world narrowed to the teasing nibbling of his soft, moist lips. The masculine scent of his aftershave enveloped her, and Tori could taste the combination of sweet pastry and chicory-laced coffee that still lingered on his tongue.

She knew she should stop him, but her curiosity was stronger than her rational mind. And on some level, she wanted to know if this man could really always affect her the way he had that afternoon. Perhaps then she'd been vulnerable, she told herself, but now, tonight, she was sure she could steel herself against his seductive persuasion.

She felt the tip of his tongue touch her full, lower lip and decided yet again that Bruce Gautreau was not only an expert at restoration, but at kissing, as well. His large hand moved at her silk-clad waist, his fingers fanning at the small of her back, lightly massaging.

Despite the cooling air, her skin felt on fire where he touched her, and her murmur of surprise inadvertently coaxed him into deepening the kiss, his tongue pushing through her lips to fully invade her mouth.

The embrace was intoxicating as he pressed closer still, crushing her full breasts against him. She tried not to react, but her body was a traitor, responding of its own accord. Hot, tight sensations streaked through her lower body, swiftly bringing her to a dangerous state of arousal, of need.

The fiery insistence of his hands and mouth were evoking a reaction the likes of which she'd never felt before.

She felt his other hand at her bare neck, massaging there, touching her soft auburn curls that she'd upswept into a twist. He used that hand to tenderly ensure his position, insistent pressure keeping her from withdrawing her mouth from his.

She felt his lower body against her own, the evidence of his own arousal hard against her leg. Another murmur escaped her throat and he answered with his own deep moan of satisfaction, his tongue dipping in and out of the beignet-sweet cavern of her mouth, echoing another penetration she knew he'd want in the future.

And she knew her body wanted it, too.

Right now.

Right here.

She'd never felt this way before, so daringly released from her tight controls. Her arms rose to link themselves around his neck, and she felt his hand at her back drop lower, boldly cupping her firm derriere, pressing her hot lower body closer to his. Another mewl escaped her throat, and he swallowed the sound into his own mouth.

Her hands tangled in his golden hair, the silky feel a pleasure to touch. Their breathing was labored, their heartbeats quickening, when Bruce withdrew his tongue from her mouth to murmur softly against her lips.

"My place isn't far," his voice whispered.

Tori's body wanted to—oh, how it wanted to—but she would not allow her head to nod yes.

His insistent hands massaged and cajoled as his lips nibbled again at her lips. "Me, I can put out your fire, *chère*." The persuasive Cajun was back. "Let me. *Droit a c't'heure.*"

"What?"

Bruce smiled. His Cajun patois was obviously too raw for the formally trained ear of Miss Avalon. "*Droite a c't'heure,*" he repeated, "right now . . ."

Like lights of the city fighting their way through the enveloping fog, Tori began to struggle through the powerful mist of her own hazy arousal. "No," she murmured.

"You want me, *chère*. I know you do."

She tried to break free of his kiss, but his hand at the back of her head tenderly insisted she stay within his power. Once more his full lips danced across hers, and a sizzling fuse tingled through her breasts and into her lower body.

"Tell me—" he demanded.

Tori closed her eyes and took a deep breath. Then, placing her palms on his powerfully solid shoulders, she pushed with strong insistence.

But he fought for his position, and his strength was more than a match for hers. Again his mouth descended, this time in a more desperate persuasion. Her lips had closed but his tongue pushed past her barriers in a forceful invasion, dipping and swirling in another intoxicating assault. Then his head rose again, locks of dark blond hair falling past his forehead and into his eyes as they looked down into her own.

"Tell me," he insisted again. "I need to hear it."

Tori pulled her head back and let her jade eyes meet his in a frank stare.

"Yes," she said clearly. "I want you. It's true. I do."

But before his mouth could descend again, before he could sweep her off her feet, into his car and his bed, she spoke again.

"But I won't act on it."

His dark eyes searched hers and read her message loud and clear. He released her slowly, stepped back, and surveyed his handiwork. Her breasts were straining against the newly wrinkled green silk. The hard pebbles of her nipples clearly outlined the evidence of her aroused state. Her lips were swelled and rouged, the lipstick partly smeared. And her French twist, usually so primly and tightly pinned into place, was now in a chaotic tumble. Long curls softly brushed the ivory complexion of her face.

Seeing what his gaze was attracted to, Tori quickly crossed her arms protectively. She wanted to tell him that they both had stepped *way* over the line; that this would *never* happen again; that their relationship would be *all* business from now on. But none of the words could get past her kiss-swollen lips.

Tori watched as Bruce placed a hand in his pocket. It seemed he was waiting for something; maybe for the words she wanted to speak but couldn't. She looked again and saw that his normal self-assured posture was somehow off balance. He ran a shaky hand through his blond hair and took a ragged breath of the cool, misty air. Studying him, Tori realized that *he* had been as affected as she by their kisses.

She wondered if it unnerved him, too. . . .

Tori's eyes looked to his for answers, but he was already turning to go.

"Bonsoir, chère," he called over his shoulder. She watched as he quickly swung himself into the sports car and fired up the powerful engine.

"I'll be in touch," she managed to call out before his sleek red car pulled out of the narrow alley, tires squalling slightly as its form disappeared into the foggy night.

With an exhausted sigh, Tori ascended the wrought-iron staircase. It had been a very long day, and she was suddenly totally drained. The door wasn't locked, and as she entered the apartment, she couldn't hold back a wide yawn. Aunt Zoe was still up, relaxing in the living room with a nightcap and some Mozart.

"Hello there, sugar," said Zoe, setting down her magazine.

"Hi."

"How was your evenin' with—"

"Don't," said Tori gently, "don't even ask."

Zoe smiled wryly. "Well, my dear, I don't believe I need to. From the looks of you, I'd say the answer is obvious."

Tori felt the warmth of scarlet staining her cheeks. "Aunt Zoe, I'll admit he's attractive in the extreme. But I just don't *trust* him, and it's a very complicated situation for me right now, seeing that I'm about to—"

"Victoria," interrupted Zoe, "you're in N'Awlins now.

Maybe you should stop analyzin' and worryin' things to death and embrace your heritage a bit."

"How's that?"

"Well, you can start by following the city's creed. *Laissez les bon temps roulet.*"

Tori glared at her aunt. "Letting 'the good times roll' is not going to get Rosegate restored."

"Hmmm, no dice, eh? Well, how about simply following the example of my favorite Southern belle?"

Tori knew exactly who Aunt Zoe's favorite belle was, and she had to admit that her curiosity was piqued. "Okay, I'll bite. What would *she* advise me?"

"My dear, she'd tell you to follow your strongest *natural* instincts."

"I don't know how safe that is where Gautreau is concerned," Tori told her aunt as she gave her a good-night peck and headed toward the guest bedroom.

"Safe? Maybe not. But, oh, how those good times would surely roll."

Exasperated, Tori turned. "Aunt Zoe, I'll make you a deal. You stop pushing Gautreau on me, and I'll adopt your favorite belle's favorite saying."

"Hmmmm . . . and what's that?"

"Why, fiddle-dee-dee," chirped Tori in a high-pitched Southern drawl. "I'll think of it all *tomorrow.*"

Her aunt's amused chuckle followed Tori into the bedroom, along with an answer to her proposition. "Sorry, sugar," she called, "no dice."

Chapter
Five

She heard drums.

Tori opened her eyes and realized she'd awakened in the master bedroom of Hestia Duchamp Arnaud's old Victorian. With surprise and delight, she saw that it was no longer a run-down, tattered mess, full of must and mildew. Dozens of lit candles revealed a room restored to its original glory—new as the first rays of dawn.

But it was not dawn now, it was too dark outside.

Tori rose from the feathered mattress of the beautiful four-poster bed. As she swung her legs over the high frame, her fingers brushed along one of the posts.

She delighted in the swirls and curves of the stylized roses carved into the smooth dark wood. She recognized them instantly as the signature buds found in Rosegate's cast-iron fencing.

Suddenly Tori heard the sound of a man's voice calling from beyond the open French doors.

But was he calling her name? Or another's?

Sleepily she stood, aware of her nakedness yet strangely uncaring. The room was warm, and a cool stream of air blew across her skin, bringing with it a feeling of uneasiness.

Hearing the voice again, she began to move her bare feet across the gleaming hardwood floor until she came to the billowing white lace curtains along the French doors.

The drums outside were still beating. They were growing even louder now, pounding with an intense, driving rhythm as she stepped beyond the doors and onto the gallery. For some odd reason, she remained unembarrassed at her nakedness.

The voice called to her again, and she looked down into the street. Through the swirl of mist and fog she could see a man standing below the glowing halo of a gas-powered streetlamp. She watched as his golden head tilted back, revealing the handsome features and intense dark eyes of a man she recognized—

But suddenly the drums became almost deafening, and her hands flew to cover her ears. It did no good, though, because the drums were no longer distant. They were moving closer.

And closer . . .

Until they were inside her own head, beating and pounding with a primal insanity.

She shook her head violently, but the beating would not stop. Then suddenly she heard a terrible scream from behind her—a woman's scream.

She tried to turn, but could not, gripped by a cold unexplainable paralysis. Then a scream finally tore from her own throat, and she was screaming and screaming in sheer terror . . .

"N-O-O-O!"

The sound of her own voice brought Tori to a sitting position, her breathing labored, her brow covered with beads of perspiration.

Where were the drums?

She listened, but could only hear the occasional car horn and distant siren of the city streets.

She glanced around her. From the dim light that slipped through the slanted miniblinds, she could see that she was not in New Orleans, but was still in New York, where she'd been for the last two weeks.

Until a moment ago she had been asleep, not on the lush bedding of the antique bed but on the firm padding of her futon.

She swallowed, took a deep breath, and wiped her damp brow with the back of her hand. Lying back, she tried to calm down. The glowing numbers of her bedside clock read 4:15.

The room around her was nearly bare, except for the dozen cardboard boxes holding the few remaining possessions she hadn't already sold or given away.

In another week Tori would be in New Orleans again. Any big change in life would cause disturbing dreams, right?

Right.

Modern psychology to the rescue.

But somehow she couldn't reassure herself. This was the *third* time she'd had this dream in the last ten days, and she still didn't know what it meant—although tonight she finally realized the identity of the mysterious golden-haired man calling her name beneath the streetlamp.

Tonight, for the first time, Tori had recognized his face.

Unfortunately, that newly revealed detail failed to reassure her. In fact, the knowledge was unsettling as hell.

The man in her dream was Bruce Gautreau.

With a final twist of the screwdriver, Bruce secured the wall outlet's carved wooden covering into place. It was the final touch on the restored master bedroom. Rising from his crouched position, he let the tool drop with a satisfying clang into its metal box.

As he ran his forearm across his brow, Bruce stepped back to admire his work. He had removed the dirty beige wall-to-wall carpeting and painstakingly restored the hard-wood floor. Likewise he'd stripped the layers of paint from the carved walnut door frame, window frames, and picture rail, which ran high around the perimeter of the room, then stained the wood to its glossy, original finish.

He'd cleaned and buffed the intricately designed Carrara marble of the small working fireplace and restored the semicircle of tiles that protected the wooden floor, replacing the damaged tiles in the process.

With the help of two part-time assistants, Bruce had steam-stripped the old wallpaper, a disgusting design of large blue cornflowers, then plastered and primed the wall with a base white. He'd have to wait on giving it a final coat until he had a chance to show his client the carefully researched color card of shades and allowed her to pick one.

His client.

Bruce kicked the toolbox shut at the thought of her. He'd been trying *not* to think of that woman for over three weeks now.

After he grabbed the T-shirt he had stripped off hours ago, Bruce draped it around his neck. Then, picking up the heavy toolbox with ease, he walked to the door of the room and tested the light switch one more time. The glare of the bulb was nicely muted by an antique crystal gaslight fixture he'd discovered in the basement.

With no air-conditioning, the house was warm, so Bruce had also installed a ceiling fan. He'd adapted the antique light fixture so that it hung just below the more modern convenience.

An electrician friend of his was the one to thank for the bit of rewiring the house needed. In fact, the man had done the small job in two days.

Bruce would gladly use him again on that big Garden District job. It would be his very first municipal project—*if* he won the damn bidding war.

Flipping off the light, Bruce left the bedroom. He walked through the now-restored hallway, its wooden floor gleaming under a fresh coat of polyurethane, and headed down the steps.

The banister had been sanded, finished, and, in places, repaired. He ran his calloused hand along the smooth wood as he descended. After crossing the entryway, Bruce entered the spacious but dreary and run-down kitchen, which, in itself, was likely to be quite a renovation job sometime in the future.

After dropping his toolbox on the cracked linoleum floor, Bruce opened the small, dusty refrigerator, peered in, and let his fingers close around the long, cool neck of a Dixie beer—his brew of choice when he was anywhere near Louisiana. He twisted the cap and let the chilly liquid drench his parched throat.

It was another hot day, and he used his T-shirt to quickly wipe the beaded perspiration from his chest. He sighed. Something was eating at him, and he wasn't sure what.

Looking again at the kitchen, he knew part of it was this job. He absolutely *hated* leaving a restoration job unfinished. He hadn't done it more than two times in the fifteen years he'd been apprenticing and working on his own. But what could he do if his client only wanted a partial job done?

It was *his* job. But it was *her* property.

He sighed again, took another long, cool drink, and tried not to remember his client's long, cool looks. He knew *she* was the true cause of this gnawing in his guts—just the sound of her voice on their three brief, businesslike phone conversations was enough to set him off. And she was due back here today. Anytime now, in fact.

Victoria Avalon.

How could a woman have insides so hot and passionate, yet a facade as cold and icy as the beer in his hands? He drank again, realizing the tang of the cold brew was almost as satisfying as the taste of Tori's soft full lips, a taste that still lingered weeks after he'd kissed her.

He thought he had already decided what to do about Tori. He was going to forget her. He told himself there was nothing to her. No matter where her youthful years were spent, her adult manner was one-hundred percent hard-headed Yankee, the kind who couldn't let herself enjoy life.

Now what would he want with an uptight woman like that?

Enjoying life was Bruce's motto, his creed. No entanglements, no complications, just take what life offers, ride out its wave, and move on—no regrets, no commitments. That was the way he'd played it for most of his life now, and it had served him well enough.

So why get caught up with a woman who would complicate things?

A derisive laugh passed his lips. "Because she's a challenge. *Éspèce de fou*," he muttered, calling himself a Cajun fool. It was the damndest thing, but Bruce could never pass up a challenge.

He knew it since last weekend, when he'd gone to a narrow alley off Bourbon Street for a little fun. His favorite jazz club, the Blue Lady, had offered the sultriest sounds and sexiest women in the Crescent City, but no amount of Jack Daniel's had made any of them sexy enough.

Even when one shapely redhead pressed her palm to his thigh and whispered in his ear some extraordinary propositions for the night ahead, Bruce couldn't bring himself to oblige. All he could do was compare her to another.

Tori Avalon wasn't perfect by any stretch. Her nose was too short for her oval face, her forehead a bit too pronounced. But her delicate skin was so soft, and the way she carried herself—so proud and independent—reminded him of the picture of Cinderella in his mother's French fairy-tale book. So sweet and innocent, so vulnerable and tragic, Victoria, he sensed, was like that girl in the cinders who'd been transformed into a lofty princess.

Ironically, the same suffering that she wanted so desperately to forget was the very thing that ennobled her, the source and essence of her beauty.

He saw it all there in her eyes. And what eyes they were . . . emerald green and exotic, almost catlike in their slightly almond shape. They shimmered with fierceness and anger one minute, then gentle vulnerability the next—constantly exposing her true emotions under that controlled, chilly facade she tried so hard to keep in place.

Yes, the other night, Bruce had been very aware of the redhead in the Blue Lady. And he had been sufficiently aroused by the feel of the woman's long, painted nails inching up his leg.

In that moment Bruce had wanted to forget all about Tori.

But he couldn't.

Instead, he'd politely declined the offer and left the Blue Lady in heated frustration.

Taking another swig of beer, Bruce walked to the tall kitchen window and lifted it, stepping through its doorsized frame. He'd forgotten how much he liked this kind of window design. It was a unique characteristic of some Victorian houses, allowing people the ease of wandering on and off the wraparound porches from practically every ground-floor room.

Bruce had to admit, he liked ease in getting into and out of things. As he walked slowly along the porch, he noticed the remains of the chalked crosshatch markings on the floorboards. The *Vo-du.*

He took a swig of beer and thought of his late mother and their rickety little house in southern Louisiana. Angelique Le Pelletier Gautreau had come from an old New Orleans Creole family. After one lusty Mardis Gras night, she'd met his Cajun father, then followed him back to the bayou, carrying his son along with her endless fascination with the *Vo-du.*

Absently Bruce's right hand reached into his pants pocket, where his fingers closed around the soft cloth of the *gris-gris* bag that his mother had once made for him. It was a charm he always carried. *Men wear gris-gris on their right side, women on their left,* his mother had told him. He smiled, the memory of her words bringing back her sweet face.

Vianney, we are traiteurs de pouvoir, she'd often remind him. Bruce knew the Cajun term *traiteurs* referred to the community's purveyors of folk medicine. *Traiteurs* ran the gamut from homeopathic herb doctors to faith healers. *Traiteur de pouvoir* was his mother's phrase for something more than that.

She considered herself a healer, but one who used physic power and sometimes even divination. She blanched at the term fortune-teller—as did Bruce. She was much more than that because she could truly read people. And, in her own way, help heal them.

People of the community would visit the house at all hours and talk at length in hushed tones. He'd watched many a distraught or hysterical person enter a room with his mother and come out with a relieved smile. Often, Bruce would try to listen at the door—though his mother always seemed to know when he did.

She'd called it "the talent," something passed down through generations. And she'd always insisted that it had been passed down to him. But for years, no matter how much Bruce believed in his mother's ability, he had denied his own. The truth was, though he'd admired how his mother had used her talent for the good of others, he'd hated how she'd used it for herself—deserately and, in Bruce's opinion, uselessly.

Paul Gautreau was away from his wife and son often. Usually for months at a time. A young Bruce attributed it to his father's job as a merchant marine. But with age came psychic abilities of his own, and he began to read correctly that his father was not *always* leaving for the sea. Nor was he always faithful to his wife.

It was a hard lesson for Bruce in how the talent could be both blessing and curse. Paul Gautreau was not a malicious man. In fact, he was a loving husband and father, when he was around. But he was a wanderer at heart, and Angelique, for all her divining abilities, refused to see the flaw in the man she loved. Instead she applied her skills to tireless searches for news of his whereabouts.

It made Bruce sick at heart.

My sweet Vianney, you must believe in the unknown and unseen forces of the universe. . . .

Believe? thought Bruce with a laugh. After his rough bayou childhood, five years in the navy, and over a dozen more kicking around the country, was it any wonder he had less than the faith of a saint?

Bruce supposed he had believed in something at one time, but whatever faith he had once carried was now gone . . . lost somewhere.

Enough hard knocks would shake anything loose from a man.

The forces, Vianney, they are what shape our destiny. . . .

"No, *Maman,* we are what shape our destiny," whispered Bruce into the heavy humidity of the afternoon. His fingers tightened on the bottle as he despaired, yet again, that his mother had wasted her life on a phantom love, a man who had not been there for her.

As Bruce walked the length of the wide wraparound porch, he put the cool beer to his lips again and tried his best to wash down his anger, wash it down to the past where it belonged.

One thing that Bruce was getting to understand as he grew older, he wasn't so certain any longer of the workings of life. And he was no longer so sure that his mother had been *all* wrong. At least about the "unseen forces."

Leaning his shoulder against a porch post, Bruce considered the two spirits flowing throughout this house. From the first day he'd entered Rosegate, he suspected that these particular "unseen forces" were set on influencing him and Victoria Avalon.

The only question now was, should he try to ward those forces off? Or help them along?

As the sun disappeared behind a bank of ominous storm clouds, Bruce's gaze idly searched the empty street. A white hatchback, towing a small U-Haul trailer, parked in front of the mansion. He watched the driver's door swing open and a long, bare leg appear.

Bruce's gaze remained fixed on the smooth, ivory skin of that leg, then slowly ascended to take in the length of the woman attached to it—the curve of the hip in the white tailored shorts; the full, rounded breasts in the sleeveless, white blouse; the long, slender neck; and the face, framed by wisps of auburn curls.

Tori was back.

His stomach dropped, and he could feel the cold beer churning inside of him. A patch of skin at the back of his neck bristled. The small *gris-gris* bag jumped in his hand, and from far away, the afternoon rains seemed to echo the growing turbulence inside of him. The clouds rumbled with a peal of distant thunder.

As the first drops of cool rain bounced off the porch roof, Bruce watched her move toward him. Sadness came over him in waves. Pain, fear, anger, uncertainty . . . and beneath it all, a longing.

They were not his feelings. But hers.

Tori crossed the sidewalk and walked up to the house, the drops of newly fallen rain glistening in her hair like tiny diamonds. Before he had time to react, she stood before him in the middle of the porch steps, her expression unreadable to the unseeing eye. But Bruce could read her like a book.

After all, though he never wanted the burden, he had to admit the truth. Like his *maman* before him, Vianney Bruce Gautreau was a *traiteur de pouvoir*.

"Well," said Tori with her blunt Yankee efficacy. "Are you going to step aside, or do I stand in the rain until I'm soaked?"

Tori had forgotten how powerfully built the man was. But as she approached the muscled, naked chest of this handsome contractor, she was reminded in a hurry. Moving close to him this way was a true test of her new vow of total self-control.

"Well, *chère*, a warm and friendly hello to you, too," said Bruce dryly, amused irony beneath his bayou drawl.

Tori knew his tone was meant as a chastisement for

being Yankee curt again, and she felt her jaw clench. It was amazing how quickly this man could vex her.

He stepped back with a flourish of his hand. "After you," he said, and she stepped up, brushing beads of water from her hair.

When she turned back to face him, she noticed the white tank draped around his neck. *What is the matter with this guy, anyway?* she wondered, trying to keep her gaze from his bare chest. *Can't he keep his shirt on?*

During three busy weeks of packing and saying good-bye to her New York life, Tori had tried to explain away her reaction to Bruce Gautreau—her breathlessness at the sight of him, her unbridled response to the touch of him.

She had told herself that her extreme reaction to his kiss had been a mere fluke; an effect caused by too much time on her own, licking her wounds after a disastrous relationship.

And that rational, psychologically sound explanation was exactly what she would cling to, Tori told herself, even as her gaze began straying toward Bruce's magnificent muscles.

So he's probably a spectacular lover . . . so what? Tori knew that no amount of physical pleasure was going to fill the void inside of her. And that's all a man like Bruce Gautreau would want from her—physical pleasure and nothing else. He'd walk away once he was through with her, like a restoration job completed. Then he'd be on the hunt again, searching for the next new challenge.

Tori knew that restoring this house would keep her busy for a while. Then, when the time was right, she'd rely on Aunt Zoe to help introduce her into New Orlean's society. That's where she'd find the *right* man. Someone stable, reliable—even predictable.

Anyone but a Cajun heartbreaker.

Any man but Bruce Gautreau.

Another peal of thunder rumbled across the sky, this time very close as the patter of rain picked up its pace.

Tori's gaze dropped and she noticed the bottle of beer in

Bruce's hand. *Great. Drinking on the job.* Tori could only wonder what the work would look like.

When her gaze rose to his face again, she noticed a golden eyebrow slowly raise. Deliberately he brought the bottle of beer to his lips and took a long drink, raising the bottle higher and higher until it was drained.

She tried not to notice the masculine bulge of his flexing tricep muscle, or the cocky twitch of a smile on his lips when he'd finished the last drop.

"Mmmm-mmm. My favorite brand," he drawled. "Like one?"

Tori was about to decline. She didn't drink beer. But then she stopped herself—it was *exactly* what he expected of her.

"Yes, thank you," she said even as her lips were beginning to form the no. With satisfaction, she caught the brief look of surprise that streaked across his expression.

She followed Bruce across the porch and into the house through the open, door-sized kitchen window.

"How was your trip?" he asked, reaching for two bottles and placing them on the scarred Formica of the cheap kitchen counter. He was about to twist off a cap for her, but she reached for it first, twisting it off for herself.

"Uneventful. How was your work?"

He eyed her a moment, then twisted off his own. "Uneventful." He watched her until she took a sip, then he took one, as well.

"Here's to uneventful events," he said, touching his bottle to hers. "That's the way you like life, isn't it?"

Tori knew he was baiting her. Well, she wasn't biting. Instead, her cool gaze swept him. "May I see the work—if any of it is finished, that is?"

She could see the fury race up his back, could see him wrestle to keep it under control. Then a smirk played across his lips as he seemed to realize she was baiting him right back.

With a toss of her head, she took another sip of the cold beer, this time a long one. Outside, the brief afternoon shower had already let up, yet the air was still muggy. She wished a breeze would dispel some of the hot heaviness in the air. But the air remained static and repressively humid.

The cool beer running down her throat was the only thing that gave her relief. She had to admit, it tasted refreshingly good. When she finally lowered her bottle and looked in Bruce's direction, he was setting down his own drink with more force than necessary. Obviously he was still steamed at her remarks. *Good.*

She watched as he flung his sweaty T-shirt from his neck and buttoned on a khaki-colored workshirt that had been draped on the back of a nearby chair.

Tori's gaze caught on a battered gray toolbox near his feet. She noticed the dozen or so colorful decals, scattered upon its sides—Atlanta, Philadelphia, New York, Chicago, San Francisco. He certainly got around, she thought, not surprised that he was the kind who liked to keep moving. It was *exactly* what she'd expected.

Suddenly a loud door slamming upstairs brought Tori's head up. She looked to Bruce questioningly.

"Is there someone else in the house?" she asked. "An assistant?"

Bruce froze, his fingers stilled in the middle of buttoning on his workshirt, his face turned toward the staircase. "No. I worked alone all day today."

Tori watched him. His entire body was tense, alert; and for a full five seconds he closed his eyes and cocked an ear as if he were listening to some silent voice.

A chill ran through her blood.

"The wind?" she whispered. But there was no wind, not even a breeze. She had just wished for one only a few moments ago.

"Bruce?" she called, but he didn't seem to hear her. "Bruce!" she tried again, louder.

He slowly turned his dark gaze to her.

"Are you *sure* that someone isn't in the house?"

"Yes," he said.

"Then what—"

"The wind." He stated it shortly, cutting off her question. Buttoning the rest of his shirt, he motioned her to come with him.

"You wanted a tour?" he asked curtly.

Tori nodded reluctantly.

For no logical reason she suddenly felt nervous about following *this* man through *this* house. Nevertheless, she forced herself to rise from the kitchen table and follow just the same. . . .

Chapter Six

"They're back. Oh, Robert! They're back!"

Marina had grown quite strong over the past few weeks. The gentleman builder had provided a consistent diet of thoroughly powerful life energy, and both Marina and Robert had fed well on it.

They had also discovered a number of tricks.

This new state of being did not carry a human voice. But when Marina got her fill of life energy, she could focus some of it enough to manipulate air molecules—what she called "color dots."

In this way she could create a kind of sound wave. Although she could not yet communicate any sort of speech on a human level, she was getting very close.

She *could*, however, communicate with her Robert. He'd helped her along with that, showing her how to "talk" through their thoughts. That also took a certain amount of energy.

On the few days in a row when the gentleman builder had been away from the house, she and Robert had slowly lost much of their strength and could barely even communicate.

Those were sad days for them both.

At one point Marina had felt so weak that she'd almost faded completely out. But Robert had pleaded with her to hold on, asserting that the two life-forms—"the lovers," as he called them—would be back any day. And, of course, Robert had been right, thought Marina, because here they were, the gentleman builder and the lady. "The lovers" were back, and their golden-warm life energy was gradually filling the house.

"Marina, we must go to them," said Robert, flowing near her.

"Yes, my love," she answered, knowing that at last she would have the chance to touch, and perhaps even kiss, her Robert again.

"We must find a way to listen to their speech," advised Robert. *"In this way, we might be able to discern their plans for the house . . . and each other."*

"And perhaps influence those plans," suggested Marina.

"By all means," agreed Robert.

"I think I've developed a method of listening," said Marina. *"I'll just reverse the method I was working on for speaking."*

"And what was that?"

"Well, it's something to do with pushing around those lovely little color dots all around us. Let's find the lovers now, and we'll try it out."

As Bruce led Tori from the kitchen to the entryway and then down the hallway to the parlor, he talked freely about his restoration work. But Tori's ears were barely listening to his list of procedures and materials once her eyes caught sight of the newly restored rooms.

In a word, they were spectacular.

It was as if he had given the house new *life.*

Tori marveled at the quality of the workmanship: from the finish on the formerly paint-encrusted woodwork, to the smoothness of the walls and the gloss on the newly sanded floorboards.

As Bruce led her up the stairs, Tori's hand caressed the gleaming banister. The rich luster of the wood dazzled her, and amazingly, no step creaked under her feet as they climbed.

As he took her through each room, Tori was more and more convinced that Aunt Zoe was right about Gautreau. He *was* a genius at restoration. When they finally entered the master bedroom on the second floor—the room she planned to claim as her own—Tori's wide eyes betrayed her overjoyed astonishment and utter admiration.

She had expected maybe two to three rooms to be fully restored, but in a little over three weeks, he had done the entire job he had outlined while sitting in the Café du Monde. The ground floor's parlor, dining room, large den, and small study were completed as well as the second floor's master bedroom. He had even thrown in the entry-way and staircase.

As Bruce spoke animatedly about the way he polished the Carrara marble of the fireplace without damaging or ob-scuring the fine details, Tori noticed his calloused hands, and how they seemed to remember the work.

She watched him reach out to touch the marble mantel, his fingers practically caressing the stone. She blinked, looking away as her mind considered other things he might want to caress.

Bruce walked to the large beveled French windows that faced the back balcony and pushed them open. The fresh-ness of the afternoon shower lingered in the air. It was less humid now, but the air was warm and still.

Tori peered out onto the wooden balcony, noticing that, though the outside of the house remained unpainted, he had managed to replace some of the missing posts on the bal-cony railing. Taking a deep breath of the fresh air, Tori turned and gazed up at Bruce. He was only a few feet from her, his arms across his chest.

The tour of his restoration work was now completed, and she wanted to say something.

"It's wonderful," she whispered, her voice revealing her joy at the first tangible evidence of her wish coming true.

Bruce's arms relaxed, and he casually let his hands dig into his pants pocket. "I know," he stated, ever the cocky artisan.

Her eyebrow rose and he smiled, crow's feet evident around his dark brown eyes. "And I'm glad you like it," he added. Then his gaze met hers. "Too bad my work is done. . . . Or is it?"

Tori wrung her hands as she stepped away from him. She paced the large master bedroom and stopped at the beautiful fireplace, her eyes drinking in the fleur-de-lys pattern in the smooth marble.

"Yes, I'm afraid it is," she finally said, her tone betraying disappointment. Tori had expected to work with him at least a little bit, hoping to pick up enough to continue the labor herself. Now he was through—unless she came up with fifty thousand bucks.

She felt him moving close to her, felt the heat radiating from his body. "It doesn't have to be over," he said, close to her ear.

Tori fought her instinctive reaction to his nearness.

"Yes," she said, "it does . . . I'm out of money. The rest of my savings I was planning to live on until the guest house began bringing in revenue. I've got the teaching position, but it doesn't start until late August, and the pay will never be enough to secure a decent mortgage."

"Have you tried the Small Business Administration?" suggested Bruce. "You have the house as collateral."

"But even with a tax credit for restoration, I've got property taxes. And if I can't make loan payments, they'll foreclose."

Tori's field of vision took in the large tanned hand near her own. She noticed the fine sun-blond hairs, the tiny scars and scratches, badges from his manual work. His finger followed hers as she began tracing the carvings in the cool marble. She watched its movements with a distracted gaze.

"You know, the fleur-de-lys design is classic," he murmured. "The word comes from medieval French and means—"

"I know," she said, "lily flower."

"*Oui, chère*, and do you know what the Victorians believed the lily to mean?"

"What?" Tori asked on a whisper, her voice clearly betraying the effect his seductive drawl was having on her system.

"The return of happiness."

Tori's hand reached to her neck, still stiff from the last leg of her long drive, and absently rubbed in thought. "But I read that the fleur-de-lys design was a stylized version of an iris bud."

Bruce's hand replaced her own as he began to massage her neck. It seemed so natural to Tori with the seductive sound of his voice. She gave in to the wonderful feel of his ministrations, and, as his other hand joined in, her eyes half-closed with pleasure.

"The lily and the iris are in the same family," he continued, his voice gentle and low. "Do you know what the Victorians thought the iris meant?"

Tori bent her head lower, allowing Bruce to rub more of her slender neck. "No," she whispered.

"Hope."

Tori smiled despite her worries, and she remembered again what she had tried to forget upon meeting Bruce Gautreau. There was much more to this man than met the eye.

She turned to face him, but his hands only lifted enough to allow her to turn, then they descended to rest possessively on her hips. She was trapped now, in a loose embrace. Looking up at his handsome features, Tori felt the air leave her lungs.

"I haven't given up hope," she said on a whisper.

He smiled down at her. "I know. You're here, aren't you?"

Tori allowed her gaze to remain on his, perhaps a dangerous choice. Since she'd entered the house, she'd tried to avoid this kind of searing exposure. She felt so vulnerable to him when she looked into the glistening darkness of his intense eyes. It felt as though he were peering right into the depths of her being.

Although the rain had stopped, Tori could swear she heard thunder rumbling in the distance as he dipped his head toward her.

His lips were mere inches from hers, barely brushing them as he spoke. "You know what I want for us," he whispered.

Tori searched his face, but she said nothing.

"Lovers," he whispered. "You and I, *chérie*. It could be spectacular—"

"I know," said Tori. "And that's what I'm afraid of."

"Don't be afraid," he said, his fingers caressing her back.

But Tori was. Her hand rose and she pushed the flat of her palm against his chest, surprised for a moment at the rock-solid wall beneath the workshirt.

"Don't," she said. "I can't . . . It's not what I want."

Bruce's head rose, but his hands tightened at her waist.

"It *is* what you want, Tori. I can read it in you. Don't you know your own self?"

Her eyes narrowed. "I know my own self very well. Well enough to keep from making mistakes I've already made." She broke away, and this time he let her. She turned, gazing unseeingly into the empty hearth. "And yes, I may *want* to sleep with you, but . . ."

"What?" he asked.

"I'm not the kind of person who makes a habit of one-night stands. Or cheap affairs."

"Uh-huh, I see. And *I* am?"

Without daring to look at him, Tori strode to one of the large windows. She noticed that it was new—a small red label was still affixed to one corner of the pane. She reached up and eased a thumbnail under one corner to peel it off.

"I think I understand, sweet."

Tori stared down at her fingers as they rolled the sticky label into a tiny ball. "What do you understand?"

"You're afraid you'll fall in love with me."

The hand that had been fingering the tiny ball now balled itself into a tight fist. She reeled on him, her eyes angrily sweeping him. He stood there defiant and confident, muscular forearms casually folded across his chest. "Why, you cocky, arrogant, insufferable, bast—"

"Well, now," he taunted, stepping closer. "Can't take a reality check, can you?"

Tori stopped dead, contemplating what he'd said.

"It's the truth, isn't it?" he prodded, moving close again.

"And what if it is," she answered. "You haven't denied that you're the sort who likes a quick turnover."

"No, I haven't."

"And you expect me to get involved with you knowing that?"

"Yes. I do."

Tori shook her head in disbelief. "I can't believe you!"

"I'm honest, sweet. I never lie to women. What you see is what you get. And, contrary to what you may think about yourself, I can see that you're a survivor. You'll be just fine no matter what I may or may not do while I'm in your life—for as little or as long as I'm in your life."

Tori tried to turn away, but he captured her wrist and gently pulled her against him. His rich, dark eyes bore into her startled green gaze and seemed to pull her soul to the surface.

"And as far as those 'mistakes' you claim to have made. I don't think you've made nearly enough to learn anythin'. In fact, I'd wager that's been your problem all along, Victoria. You try so hard *not* to make mistakes that you make big fat ones all the time."

His head lowered as he spoke. "This house was your first big risk, but it shouldn't be your only one." Tori felt his other hand at the base of her neck, coaxing her mouth even closer to his own. "Don't you understand, Tori, all that beauty and fire needs passion in her life—not safety. You need me like you need this house."

This was a snow job, she told herself, trying to believe it, trying to believe he used these same lines on all the women he wanted in his bed. Yet his words . . . they seemed to be so true for her. He'd just met her a few weeks ago, yet he was able to read her like a freshly inked blueprint. Now how could that be?

She looked into his dark, intense eyes, wanting to resist him . . . yet something seemed to be prompting her to taste him again. It gnawed at the edges of her thoughts, beat at the base of her brain. . . . Okay, so maybe she'd allow a kiss.

Just for a moment.

She did not move away as his lips brushed hers in the lightest of fluttering kisses. Tiny pearls of heat seemed to roll through her veins at the expert touch of his full, soft lips. Her entire body tingled with fire and life at his nearness.

She wanted so much to feel cold and distant from him, but she couldn't. And at this moment Tori could no longer deny that her reaction to his touch three weeks ago hadn't been a fluke at all.

This moment she was feeling the same intense heat, the same burning need . . .

He pressed closer, his lips hungry for more of her, and the scent and taste of him enveloped her like mist. She felt his hand move from the back of her neck to lightly cup the side of her jaw. The flick of his tongue brought a blatant, shameful response to her breasts, and a liquid heat to her lower body.

The reaction was almost unreal in its immediacy—no other man had ever generated an arousal in her so quickly or so powerfully; in fact, every cell of her entire form was responding in an almost magical dance to his touch.

Yes, it did seem magical.

And vaguely, Tori realized there was something else extraordinary here: the air. It had been still and warm in the room, but now as Bruce kissed her, Tori felt a draft. A cool stream of air seemed to be circling their entwined bodies, and Tori could feel the chilly flow as it seemed to brush her bare legs, then swirl around Bruce and back up across her cheek.

The windows were open, but strangely enough, this air stream seemed to be coming from *inside* the house.

Suddenly her hand raised, almost of its own accord, and coiled around his neck. It seemed crazy, but the cold stream of air began swirling faster around them, making her dizzy with a need to touch him. Boldly she began to unbutton his work shirt, her hands rejoicing in their contact with his broad hard chest and the silky golden curls that covered it.

Before she knew what was happening, Bruce's long fingers had found the buttons of her own white cotton blouse. His lips were still on hers, hot and insistent, distracting her from the fingers that were slowly exposing more and more of her skin.

She didn't even hear the unsnapping of the front clasp on her thin, lacy bra. All she felt was the exquisite sensation of Bruce's hand at her full breasts, tenderly cupping and caressing. Then his fingertips—still cool from the beer—rolled and pinched the dark pink nipples into taut signs of her own mounting desire for him.

As his tongue penetrated her mouth in a tender exploration, she felt his hand move lower. Without invitation, he undid the top of her shorts and reached his calloused hand inside.

Tori's breathing was rapid, her heartbeat driving now with the same incessant anticipation of those drums in her dreams. In fact, she almost felt like that now, as if she were in a dream.

She reveled in the masculine taste of his lips, the tang of his aftershave, the tartness of the beer, the salty scent of his perspiration . . . all combined with the cloying aroma of magnolia from the garden to create a dizzying cloud of bliss. Her own tongue wanted more, and she pushed it past his lips, her reward a groan of pleasure.

The hand at her back now moved lower to caress her waist, just as his other hand slipped into her lace panties. Tori felt the rough calluses of his palm against the smoothness of her belly—his hand felt so hard, so masculine, and it made her feel that much more feminine. She gasped when she felt his long, work-roughened fingers dip even lower and tangle in the tight feminine curls hidden beneath the silky lace.

Too mesmerized to put a stop to his boldness, Tori merely closed her eyelids and tightened her arms around his broad shoulders for support as her knees went suddenly weak.

"It's always wise to christen a bedroom," whispered Bruce. Then his mouth descended again, this time more forcefully. And as the drums from her dreams continued to haunt her, she felt his rough fingers dip into her soft folds.

The driving rhythms moved through them both, and Bruce caressed Tori with the same gentleness and patience that had made him a master artisan. Gradually he brought her to the very brink . . . then with two long fingers, he plunged deeply into her.

And like her dream, she screamed. But this time with pleasure, not terror.

As his mouth swallowed the bright sound of release, Bruce used his strong arms to clasp her waist against him, supporting her body as it rose and fell on waves of pleasure.

He held her tightly to him for long moments, waiting for her breathing to slow from its rapid pace, her heartbeat to calm. She clung to him now, burying her face into his shoulder.

Every kind of emotion washed over Tori in those few moments, but the strongest was the one that now brought dampness to the shoulder of Bruce's workshirt and racking movements from her own slender form.

Bruce held her tightly as she cried.

Tori was surprised that he didn't ask what was wrong. It

was as if he knew. She clung even more tightly to him for that, to his strength and sureness—the bedrock beneath the cockiness that had so annoyed her at first.

When she was through, she raised her head, her green eyes glistening, her cheeks damp. His brown eyes drank her in, his serious expression melting to longing as he surveyed her face.

"I don't make promises. But I'm always honest," he whispered, brushing at the damp tracks of tears on her cheeks. "And, no, I don't stay forever. I can't. But I can stay awhile. I can help you find what you need."

She swallowed. He couldn't know the specifics of her life, but now he clearly knew how much pain she had been trying to cover.

"I don't know," she managed on a weak voice.

It was at that moment they heard it. A loud crash two floors above them. Both froze, but Bruce was the first to move. He walked to the stairs to listen.

"Stay here," he commanded, then quickly ascended the steps.

Of course, Tori stayed—right on his heels. She rushed to catch up, buttoning her blouse and shorts as she went. And then, on the third-floor landing, Bruce stopped so quickly that Tori ran smack into his broad back.

He turned to her with a finger to his lips. "Listen."

She did, and couldn't believe her ears.

Sure, plodding feet were pacing above them, the boards creaking with every step. The footsteps were strangely measured, and echoed through the house with an eerie resonance.

The strained look on Bruce's face confirmed her own fears.

Someone was in the attic. Or some*thing.*

Chapter Seven

As Robert's filmy essence hovered in the musty cluttered attic of the old Victorian, he was aware of many things— mainly, four generations of collected junk.

From mildewed footstools and broken lamps, to dusty firescreens and damaged desk chairs, these were not the possessions of his time, but trappings of other lives.

Oh, he was aware of *some* possessions from his time. They were collecting their share of dust here. But, for the moment, it was only one particular item that concerned Robert's awareness. It was an objet d'art. One of some value, as he recalled. Unfortunately, the thing was now well hidden in the old attic.

It was incredible how different this space was from the brand-new attic he recalled building. That had been a place of order and neatness.

It was also incredible how oddly the details of the past came back to him—like erratic brush strokes on a blank canvas. He had yet to see the entire picture of it. Yet one thing was certain. He could recall nothing beyond his wedding night. Nothing came back to him beyond holding his beautiful new bride close—

Sudden movements of the nearby life-forms drew Robert back to the business at hand. He became aware of the gentleman builder and the lovely lady. Their warm bright energy grew perceptively stronger as they moved to investigate the noises that he and Marina had been making.

Robert observed his ghost bride, flitting about and using her energy to conjure ghostly footsteps on the floorboards. It occurred to him that she was getting a bit carried away with her newfound ability to . . . *haunt*. He nearly cringed at the word.

In life Robert never thought himself a snob, but it struck him now that the entire idea of actually *haunting* a house in this manner was rather . . . well, gauche.

"Marina, that should be enough—"

"Enough?" asked Marina, making a few more creaking floorboards keen and cry like screeching alley cats.

"Yes, they are coming now. For heaven's sake, stop."

"Robert, it is precisely for heaven's sake *that I'm doing this,"* returned Marina. *"This house will be like a hell for us unless it is set right again. And you know we must find a way to keep these two together—"*

Marina carefully refocused her energies, this time onto the attic door. The worn wood had no sooner creaked open slowly and banged shut than Marina was searching for another disturbance to lure the lovers closer. A large, mildewed red velvet armchair provided the perfect vehicle. Upending it, she found, would create a splendid loud thump against the floorboards.

"Quite effective! Isn't it, Robert?!"

"Marina, I tell you, that's enough!"

"Oh, just one more thing. Please, Robert. To have such an effect on the living, doesn't it make you feel grand?!"

Grand. Robert did not know whether it was Marina's phrasing or his sudden sighting of a completely tarnished yet familiar-looking cat-shaped brass vase. But whatever it was, for a moment Robert's memory removed him from the musty old attic of the twentieth century and brought him back to a bright street in the 1890s Quarter.

It had been midday; and upon meeting him in the street, Marina had dragged him down some little alley and inside a small shop, where the word CURIOS had been deceptively painted on the window. To Robert's mind JUNK should have been a more accurate label. Marina, however, did not care about the quality of clutter she was purchasing. She merely wanted *clutter,* taking him to task for having too neat and orderly a household, which she had surveyed at his house-warming *soirée* the week before.

Well, what did she expect? Robert thought at the time. With no living mother nor sister to guide him, he'd spent over seven years of his adult life as a bachelor abroad. This, he assumed, was the driving force behind the well-meaning Marina's guiding hand. He later discovered that her motivation was not merely a female taking "pity" on a hardened bachelor, but a deeper interest, one that would blossom and flourish in the months to come.

And he himself would soon discover that his initial physical response to her fresh, somehow exotic beauty at a Mardis Gras masque ball would only be a prelude to a more profound attraction . . . and an eventual realization that he had no interest in living life without her. . . .

Such deeper discoveries, however, were far from apparent on that bright day at the junk shop. No. On that day the *house* was the thing they talked of, and what his spanking new abode needed, she insisted, were lovely little adorning items. These trinkets would provide a "lovely clutter" and make his cold barren structure seem more like a house.

He found himself agreeing, not particularly with the idea of clutter, but with the chance to spend a bit of time in the presence of this exotically beautiful young woman. While the clop of hooves had echoed in the narrow flagstone street outside, she went about helping him pick out a number of items: ornate lamps, gilded picture frames, peculiar statuary, that brass vase in the shape of a cat . . . and then she saw the small music box.

It didn't work, and it was overpriced, but the top of the box was painted with apple-cheeked Renaissance cherubs heralding the morning sun with small golden trumpets, and Marina had loved it so. *Just one more thing, Robert. Just to look at it . . . doesn't it make you feel grand?!*

But he had laughed and said they'd bought enough. They'd left the shop with delivery instructions, but Marina had turned back once more to look at the music box.

What joy it could have given her—to place that box in just the right spot. What joy it could have given him—to see that box and recall her fleeting joy. . . .

Perhaps he could have repaired it. And they could have danced to the tinkling notes, marveling at what melody it might have played . . . might have . . . but back then, in that little shop, he had simply checked his pocket watch and declared himself late for some appointment.

What the appointment had been, he could not now recall. Over a year later, however, after they had become lovers, he had returned to that street. The shop was boarded up. Out of business. The music box gone with it.

Such were the moments of a life, he supposed. Forever fleeting. Perpetually passing. Back then, he'd scoffed at the notion that there was some great trick to mastering it all. But from his present perspective, he felt that maybe there was a skill to it. Yes . . . if the whole noisy affair came down to so many moments, then perhaps the true trick of living was coming to understand which were the moments that, in the end, didn't matter a fig, and which were the ones that . . .

"If only I had bought you that music box."

"What?"

"Off Chartres Street," explained Robert.

Marina was unaware of Robert's reference and was without time to explore it. The lovers' footsteps were louder now.

"They're coming!" exclaimed Marina.

"Yes, my love, now remember, we must not alarm them when they reach us. We want them to find what is hidden."

"Oh, Robert. Do you think she will use its value to hire the gentleman builder?"

"I hope so, my love. I hope so. . . . "

"Tori, didn't I tell you to stay downstairs?"

"Tell me? Tell me all you like, Gautreau, but this is *my* house and I'll do what *I* wish, not what you tell me."

"Mmmmm-hmmmm." Standing on the bare wood boards of the third-floor landing, Bruce bristled again at Tori's Northern royalty act, especially with it coming so quickly on the heels of their shared intimacy. But then again, what else could he have really expected of her by now? *How about some civility? Or maybe some sign of a chink in the pristine armor?*

A sudden banging above made Tori's form jerk with a start. "That's the attic door," she whispered.

Bruce was cocking an experienced ear. "So it is."

"Who's up there?"

Bruce was about to say *no one*. But on second thought he knew that wasn't altogether accurate. "I don't know."

"Well . . . what should we do?"

"We?" Bruce took pleasure in turning to face down Tori. Her hair was disheveled, her lips kiss-swollen. He wanted her.

Bruce hadn't a doubt that she was his for the taking. But there would be consequences with this one. He knew that now. And that reason was the chief one he turned his attention to the attic.

"It's *your* house, Miss Avalon," drawled Bruce, backing up and gesturing to the staircase before them.

With agitation, Tori watched the edges of Bruce's mouth begin, ever so slightly, to defy gravity. "Don't you smirk at me, Gautreau. We'll go up together."

"Bien sûr, your highness. *Après vous."*

Tori glared at Bruce. Obviously she'd stuck her foot in it. Gautreau now expected her to go up first. Well . . . what could she do now but go forward? There'd be no facing him, otherwise.

Taking a fortifying breath of warm, humid air, Tori began moving up the steps. About halfway up she felt a hand on her arm.

"Okay, *chère* . . . far enough," murmured Bruce. "I'll take over."

"You'll do no such thing," snapped Tori. "I can—"

"I know you can," interrupted Bruce. That's when the loud THUMP-THUD sounded above them.

Tori swallowed uneasily, and Bruce quietly slipped his large calloused right hand around the slender soft fingers of her left. She was secretly grateful for the gesture.

What's the matter with me, anyway? Tori had never before thought of herself as some delicate magnolia, ready to swoon and faint at the slightest provocation. But these noises, they really had her spooked. No . . . not *spooked*—that was an unfortunate word choice. She was just *nervous*. After all, there could be an intruder up there, a burglar. It was an upsetting prospect, but nothing she was going to shrink from—certainly not in front of Bruce Gautreau.

As they mounted the last step and she placed her right hand on the doorknob, she paused a moment to listen—or maybe to reassure herself, yet again, that she did not believe in the existence of ghosts.

But there was no sound. No noise.

It seemed the entire house had fallen into a deep slumber. Then Tori felt the warm touch of a hand over hers. Bruce was gently guiding her to turn the doorknob. Tori swallowed uneasily as she heard the click at the jam.

Bruce nudged the scarred old door, and with its opening came a slow creaking yawn. The tone's unsettling pitch reminded her of her own ill-fated efforts to learn the violin—one of the many things she'd attempted to try to please her father. . . .

Tori's moment of distraction gave Bruce the chance to step by her quickly and enter the attic first. She said nothing as she followed him, her gaze quickly surveying what was once a functional servants' quarters but was now nothing more than a storage area.

As a rule Victorian attics were nothing like the dark, tiny spaces in more modern houses. Aunt Hestia's attic followed the pattern of most Victorians. It was large, with nice-size windows, which at this moment were boarded up. Luckily, rays of afternoon sun could slip through the inch left open at the top of one window. The dim light, suffused with dust particles, was enough for Bruce to stride to a hanging lightbulb and pull the string.

"No one," said Tori in relief as she looked completely around.

Bruce stood stock-still. The expression on his face was tense, and his breathing seemed irregular.

"We can go back down now," suggested Tori hurriedly.

"We can?"

"Yes . . . you can see there's no one here. So the noises must have just been . . ."

As Tori's voice trailed off, Bruce turned his gaze to an item across the musty, cluttered room—a big overstuffed armchair, its red velvet torn and mildewed. The chair had been awkwardly upended, and Bruce leaned over to examine it, then turned back to Tori.

"Mice?" he asked sardonically, a golden eyebrow rising.

"What?" asked Tori.

"Do you think, *chère,* that mice did this?"

Tori hesitantly walked closer to the upended chair. "That chair has probably been lying there like that for—"

"Minutes? Seconds?" Bruce crouched low and gestured toward the dust-free area where the large chair had obviously been sitting upright for years. Clearly that area was newly exposed. Slowly he ran a finger across the clean floorboard, then into the undisturbed half-inch caking of thick dust.

"Okay, so it wasn't mice. And it wasn't the wind," she said, her fingers snapping at the boarded up widow. "Then it was the house settling. As long as it's not an intruder, I don't care."

"Fine, sweet. Then go if you like," offered Bruce. "But I'm havin' a look around."

Tori's arms crossed her chest and she propped her hip out defiantly. "I'll wait."

Bruce bit his cheek to keep from laughing at Tori. She was quite attractive when she was trying desperately not to show her true emotions—in this case, stark fear. He could feel it coursing strongly through her just under the surface. But strong emotions were like powerful currents, sometimes they swelled and overflowed, as sloppily as the flooding banks of a muddy river.

Rubbing his dusty hand over his pantleg, Bruce turned his attention back to the question of the attic noises. He rose to his feet and stood silently a moment, just listening.

The presence was here—at least one, anyway—or maybe the two were so close together, he could only judge them as one. Bruce could actually *see* nothing. He could *hear* nothing. But another sense, his Cajun mother's sense, was somehow aware of the energy source. It drifted in a far corner of the room like a hovering cloud. Ironically, he got the sense that it, too, was watching.

We were called up here. Bruce knew it, not from logical deductive reasoning, but suddenly, like his nose telling him that a certain whiff on a certain street near the French Market meant that Odette was baking her crusty baguettes. He had no doubt that the presence—or the two—had *called* them to the attic. But why? Bruce asked as he began to move through the clutter.

To find something . . .

"Look around, Tori," suggested Bruce at once.

"Look around? I don't under—"

"Just look." Bruce didn't know quite what they were supposed to be looking for. He just felt the need to follow the sudden suggestion in his head.

"Look?" Tori did nothing of the sort. In fact she didn't move a muscle, other than the tapping of her foot, but simply regarded Bruce impatiently as he alone poked around the attic.

Old magazines, books, cheap broken furnishings—none of it seemed significant to Tori, other than the notion of the clutter being a fire hazard. She made a mental note to take care of clearing it out and installing first-rate smoke alarms.

"There," Bruce murmured as he walked toward one of the walls, covered with dingy striped wallpaper. His gaze took in the slant of the roof as it met the wall. It didn't look right. He knew the room below extended farther out and the roof above did as well. . . .

"What is it?" asked Tori. "What are you—"

"I'm not sure. Help me move some of this."

After a box of old Mardi Gras trinkets and a rolled-up rug were pushed out of his way, Bruce moved to a section of the papered wall and tapped his fingers against it. Then he moved lower, tapped again, and began to feel along the papering. When his hands reached an edge, about knee-level, he knocked. The hollow sound followed his hand as it tapped and knocked, knocked and tapped until he'd gotten a good notion of the outline.

"Bruce?"

Pulling his Swiss Army knife from the pocket of his khaki work pants, Bruce glanced at Tori. "There's a false wall here" was all he said before flipping open a cutting blade, then bending over to slice at the paper. He made three quick square incisions—two that measured about four feet across and one four feet vertically.

"A door," said Tori, amazed.

"Looks like a blocked room," offered Bruce as he used his muscles to pull the stiff door all the way back. He tried to peer into the blackness but only caught a whiff of stale, hot air, full of enough dust to make both of them endure a terrible coughing fit.

"What . . . what are you doing?" Tori asked between dissipating coughs when she saw Bruce digging into his pocket, then crouching.

"Going in," said Bruce, flipping on the same small flashlight he'd conveniently carried the first day they'd met.

"Maybe you shouldn't—"

But Bruce was already moving through the low door.

"Well?" Tori finally asked after a few moments of silence. "What do you see?"

"Furniture," he answered.

"Oh, is that all."

"No. It's not like the other things. This is—"

Bruce's voice broke off and Tori grew curious.

"Is what?" she asked, finally moving through the door herself. For a moment she hesitated, not really wanting to walk into a stuffy, pitch-black room. But when she did move inside, she was happy to see that Bruce's small light illuminated much of the space—a snug ten by twelve box with a narrowly slanted roof.

Tori was surprised at the neatness inside the space compared with the chaos of the main attic. There was a set of furniture inside, each item carefully shrouded with a heavy white dropcloth.

Bruce had already unveiled a beautifully carved chest, a sealed wooden crate, and an ornate armoire with a mirrored door. Tori lifted the cloth on the remaining items to find two nightstands, and a velvet covered *prie-dieu,* or prayer kneeler.

She looked over to find Bruce crouching by a large bundle. He was pulling back the protective cloth to reveal pieces of some sort of dismantled furniture.

"Looks like a bed . . . a four-poster," said Bruce. "All of these pieces look like quality antiques. Let's move them into the main room and have a better look at them."

Tori agreed, but after they moved the items and she got a closer look at the mahogany and rosewood bedroom set, she felt her limbs go numb. Backing up, she collapsed on a ratty old footstool.

"What's wrong?" asked Bruce, eyeing her curiously.

"This bedroom set . . ."

"Yes."

Tori recognized the intricately carved swirls in the wood, the pattern of budding roses mingled with fleur-de-lys. The design was the same one found in the mansion's signature cast-iron fencing.

"It's the Rosegate rosebuds," said Tori with a shaky voice. No, there could be no mistake. This was the *same* exact bed that had been in her recurring dream . . . the one that included Bruce. . . .

"Was it your aunt's bed?" asked Bruce.

"No. Believe me, I'd have remembered seeing this before."

Tori moved to the chest and tried to open it, but couldn't.

"Let me." Bruce used his knife to jimmy the lock, and Tori gasped softly when she saw what was inside. Lace curtains, bed linens, and tasseled pillows had been carefully preserved inside. Below them she found a fine porcelain pitcher and bowl, and a bound leather book, the initial *M* hand-tooled onto the cover. All were part of the master bedroom in her dream—and the master bedroom had unquestionably been Rosegate's.

Bruce watched Tori as she lifted the leather-bound book and used her finger to outline the engraved *M*. Her face betrayed little emotion, but he knew feelings were wreaking havoc inside her.

"You *do* recognize these things," said Bruce, studying her carefully.

Tori noticed that it was not a question. And not for the first time, she realized that Bruce could read her quite deftly. She shifted uncomfortably. No person in her adult life, except perhaps occasionally her two aunts, had been able to see through her practiced masks. Not even Edward Halloran, whom she'd lived with. *And remember how wrecked you were when that ended,* chided her own embittered conscience. *Face it, you're still not over it. . . .*

Tori lifted her emerald gaze to search Bruce's chiseled face. The room was stuffy and they'd both been perspiring. His forehead was glistening, locks of sun-gold hair had been darkened by the dampness. Suddenly she was aware of the moist stickiness on her skin causing a revealing cling to her blouse.

Her eyes met his and she felt a tingling in her body. Too vividly she recalled the caress of his work-roughened hands

across her body, his hungry kisses—and her uncontrolled
release.

She also recalled his offer when it was over.

He wanted further involvement with her, further opportu-
nities for physical intimacy. And yet, his offer had been
couched within a qualifier, hadn't it?

Yes, she realized. Bruce Gautreau hadn't made a declara-
tion of love. He'd made one of limits.

Or perhaps it was a plain old-fashioned proposition,
snapped her biting conscience.

"Tori, don't—" Bruce spoke up suddenly. But after those
two sharp words, he stopped himself and simply closed his
eyes, his posture sinking in on itself.

Tori studied his fallen face. "Don't what?" she prodded.

What could he say? thought Bruce. *Don't turn a beautiful thing into an ugly thing. Don't crush a bud under your
heel because you know that after it blooms, it will die. . . .*
He could read the general direction of her thoughts, and he
wagered he'd have a better time changing the direction of
the Mississippi.

A sudden loud thump sounded inside the pitch-black
room that they'd just opened up, shocking both Tori and
Bruce from their internal debates.

"What the heck?" blurted Tori.

Their heads turned simultaneously, but neither could
make out anything clearly in that black box of a room
they'd just left.

Bruce's steady gaze move to Tori's face. "Mice."

Tori smirked and started for the room, but he caught her
arm. "Wait."

"Why?"

"Listen."

Tori did, and she heard nothing for a moment, but then
something. It was a strange eerie thumping against the floor
and wall inside that small room. It was measured out, like
code.

Three thumps, then two, then three more.

She bit her lower lip, her limbs becoming rigid, her heart

pumping blood at twice the usual rate. "What is it?" she whispered.

Bruce glanced down into her face, the edges of his lips again beginning to defy gravity as if he knew something she did not.

"Gautreau? Answer me. Do you know what it is?"

"If I tell you, Miss Avalon, will you believe me?"

Tori hesitated, but before she could answer, another loud BANG! sounded, and that was enough for her already frayed nerves.

Breaking away from Bruce, she flew for the attic exit. The metal doorknob slipped almost sinisterly in the sweaty palm of her hand, and she cried out softly as she worked to turn it.

Finally the knob moved. She shoved at the wooden door, then stumbled down the first few steps. After catching herself hard on the banister, she returned to her speedy flight downward.

Bruce caught up with her as she entered the sun-washed master bedroom. He walked slowly to where she had sunk to the floor, her back against the wall, her breathing labored. It wasn't until he'd sat down beside her and softly spoken twice that she realized she was holding something in her arms.

"Tori, I said, let me see what you have."

Glancing down, Tori saw the leather-bound book with the *M* hand-tooled into the cover. It was clutched to her chest, and she had to consciously order her white-knuckled fingers to release their death grip. "I . . . didn't realize. I mean, I don't know what's inside," said Tori, handing it to him.

Bruce inspected the outside of the old book and then opened it. Beautiful script filled the yellowed pages, the black ink swirling and looping across each line, an occasional black ink splotch marring the delicate hand.

"It's written in French," murmured Bruce.

Tori reached for it and turned to the first page.

* * *

LE 18 FEVRIER, 1896

JE RENCONTRE LUI . . .

"February eighteenth," she translated aloud. "Eighteen ninety-six. I met him . . ."

"It's a diary, then?" asked Bruce.

Tori nodded. "It appears." Drawn back to its first page, she continued translating aloud. *"And so I begin this book because it is my birthday. It is not the date of birth, it is the date of Mardis Gras. Yet, on this day and year, I feel as though I have begun my life. Begun it at the age of nineteen because it is the day, or rather the night, I have met him!"*

Tori paused to leaf through the book. "It's a young woman's diary. A French Creole . . . of high social station, considering her language usage. It's quite proper, no patois. She was well educated . . ."

"And it's a century old?"

"Looks authentic to me," said Tori. "Which means I should turn it over to the Historic New Orleans Collection."

"Let me see it," said Bruce, examining it again. "You might want to think about selling it to a private collector instead. Maybe those Historic New Orleans folks can give you an appraisal."

"Well, actually, the Internal Revenue Service won't let *them* do that, but they can probably recommend some appraisers," said Tori, taking it quickly back into her hands. "But I'd like to translate it myself first, anyway."

"Sure . . ."

"Maybe a small press will buy the rights." The whole idea of money brought Tori back down to reality. "Uh . . . Mr. Gautreau—"

"God have mercy, sweet is calling me *Mister*. Look out, son."

"Bruce—"

"Hmmmm, first name could be just as dangerous."

Tori ignored his Cajun teasing and plowed onward. "I

don't have the funds to hire you beyond what you've already done, but—"

"Don't tell me now, you've always relied on the 'kindness of strangers.' "

Tori took a deep breath. Leave it to Gautreau to quote from a play with the word *Desire* in the title. "I assure you, Bruce, I'm no foolishly romantic Blanche Dubois. At least, not anymore."

"I wouldn't be so sure of yourself, Victoria. The world's turned into a mighty cruel place. You'd do well to think twice before you turn down offers of kindness from anyone." *Or an offer to fulfill a true passion,* added Bruce silently.

"Listen . . ." she began, then paused, fingering the edge of the leather-bound diary. Her next words had to be weighed carefully. She was well aware that, in many respects, Bruce Gautreau was an amazing man. Virile. Sexy. Smart. Skilled. But he was not the kind of man she could trust, and certainly not the kind she felt she should get involved with.

Once again Tori reminded herself of her carefully chosen plans. At some point, when she felt more settled, she'd ask Aunt Zoe to introduce her around New Orleans—to the right sort. Tori wanted a relationship. But one with a stable, settled man. Someone who was a bit more genteel, and wouldn't provoke her emotions so much.

On the other hand, at this moment in time, Tori needed Bruce's help. She wished to God she had the money to hire him, but she didn't. And she certainly didn't want to give him the wrong impression, leading him on when she really had no intention of getting involved—

"Bruce . . ."

"*Oui, chère.* I'm waitin'."

"I need your help."

"I know."

"And I don't have the money to pay you."

"I know."

"So, I think we should work out a deal . . . of some sort."

"A deal, *chère*? Or a . . . proposition?"

Tori sighed with frustration. She rose to her feet and walked the length of the room. At the French doors she took a deep breath of fresh, aromatic air. The newly moistened greenery of the overgrown garden seemed to steady her nerves.

"Friendship is all I want from you, Bruce," she said plainly. "If you're willing to extend it, that is. But I need a *friend* now more than a lover."

Bruce remained seated on the floor. He surveyed Tori's attractive form and considered his response. "That's a lie," he finally said softly. "You want a lover, *chérie*. You want me. But you just don't want to admit it. . . ."

Tori never blinked. She blatantly ignored his challenge and continued on as if he hadn't even spoken. "Here's my offer: I can't hire you to *do* the work, not yet, but I can go forward with it myself, a little at a time. I only need you to oversee it. Teach me the proper methods."

Bruce slowly smiled, a mischievous glimmer making his dark eyes shine like lacquered stones. He knew in his heart that he wanted to finish this job; and he knew, in other parts of his body, that he had other unfinished business under this roof.

"I'll teach you my methods, sweet. Don't know how 'proper' they are, but I'll teach you."

"Good," said Tori brusquely, walking toward Bruce with her hand outstretched. Bruce rose and shook it, the physical contact alarmingly potent to them both. "I'll keep a running tab for your services," promised Tori. "You *will* be paid. Once I find a way."

The glimmer returned to Bruce's gaze as he continued to hold Tori's hand. When they finally broke contact and started down the stairs, Bruce asked about the bedroom set and sealed crate.

"Do you need help moving those things down?" he asked. "You might try getting an appraiser here to look at those pieces."

"Thanks, that's very nice of you. Maybe in a little while,

when more of the house is in better shape." Tori knew very well that she could try to sell the pieces for part of the money she needed, yet part of her was reluctant. They were so beautiful . . . and there was something else about them, something unsettlingly familiar, that made her hesitate. If she *had* to, she'd sell. But she wanted to try finding the money another way first.

Bruce tried offering to help her move her things in, but Tori seemed intent on ushering him out of the house for the evening.

Yet before walking out the kitchen door, he turned to stare into her pensive face. "Well, Miss Avalon," he remarked. "Looks like I have my work cut out for me."

Tori caught Bruce's amused look and got the instant impression that he was referring to something more than the house.

"Yes," she answered warily. "I suppose so."

"What happens now?" asked Marina.

She hovered close to Robert near the mansion's back door. The ghosts had followed the living couple down from the attic and were trying to monitor the situation.

"I believe," answered Robert, *"that the gentleman builder has agreed to come back many times. He will help the lady restore the house little by little."*

"But what of their involvement? Will they become lovers?"

"I don't know," said Robert hesitantly.

"Oh, blast it!" exclaimed Marina. *"I wish they would have found what we'd wanted them to up there. . . ."*

"Yes, it was unfortunate. The gentleman seemed perceptive to our suggestions, but he got sidetracked. If only the lady hadn't rushed away."

"We must simply try again," decided Marina. *"We will get them back to the attic somehow."*

"Yes," said Robert. *"But not right away. We do not want to frighten the lady away entirely, and after all, they* are

going forward with their work on the house, which was the whole point of our previous efforts."

"Yes," conceded Marina, *"but I'd be much happier if they were also going forward with work toward a love affair."*

Robert felt a thing like laughter course through him. It produced a series of small energy bursts, bubbles forming, then popping in the air with a sound like champagne corks.

"Robert, are you . . . laughing?"

"Yes . . . I believe I am."

"In heaven's name, why?"

"Because of your comment, my dear. You see, they are working toward that. Or haven't you been listening as carefully as I?"

"Well, I suppose I was listening more to the lady."

"Ah . . . that explains it."

"Explains what?"

"I was listening to the man."

Chapter Eight

LE 18 FEVRIER, 1896
JE RENCONTRE LUI . . .

Tori found herself drawn back to the diary that night. Sitting on her futon on the bare floor of the empty master bedroom, she leaned back against the wall and began to write out the translation in a spiral-bound notebook.

At the masque ball, he asked me to dance. I shall never forget what he looked like. He was dressed as a Musketeer with a red silk mask tied across his eyes and a white plumed hat atop his golden head. His strong physique was dressed in a cape and flowing white shirt. His breeches were tucked into shiny black boots, and a sharp foil hung at his waist.

There was one more item to his costume—a long faux

nose. I asked him what it meant, and he said he was Cyrano de Bergerac, a character in a new play that he'd seen last year in Paris.

I was dressed as an Indian princess in a white fringed dress of doeskin with a white feathered mask and a beautifully beaded headdress. Stepmother said I was the most beautiful girl at the ball, but it was not until I saw it in Robert's eyes that I finally had a mind to believe it.

Robert is like no other boy I have ever met, and I have met many in the last year since my coming out. But I should not call Robert a boy. He is a man. At least twenty-five with golden hair and dark brown eyes . . . and so very handsome. I tell you truthfully, diary, when I shared my piece of King Cake with him and he removed his nose and mask, I nearly swooned.

He describes himself as Bohemian in spirit, yet bourgeois in background with an eye for maintaining a conventional profession as an architect. He says he has come back to the nest to settle down in his own business, and his dream is to work with gifted artisans here in New Orleans to create elegant homes.

I asked if I would know any females in his family, and he regrettably informed me that his mother and two sisters perished when he was a boy. Yellow fever (which Father says also struck down members of our extended family).

Robert says the yellow fever is why his late father sent him to France for schooling in the study of fine art and architecture. Perhaps this is the reason I find him so fascinating. He does not think and speak like the other boys I have met. His mind is quick, and he is fascinated by more than petty squabblings over which carnival krewe has put on the finest ball or other such gossip.

Like me, he seems to enjoy thinking through larger issues . . . like the question of our spiritual state versus our physical being. . . .

Even before my come out last year, I have pondered questions concerning the nature of our human condition, the sense of our social customs, even the origin of our religious rituals. Until recently, I would never have dared risk uttering such ponderings aloud. I have, for my entire life, been a good unquestioning Catholic: Holy Communion, convent schooling with the Ursalines, etiquette instruction, piano study. And yet, in my observation of the world of late, I find myself barely satisfied.

There is so much more beyond the walls of home, so much I would like to see and understand. And yet to even speak of questioning—it is like a crime to so many.

But not to Robert.

He picked right up on a small game of mine at parties, my own way of expressing my internal questioning. What I do is ask, in an amusing fashion, the need for this or that convention. In Robert's case, after I had been properly introduced, I asked him about the gilt mirrors in the exquisite St. Louis Hotel ballroom. I recall every word of our first little conversation.

"Being an architect, what do you think the reason for these hanging mirrors could be?" I asked him.

He smiled, patronizingly at first. "Ornamentation."

I instantly challenged him. "Beautiful murals or paintings would certainly suffice on that account, wouldn't they?"

Robert's golden eyebrow rose at my response. He studied me a moment and then agreed. "Yes, of course. That's true." Then he gestured to the elegant lighting. "Perhaps the answer then lies in the choice of these chandeliers."

"How?"

"Well . . . they were brought directly from France."

"I don't understand. How would that explain the mirrors?"

"Have you not heard of the great Hall of Mirrors at Versailles?"

"Ah, very good. So we in New Orleans are merely imitating. But then that begs the question of Versailles' mirrors. . . . Why the need for a ballroom to be lined with reflecting glass?"

"There is the lighting," offered Robert. "Mirrors reflect

*the candles or, even now the electric lights, and create
more of it."*

"I see, but then, why not simply provide more lights?"

*"Well . . . I should think it is also vanity. The peacocks
like to watch themselves showing off the plumage."*

*"That is an obvious answer," I chided, curious that the
conversation had actually continued this far. The usual
boy, by this time, would either take offense to my chal-
lenges or simply give up on the idea of riding a train of
thought to an unknown destination.*

*I wondered if Robert would give up entirely and excuse
himself or simply turn the conversation to a nice, safe topic,
like this year's costumes or the weather.*

*Happily, he did neither. Instead, he smiled, his eyes be-
hind his mask sparkling. "If you don't like the obvious answer, then perhaps I shall try this one: Man likes to see
himself in reflection because it helps him define who he is."*

*I grinned. "A better answer. And one I can agree with.
You see, I feel the comparison of humans to peacocks has
always been a poor one."*

"And why is that?"

*"The peacock does not question that he is one of God's
creatures and therefore beautiful. Humans, I find, constantly question their worth, and are so uncomfortable with
their feathers that they resort to eyeing the glass to confirm
the beauty on the outside of them that they cannot see
inside. . . ."*

*Robert laughed at this and told me that my Catholic up-
bringing was showing. "You have only to meet a true
Dandy, strutting about the Paris salons, to understand that
what you say does not apply to all humankind."*

*Then he asked me to dance and so began a long wonder-
ful night. Once he seemed comfortable with my ability to
listen, he began to talk, and, oh, how I enjoyed his mind's
workings! He spoke of women and men and the new order
of things as we approach a new century. He talked of his
passion for the individual, and the assertion of his or her
mark on society . . . To will, to achieve, to live!*

It was so glorious to talk with him!

He told me truthfully that he thought he would be bored stiff by the party. He had returned from abroad late last summer and had applied himself quite single-mindedly to his building of a large house, which was just completed. It was a showplace, he confessed, to test and perhaps show off his abilities as an architect.

The house was much like one he'd admired while vacationing one summer in England—a style called Queen Anne.

"Where is this house?" I asked.

He named a street in the Quarter near Congo Square. He said his late father already owned a large lot there. An old Creole cottage had sat upon it for decades. Robert confessed his grandfather had once used the place as a home for his quadroon mistress—a free woman of color—and their two children.

I nodded, knowing this was common behavior in the early part of this century, before the War Between the States. Creole gentlemen would often go to Quadroon Balls, where they would select a mistress.

It was all very elegant and civil, with the gentleman making proper financial arrangements with the quadroon's mother. I also understand that when the Creole gentleman finally married, his wife would often expect the relationship to end.

Sometimes it did, but sometimes it did not, depending on the inclination—and heart—of the gentleman. Certainly, many a French Creole had fallen passionately under the spell of his mistress, but still, I find it alarming that so many gentlemen would find themselves with two separate families. . . .

Anyhow, Robert said that this cottage was in a bad state of disrepair, and he decided to raze it and start from scratch with something brand-new.

"Whatever happened to your grandfather's children?"

"Well . . . uh . . . the mistress passed on . . . as far as I know," said Robert, seeming a bit uncomfortable. "With *the coming of the War, the two boys took our family name and went off to make their own way in the world."*

"Doesn't it make you wonder, though, about these two relatives you may have?"

Robert eyed me closely. "I suppose you could ask the same question of many families around here . . . but the only answer you'll get from them is the one you'll get from me. . . ."

"What's that?"

"Whatever will be, will be."

I shook my head. "That is no answer."

Robert simply shrugged his shoulders, looking away. "I have my own life to build . . . and since my return, I have been primarily occupied with constructing the house. In fact, I am nearly done, and if not for the insistence of friends at my club, I would not even have come to this particular ball."

As I write this now, I see that I owe a debt to that group of friends! Oh, yes, I do . . . but I am so tired now and sleep comes like Rex, the King of Carnival, waving his scepter at midnight and declaring the festivities at an end. . . .

I shall write more of Robert tomorrow.

Tori continued to turn the dry delicate pages with care and resumed translating with interest. . . .

FEBRUARY 19, 1896

The ashes on my forehead itch, but Stepmother insists we must all wear the black cross until it rubs off or else until the next morning's ablutions.

Ash Wednesday has often been a time that makes me turn inward. I stand before the priest as the sign of Christ's suffering is etched upon my forehead and he recites, "Remember, man, from dust thou came and unto dust thou shall return. . . ."

I think to myself, here we all are, good Catholics, filling the Cathedral pews, lining its aisles, and yet how many of us really consider this? There is so much I wish to experience, to know, before my own body returns to the dust. . . .

I thought of Robert through the day and even through mass. I considered the time I spent with him at last night's masque ball to be the most alive I've ever felt. Honestly, I have tried to gently draw out other boys who have shown interest in me. I have attempted cautiously to express my ideas. But they merely laugh at my notions, saying I should settle my mind on things domestic, of fulfillment through family life. One boy was so put off, he practically advised me to visit a confessional!

I have never spoken of such things to Father and Stepmother. I may be at times a romantic girl, but I am far from dim-witted. I know, of course, what they wish. They wish me not simply to marry, but to marry well.

Last year's Mardis Gras marked my debut, and at first I was so swept up in the gowns and lights and festivities. But now I count a full twelve months gone, and for each of those months at least one young gentlemen has made an inquiry toward an engagement—even despite what they have cited as my "strange" discourse with them. But Father has turned them all down, saying within only the four walls of our parlor the true reasons.

One evening last month I listened secretly as Father turned away the latest young suitor.

Stepmother entered the parlor and spoke gently to him. "Etienne, do not wait too long to allow her to marry. Marina is young, but showing her off beyond two seasons is not wise."

Father answered quickly. "I will not hand her to a mediocre son of a shop owner. I tell you, she has the kind of exotic beauty and sharp mind that should be treasured . . . and will be."

After a long pause, Stepmother spoke up again, but very softly. I had to strain to hear. "Then you are waiting for the interest of a man with greater . . . resources?"

"There is a man. He is interested."

"Then let them meet," suggested Stepmother.

"In time."

"But . . ." Stepmother hesitated, then gently put forward, *"Dearest . . . who is this gentleman?"*

"A businessman. Very successful. I am beginning to plan some investments with him. You will know in time," said Father, a bit tensely, and then that was the end of it.

As far as I was concerned, *"time"* was fine with me. Before Robert, I had yet to meet a boy to whom I could honestly feel any sort of connection, and I was in no great hurry to enter a union of bank accounts alone.

But this mysterious wealthy suitor who had an *"interest"* in me never did come around. I surmised that whoever it was had found some other young woman of greater interest. I turned back to my reading, and studies of music and painting. And then Mardis Gras came and I met Robert!

I must get back to describing last night. . . .

After we danced, we took a stroll around the crowded ballroom, and he asked me if I had a beau. I told him no, not really, but I quite boldly confessed that I had made a prayer for a boy to love.

"To love physically?"

I was so surprised that I felt my face warming with a flush. I tried my best to control it. *"I . . . had . . . not made the distinction. Not to God, anyhow,"* I stammered.

"Good heavens, I've managed to fluster you! Well, good for me. You're not an easy girl to catch off balance."

"Thank you," I said. *"Or am I being dim?"*

His smile was warm. *"No, you are not being dim. You are, in fact, one of the sharpest girls I have ever met—if a bit naive. But what I said I meant as a compliment."*

"What do you mean that I am naive?"

"Oh, please don't take offense . . . it's just that I have met young women in Paris—of good standing—who are not so put off by the idea of physical love."

"I am not put off by it," I returned quickly. *"I am simply . . ."*

"New to it?" put in Robert gently.

I lowered my voice considerably. "Of course. I am Catholic and must remain a virgin until I marry."

"I am Catholic as well, but let me ask you this. The man you marry, should he be a virgin?"

"According to the church, he should."

"But he is not usually."

"I am not supposed to know of such things, but I do know that there are many places for young men to . . . find experience."

"And not young women?"

"Of course not."

"Now there *is a contradiction worth thinking through. I'll quote you a passage from a seventy-year-old book. 'It is a far greater sin against modesty to go to bed with a man only twice seen, after three words of Latin in a church, than to surrender despite oneself to a man adored for two years.'"*

I looked upon Robert's face in that moment and something odd happened. Around us, the dancers swirled on the floor, the music played, the libations flowed, and yet I felt as though something were suddenly drastically different. It was as if I had been standing in a dimly lit room that had just been flooded with light.

"Who wrote this?" I asked in earnest.

"Stendahl. Have you read him?"

"I regret I have not."

"He makes a grand study called Love. *It boils down to his obsession with a woman, Mathilde Viscontini Dembowski. Stendahl tries to exorcise himself of it by dissecting his feelings. But it makes for a dissection of universal passion. Quite a thought-provoking read, I'd say."*

"It sounds fascinating."

We were interrupted the by the cutting of the King Cake.

One of the ball's court jesters handed me a slice of the cake and I held it up to Robert. "There is a gold bean baked into the cake," I explained, "and every lady at the ball receives a slice. The lady who strikes gold at this par-

ticular krewe's ball is named queen for next year's Mardis
Gras."

"Good lord," he joked, "I hope there aren't too many
queens with missing teeth!"

I laughed and split my piece, holding it out to him.
"Here, you should sample our tradition, kind Musketeer."

"Why, thank you, m'lady," said Robert, bowing and taking the slice. "But what if I find the bean?"

"Then you will be queen, I suppose."

"Good heavens. I had better coif my hair then!"

I laughed as he tried to bite into his piece. He could not,
his long "Cyrano" nose was in the way. He pushed it up
and the rest of his mask went with it, revealing his handsome face. It was the first time I had seen it, and as I wrote
before, I nearly swooned at the sight.

I was already so taken with his mind and spirit that I had
not really thought of his physical appearance, and so I was
not at all prepared for the revelation of his good looks.

Suddenly a happy cry rose through the crowd as a young
woman dressed as Joan of Arc stepped forward, holding up
the golden bean. The commotion allowed me to compose
myself. I placed a bit of the sugary cake into my mouth and
chewed without really tasting it.

"Well, I suppose we no longer have to worry about
breaking any teeth," teased Robert.

"No," I said after swallowing. I smiled, but was at once
unsettled. It was odd to see his face now. I felt free when he
was masked to speak of private things, but now, I was embarrassed. In an odd way, the revelation of his good looks
was for me as unnerving as if he'd been grotesque.

Here was the undeniable evidence that this was a physical man standing here next to me, not simply a complex
bundle of thoughts and ideas.

"Is something wrong?" asked Robert beside me.

"I confess, something is wrong," I said and then removed my own mask.

He studied my face for a long moment. "You are a beautiful creature," he said in a hushed voice.

"Isn't it odd," I said. "Suddenly we are awkward with each other. As if we are just meeting again. I don't understand. . . ."

Robert smiled. "You should. What have we done just now? Removed our masks. Now, you see, there are no artificial barriers. And when the safety of barriers is removed, social conventions come down like protective stage curtains."

"Yes, I suppose you are right," I said.

The band struck up a lively tune then, and Robert asked me to return to the floor. I readily agreed. We danced and danced until the night was almost through.

Tante Camille, my widowed aunt, was not happy with my spending so much time with one gentleman. She watched from a comfortable chair in the crowded room, but was soon so distracted by the ball's festivities that she did not press her usual cautions.

Father and Stepmother had come as well. I was very aware of the time, and knew my parents would soon be summoning me to leave by their carriage. I began to wonder if I would see Robert again.

"Stendhal . . ." I asked him as we took a final stroll around the room. "Did he believe in love at first sight?"

"Yes. One section of his book on love is titled 'The Thunderbolt,' though he qualifies that it is a ridiculous word."

"I see."

"He also cautions something," Robert said, then paused and spied me carefully. "He says that the young and overfervent may make the mistake of hurling themselves upon the experience of love instead of waiting for it to happen naturally."

"What does that mean, exactly?" I asked.

"The young and untried often invest the love object with imaginary charms, which they conjure up in their heads . . . but then they are later disappointed."

"Oh, yes, I see. I've done that."

"You have?" asked Robert with surprise, but I suspect

*he was really surprised by my ready admission of so naive
an endeavor.*

"Oh, yes, though I hesitate to tell you with whom."

"Tell me."

*"You won't tell a soul?" I could not believe I was admitting this to him! Yet there was something about Robert that
made me want to tell him everything about my thoughts and
feelings.*

"I swear."

*"Well, I conjured up an entire romantic fantasy about a
young priest in my parish."*

*Robert's eyes widened. "Marina, what a good Catholic
you are! You even fall in love with your priest. Or was it
more akin to lust?"*

"Well . . . truthfully . . . both."

*I took no offense at Robert's laughter. I could certainly
see the humor. "I had no intention of defrocking the clergy,
you understand."*

*"Oh, but did you tempt him? That's what I wish to
know!"*

"I did not!"

*His face was flushed from the amusement, and he invited
me to sit down on an embroidered settee. "Oh, Marina, you
delight me so!"*

*"I am glad. You are a delight to me as well. But tell me
now, Robert," I said, flicking at his long nose, "why did
you choose this long-nosed Cyrano for your costume?"*

*"Well, he is a grand character, part of a new play, written by a friend of a friend, who is putting it up next year in
Paris. I saw an early performance."*

"It must have made quite an impression."

*"Yes, Cyrano is the bravest, most clever and skillful of
all the Musketeers in the King's charge, but he is deformed
by this unnaturally long nose and so believes himself unlovable. Yet, he has fallen in love with the most beautiful of
women, named Roxanne, who is terribly clever and kind.
Roxanne, however, falls in love at a distance with a dash-*

ing young Musketeer named Christian, who has no brains in his handsomely empty head."

"What does Cyrano do?"

"He loves Roxanne, and wishes her to be happy, so he puts brilliant words into Christian's mouth, writing letters for him, even speaking for him. In this way, Cyrano at least is able to express his love."

"So in the end Roxanne loves Christian—and not Cyrano?"

"She makes love to Christian's body, but only because she falls in love with Cyrano's mind and heart."

"But is not the love of mind and heart the truest love?"

"It is the truest," agreed Robert. "But on Earth, is not the physical a part of our human condition?"

"Yes," I had to agree. "I suppose it is."

"Then a woman must have a mental and physical connection to a man?" Robert's hand fell upon my leg, just above my knee. The suddenness of the gentle touch unnerved me instantly. The warmth of his palm and fingers penetrated the material of my skirt and reached my bare skin. The tingling seemed to race past my thigh and higher until it warmed my very core. The sensation of the physical with the teasing question undid me.

He leaned closer. "Mental and physical. Don't you agree?" he whispered in my ear, and I swear I nearly swooned with wanting him. It took me a moment to get hold of myself.

"I . . . must see this play, and read your Stendahl," I managed.

Robert smiled and leaned back. "Yes, Stendahl. I had been skeptical of him in previous years. For instance, he believed that in a romantic situation, love can conquer at first sight."

"Stendahl believed it," I said, gazing up at him. Then I paused to gather courage. "But what is it that you believe?"

"I believe what I experience."

"I see."

"So, as of this night, and these last few hours, I would

have to say, that I finally agree with Stendahl in this matter. Shall I lend his book to you?"

For a moment I was without a tongue. Had Robert admitted what I thought he had? I simply stared at him, my tongue frozen solid to the roof of my mouth.

"Shall I come calling? At your house . . . to lend it?" he asked then, a certain glimmer in his gaze.

"I . . . yes . . . I should like that. Very much," I said, finally finding my voice.

Then something happened that I shall never forget. Ever so gently, he cupped my chin in his hand and whispered two lines of a very old poem. "There is a garden in her face/Where roses and white lilies grow . . ."

Before parting, he stood and gallantly bent over my hand, his gaze never leaving mine. Oh, I do think I will carry that moment with me, even beyond the day I die. . . .

"Roses and white lilies," whispered Tori, realizing she may have finally found the origin of Rosegate's signature designs.

She yawned and realized that her scrawling longhand was growing sloppy. She stopped writing out the translation and instead began simply reading a little further on.

According to the diary, Robert had come calling—with Stendahl in hand—and met Marina's austere father. Once the man learned of Robert's generous inheritance, his fine education, and prospects as an architect, the coveted blessing was given for courtship.

Robert held a housewarming party the next week. He was very proud to show off his skills and invited Marina and her parents to meet his extend family, some new artisan friends, and business associates. In the diary, Marina's description of the house was particular enough to convince Tori that it was indeed Rosegate. . . .

Finally Tori's eyelids began to grow heavier, and though she wanted to continue, she knew her long day was finally at an end.

She closed the leather-bound book, flicked off the small

lamp, and pulled a light sheet over herself. But just before she drifted off, Tori heard a strange noise outside the room.

It sounded like a measured thumping.

Two thumps . . . then three . . . then two again.

Tori's heart immediately began to race, and she felt her fear returning, but she refused to give in to it.

She'd spent months of anxious thinking before she'd made the difficult decision to change her life. But she'd gone and done it. She'd come back home to build afresh. *This* was the life she wanted, in *this* house—and nothing was going to make her abandon it.

Resolutely she pushed back the sheet and rose. Grabbing her robe from a chair, she slipped it on and stood by the open bedroom door to listen again.

It was a kind of coded tattoo all right. From down the hall.

THUMP-THUMP . . . THUMP-THUMP-THUMP . . . THUMP-THUMP . . .

She swallowed nervously.

"It's just the pipes . . . or something," she told herself aloud. "The walls are just settling . . . or whatever . . ."

But despite her attempts at creative rationales, Tori knew she wouldn't be able to sleep until she had at least checked out the noises. Barefoot, she stepped outside the bedroom's threshold and walked slowly down the hall.

She stopped and listened again, but there was nothing.

She flipped on a light and opened the hall closet.

Nothing.

She checked the first bedroom on the hall.

Nothing.

The bath.

Nothing.

The next bedroom appeared normal, and she was feeling stupid.

With one last bedroom to check, she gave it up, turning back for the master bedroom and some much-needed sleep. That's when one sharp *thump* suddenly sounded from that last bedroom.

Tori walked toward it, her palms sweating.

The door was closed and she stared at it a long moment, this time hearing another loud thumping—her own heart.

She swallowed down her fear and put her ear to the wood.

For a full minute, all was silent.

Finally she turned the doorknob and opened the door. The hall light fell into the room, and Tori could see that there was no one here at all. And no more thumping.

"Good night, then, you mice," she said aloud, then stopped.

There *was* something in the room after all. She opened the door wider and stepped forward, incredulous.

There, in the middle of the empty bedroom, stood a little painted wooden horse, just like the one her mother had once given to her. Tori rushed to it and took it in her hands. She knew this horse wasn't Champlain, but it was a close facsimile.

She shook her head, amazed and delighted with this reminder of a time when her childhood had been so very happy—and everything seemed possible.

Then she noticed a card attached to a string around the horse's neck. She brought the toy into the lighted hall to read the note. It held only a few handwritten words:

He needs a home . . .
—V.B.G.

Tori actually smiled.

After flipping off the hall light, she made her way back to the master bedroom.

Gently she placed Champlain Deux on the pillow beside her; and, with the smile still on her lips, she drifted off to sleep.

In the back of her mind Tori knew that the thumps had somehow led her toward finding this gift from Vianney Bruce Gautreau, but she couldn't think of that now. She was much too tired.

She would think of it tomorrow. . . .

Chapter Nine

"Tori, forgive me, but you don't look well. Are you working too hard?"

From the moment Zoe Duchamp had seen her niece that morning, she'd been concerned. To a casual observer, Tori Avalon would appear a beautiful, well-dressed young woman having a pleasant lunch at a trendy restaurant. But Zoe saw the thin lines of strain around her niece's mouth, the tired look to her eyes.

Over three weeks had passed since Tori had begun working on Rosegate, and Zoe hadn't seen hide nor hair of her niece in all that time. So she'd stopped by this morning to force Tori to take a break from the endless sanding, staining, and painting.

Zoe had chosen Nola's for lunch, a hot young restaurant in the Quarter. The exposed brick and partially open kitchen made the main dining room feel modern yet cozy, causal yet classy.

"I'm fine," said Tori, opening her menu. "What's good here?"

"Absolutely everything," pronounced Zoe, still studying her niece's face. "I adore Emeril Lagasse."

"Who?"

"The chef and proprietor."

"Isn't it someone named . . . Nola?"

Zoe smiled. "NOLA is *N*ew *O*rleans *L*ouisian*A*. You really should get out more, sugar. Enjoy yourself a little."

"I don't have the time," admitted Tori. "Right now, anyway."

"It's no wonder, the way you're pushing yourself. . . ."

After they ordered, Zoe decided that they were comfortable enough for her to get down to brass tacks. "Tori, tell me what's wrong—no use denying it, now. Is it the work?"

Tori sighed. "No, I like the work. I'm just . . ." She hesitated a moment, looking away. "I'm not getting enough sleep."

"Oh," said Zoe, deciding that if it were just *sleep* she was missing, then maybe she was enjoying herself after all, especially if it involved Bruce. "So, how is our Mr. Gautreau treating you?"

"I hardly see him. Every few mornings he comes by to get me started on a section and then in the evening he'll stop over to check the work I've done—"

"That's quite a lot of visits by my calculation. I'd *hardly* say that you *hardly* see him! Is that why you're not sleeping well?" asked Zoe hopefully.

"What do you mean?"

"I mean, does he *stay* after checking the work in the evening?"

Tori shrugged. "Sometimes I invite him to eat dinner with me. Usually, he does stay for a bite—"

"And—"

"And nothing. He leaves after dinner."

"I don't believe it."

"It's true. We're simply working together, Aunt Zoe,

that's all. And I'm keeping accounts to pay him for his time."

"A pity. A man as handsome as all that . . ." said Zoe with disappointment, then she leaned forward, her tone trying its best to sound light. "But speaking of payment, why don't you reconsider taking the money I've offered?"

"Aunt Zoe, I've already taken enough. Five thousand has given me a good start on materials and furnishings, and I mean to pay back every penny. Once my teaching job starts—"

"Tori, part-time teaching will pay peanuts, and it would be worth it to me to see Rosegate in her glory again. You've already done some amazing work. I can't get over it."

"Yes," said Tori, pleased and proud that both the first and second floors were now beautifully restored. "Without Bruce, I don't know where I'd be."

"You see there," said Zoe. "Mr. Gautreau isn't so bad after all. If you gave him a bit of encouragement, I'm sure he'd—"

"*Encouragement?* Oh, no, Aunt, you don't get it. The man has already declared his 'romantic' interest. *More than once.*"

"He has?" asked Zoe, her eyes opening widely. "I *knew* he was smitten with you. I *knew* it. And?"

"And I've said no—*more than once.*"

"*No?* My heavens, the man expressed interest and you— you turned him down?" Zoe couldn't believe Tori. The girl was so doggone stubborn—and shortsighted. *She was just like her mother!*

"For heaven's sake, don't make it sound like I've shattered his fragile ego. Remember that old saying of Uncle Richard's?"

"What?"

"*You can tell a Cajun from a mile away, but you can't tell him a thing up close.* That's very true of this particular Cajun."

Aunt Zoe sighed. "I know Bruce can be headstrong, but

so can you, my dear, which shows how right you are for each other—"

"Well, by that rationale, maybe *you* should take up with him. You can be quite the bullheaded grand dame, you know."

"Yes, well, it runs in the family." Zoe took a sip of her Chardonnay. "But I'm not about to throw my vintage self at Bruce Gautreau. You, however, are a bouquet more to his liking."

Tori sighed. "Gautreau is another Edward. It's clear as day, and I'm not going through that again."

"I see," was all Zoe said.

Tori had a feeling her aunt did see—right through her. Tori *did* want Bruce Gautreau in her bed, and that's why she wished she could show the man the front door for good. Then at least she wouldn't have to fight the awful temptations that came over her like a strange chilly fever.

So far, *hands off* had been their unspoken pact. But it hadn't been easy—at least on her part. Lately, she got the feeling that Bruce had lost interest . . . or perhaps found it elsewhere.

"Aunt Zoe, maybe this is a good time to ask your advice."

"By all means."

"I admit that I *would* like to meet a man, but I'd like it to be someone of the . . . well, of the right sort, you know what I mean?"

"I know what you mean." *Yes,* thought Zoe, *just like Coco.*

"I want someone stable. A man who's looking to settle down, raise a family. As attractive as Bruce is, you and I both know he's not the kind to settle down."

"I know nothing of the sort."

"You do so."

"Well . . ." Zoe hedged. She took a long sip of her wine. What could she do to convince Tori that she was headed down the wrong road? This would have to be done delicately. "About this imaginary man. I suppose you want him to have a good family background?"

"Yes."

"And money? Money wouldn't hurt?"

"Aunt Zoe. Money isn't . . ." Tori took a deep breath, determined to make things clear. "Listen, I'm not gold digging. I just think that a man who's already established with the community—one who's led less of a wanderer's life, maintained a long-term career here—he's more likely to be happy settling down, you see?"

"Tori, do you realize you sound just like Coco at your age?"

"My mother?"

"Yes . . ."

That disturbed Tori. Coco Duchamp Avalon had made a happy marriage, at first, but things had turned terribly dark for her terribly fast. Still, what did that have to do with Tori, really?

"Aunt Zoe, let's leave my mother out of this. I'm my own person. And there's nothing wrong with the things I've listed."

"Yes, dear there is. They're superficial."

"They're practical signs of a man's intentions."

Zoe raised an eyebrow. "Be careful of placing a high value on the superficial, my dear," she said softly.

"I don't understand—"

"True love is worth more."

The food came then, and they ate. The entrées were so good that Zoe insisted they see the dessert menu. Tori was horrified when her aunt actually ordered the entire list of ten desserts for the table.

"Aunt Zoe, what are you doing to me?! Don't you remember my childhood?"

"You were full figured," said Zoe tactfully.

"I was the Pillsbury Dough Girl!"

"Oh, now, honey, those years are behind you. We'll just take a sample bite of each item. After all, it *is* my business. Got to stay on top of the competition."

"*You* stay on top. I'll just have coffee."

Zoe sighed. Tori *was* headstrong. And Zoe knew that the more she'd try to guide her niece, the harder that girl would dig in to her own position. That's the way it had worked with Coco, all right. Zoe stopped a moment. Perhaps she had just stumbled into a solution: Instead of ranting about how Tori shouldn't go down the wrong road, maybe Zoe should try to *push* her down it. Yes, then perhaps Tori would be the one to put on the brakes and start reading the road signs for herself.

"Now, let's talk about this wish of yours, to meet the 'right' sort," Zoe began with a renewed purpose. "I have a good idea for helping you meet some eligible men 'round town."

"You do?" asked Tori, almost afraid to.

"We'll throw a party at Rosegate."

"A *party?* At *Rosegate?* Are you crazy? The first and second floors are finished, but, Aunt Zoe, the rest of the house is a wreck. The kitchen isn't even remodeled yet!"

"Oh, my dear, use your creative belle spirit. We'll call it a Halfway-Through party, and we'll have it on a Wednesday, halfway through the week. It's brilliant—my old sorority sisters would be so proud!" exclaimed Zoe. "And I know just who to invite from the New Orleans Chamber of Commerce. Pierre will cook, and I'll have a few of my waiters serve, and . . ."

Zoe went on for another few minutes, and Tori sat back helplessly, as if a Gulf hurricane were blowing past her head.

"Well," said Tori when Zoe finally took a breath. "I can see what they say about New Orleans is absolutely true."

"What's that, honey?"

"You people will find *any* excuse to have a party."

"Damn right." Zoe threw a wink at her niece. "So don't you think it's about time you joined the tradition?"

A wide yawn interrupted Tori's laugh, and Zoe's eyes narrowed with concern. "Tori, tell me the truth now. Is the money for the house what's keepin' you up at night? Because, as I say, I do want you to take a bigger loan from me—"

"No more money talk, Aunt Zoe, you've done enough! And the truth is . . . well . . . you'll think I'm crazy. *I'm* beginning to think I'm crazy, but it's the *house* itself that's keeping me up."

"What do you mean, the *house*?"

"I hear things at night. Noises. They wake me at all hours."

Zoe leaned back in her chair and put a finger to her lips in thought. "What sort of noises?"

"Thumping. But not just pipes knocking. I remember after I moved out of the New York University dorms to live with Edward, his place was in this old building. The steam pipes knocked like crazy in the middle of the night during the winter. It's not like that at all. This thumping is measured out. Like someone knocking at a door to call your attention—besides, there's no steam heat in the house this time of year."

Zoe nodded. "Unless it's coming in off the sidewalks. What else?"

Tori shifted in her seat, hoping her aunt wouldn't have her committed. "Footsteps," she said, her voice low. "Usually above my bedroom. The floorboards creak as if someone is pacing. And sometimes a door slams. I tried checking them out many times, but there's never evidence of anything out of the ordinary."

"Mmmmmm. Interesting," said Zoe.

"So, what do you think?"

A long pause followed as Zoe examined her niece's worried face. Then she leaned forward, her eyes staring with serious intensity. "My dear, I'm afraid there's only one explanation I can think of—"

Tori leaned toward her aunt. She felt a terrible knot of stress form in the pit of her stomach as Zoe opened her mouth to finish her thought—

"Zoe Duchamp! Why, fancy meeting you here. How are you this fine day?"

The male voice shattered the tense moment, and it took Zoe a moment to respond to the fortyish man now standing next to their table. "Franklin . . . Franklin Morgan?" Zoe finally pronounced, a practiced smile touching her lips as she extended her hand. "Good day to you."

"You as well," said Franklin, smoothly squeezing her aunt's four fingers. "And who is your charming companion? I don't believe I've had the pleasure . . ."

Tori carefully watched the interaction. For a fleeting moment, Zoe hesitated. Only someone who knew Zoe as well as Tori would have observed the reluctance at all in her aunt, whose skillful social manner was usually as smooth as opaque glass—and just about as transparent. "Franklin Morgan, this is my niece, Victoria Avalon."

The first thing that struck Tori about Franklin Morgan was his sharp gaze. As he turned it on her, it appeared coolly haughty, his eyes pale as blue crystal. For a moment, he seemed to be critically evaluating her. Then the twin ice chips of his eyes seemed to melt.

"Very nice to meet you, Miss Avalon."

Clearly warming to Tori, Morgan extended his hand and she took it, deciding that the lean angles of his face were quite handsome. Without thinking, Tori found herself holding this man's image up to that of Bruce Gautreau's. The idea of it annoyed her, and yet she continued the comparison just the same.

Where Bruce's face was more ruggedly chiseled, with a sailor's set square jaw, this man's bore the classic angles of aristocracy. His jet-black hair was short and neatly combed, betraying a distinguished hint of gray at the temples. His trim blue summer suit and silk tie with a tastefully expensive fleur-de-lys tiepin were perfectly tailored to his lean physique. And his smile was as dazzling as a *GQ* cover model.

"Franklin's a local financier," supplied Zoe.

"Yes," put in Franklin. "I have the pleasure of sitting with your aunt on a local committee."

"Oh?" Tori's gaze casually traveled over Franklin's hands. No wedding ring. "What committee is that?"

"The Garden District Committee to Save the Lafayette Cemetery Library."

"*Cemetery* Library?" asked Tori, intrigued.

"Cities of the dead," put in Zoe. "You know the cemeteries here in New Orleans are amazing pieces of history."

"You see, Miss Avalon—" began Franklin.

"Call me Tori."

"Of course." The Southern-Gentleman smile flashed. "Tori. And call me Franklin, by all means. You see, many historians have attempted to research the funerary architecture of the older tombs. May I?" he asked, gesturing to the chair next to Tori.

"Of course," she said, a little thrill shooting through her as his pantleg brushed her thigh underneath the small table.

Zoe motioned over the waiter, slight strains of annoyance barely evident around her mouth and eyes. "Please bring a cup of coffee for our guest," she instructed the young man, who conjured a cup in an instant.

"The committee is sitting pretty at present," Franklin explained to Tori, a handsome sparkle in his blue eyes clearly saying, *as pretty as you.*

Tori felt a pleasing warmth creep into her cheeks.

"It's true," added Zoe. "Our Cemetery Library Committee has raised generous funds. And they'll be matched by the city."

"And what are the funds to be used for exactly?" asked Tori.

"To convert an old mansion into a library," explained Franklin. "Unfortunately, the building was partially destroyed by a fire last fall. But once it's restored, it will be a place where historians and restoration specialists can do their research."

"Fascinating," said Tori, suddenly thinking of the New Orleans cemetery where her mother was buried. Tori was young when her mother died, nine years old, but she still vividly recalled walking in the funeral procession and seeing that angel.

Up until that day, the only depictions of angels Tori had ever seen were always serene and glorious. But this winged statue in flowing robes stood alone, bitterly weeping at the door of a stark white tomb.

It had struck Tori how right it was to see an angel crying that moment. She hadn't shed any tears of her own at her mother's burial. In fact, for the rest of her life, she'd always felt as if that angel were doing the crying for her. . . .

". . . and I believe all bids for the restoration will be in soon," Franklin explained, nodding at Zoe.

"Yes, Mr. Morgan," she replied, a bit tensely. "We shall indeed have our work cut out for us."

"Oh, now, you know what my philosophy is: *Go with who ya know.* Wouldn't you agree, Miss Avalon?"

"Well, I—"

"Now, don't go draggin' my niece into our little argument, Mr. Morgan." Zoe turned to Tori. "You see, *I* feel that Mr. *Gautreau* will do a fine job. Mr. Morgan, however, would rather champion another contractor." Smoothly Zoe returned her focus to Franklin. "But I warn you, Mr. Morgan, my niece is liable to take my side. You see, Mr. Gautreau has been working with her on Rosegate."

Franklin's expression seemed to still for a long moment. "Rosegate," he finally said, fingering the edge of his coffee cup. "Surely you don't mean the Brevard House on First Street? Didn't that famous writer of vampire novels purchase that residence?"

"No, that house is in the Garden District," said Zoe. "There's a *second* Rosegate in the Quarter, and Tori is working her fingers to the bone to restore it—*with* Mr. Gautreau's help, of course."

"I see," said Franklin. He turned to Tori. "And what do you think of our Mr. Gautreau?"

Tori's fingers tightened around the linen napkin in her lap. Why was it she couldn't get out from under conversing about this man? *I must be hexed.* "He's quite capable."

"Is he? Well, I hear the man can be capable of quite a lot of things, Tori. I'd take care. He does have a reputation—"

"Mr. Franklin, won't you have some dessert?" chimed Zoe at once, cutting him off quite pointedly with the thrust of a small green dessert menu.

From then on, talk was rather innocuous. After an array of tarts, pralines, and ice-box cakes made their appearance on the table, the conversation came back to Rosegate. Tori found herself recounting the story of the noises and thumps to Franklin.

"Sounds like you're inhabiting one of the city's many 'haunted' houses, doesn't it, Miss Duchamp?"

Finishing her coffee, Zoe nodded. "I'm afraid it does."

"*Haunted?* You really believe that?" asked Tori. "Both of you?"

"Why, Tori, of course—" began Zoe.

"Of course *not,*" interrupted Franklin with a chuckle. "I was simply joking. It is amusing, isn't it? The number of so-called ghost stories circulating in this city—"

"Actually there are many documented cases," insisted Zoe. "New Orleans is the most haunted city in America. Why, you can't go two blocks without finding someone in the Quarter who's experienced a supernatural encounter."

Tori shifted uncomfortably. "I remember some ghost stories from my childhood, but aren't they just tourist mumbo jumbo?"

"Yes," said Franklin. "Take that famous story of the octoroon mistress—"

"I haven't heard that one."

"I know it well," said Zoe, a strange tone of somberness in her voice.

"Tell me."

Zoe hesitated a moment and then began. "A beautiful woman of color became the mistress to a wealthy Creole aristocrat. She lived in an elegant townhouse and enjoyed a sophisticated life of parties and entertaining. Eventually, though, she wanted her lover to marry her. She wanted a real life with him, you see, not just the trappings of one."

"Did he marry her?" asked Tori.

"Of course not," Franklin scoffed. "In the early eighteen hundreds it was unheard of for a man of his status to marry a woman of color."

"But he did love the girl," continued Zoe, "so he gave her a challenge that he thought would stop her marriage talk. He told her to spend the entire night on the roof stark naked. Only then would he take her as his wife."

"Did she do it?" asked Tori.

"She did, but it was December, and freezing rain lashed her body for hours. The man retired, certain that his mistress would give up and return to her warm bed."

"But she didn't, did she?" whispered Tori.

"No," said Zoe softly. "She stayed on the roof all night. And her horrified lover found her body in the morning, frozen to death. Now they say on rainy nights you can still see her naked form walking that roof."

"That's quite a legend, I grant you," said Franklin. "But it sounds to me more like a cautionary tale than anything else."

Tori turned to Franklin. "How so?"

He took a sip of coffee. "Woe to the mistress who asks for legitimacy. Better to stay alive in a gilded cage—"

"I don't know that it's just a tale, Mr. Morgan," interrupted Zoe. "A parapsychologist has written about the case and documented neighbors who've seen the girl's ghost between midnight and dawn on inclement December nights."

"Yes, well, I always enjoy talking over these old tales of New Orleans, but—" Franklin motioned over the waiter. "I'm sorry to say, I must leave you two. It has been quite enjoyable."

"Yes, Mr. Morgan," said Zoe. "But, please, this was our lunch and it is *my* treat."

"Nonsense—"

"No, I insist," tried Zoe with tension, but Franklin had already placed his platinum credit card on the waiter's small silver tray.

"Thank you," supplied Tori, wondering why her aunt

was so uneasy about accepting such a kind gesture from Franklin. "Won't you stop by Rosegate sometime? I'm actually planning a party to celebrate the partial restoration." Tori glanced at her aunt and didn't like the look she received in return. Quickly she turned her gaze back to Franklin. "I'd be so happy if you could stop by."

"Why, I'd be delighted. Just let me know the date and time," he said, slipping his business card smoothly into Tori's fingers. "I do hope I'll be seeing you again. And soon."

"So do I," said Tori, a little thrill running through her.

Franklin's blue gaze held Tori's a long moment. "Come to think of it, if you're free tomorrow evening, perhaps I can show you a project I've helped get underway. You might find it interesting."

"A project?"

"A casino," said Zoe flatly.

"That sounds interesting," said Tori, trying to be polite in the face of Zoe's indifference.

"And, of course, you'll be my guest for dinner."

Tori's eyebrows rose. "Well, then, I guess it's a date."

"Yes." Franklin rose, then took Tori's hand in his, giving it a warm squeeze. "Until tomorrow then."

Tori's gaze followed his movements away from their table and out the restaurant door. Her fingers were steepling confidently on the table, her lips half-bent in a curious smile.

"Get that look out of your eye," advised Zoe.

"What look?"

"The look that says you're interested in that man."

"And why shouldn't I be? He's just the type of man I was talking about."

"Victoria, you know very little about him." Zoe knew she had to be extremely careful. The last thing she wanted was to make the same mistake with Tori that she'd made with Tori's mother.

"And what else should I know, other than he's obviously handsome, charming, sophisticated, successful—"

"He doesn't believe in ghosts for one thing."

"What?"

"A man who doesn't believe in ghosts has no thought, and therefore no fear, of the hereafter."

"Aunt Zoe, *what* in heaven's name are you talking about?"

Zoe shook her head. "Trust me, sugar, find a man who believes in ghosts and you've got a man with a true soul."

"*I* don't believe in ghosts."

"Oh, but you should, my dear, you must."

"Why?"

"Because it's clear enough to me that Rosegate *is* haunted."

Chapter Ten

That afternoon Tori had done a bit of work cleaning out a third-floor bedroom, but even before the sun descended, she quit for the day. The big lunch at Nola's had slowed her down, and she found herself troubled by her aunt's assertion that Rosegate was haunted.

"Aunt Zoe, do you really think there's something to it?" she'd asked before they'd parted after lunch.

"It's not just me, dear. Ask Bruce, he'll tell you the theories he's come across. You see, it's all in the water—"

"The water?"

"Just ask him. Bye now!"

After showering and changing into a pair of worn cutoff shorts and a thin white tank top, Tori settled into a chair on the front porch, her trusty spiral-bound notebook on her lap. She was drawn back, yet again, to translating the leather-bound diary she'd found.

As the sun neared the rooftops of the Quarter, she was

soon contemplating a gap in the dated entries. In August, Marina had written of a family picnic in the park with her handsome beau, Robert. But no other entries were recorded until October.

Tori closely examined the book. No pages were ripped out, yet the diary had never before skipped *months*. So she began translating, looking for an explanation in the pages.

OCTOBER 5, 1896

"Wait for me."

For two months I have lived with Robert's words, the last words he'd spoken before leaving. . . .

Oh, how I wanted to go with him to Paris. He explained the situation—that the professor to whom he owed so much had taken ill. "He is like a father to me. I must go to him. Like me, he has no immediate family left, and I am like a son. Come with me."

"Yes, I shall. Let us announce our wedding date this instant, and once we are married, we shall both go to him."

"No, Marina, I cannot risk taking any time, not even a day to arrange a wedding. Come now and we shall wed upon our return."

I looked at Robert in shock. Yes, I had thought of myself as forward thinking. I had thought of myself as devoted to this man. But to go with him like that, without a wedding? All I could think was: What will Father say? Even if I could convince Robert to consent to a small hasty ceremony, my father would never agree.

A hasty wedding and then a speedy departure would incite ugly gossip. It would be a disgrace to Father, a man of standing who had spent his life bolstering his status in the community. And Robert's outrageous suggestion that we put off the big ceremony until our return produced a loud and terrible reply from my father. He was outraged, insulted. The voices raged from the parlor, and then finally, I heard my name being called.

It was Robert, his voice intruding on every room in my father's house. "Come with me now, Marina!"

He was at the door of the parlor, my father standing behind him, his face as red as a beet. Stepmother's face looked ashen.

"You are a grown woman," asserted Robert, "and I wish you to accompany me to Paris."

"Marina, go to your room!" demanded Father. "No respectable girl would consider such an offer."

I looked upon this scene in horror. So deeply torn. How could I say no to my love? And yet, how could I abandon my family and risk shaming them? I was paralyzed, teetering between a past I loved dearly and a future I wanted desperately. I was lost—

And then I felt hands on my shoulder. It was Tante Camille, father's widowed aunt. "She will wait for you, Monsieur," said Tante. "She will wait and you will return for a proper wedding."

Both Robert and Father glared at me. I felt that neither was happy with this decision. Yet neither disagreed.

"Wait for me," was all my Robert said before he banged the front door shut behind him. Then Father turned angrily and walked to his study, slamming its door in turn.

I ran to my room, crying on my pillow until I had fallen asleep. When I awoke, the mosquito bar had been drawn around me. The filmy white netting, attached to the tester above my bed, made the room appear as if a cloud had descended upon me. But even without the netting, a cloud had indeed descended—for my love was gone. Robert had caught a steamer for France, and I was left to pine for his return.

It was only tonight, after dinner, that I realized for the first time that there could be terrible consequences from Robert's leaving. More than just my pining. . . .

Tonight, I overheard Father talking to Stepmother. It seems to me that they are skeptical IF Robert will ever return.

"Give it more time," said Stepmother. *"She cares deeply for this one."*

"I know," said Father sadly. *"But I must think of what is best for her. I must think of her future well-being."*

I dread what my father has in mind. I have written a missive to my Robert, urging him to state when he will return. I only pray that Father be patient. I will not marry any but my Robert. I do not care if I should die an old maid!

OCTOBER 25, 1896

Something is happening. Even my little brother knows, and he is barely ten.

Dinner had been strained for a week now. Our eyes are cast down on our plates like nuns at prayer. I think it has to do with money. And the Americans—that is the term we French Creoles use, "Americans."

We are all Americans, of course, but we Creoles have always felt that the "Americans" are those who have settled into our city since the War Between the States—not that I was even alive for it. I just hear stories from the older ones. As Tante Camille says, "They do not speak a word of French, and they have taken over everything!"

I know Stepmother is upset. She and Father have many hushed conversations in the parlor. From my eavesdropping, I gather Father's brokerage business is in trouble. He is now concocting importing schemes with American businessmen to secure his finances.

After dinner this evening, the table emptied quickly, Father was off to another business meeting—at his club, he said—and Stepmother had gone straight to her room. Tante Camille was instructing P'tit-Boy in Catholic Catechism, so I wandered out to the kitchen, where Liberté was cleaning the pots.

Liberté.

Isn't that a fine name? It was the name she chose for herself. She told me that the day she heard of President

Lincoln's signing of the Emancipation Proclamation, she changed her name from one she never liked.

What a fine idea . . . choosing your own name for yourself!

She says her freedom after the War left her nearly terrified at first, but she left the plantation anyway. Her parents would not go, but she left.

I think that she must be the bravest person I know. She came to New Orleans all by herself and found a job with Father's family. For years she worked for my grandfather as a cook and nanny, and after he passed on, she agreed to work for Father.

"Do you know what's wrong?" I asked Libbe as I sat down on a kitchen chair."

"Wrong?"

"Yes," I told her. "Everyone's so upset . . ."

"Your father, it seem to me, he havin' money troubles," said Libbe. "Dat what you mean?"

"Yes . . ."

"Don't go upsettin' yo'self, now. Your father is a smart man. He find a way to take care o' you. . . ."

"I'm not worried about me. I am beginning to rest easier that my future will be fine—once Robert returns, of course. You do like Robert, don't you?"

Libbe smiled at me, her dark eyes shining with mirth. "You in love, chil', o' course your future look rosy to you. An' yes I like yo' Monsieur Robert. He a handsome fello'. But what more import'nt is dat he love you. I see it in his eye."

"Do you think my mother would have liked him?" I asked.

Libbe is the only one I can speak to about my mother. Father is not comfortable speaking of her, but Libbe will— quietly though, when Father is not around. She likes to tell me how lovely Mother was, with a flowing fall of red-brown hair like mine.

I was eight when she passed away. Libbe says she is still

in my life, watching over me, as one of my guardian spirits. Libbe says her "Vo-do" assures her of this.

I find Libbe's Voodoo fascinating. I know she believes a good gris-gris can overcome bad magic. I actually believe this, too, and keep the small gris-gris bag that Libbe made for me under my pillow—though Father would have a fit if he knew!

He says Voodoo is flubdubbery, but I think there's something to it, maybe because I love Libbe so much . . . and I do wish to believe what she said about my mother's still looking over me, even though she is dead.

Anyhow, when I asked Libbe about my mother liking Robert, she came to the kitchen table and sat down with me. She took my light-skinned hands in her dark ones. "Your mama would have loved him, chil', I'm sure . . . because she could see dat you love him. An' I know you don't remember her much—"

"I remember her. She was lovely, and kind. But, you see, I don't think Father understands how I feel about Robert."

Libbe shook her head. "Chil', yo' father understan' 'bout love, believe me. He love yo' mama with all o' his heart."

"But Father acts as though he doesn't understand."

"You his chil', dat why. He want what best fo' you. Trus' me, though, he understan' 'bout love. . . ."

I hope Libbe is right.

NOVEMBER 13, 1896

I am terribly afraid.

Robert has sent another letter, but it predates my letter to him and, therefore, does not answer my pleas. He speaks of his love for me, but he does not affirm his return.

Things are bad with the family. Father does not even try to hide his worries any longer. He closed his Baton Rouge office, and his New Orleans office is not doing well.

He has made a close friend of one of the Americans. His

name is John M—. It seems as though they've known each other a long while and lately have stepped up these import-ing schemes together.

John M— is quite wealthy. His shipping business is one of the strongest in the South. I think he is using my father to secure ties and investors in the Creole community.

He often comes to our house now for dinner. He is near my father's age, middle forties I should think, with dark hair and an attractive face with blue eyes. Yet from the mo-ment I met him, I did not like him. He looked at me in a se-cret way, not proper at all. He made me want to throw a shawl around myself.

Tonight he joined us for dinner again. He and Father usually talk and smoke in the parlor after dinner. And tonight, as I left table, I overheard the man speak low to my father. He said my name.

Why would he speak my name in private to my father?

I have a terrible feeling . . . I only pray it is wrong.

DECEMBER 19, 1896

My fears about John M— are confirmed. I dreaded this would happen, and so it has.

It began at the party. Tonight the family was in a festive mood with Christmas so close. Despite Father's money troubles, we hosted a small soiree.

When John M— arrived, he gave the immediate family gifts. To me he gave a fine perfume in a beautiful crystal bottle shaped like a swan. He said it was from Paris. I thanked him, but I did not like the way he looked at me as I opened the gift.

"Do you like it?" he asked, stepping close.

I stepped back quickly, answering in French to underline the difference between us. "Oui. Merci, Monsieur."

"Call me John, Marina. You are such an innocent," he murmured then. "Such a sweet thing, like a fresh little

flower." He reached out then to touch a fallen curl, but again I stepped back.

I excused myself and left the parlor. Somehow with all the commotion of arriving guests, he managed to follow me as I headed down the hall toward the kitchen. He caught my arm, startling me, and led us a few steps into Father's study.

I was puzzled at first, not wanting to argue, even when he closed the door and insisted I try the perfume still in my hand.

I was terribly nervous. It was not proper to be alone with him like this, and I tried to step around him, but he blocked my way. He appeared unaware—or unconcerned—with the impropriety.

I looked into his face and there was an odd expression there. Now that I think back, it almost seemed as if he were enamored of the apprehension he saw in me. That is a strange thing to consider . . . but in my soul I know it is the truth.

I stood there, not knowing what to do. I could not cause a scene. This was Father's business associate, a wealthy, respected gentleman. I told myself that I was acting like a silly schoolgirl. Clearly, the man had some romantic interest in me. He was not an unattractive man, I told myself. And perhaps he did not mean to be improper. Perhaps he was simply clumsy in his pursuit. After all, the Americans were less formal, less traditional than we Creoles. I decided to be agreeable, but take the first opportunity to set things right between us.

"Try it on," he said again; and again it was far from a tender entreaty. His voice was rough, commanding, as if he was used to ordering people about; as if no one had ever denied him.

Because I planned on rejecting his advance, I decided the least I could do was oblige trying his generous gift. I pulled on the swan's long neck, which served as the stop to this ornate crystal bottle. The underside of the stop carried *a glass applicator that arrowed downward into the expensive liquid.*

I gently touched the tip of the applicator to the inside of my wrist. My hands were shaking a bit and I was embarrassed by this. Again, I scolded myself for acting like a silly child.

John M—'s eyes were intense as they looked upon me. He reached out and took my wrist in his hand. I resisted a moment, but his grip was insistent, so I yielded, allowing him to draw it toward my face.

"Sample it," he ordered.

I inhaled. The fragrance was sweet but cloying—much too overwhelming for a girl of my years.

"What do you think?" he asked.

"It is very nice," I lied. "A generous gift."

"Yes, it was. That particular bottle would cost over fifty dollars at a department store."

My eyes widened at this. "That is . . . too great an amount. . . ." I managed. "You must not spend it on me. You should take it back. . . ." My left hand held the bottle up to him.

"Do not worry your pretty head," he said. "I am an importer. It cost me a fraction of that amount . . . but it is an expensive item. I just wanted you to see how easily it is for me to acquire the best—at a reasonable price."

"Well, I do hope my beau will like it," I tried, emphasizing the words "my beau."

John M— stared me down, his eyes seeming to glitter. "Yes . . . I'm not surprised you have a beau. I've heard you have had many young blades sniffing around here, haven't you?"

"I—"

"But, you see, my girl, you must learn how to wear the perfume proper . . . for your 'beau.' Let me show you. . . ."

John M— then took the applicator from me. He dipped it in the perfume bottle still in my hand. I thought he was going to apply it to my other wrist, but he did not. Instead he reached up, past my exposed shoulders to touch the skin behind my left ear.

I was wearing one of my lovely white Paris gowns for the holiday soiree. It was not a new gown. I had worn it during last year's round of Mardi Gras balls, but it was lovely. The lace décolletage was daring yet tasteful. My flowing auburn hair was pinned up, of course, so it was easy for John M— to gain access to the soft flesh behind my ear. The glass point of the applicator felt cool, and I tried not to jump as he rubbed it across my skin.

"Yes . . . that's where it should go. . . ." he said low, a patronizing edge to his tone. "Now when your 'beau' moves in close to you, he can smell the invitation of the perfume. You see?"

I was unsettled by his closeness now, but I tried to act like an adult and not show girlish fear.

"And of course you must put it behind the other ear. . . ."

"No," I said, backing up a step. This was getting out of hand! For one thing, I was going to smell like a perfume shop. And for another, he seemed intent on physically advancing on me. I backed up, but he pursued until I had reached a corner of the room, trapped against one of the study's heavy bookcases.

"Yes," he insisted. "The other ear."

Uneasy, I allowed him to apply the applicator once more. But this time as he drew his hand from my right ear, I reached up to snatch the applicator from him.

Quickly he pulled up his hand, holding it just out of my reach. Then, as I lowered my hand, he dangled the applicator in front of my eyes, teasing me to try grabbing it again.

I did try again, and again he pulled it up, out of my reach.

"It's a game, then, isn't it?" he asked, laughing at me. "Good. I like games, too. And you should learn what I like—"

"It's not a game. Let me by now—"

"One more spot, my sweet girl . . . and you are sweet, aren't you?" he murmured low. "And innocent. And beautiful. The most fresh and beautiful belle in the city, they *say—one whose father thinks her too good for the eligible gentlemen of this town—"*

"Monsieur, you must stop now," I whispered harshly in a scandalized tone. "I beg you. Please, do not be angry, but I tell you, I do have a beau—"

"Just one more spot," he said, calmly ignoring me.

His ice-blue eyes seemed to trap my wide green ones as he then took the applicator's tip and brought it slowly to the lowest point where my neckline plunged. His gaze followed the cold pointed tip as it made contact with the warm skin of my cleavage.

I was paralyzed with pure shock at this vile violation. And if that weren't enough, he began to rub the tip back and forth there, dipping into the neckline of my dress.

I am young, but I am a grown woman, and I vowed to handle this offense with dignity. Only one of my hands was free, the other still holding the crystal perfume bottle. I used my free hand then to try slapping his away, but his free hand captured it, forcing it behind me as he continued to slowly rub back and forth. The scent of the heavy sweet perfume now rose from the skin of my breasts like a smothering cloud, sickening me.

"Monsieur, you have overstepped the boundaries of propriety," I manage to bite out. "I demand you release me."

He said nothing. He stopped rubbing the end of the glass applicator between the swells of my breasts, but he did not remove it, however. Instead, he brought his sharp gaze up to bore into mine, then he pressed the point hard against my skin, not enough to pierce it, but enough to leave an angry red brand.

Then he began to smile. It was an unholy smile, drawing sustenance from my shame and barely hidden fear.

"There," he said low, his tone ugly. "You are ready now. All ready for"—he paused—"your beau."

He stepped back then, and the moment his strong fingers released my small hand, I swung hard to slap his face. But even the sting of my palm failed to alter his terrible smile. In fact, it was then he began to laugh.

When he released me, I bolted, and this time he did not stop me. I set down the perfume bottle on a side table as I fled the room. I wanted nothing more to do with it, or him.

I went to the bath and immediately scrubbed at the stench, but the perfume was strong and hard to completely remove. I went back to the soiree, avoiding John M— most of the night, taking care to always remain in the company of cousins or friends.

But I could not speak a word of this to anyone.

Father needed his association with John M— for his business, and I knew that relating such a scandalous encounter would cast doubt on me and even my love for Robert. My own behavior would immediately be questioned. Did I somehow tempt him to such behavior? People would wonder. So I said nothing, praying the whole ugly scene would fade with time.

But tonight, after the soiree, when I returned to my room, I saw an omen that sent a shiver through me. There, sitting near the pillows of my bed, was the evidence that John M— was not through with me: It was the crystal swan.

I flung it out the window with all my might, wishing that all my worries could be flung away so easily. . . .

JANUARY 6, 1897

My life is changed forever. No matter what happens to me now, I have learned a thing tonight that has left me a different person.

Just last night my chief worry was Robert. I have not heard from him for two months now and am beginning to fear that something terrible has happened to him.

Over the holiday I managed to avoid John M—. Even when he came to the house, I made excuses, then hid. Tonight, though, I could not avoid him. He came to the house for our celebration of the Epiphany. After we fin-

ished eating the traditional King Cake, it finally happened. John M— asked for my hand.

The guests had left and most of the family had retired when Father and John M— reclined to share a drink. I went up with the rest of the family, but snuck back down to my hiding place in the shadows of the dining room, just outside the double doors of the parlor. I listened intently and wrung my hands at the planning of my entire life's fate. . . .

"She's a pretty little thing," John M— told Father. "And you know I've been interested for some time. I want her hand."

"Yes, of course you do," said Father. "But you see there's a young man who has expressed interest and he's in Paris—"

"Now, you said the same thing to me some time ago, but where is this suitor? Seems to me he's left your Marina high and dry."

"He has given his word that he will return for her."

"When?"

"Soon . . . "

"Ah, Etienne, you and I have known each other for over a year now . . . and I can tell when you are not being completely forthcoming. I hope you aren't deliberately trying to make me unhappy."

"No, no . . . of course not—"

"I'm a formidable man when I'm unhappy."

A long pause followed and Father then carefully said, "That's what I've heard. . . ."

John M— laughed loud and long. "You heard right."

"I love my daughter, and I want her to be happy."

"Yes, yes, she'll have the best of everything. The finest clothes, the gaudiest jewelry. And besides, we've worked out a nice little operation over the past months. It would be good for me to marry again—especially into your family. Your Creole community will be more accepting of me. And you know it would be far better for your family financially if you solidify our connection."

"I grant that you are not wrong. But—"

"Don't make me unhappy now—"

"No, no. I'm sorry. I'm just trying to say . . ."

I listened with an odd realization dawning over me. All of my life, Father had always seemed in utter control. Under this roof, he was the man who laid down the law and set the clocks. Yet, now, for the first time, I saw my father struggling to keep control. Under his own roof, my father was actually pleading.

". . . and I believe we should wait a little longer—just a little longer. If we have not settled the matter with the other suitor by, say, Mardi Gras, then I will happily speak with you about an engagement. How is that then, John? That's not asking too much, is it?" finished Father.

John M— did not sound happy, and though his words were that of acquiescence, it seemed to my ears more like a threat. *"I see, Etienne. I suppose then, you give me no choice."*

"Then you understand?"

"You know, you have a pretty high opinion of that girl of yours."

"Well, of course, John, naturally I do. We are an old and respected New Orleans Creole family, and she deserves the best. . . ."

"I'll make this more plain. There's a piece of rumor I picked up in Baton Rouge."

"What rumor?"

"A rumor that tells me your girl there may not be quite the purest snow. A rumor that says her mother, your first wife, was—what's the term you Creoles like to use?—café au lait."

I tried not to gasp when I heard those words. My hand flew to cover my mouth, and I was terrified that I would make a sound.

"Sir, I think you should leave now," said Father bluntly.

"Don't be so hasty—" warned John M—.

"Please, sir, I think you should leave."

For a long time I sat alone in the darkness in shock. My

*mother? Café au lait? A quadroon? And that would mean I
would be an octoroon . . . one-eighth colored. . . .*

*My God, I thought, if this were true, it would ruin us. It
would mean my father had colored children and he had
dared to try passing them off as white—dared even to try
showing me off for marriage in the white Creole community! This was scandalous!*

What, by heaven's name, would Robert think?

*I sat so quietly in the dining room corner for so long that
I nearly cried out in surprise when I heard voices again
through the door to the parlor. This time it was Father and
Stepmother.*

*"He knows the truth," said Father, his voice the weakest
and saddest I had ever heard it.*

"You did not admit it to him," argued Stepmother.

*Stepmother knew, too! I realized with even greater
shock.*

*"Of course I did not admit it," said Father. "But he is a
powerful man. If he wanted to ruin the family's reputation,
there is not much I could do. . . ."*

*"We must wait and see what happens then," suggested
Stepmother. "And we must do what we can to fight him."*

*"Perhaps I should marry her off to him," speculated
Father.*

*"Give it a little more time. By Mardi Gras, the young
man should return from Paris. He has said he will return
for her. . . ."*

*"I do not like this game of risk . . . but I will agree to
that. Until March the second then . . ."*

*I still cannot fathom it. I stood in front of my armoire
mirror for a long time. I dared to strip naked and examine
my whole body, looking for signs of being colored. . . .*

But I am still me.

*What I know now does not change who I am, and yet the
truth would change everything about the way the world will
see me . . . will treat me. . . .*

Now I wonder about my mother in a new light. Had she

been a part of New Orleans' large community of free persons of color? Or had she descended from slaves?

From what Libbe said, Father met Mother here in New Orleans. Marie Lisette, my mother, was supposedly an orphaned child, living with an elderly aunt, and Father fell instantly in love with her.

Suddenly I realized why he may have left New Orleans; why he had set up his household and second office in Baton Rouge. No one would know my mother there . . . no one would suspect, just looking at her, that she was a person of color.

With a heavy spirit, I think again of my mother's position in life and wonder about her family. What would my position be now if Mother had been the daughter of a slave and the War Between the States had not come?

I would have been owned, too, of course . . . like Libbe.

And what would I have done if my master were a man as vile as John M—?

My spirit cringes at the very idea, for I feel a shadow over that man's spirit—a sinister, cynical darkness. When he looks at me, I see a vulgar lust at the surface. There is no genuine caring there. No interest in my spirit, no respect for my person.

He is nothing like my Robert.

John M— seems only to harbor an ugly desire to possess. Whether it be items imported from Paris or my innocent youth, it seems there is little difference where he is concerned.

And if such a man would marry me, knowing of my mixed blood, then what does that mean?

The answer comes to me from a place deep inside: This vile man means to have a wife he can control. Yes, if I am forced to marry him, then my life will truly be over.

My fear of his revealing this terrible secret will become my bondage, my chains, and he will have in me a wife, who is by all accounts but legal ones, his slave.

FEBRUARY 2, 1897

I am lost. I am finished . . . there is no recourse . . .

Father has promised my hand to John M— and I cannot fight it. Both The Louisiana Gazette *and* The Picayune *have announced our engagement. We will marry on Saturday, May 1.*

Father has made it plain to me that he would have been ruined if he had not agreed to the match. A large, very valuable shipment of goods was lost at sea the third week of January. John M— would not extend to my father a credit for the future. Investors have lost a great deal, my father nearly everything. He says that if he did not give my hand to John M— the family would have been ruined, his business finished, even our house gone to creditors.

I love my family, but I am outraged that they have used me this way. I cannot be resigned, as they are, to Robert's abandonment. . . . I feel in my heart and soul that he will return. And his wealth could have helped us through . . . yet there has been no word from him for so long, no answers to my many letters. . . .

I am beside myself with grief at this turn of events, but my family is desperate now, and so I am forced into this decision.

I am forced to live a life that would have been my destiny not so long ago. And now I will know what Libbe felt. Now I will know what it is to be bartered into a life against my will, a life far from one I would ever freely choose.

Chapter
Eleven

"Good read?"

Tori looked up from the diary to find the sun had sunk well below the rooftops of the Quarter, casting its remaining light in a gentle array of soft pastels.

Bruce Gautreau was standing on the porch steps of Rosegate, one muscular arm casually leaning against a tall wooden post.

For a moment Tori found herself speechless.

Over the last hour she had become completely wrapped up in the intimate emotions of the Creole girl's diary. She hadn't even heard Bruce climbing the front porch steps.

Now he stood gazing at her with mild amusement—and something else Tori couldn't quite define.

Bruce slowly crossed the porch, unable to take his eyes off the long bare legs stretched out in front of him . . . then suddenly he saw those same limbs wrapped around his body on a soft mattress. Her head was thrown back in ecstasy, her glorious auburn hair streaming out across a white pillow like rays of dawn.

Bruce stopped a moment, closing his eyes with the image. It was not a red-blooded man's wishful thinking, it was the *traiteur de pouvoir* inside him, the divining of what would be.

A smile of anticipation touched his lips as he opened his eyes. Tori was staring at him, curiously. "What are you smiling about?"

"The future."

Tori shook her head in exasperation. "Right, Gautreau, that makes perfect sense." Snapping shut the diary, Tori rose from her porch chair and started for the house. "Have you eaten?"

"If I say no, will you feed me?"

"Well, Aunt Zoe already provided dessert—last night's specials at Duchamp's—so I decided to mix up some dinner." She made her way through the restored dining room and into the still-run-down kitchen.

"Home cooking, huh?" remarked Bruce. "I can hardly believe it. Seems to me you've been livin' mostly on cold cuts and canned soup for nearly a month. Hey, now, somethin' smells yummy in here."

"Shrimp Remoulade."

"*Non!*"

"*Oui.*"

Bruce sauntered over to the table, where Tori had set out the plates. "May I?" he asked.

"Please."

Bruce picked up a fork and took a bite of the spicy shrimp salad. It was heavenly. "Mmmmm . . ."

"My aunt used to whip this up on hot days. Guests would rave, as I recall."

"Mmmm-mmmm. They weren't wrong. Is dinner served, then, *Mademoiselle*?"

"Yes. Take a seat."

"Well, before I do, I've got something."

"What?"

"Be right back."

Tori waited only a few minutes as Bruce ran out to his pickup truck—she knew by now that he preferred it to the Porsche on work days. When he returned, he held a cardboard box with holes in it and a large container of Kitten Chow.

"What the—" she began, but then she heard a small sound, like mewing.

"For you. And the house," said Bruce, setting down the box and opening the lid.

Two small striped heads peeked out, four tiny golden eyes blinked. And Tori's heart immediately melted.

"Oh, they're adorable!" she exclaimed, stooping to pick up the two nearly identical orange-striped kittens.

"My landlady's cat had them about three months ago. Tony and Cleo. Okay with you if they take up residence here now? I'm sure they'll earn their keep with mousing, and you did mention you're uneasy here alone at night."

"Oh, they're adorable!" repeated Tori, pressing their furry faces against her cheeks. Both kittens purred with the attention.

"I guess that's a yes."

After dinner Bruce leaned back in his kitchen chair. "Ready for me to take a look at what you've done today?"

"There's not much for you to see, I'm afraid," said Tori, grabbing their empty plates as she rose from the table. "I had lunch with Aunt Zoe. Finally took a day off. But maybe you can help me get that antique bedroom set down from the attic."

"Sure. What's the occasion? Have you found a buyer?"

"No. I've decided to keep it. Set it up for myself."

Bruce nodded. "I'm glad. It seems to belong here. . . ."

"Yes, I know what you mean. Maybe it's the diary. I'm feeling a kind of, I don't know—a connection to the people who lived here. Does that sound odd?"

"Not a bit. Happens to me when I work on a place." Cleo, the female kitten, had finished her dinner and was now brushing against Bruce's leg. He reached down to scratch behind her ears.

"You feel a connection?" asked Tori.

"Yeah, a lot of times I can feel the presence of the previous residents. It usually helps in the restoration, bringing back the former glory, remembrance of things past and all that—but, listen, I'm glad you took time off. You've been working too hard."

"That's what Aunt Zoe said. It's funny, though, it doesn't seem like *work* to me. I grant you it's taxing, but I'm beginning to understand why you do this. . . ."

"You are?" Bruce eyed her as she finished rinsing the plates in the sink, then began to make coffee. "Enlighten me, then, because I'm not sure why I do much of anything."

"Well, it's so satisfying to accomplish something that you can actually *see*—a result that comes from your own efforts," explained Tori, letting the water run into the coffeepot.

Bruce noticed the boy kitten jumping onto the kitchen counter to watch Tori's every move. Bruce was watching, too, and feeling. Something was roiling just beneath her surface. In fact, he sensed that her insides were like a pot of gumbo about to boil over. . . .

So what would be the harm in lifting the lid a little bit?

"Uh, Tori, are you talking about something else here? Besides the house?"

Tori was silent a moment as she poured the water into the drip coffeemaker. "Yes, I suppose so. I mean, I'm just beginning to realize that I never felt so *good* about my work before."

"Is that why you left New York? Because you didn't feel good about your work?" Bruce sensed the answer had something to do with a man named Edward. He wondered, though, if she'd tell him the truth.

"Partly . . ." was all Tori said, completely avoiding the subject of Edward. Bruce let it go—for the moment. He figured it was better if he just let her talk. He'd lead her back to Edward eventually.

"I mean, I didn't find satisfaction studying for a doctoral degree," explained Tori. "I never believed my studies would ever amount to anything. So I left them and tried the business world. I worked on a corporate newsletter for two years, but office politics were hell, and the company had this neurotic fear of recognizing efforts—"

"Wait a second there," interrupted Bruce as he picked up Cleo and placed her on his lap. "A *company* had a neurotic fear?"

"That's about the size of it. A pat on the back might lead to the expectation of a financial bonus, and they couldn't have that." Tori began scooping coffee into the filter. "I guess it was some thrifty CEO's sick business theory that he would never have to pay people what they were worth if he never let on that he *knew* what they were worth."

Suddenly she stopped scooping, then turned to face him. "But, Bruce, what I've done *here*, on the house. It's *clear* what I did by my own hand. I can be proud. Do you see?"

Bruce nodded his head. He slowly stroked the soft fur of the kitten, feeling the sense that there was a father figure somehow mixed up in all this talk of pride of accomplishment.

"Come to think of it," said Tori, still staring at Bruce. "My father used to act just like that CEO."

There it is. Bruce studied Tori. "He never wanted to give you a raise?"

Tori smiled. "Forget it, I don't know why I—"

"No. You brought it up. What do you think the connection is?"

Tori shrugged. She placed the coffee filter into the machine and flipped the button on. "It's stupid. Must be the coffee making. Did you know French Creoles used to consider this so significant a rite that in most homes the father of the house used to make the coffee?"

"Tori, I'm sure that's fascinating, but that's not what you were—"

"The pot's top held the grounds and the bottom held the final brew. Just a little bit of water was poured over the grounds at a time—"

"Tori, don't—" tried Bruce again.

"They even roasted their own beans—"

"Tori, *ça c'est assez!*" Bruce exclaimed, his hands going to his temples as the kitten quickly scampered off his lap. A moment of tense silence followed and then Bruce spoke again, this time softly repeating his words in English. "That's enough."

"Enough?" asked Tori in a puzzled voice, startled by Bruce's seemingly unprovoked outburst.

"If you don't want to talk about your father, that's your business, but don't shut me out like that. It gives me a headache."

"What . . . what do you mean, shut you out?"

Bruce stared at her. "Tori, I'm—" He stopped a moment. "My mother was . . . what you'd call . . . psychic."

Tori felt her limbs going numb. *"What?"*

"She read people. Sometimes their thoughts. Sometimes their inner map, so to speak. She tried to use it to help folks navigate through their problems. I picked up some of her . . . talent."

Tori found she needed to sit down. So she did. "What do you mean? You can read my mind or something?"

"Yes."

"And you expect me to believe that?"

Bruce sighed in disgust. "Believe what you want, sweet, it won't alter my reality."

Tori sat and considered this for a long time. "Okay, what am I thinking?"

"How should I know."

"But you just said—"

"I'm not a circus performer, Tori, I don't do tricks. Whatever it is I have, it kicks in of its own accord—"

Sure it does. Just like your libido.

"Just like my libido."

"What!?"

"That's what you just thought, didn't you?" asked Bruce.

"Oh, my God."

"You want to think of a number between one and forty-five?"

"Don't be silly." *Thirty-nine.*

"Thirty-nine, *chère,* is that the age you fear most?"

"Oh, my God, how did you do that?"

Bruce showed his palms to the ceiling. "God's blessing—and curse."

"What do you mean *curse*?"

A harsh laugh escaped his throat. "It's not always an advantage to be a sensitive. Why do you think people put on masks, Tori? Often it's to protect themselves, but sometimes it's to protect the people around them."

She considered this, then shook her head. "Is the truth such a harmful thing?"

"That CEO of yours apparently thought so."

"That's manipulation. Not truth. Manipulation for someone's own self-serving purposes. Just like my father and—"

Tori stopped and Bruce studied her face. "Please go on," he said softly. "Maybe I can help you . . . sort things out."

"I don't know what to say. . . ."

"Tell me what your father was like when you were growing up. You said your mother passed on. What was that all about?"

Tori swallowed uneasily. Bruce could tell how hard it was for her to open up. He watched her for a long moment as she folded and refolded a paper napkin, struggling with whether or not to trust him with her most private thoughts.

"Well . . ." she finally said, glancing into his handsome face with timid guardedness. "I'll just start from the beginning. Okay?"

"*Oui, chère.* Whatever you want." Bruce tried to contain how pleased he was that she was at least going to try.

"They met here in New Orleans," she began hesitantly, her voice very soft. "They got married and I'm told were very happy for a little while. Then I came along. . . ."

Bruce nodded.

"From what I've gathered, Stanton, my father, he began to feel as though he were missing out on something. A more exciting life, I guess. Most of what I know is from my late aunt Hestia. I asked her about them when I was a teenager. You see, by that time I was living here at Rosegate."

"What happened, Tori?"

"When I was about seven years old, my father's business contacts offered him this high-powered job with a big New York law firm. But Mother refused to leave New Orleans. She said she didn't want me growing up in New York. . . ."

Bruce felt something inside of him move as Tori talked. He could feel her reaching out to him. But it was more than that. She was accepting his talent so innocently now, with so much trust. It felt as if, after weeks of knocking and waiting, a mansion's front door had finally been unlocked to him. Bruce liked this feeling, liked knowing her this way . . . like being let in. . . .

"But Father didn't care what Mother wanted. He took the job in New York anyway, leaving her—and me—behind in New Orleans. They never divorced, just separated for about half a year. Then Father began to put a lot of pressure on Mother to join him. . . ."

"Pressure? What kind of pressure?"

Tori's body tensed. Bruce watched as her fingers began to uneasily wring the paper napkin in her hands.

"He threatened to take me away from her. He was an attorney, you see, and he had resources at his disposal. . . . It must have been pretty awful for my mother. . . ."

"So, what happened?"

"She gave in, and we moved into a big house in the suburbs north of Manhattan. But Mother was so unhappy. She began to . . . get depressed." Tori's fingers ripped at the napkin in her hands. "She drank a lot. And within two years she was dead. I still can't believe how fast it all came apart. . . ." Tori's voice just trailed off, her gaze unfocused, her fingers releasing what remained of the thin shredded paper.

"What happened then?" asked Bruce gently. "Were you sent here to Rosegate?"

"No. Father sold our house in Westchester, then he and I

and the housekeeper moved into this big Park Avenue apartment in the city—"

"And how was your relationship with him?"

"Oh, I don't know," said Tori. "He'd always been reserved."

Not just reserved, sensed Bruce. *Cold.* "Was he that way just to you? Or to everyone?"

"I . . . never thought of that before. I mean, to everyone else he seemed—"

"Seemed?"

Tori shook her head. "He laughed with other people. I remember that much. He'd have people over to the apartment in the evenings. I wasn't to come out—it was grown-up talk, you know. But he *laughed* with them. Had a lot of slap-on-the-back, let's-have-a-drink sort of evenings."

"But that wasn't the side you saw?"

"No."

Bruce's ears heard a very controlled voice, but his eyes saw the signs of anguish in Tori's face and felt the anger and frustration beneath the surface.

Tori shook her head. "Maybe things would have been better between us if he had just sent me down to my aunt and uncle right after Mother died, but he must have felt some obligation. Though I sometimes wonder . . ."

"What?"

"I wonder if he ever blamed me," said Tori in a terribly weak voice. "Blamed me for Mother's death."

Bruce heard the words, but read something else. Deep inside of Tori, there was a tremendous heaviness of heart, a sense of guilt, sorrow, and rage—all directed at herself.

It wasn't her father's blame that cut her so deeply. Tori Avalon blamed *herself* for her mother's death.

"On the other hand, there was so much more to blame me for—I mean, *after* her death."

"What do you mean? You were just a kid. What could he blame you for?"

"Well, appearances were so important to him, and I could never do anything right. I was a complete screwup. I'd keep going back to try harder and harder, but nothing ever worked—it was pathetic. *I* was pathetic."

"I don't understand, Tori. What were you trying harder at?"

"Everything! My father wanted the best for me: education, clothes, friends. He really tried to make me happy. I mean, there were dozens of lessons that he spent a fortune on: violin, ballet, speech—because I began stuttering—and then there were the doctors—because I began to eat myself out of dress sizes. My God, after two years, I was a walking disaster."

"Is that what your father told you?"

"He never had to *say* it, for God's sake. I mean it was so *obvious*! My father was handsome, erudite, successful, and I was nothing like him. I was an embarrassment, a failure. You know, I don't even blame him for finally giving up on me. It's no wonder he sent me back down to New Orleans to live with Aunt Hestia and Uncle Richard—" Tori shrugged. "You see, *that's* how I ended up here at Rosegate. Pretty pathetic story, don't you think?"

Bruce leaned back in the kitchen chair and crossed one leg over his knee. "And you think that's why he sent you back down here? Because you were a failure at—what age?"

"Let's see, I guess I was . . . twelve."

"And your father . . . was he seeing any women during this time?"

"Women . . . well, yes . . . there were a few, I think."

"There's one woman in your mind. A woman named Barbara?"

Tori's eyes widened. "How did you know that name?"

"I—" Bruce stared at Tori a long moment, then sighed with frustration. *"Lucky guess."*

"Sorry," said Tori softly, realizing she'd insulted Bruce. Well, it wasn't so easy talking with a mind reader. "Father married her, after I was sent to Rosegate."

"I see . . ." Bruce felt the confusion inside of Tori. "So you've been telling yourself you were unloved and unwanted by your father, because you were a failure."

"Well—"

"At twelve."

"I—"

"Have you seen the twelve-year-olds from the school down the block, Tori? Do you realize how young they are?"

"No, I guess, I—"

"Is that why you went back up to New York for college? Because your father was still up there?"

"I tried to reestablish contact with him, yes. But—"

"He was still cold to you, wasn't he?"

"Yes."

"And this Edward person you keep comparing me to in your head: He was a young associate in your father's law firm, right? And you became lovers. Was he a part of this struggle? Was he your way of proving something to yourself and to your father?"

"Shut up! How do you know about Edward? Shut up!" Tori rose from the table, suddenly enraged. "How dare you invade my private thoughts! How dare you jump to conclusions like that! How dare you—"

"Calm down." Bruce knew instantly that he'd made a mistake; he'd pushed too far, too fast, and set her off. Actually, he wasn't in the least perplexed by Tori's tirade. He'd seen worse. Some women actually began throwing things at this point.

CRASH!

Bruce ducked under the flying salt shaker and bit out a silent curse. Now she was going for the pepper mill.

"Tori!" Bruce rose and placed a firm grip on her arms. "That's enough! *Ça c'est assez!*"

When he'd finally gotten her to sit back down, he rose and crossed to the counter. Silently he poured her a cup of coffee. Then he reached into the cupboard, his fingers closing around the neck of the bourbon bottle he'd brought to the house weeks ago. A shot splashed into her cup and, after a second's consideration, another went into his.

"Here, drink this. And take a deep breath."

Reluctantly Tori did.

"Listen to me, *chère*," began Bruce as he sat down at the table. "*I'm* not coming up with this stuff. *You* are. I don't know if it's right or wrong in the scheme of things. I don't know your father, and I can't look into a crystal ball to see what the real *truth* of the past is. But what I can do . . ." His voice grew soft. "*Chère,* what I can do is look inside you and see what past *you* carry around inside. I can see how it all adds up in your head. *Compris?*"

"No. I don't understand," countered Tori. "*I* can certainly add it all up in my head for myself."

"Can you? Well, God bless, then, because *I* can't. I can read other people, but I can't know my own self. We're too smart, you see, we like to play tricks on ourselves. It's like putting writing up to a mirror. Seems like the reflection is clear enough, but then you look closer, it's completely backward."

Tori considered this for a long moment. "Edward was a shit."

"But you still love him?"

Tori shook her head. "I still love the idea of him, maybe."

"What happened?" Bruce asked carefully, hoping she wouldn't stop trusting.

Tori studied Bruce a long moment, not sure why she was telling this man so much. But then maybe she did know why. Over the past weeks, as she began to feel more and more connected to Rosegate, she was also feeling more and more connected to a new life.

In his own way Bruce had been a good friend, and an important part of her new life.

Perhaps he was right . . . she couldn't sort all of her feelings out herself. She needed a friend to help her. And besides, now that she was starting to catch hold of some shining new dreams, she was feeling the need to let go of the old tarnished ones.

"I met Edward through my father," said Tori softly. "Father's wife, Barbara, seemed to like me. During the years I was at NYU, Barbara often invited me to their place. A dinner here, a party there. Nothing ever helped my relationship with my father. He just didn't like me. I simply didn't measure up—or maybe he still blamed me for Mother's death. I don't know. But at the time I would have done anything to make things better. I just didn't know how. . . ."

"But then you met Edward."

"Yes. He was at one of their parties. It was some sort of celebratory fling for my father's firm. Edward swept me off my feet. He was charming and handsome and"—Tori shrugged—"my first lover. I fell fast and hard. As it turned out, much too hard."

"What happened?"

"Oh, one day, after we'd secretly moved in together, I found him in bed with a senior partner's secretary."

Bruce took in a sharp breath. He could still feel the painful cut of the memory inside of Tori.

"At first, I thought it was promiscuity, you know. The affair he needed to get out of his system . . ."

"But it wasn't."

Tori shook her head. "When he let the secret out at the office—that we were living together and planning to get married—he discovered that I was far from the apple of my father's eye. In fact, his relationship with me was more likely to *hurt* Edward's ambitions, not help them."

"So he found a way to make you walk out."

Tori nodded her head. "And make it with a better prospect in the process—at least the secretary could feed him semireliable office gossip. Two birds with one stone, so to speak." She laughed bitterly. "He was such a shit."

"But you still have feelings for him, don't you?"

"I have feelings for what I *thought* we had. But what did I know? I fell in love with an elaborate act . . . a phantom."

"Tori, are you aware of *why* you got involved with Edward in the first place?"

"Sure . . . like I said, he swept me off—"

"He was in your *father's* firm, wasn't he?"

Tori eyed Bruce. "What are you saying?"

Bruce watched Tori shift in her seat. He saw something

inside of her that he felt she needed to know. For a long moment he tried to puzzle out how his mother would handle it.

He recalled Angelique's sessions in their little bayou house and remembered that she never pressed her visions on anyone. *Asking hard questions, Vianney, is a much more powerful healing method than providing easy answers.*

"Tori," he finally began gently, "when you look in the mirror, what do you see?"

"I don't understand."

Bruce leaned forward. "Do you see what I do . . . an accomplished, intelligent, and beautiful woman? Or do you see the awkward, unhappy twelve-year-old being sent away by her father?"

Tori stared into Bruce's open, rugged face for a long moment as she honestly considered his questions. Salt water began to fill the ducts of her emerald-green eyes, making them glisten. A small drop brimmed over the edge and slipped loose, traveling a crooked course along the outside of her cheekbone.

For Bruce, it was all the evidence he needed that he'd broken through. But it was also a sign that she now needed to *think* everything through.

"Would you like me to leave now?" he offered.

"No." Tori shook her head, brushing at her wet cheek. "Please don't."

"Sure, sweet." Bruce smiled, wanting nothing more than to take her in his arms. And yet, he couldn't. Not yet. He sensed she needed a little more time. "You still want me to tackle that attic with you tonight?"

"The things in the attic." Tori nodded. "Yes. That's a good idea."

Bruce gave her a wink. "Then let's go to it."

Chapter Twelve

"Robert, are you quite sure we shouldn't?"

"Yes, I'm sure. Don't you recall what happened last time?"

Robert and Marina watched as Bruce and Tori began to move the old furniture down the stairs from the attic.

Marina wanted to try her ghostly hand at loud haunting again, thumps and bangs, to lead them to that valuable object they'd failed to find weeks ago. But Robert stopped his ghost bride.

"I don't want you scaring them away," he said. *"Or worse, scaring them* apart. *This evening I sense that they are more open to each other than ever before . . . perhaps tonight . . ."*

Robert was terribly concerned that the love affair had not yet begun between the living couple. For weeks the ghosts had been trying to enter their bodies and attempt to arouse their desires; but the human beings were bent on fighting their passions.

Most of the time, it was the lady who would not give in, but often it was the builder, as well. He seemed to be just as cautious during these weeks, and the willpower they exhibited was strong. As long as they were *actively* resisting, the ghosts could do nothing to force them together.

"Remember, Marina, they must be open *to physical contact. As soon as they are open to it, we will have a chance of influencing them. Otherwise, I don't know what we'll do."* Robert could not bear this pain much longer—to be so close to Marina and yet unable to kiss, to caress . . .

Marina could feel the despair coming over her darling Robert. She hovered close, wanting desperately to be able to reach out and touch him, hold him. Her own desire was as great as his, and yet she could do nothing to force Tori to love Bruce.

Marina could not fathom it. This Vianney Bruce gentleman was as handsome as her Robert. He appeared kind and gentle, but with a hot-blooded appetite that was quite appealing. Why didn't Tori give in to such obvious temptation?

Thus far, *haunting* Victoria Avalon at night had been Marina's last resort. Although Robert had been averse to the idea, Marina truly believed that her haunting was finally unsettling this proud, independent lady.

Waking her with ghostly footsteps and noises in the dead of night was the only thing Marina found could shake Victoria's headstrong stubbornness—the only way to begin shaking open her closed and cautious mind and heart.

As Tori and Bruce traveled down the stairs for the last time and began arranging furniture in the master bedroom, the ghosts followed, hovering near the ceiling. They watched as the two positioned each of the specially made mahogany and rosewood pieces.

No! Not there, whispered Marina to Vianney Bruce. *Place the mirrored armoire next to the other wall.*

The chest should go at the foot of the bed, conveyed

Robert to the sensitive ear of the man. *Oui, that's as it should be.*

"Robert, it looks almost like it did on our wedding night, doesn't it?" asked Marina with growing excitement. "It's hard for me to recall, but seeing the room again this way . . . I can begin to remember more clearly . . ."

"The details . . . yes . . ." said Robert. "Like everything else, it comes back in puzzle pieces, out of order, but here . . . now . . . I can begin to remember. I had left you here in your white gown."

"Yes. You left and I was anxious. I heard the drums outside . . . in the park. The Voodoo drums . . . and I took off my clothes, feeling the pulse of the rhythm through my blood."

"You were so beautiful." Robert felt a longing in his spirit so intense, so deep that it flowed through his form and into the room in waves. The electricity in the room pulsed and the lights actually flickered.

"Why did you leave me then?" asked Marina. "Oh, wait . . . I seem to recall now . . . you were going to get—"

"My wedding gift to you."

"But didn't you give me the gift already? Your house. This *house.* Wasn't that the gift?"

"No. I mean, I did give you the house. I was concerned that you would always have a place in your name, no matter what happened to me—there were threats, yes, now I recall. There had been threats to me, and to you. Remember?"

"I do not . . . but perhaps I don't wish to—"

"I showed you all of the legal papers drawn up in your name. I showed you these the day before our ceremony, didn't I?"

"Yes, yes . . . that's right. But then why did you leave on our wedding night?"

"I had another gift. Something else, something special," said Robert, not quite able to bring back the memory of exactly *what* it had been.

"Something special," said Marina. *"What was the gift, my love?"*

"I recall commissioning an artisan friend to make it. I knew it would please you."

"But what was it? Why can't I recall opening it? Seeing it?"

"I don't know," said Robert, perplexed. *"I am trying to think . . . to remember . . ."*

"Bruce, did you see that?"

"What?"

"The lights flickered."

"So?"

"So . . . I thought you said you had the house rewired?"

"I did."

Bruce didn't even look up from his work assembling the four-poster bed. He'd felt the spirits close by, felt the suggestions in his head to place each piece of furniture a certain way, and he well knew the flickering had nothing to do with the wiring.

"That's it," said Bruce, rising from the floor and dropping a screwdriver into his toolbox with a loud clang. "Now you've got a *real* bed."

"It's so . . . beautiful." Tori was beyond pleased as she stepped forward to run her fingers up and down the intricately carved rosebuds in the heavy mahogany and rosewood posts.

Next she stepped back and studied the rest of the bedroom set. Two nightstands, an ornate armoire with a mirrored door, a velvet covered *prie-dieu,* and a cedar-lined chest. Finally her room looked like a French Creole's master bedroom. She'd already put up white lace draperies on the window and French doors and found a light throw rug. But with these gorgeous antiques in place, the room looked finished at last.

"If I had lived a hundred years ago, I'd have a mosquito bar. . . ." murmured Tori, gazing at the bed.

"Well, sweet, today you've got that much-less-romantic

invention of window screens. But you *are* missing something vitally important for a good night's sleep. . . ."

"What's that?"

"A mattress."

Tori smiled. "I had one delivered. It's in the next room."

Bruce followed Tori down the hall, then helped her carry the mattress set into the master bedroom. She grabbed fresh linens from the closet and began to make up the bed. Bruce stepped up to help.

As they worked to slip on the fitted sheet, a slow smile spread across Bruce's face. A vision came over him slowly, like a sultry cloud of mist. He saw two entwined bodies on this bed. The image was hazy, as if the gauzy mosquito netting used in the previous century were drawn around the couple. He wasn't sure if this image was from the past or the future, but it affected him. He felt his own body tighten with a sudden need. . . .

On the other side of the bed Tori noticed Bruce's form still, his eyes glaze for a long moment. Then his rich brown gaze looked at her with a burning intensity. Slowly it caressed her slender figure, the round, soft swell of her full breasts, the long bare legs in the cutoff shorts.

"Bruce?"

"I was just wonderin' . . ."

"What?"

His calloused hand ran along the smooth white sheet. "Do you want any help . . . breaking it in?"

Tori shook her head, then snapped open the top sheet. It hung in the air an unnaturally long moment, like the white wings of a seagull holding a stiff breeze. Then, finally, it fluttered downward, covering Bruce's hand.

"Well?" murmured Bruce with a quirk of his lips, the touch of the thin cool sheet tickling his skin.

"You never give up, do you?" said Tori, unable to stop herself from returning his small smile. What else could she expect in any room containing Bruce Gautreau *and* a bed?

"Ah, *chère*," said Bruce, sitting down on the mattress.

"Haven't you heard that old sayin'? You can tell a Cajun a mile away—"

"But you can't tell him a thing up close. *Yes,* I have heard it, but I never believed it—"

"Till now?"

"Till you." Folding her arms over her chest, Tori glanced around, desperate for a distraction. Salvation came in the form of a wooden crate. "So, Bruce, what do you think is in here?" Abandoning the bed, Tori walked over to the corner of the room, exaggerating her curiosity at this last item that they'd brought down from the sealed-off room.

"You want me to open it for you?" he asked, glancing at his watch. "I'll have to grab a crowbar from the truck."

Tori didn't want to trouble Bruce any further. The sun had set and she was beginning to get the feeling she had no reserves left in her when it came to resisting this amazing man.

"It's no trouble," said Bruce, reading her train of thought as he headed for the door of the bedroom. He couldn't stop himself from turning back a moment to tease her. "And you don't have to worry about resisting me, *chère.* Not *tonight,* anyhow. I've got an appointment in less than an hour."

"An appointment?" whispered Tori after he'd gone. *With whom? A woman?*

Of course it was with a woman, she thought, answering her own question. Darkness had descended on the Quarter and a silvery moon had already risen. No way it was a *business* appointment this late in the day. Not in a city called the Big Easy. Not when it involved a man like Bruce Gautreau.

He was going to an appointment for pleasure, Tori decided. And for Bruce, that had to mean a woman was involved. The idea of it disturbed her. And the realization of her own possessiveness toward him shocked her. She wanted to cast the feeling off—tried to tell herself it was not her business.

But she couldn't.

The fact was, she couldn't stop herself from actually

playing it all out in her mind, like a jazz guitarist experimenting with a new riff. . . .

Jazz. That was it, thought Tori, recalling Bruce's mentioning a place he frequented on Bourbon Street. Pacing the room in agitation, Tori imagined him with some sexy blues singer, shapely and red-lipped, her fingernails painted a bit too brightly, her dress a half-size too tight.

This diva of dives would probably croon to him most of the night while he sat on a barstool. Then, between sets, she'd blow him a kiss and crook her finger. He'd follow her up the back stairs to her cluttered apartment—probably borderline seedy, but like the run-down sections of the Quarter, seedy became sultry after sundown.

Tori knew this well about her hometown. The harsh light of day pronounced a cruel indictment on the grande dame that was New Orleans—revealing every wrinkle, unmasking every flaw. But in the magic and mist of a shadowy, gaslit New Orleans night, block after block of worn-down old Creole cottages were transformed into a living slice of romantic history. She could almost see hot-blooded Frenchmen challenging each other to duels in the garden behind St. Louis Cathedral; or lusty riverboat gamblers taking their winnings to the notorious parlors of Storyville for some fleshy companionship.

And Tori knew that through the shimmering veil of a New Orleans night, the tattered apartment of some well-endowed blues singer could easily become a sexy scene of seduction for Bruce Gautreau. She could see it all too clearly. The woman would pour him a drink and then he'd slowly lift her tight dress. Her hand would find the hard evidence of his arousal, and she'd caress him through the thin layer of his slacks.

That would probably drive his own hands to get busy. In no time he'd have them both half-naked; too impatient to find a bed, he'd back her against a wall. Then he'd lift her soft thigh with his calloused hand and push roughly forward, taking her with demanding strength.

The wail of a jazz horn would echo from downstairs as

an instrumental jam picked up, and the lovers would move
to the rhythm. The diva would shout out with decadent
pleasure as he moved deeper into her . . . all that potent
power, all that hungry need . . .

Tori's breath was coming out shallow and harsh. She
walked to the end of the room and stopped at the velvet
prie-dieu. She stared at the kneeler a long moment, trying
to get a hold of herself. This wasn't like her . . . this whole
train of thought . . .

It's the city, decided Tori. Night after night of hearing
shouts of revelers, jazz horns, the clopping hooves of mules
pulling carriages where lovers' hands roved over each
other—

Or maybe . . . it was simply Gautreau.

Tori stared at the kneeler and took a deep breath. The
pale mauve velvet of the kneeler looked somehow a ghost
of itself—less than purple, yet more than brown. Whatever
it had been, time had clearly robbed the velvet of some
brighter shade, a hue carried with more certainty when it
was new and unused.

Tori's gaze caught sight of Bruce's scarred metal toolbox
across the room. It was covered with colorful luggage stick-
ers—signposts charting the life of a wanderer, a man who
would not stay for long, certainly not for her.

Reaching into her pocket, Tori's fingers automatically
closed around a small white business card. Since lunch,
she'd been carrying it around like a talisman, hoping it
would bring something wonderful to her life.

Franklin Morgan
Financial Consulting

With a deep intake of breath, Tori made a decision. She
needed the physical in her life again. She needed a man. So
she'd better get close to the *right* one before she let herself
fall into bed with the wrong one.

Bounding footsteps sounded on the stairs, and Tori set
down the card on the nightstand, near the phone. Maybe

she'd call Franklin tonight. She needed to find out the time of their date tomorrow, anyway, and it would be a good way to begin making headway with him. Yes, she'd make the call after Bruce left—for his "appointment."

The moment Bruce stepped into the bedroom, he knew something was wrong. He gazed at Tori and felt a chill, like every door and window in her soul had been slammed shut.

"What's wrong?"

Tori wouldn't meet Bruce's gaze. "Nothing. Would you help me open this then?"

Bruce studied Tori but could read nothing. Reluctantly he moved toward the crate. After positioning the crowbar, he levered it carefully under the first slat, working it until the nails gave way. Quickly he moved to the next one and the next . . .

Tori found herself watching Bruce. No more than that, surveying him, as if she were trying out a new pair of eyes. Suddenly she saw things. Like his frayed white T-shirt sporting the boast "Breaux Bridge: Crawfish Capital of the World" in fading red letters—*Was that where he'd grown up?* Suddenly she noticed how it clung to his muscular form and how that form was slightly asymmetrical, the right side a tad more developed than the left.

For the first time tonight, she noticed the cropped golden hair at the back of his neck, and decided he must have just gotten it cut—*Just for the "appointment" tonight?* She caught sight of the white splatter of spackle on his olive work pants—*What job was he working on these days?* And she saw the small crow's-feet that formed at the edges of his brown eyes when he squinted in concentration, or smiled at her "Yankee-acquired" eccentricities.

Yes, Tori looked at Bruce with new eyes—the eyes that saw, for the first time, what it was she was giving up to another woman.

"That's it," said Bruce with the lifting of the last slat. After putting down the crowbar, he bent over the crate and began to dig in. "Whatever's in here, it's packed damned good," he noted as he pulled out gobs of cushioning material. Finally he reached a hard, thin round object and pulled it out, setting it on the floor and crouching next to it.

"How odd. It's wrapped . . . like a gift," murmured Tori, amazed.

"Still wrapped, after all this time? That's strange." Bruce looked up into Tori's face. "You want to—"

"Yes." Tori knelt down. Carefully her fingers loosened the fabric ribbon and tore at the fragile paper. When she'd finally pulled the wrapping away, both she and Bruce simply stared in stunned silence for a very long time.

"She looks . . . like you. . . ." whispered Bruce at last, feeling a sharp draft of cool air brush across his skin as a strange sudden darkness filled his spirit.

Tori blinked in complete and utter amazement. In perfect condition sat a round stained-glass window about three feet in diameter and expertly framed in metal and wood. The workmanship was clearly exquisite with a motif of lilies and white roses embedded in royal purple, and at the center of the circle was a woman's face. She had fiery auburn hair that flowed around her like a Greek goddess. And she looked very much like Victoria Avalon.

"Oh, no . . . Oh, God . . ."

Marina heard Robert's lament, but she did not know why. Instantly she hovered closer to the beautiful stained-glass window. The central image was a sharp reminder of her visage in life—her physical form.

"Oh, Robert . . . that was me, wasn't it? Look . . . I had long auburn hair . . . and green eyes . . . and smooth, ivory skin . . . Oh, yes Robert, seeing this beautiful stained glass helps me to recall now. . . ."

"You were beautiful, my love, and I wished this house, our home, to carry your image beyond our—"

"Oh, no . . . Oh, Robert! Our deaths! Our deaths!"

"Yes, my love."

"That is why I never saw the gift, it is all coming back in a rush! Oh, Robert, we were shot, we were killed, cruelly and terribly slaughtered—on our wedding night. . . ."

"Yes."

Though she was only energy, only spirit, Marina felt a terrible misery envelop her. Finally she understood a fact that had been mercifully muted from her spiritual memory. She and her love had been *murdered*—their end had come ruthlessly, not by nature's gentle hand, but by a cruel and deliberate act of human will.

Such a fact, charitably silenced, had, up to now, rendered Marina and Robert a tenuous existence, like a quiet purgatory, but now . . .

Now that the ghostly lovers were reminded of what had been brutally ripped from them, they were undone. The twisting dagger of the truth tortured them, casting them into a state of hellish agony.

"Oh, Robert—" cried Marina as wave after wave of sorrow shook her.

Robert felt the sorrow, too, and the pain, as he considered the details he could draw forth. He had been holding his naked, wanting bride in his arms, reveling in the feel of passion in his own loins, and then suddenly he heard the door and a loud report from a firearm. Searing pain was next, along with screams—were they Marina's?—and blood, so much red, flowing crimson . . . and then darkness.

Robert tried to recall the image of the murderer, but it was a blur. He could see a man—no, two—but he did not recognize either. Was it because of the blur of faulty memory? Or was it truly that he did not know them?

"Oh, Robert . . . look at your gift to me . . . look how beautiful it was. . . ."

Robert sensed Marina's terrible sorrow. She was now hovering near his wedding gift to her, and he felt his own sharp pain turning to slow, burning anger. How he wanted to hold Marina. Comfort her. But he could do nothing. He was mere energy. Pure spirit. The physical had been prematurely ripped from him, unfairly robbed from her.

"Marina . . . listen," whispered Robert. *"Do not despair. Look how these living beings are admiring the window. Look how the woman resembles you. . . ."*

"Yes," said Marina, still racked with pain. *"Do you suppose they will put up the window, just as we would have?"*

"Yes, my love, they will. And think of it. All who enter will now know what a beautiful mistress this house once had . . . even if for the briefest time. My wedding gift to you will finally take its rightful place here. In our home."

Marina felt herself able to take comfort in Robert's words.

"Oh, dearest," whispered Marina. *"How I wish I could hold you."*

"As I, my love. As I."

"I'll sell it."

"What?"

"It's got to be worth quite a bit—"

"Tori, no—"

"I might get enough to start exterior restorations—"

Bruce exhaled harshly. "Tori, you can't sell it."

"What? Why not?"

"Look at it. The central image. The face. It resembles—"

"That's *exactly* why I want to sell it. It's unnerving. I don't know anything about this window, maybe I'll ask Zoe—thought I doubt she'll have a clue. But it's spooky. I don't like it."

"But—"

A lightbulb in the room began frantically flickering.

"What the—?" Tori turned to see the lamp on the nightstand weirdly blinking on and off. "That's odd, the overhead lights are fine and yet—" Suddenly the bulb violently shattered, shards of glass sprinkling down onto the table and floor.

It startled Tori, and she turned to Bruce. "Was . . . was that the wiring?"

"No."

"How can you be so sure?" Tori was overwhelmed with apprehension. "Maybe it was a power surge."

"The wiring is fine," was all Bruce would say.

Tori studied his face a long moment, trying to understand

some secret he seemed to know. Giving up, she turned her attention back to the window.

"I need the funds to finish restoring Rosegate," she asserted in a quiet voice, "and I'm sure this will bring a good amount. I'll get it appraised." She began to cover the window with the wrapping paper again, not wanting to look at the central image any longer.

Bruce leaned forward, stilling her busy hands with his strong ones. "Don't sell it, Tori. Please."

Tori sat back on her heels, perplexed. "What's gotten into you? *You* were the one to suggest I sell that old diary for funds. Now you want me to keep this? You're crazy. *This* is the thing that will bring the real money—I mean, it's exquisite craftsmanship. . . . Don't you think I could get at least six or seven thousand?"

"You shouldn't sell it, Tori, it obviously belongs here . . . like the bedroom set—"

"The set is useful. Practical. It makes sense for me to keep it, but this window is just ornamental. And I need the money."

With frustration, Bruce watched as Tori began rewrapping the window. Then she stopped.

"Changed your mind?" asked Bruce hopefully. He tried to get a sense of what she was thinking, but ever since he'd left the room to retrieve the crowbar, he'd been unable to read Tori. He wasn't sure if it was his sudden blindness or her cold will to shut him out. Either way, he didn't like being left in the dark.

"The *party*," murmured Tori, almost to herself. "I can surely get some offers for the window at the party. I'll just display it on an easel and Zoe will help me chat it up with the guests—"

"What party?"

Tori hesitated a moment. *Damn.* She hadn't told Bruce about the party—she honestly wasn't sure if she should. But now that the cat was out of the bag . . .

"Uh . . . Zoe and I are throwing a Halfway-Through party. For the house—"

"Ah . . . I see. You weren't planning on inviting me?"

"No, I mean, yes. I mean, I had forgotten to tell you. We just came up with it today." *So I can meet some suitable bachelors from around town.*

Bruce didn't need to be a mind reader to get the drift, but he suddenly heard Tori's last thought loud and clear. *Suitable.* A chill filled his soul and he rose from the floor.

"I've got to get going," he said, walking across the room, careful to step clear of some of the sprinkling of lightbulb glass. "Mind if I borrow your phone, check my machine?"

Tori instantly recalled Bruce's "appointment" and her back stiffened. "Go right ahead," she said pointlessly—after all, he'd already begun dialing.

Bruce heard his own phone buzzing and felt his blood's temperature rise a few degrees with each ring. He prayed there'd be a message canceling his appointment. The last thing he wanted to do now was talk business. He was agitated and angry and he was feeling the need to tie one on—and maybe, finally, visit the Blue Lady, and let off a good dose of physical steam. It had been mounting in him for weeks, ever since he'd met Tori. . . .

The machine beeped and Bruce pressed a digit to program the message playback. Nothing. *Damn.* He'd have to go through with the meeting. *Bon Dieu, I'm hungry for a woman.*

He'd been stupid enough to subscribe to that old idea that hunger was the best sauce, and in time he thought he'd be savoring Tori Avalon like a fine gourmet dish. But Bruce could begin to see that he didn't have the pedigree to share a table with this princess.

To hell with her, thought Bruce angrily as he hung up the phone. He'd dine elsewhere.

Oui. After his appointment he planned on enjoying a veritable feast. *A la dépêche*—yeah, in a hurry, all right.

He was about to turn when his eyes caught a card on the nightstand. A few shards of broken glass had dropped onto the card, and he felt a prick to his finger as he reached for it.

"Franklin Morgan," he read aloud.

"Put that back," snapped Tori quickly.

Bruce eyed her. "How do you know this ass?"

"Excuse me? Is it *any* of your business?" She stepped up to Bruce and snatched the card from his hand. A small teardrop of blood had stained the edge.

"I get it. Is he *suitable* enough to consider fucking?"

"Get out."

"Gladly."

Chapter
Thirteen

A small dark bar sits on the corner of St. Philip and Bourbon. To the casual observer it appears to be little more than a run-down shack. Yet the place remains a point of interest to most of the French Quarter's walking tours. And when the hustling carriage drivers manage to rake in a fare, this is one of the many sites they trot their faithful mules past.

Bruce Gautreau approached the brick and mortar construction, bearing the unassuming sign LAFITTE'S BLACKSMITH SHOP. As his eyes scanned the walls, he couldn't say whether Jean Lafitte had actually conducted smuggling here, but he could verify the historic integrity of the building. The bar's stucco was now mostly worn down, exposing the vertical and diagonal wood posts that were used to reinforce poorly made local bricks and mortar—the telltale construction of an eighteenth-century New Orleans cottage.

Atmosphere, noted Bruce as he eyed the worn wooden shutters, warped and splintered, a few slats missing and never replaced. The cottage still *looked* like a place where Jean and Pierre Lafitte would meet to plan their slave smuggling—a lucrative business after 1807, when the importing of slaves was outlawed. And that's just how the brothers would have gone down in history, too, thought Bruce, as slave smugglers; privateers; thieving pirates. It was damned lucky for them the War of 1812 broke out.

". . . and ovah here, dat buildin' once house de blacksmith shop o' de famed pirate Jean Lafitte. Yeah, he de hero who help Andrew Jackson whip de hell out o' dem Brits in de Battle o' N'Awlins. . . ."

Bruce caught that much of a carriage driver's shout to the two gawking tourists riding behind him. The echo of his voice joined the clop of mule hooves as the carriage made its way down the dark street. Mist was beginning to roll in on this warm night, and the carriage disappeared into it, as if swallowed up by the past.

The past . . .

Bruce considered his own and thought of his mother's sweet face. *My Vianney, the unseen forces of the universe . . . they are what shape our destiny.* "Well, *Maman*," Bruce murmured softly, "I'll give you this, 'the forces' certainly had a hand in the destiny of Jean Lafitte."

Bruce didn't particularly care this moment what those same "forces" had in store for him—with one exception. Tonight, he hoped they'd put him in quick contact with a willing female body. *Any* body . . . as long as it got the burning desire for Tori Avalon out of his system. . . .

But first, he had to take care of a little business.

As he made his way into the half-empty bar, Bruce let out a sigh of frustration. He didn't want to be here. The really hopping section of the Quarter was farther down Bourbon, closer to Conti and St. Louis. That's where he'd be heading after this little meeting. *Yeah, me and the Blue Lady have a little unscheduled rendezvous, all right.*

He walked up to the bar and ordered a bourbon. He didn't notice any blondes sitting on barstools, let alone one wearing a yellow dress. Mostly men occupied the severely dark room, a few gathered around the glowing neon of the poker machine at the back. A few more were at tables, although it was so dark in the bar it was hard to recognize faces. He supposed that was the point.

Bruce sipped his bourbon and checked his watch. It wasn't that he needed another restoration job—after all, he was already working with a crew on an apartment building on Esplanade Avenue, and, from what Zoe told him, he'd probably win that bid on the Cemetery Library restoration in the Garden District. But the woman who'd called him early this afternoon had sounded emphatic about meeting. She said she wanted a bit of work done on a Creole cottage facade, and she was willing to pay handsomely.

"I should've gotten her number and rescheduled," Bruce mumbled impatiently to himself as he gulped another sip of bourbon and rechecked the door. Guess that was the price of not having a proper office and a full-time secretary. Hell, his phone machine had always been the best secretary, as far as he was concerned, and his apartment—or a nearby bar—had been the only office he'd ever wanted.

Right now his third-floor apartment down the block was reasonably priced and he didn't have much savings. Money seemed to slip through his fingers, he had to admit, so why spend a dime on an office? But then, he never liked to stay in one city for more than a few years, and he'd never actually needed one.

Maybe, if things picked up for him . . . if he won that Garden District bid . . . maybe then he'd think about something more permanent. Otherwise, it was *You have reached Gautreau Restoration Services please leave a message at the beep. . . .*

"Excuse me, are you Mr. Gautreau?"

Bruce turned to see a thirtysomething blonde in a yellow dress. "Yeah. You lookin' for a contractor?"

The blonde raised an eyebrow. "Among other things."

Well, well . . . maybe he didn't need to be headin' down the street after all. . . . "What do you drink?"

The blonde sidled up next to Bruce. "Whatever you're havin', honey."

He ordered another bourbon as she sauntered over to the silent corner jukebox. His gaze enjoyed the sight of her round derriere as she bent to slip a few coins in the slot. A few seconds later the place was pulsing with Boozoo Chavis's jazzy zydeco, "Son of a gun, we're gonna have big fun on the bayou. . . ." and Bruce was studying the woman walking toward him.

He liked the face well enough. She was attractive with a worldly-wise look to her blue-gray eyes. And he liked the bod. Definitely liked the bod, so full and shapely in that tight yellow dress. She had some money, too. That was evident in the expensive diamonds glittering in her ears and the small but expensive-looking leather bag she carried. Yeah, he liked it all well enough. But . . .

He couldn't read her.

Nope. This was one closed lady.

And Bruce did hate to be left in the dark.

"So what's the job, then, Mrs.—?" asked Bruce, handing the blonde her bourbon.

"Miss," said the woman, taking a sip. "Mmmm, that's good. Just call me Charlie—it's short for Charlene."

"Okay . . . Charlie. What's the job you'd like to discuss?"

"Oh, now, *must* we get right down to business, honey? I mean, when you were recommended to me, I never expected to see such a good-lookin' slice o' man—"

Bruce quirked an eyebrow. *Maybe the dark wouldn't be SO bad.* It was likely that he'd find *feeling* way more fun than *seeing* anyway—at least for a few steamy hours. . . .

"Okay, Charlie, we'll table the business for the moment," said Bruce with a quirk of his lips. "But what *exactly* did you have in mind?"

"Well . . . you could come on over to my place. It's not far. And you could give me a quick appraisal . . . or maybe a nice, *long, slow,* appraisal. It's up to you, baby. All depends on how you like it." The woman sipped the bourbon slowly, tilting back her head to let the burning heat trickle down her throat. "But I do know I'm feelin' the need for a good, frank . . . appraisal. How 'bout you?" she asked, her blue-gray eyes suddenly meeting his.

Trouble. The feeling shot through him like a bolt from the sky. *Oh, Maman,* thought Bruce, *why am I cursed with knowing too much?* It was a sick irony. Just a few moments ago he was lamenting not being able to read this woman. And now . . . now that he got a clear message, he'd have much rather been left in the dark.

Screw the warning, thought Bruce, anger still simmering inside him. "Yeah, sweet," he drawled low, "I'm feelin' the need for a good, frank *something* at that. You go on now and lead the way . . ."

"Fine," she said, her crimson lips smiling slyly. "There's jus' one thing, though, that I'd like you to do before we have some fun."

"What's that?"

"There's some friends o' mine here. They wanna talk to you fo' a few minutes. . . ."

Big trouble. Bruce sighed. "Sorry, darlin', changed my mind, gotta go. . . ." He lifted the glass and quickly knocked back the remainder of his bourbon. He was just about to turn away when he heard an all-too-familiar male voice close behind him.

"Havin' a nice evenin', Vianney?"

It was Gil Vonderant, a minor thug and a major threat to the survival of his business.

"I *was.*" Bruce turned his head enough to glare at the blonde. "How much are they payin' you?"

"Enough," said Charlie after a moment's pause, then she looked him up and down with a catlike smile of satisfaction. "Gotta tell ya though, honey, it'll be *my* pleasure."

"C'mon, Vianney," said Gil Vonderant. "Let's talk a little bit, and then you can have some fun—on us."

Bruce set down his glass on the bar, his form unmoving.

"Get him another," said Gil shortly to the bartender.

When the second bourbon appeared, Bruce stared at it a

moment. *What the hell.* He brought it to his lips and sipped, then turned to face the thick blunt features and yellowish hazel eyes of Gil Vonderant.

"Our table's ovah here," said Gil. "Charlie, wait fo' him at de bar."

Bruce silently followed Gil, not surprised to find René sitting behind a pitcher of beer. Gil was the older of the two Vonderant brothers, most likely in his late thirties, and he was definitely the better dresser. An expensive summer suit appeared expertly tailored to his stocky form.

The younger Vonderant, René, was a good ten years younger and much better looking, but his handsome face was marred by the severity of his buzz-cut dark hair and the flashy arrogance of the gold chains shining against his black T-shirt.

"Gautreau, you lookin' a little tense tonight," remarked René. "Drink up."

Bruce gritted his teeth. He could almost stomach dealing with Gil, but something about René made his hair stand on end.

"Quoi tu veut?" Bruce bit out shortly in Cajun French.

"Ahh," said René, turning to his brother. "De man here want to know what you want? I think he impatient to get himself into some o' dat soft flesh over dair, *tout d'suite.* Hey, Gautreau, what say we make it a two-man dance with de little blonde? Less o'course you worried 'bout de younger comp'tition—"

"Ren, *arrête tes bêtises!*" snapped Gil to his brother, a sharp look punctuating the remark.

Quit your foolishness, Bruce translated the rough Cajun French in his head, quirking an eyebrow at Gil's impatience. Whatever the man wanted this time out, it looked like he was serious.

"Vianney, have a chair," suggested Gil with extreme civility.

"Okay, Gil . . ." said Bruce, his curiosity getting the better of him. "It's your party."

"So it is." As Bruce sat down and sipped more of his

bourbon, Gil took a moment to pour himself a beer. "Vianney, as you know, we been wantin' you to take it easy on the work 'round here, like dat dair Garden District job. Dat's *our* company's job, y'see. We made dat clear enough to you in de past, *non?* Now we wantin' to know why it is you has not yet withdrawn your bid? Why is it you not gettin' our message?"

"Oh, now, Gilbert, I got de message, aw right. Loud and clear, yeah," drawled Bruce, letting the Cajun in him take over his tongue. "Me, I jus didn't agree with it, is all."

A loud sigh of disgust came from Ren, but Gil threw him another sharp look.

"Vianney," tried Gil, "you and me, we both from the same stock . . . and I t'ink we understan' each other, *non?*"

"Oui," admitted Bruce, bringing the bourbon to his lips for a long drink. He liked the burn in his throat: It distracted him from the slow burning of his temper.

"A man's territory . . . dat a sacred t'ing to him." Gil leaned forward. "Let me tell you 'bout a sign I saw on a fence north side of Lafayette Parish. Some Cajun put it up on his property. Know what it read?"

Bruce stared.

"'Trespassers will be shot. Survivors will be shot again.'"

Bruce let a half-smile touch his lips. "Well, now, let me tell *you* somethin'—a story 'bout my grandfather on my father's side, Jean-Baptiste Gautreau."

Gil quirked an eyebrow.

"Used to run with a rowdy group, ol' *Grand-père* Jean. He like attendin' different dances along Bayou Lafourche . . ."

"Mmmmm."

"Grand-père Jean, he weren't no troublemaker, *non,* but he knew all 'bout troublemakers, him. At one of de dance halls, dere was a man used to go every week. Dat man, he jam his knife into de wall, then hang his hat on dat knife. Markin' his territory, see?"

Gil sipped his beer and stared at Bruce, who casually

rolled up his T-shirt sleeve—enough to show off the small blue navy anchor tattooed there.

"One day *Grand-père* and his friends come to dat dance hall. Dey weren't troublin' nobody. But de man with de knife in de wall, he like to make trouble. He get all in *Grand-père's* face and tell him to leave. But it were a *public* dance and he say, nobody own dis here hall. We not botherin' you, *non*. But dis man with de knife, he come at *Grand-père*. So dey take de fight outside and dat be dat."

Gil put down his mug of beer. "*Quoi t'a dit?* Dat be what?"

"*Grand-père* slit the man's throat with dat man's own knife."

Gil eyed his opponent a long moment, as if considering what he was up against. "Vianney . . . I can see you a . . . reasonable man."

"You can?"

"And I can see you be wantin' to stay independant. But we t'inkin' you might be needin' some *help* here in N'Awlins. Help with say, some buildin' materials at lower rates, *oui*? And maybe some nice, expensive jobs thrown your way . . . real easy like . . . whenever you want 'em?"

Bruce just shook his head. "You got to understan' somethin' here. I *like* bein' independent."

"You can't use a discount on materials?"

Bruce eyed Gil a long moment. "Know what my *grand-père* used to say? *Qui vole un oeuf peut voler un boeuf.*"

"Whoever steals an egg might also steal an ox?" broke in René loudly. "What the hell are you talkin' 'bout, Gautreau?"

Gil stared down Bruce. "He's sayin' we *steal* our materials."

"Now, did I actually *say* that, Gil?"

A sly smile escaped Gil's lips, then he let out an amused chuckle. "Y'know, Vianney, I like you. And I want to see us do bizness."

Bruce took another sip of bourbon, then leaned toward

Gil. "I'm not about to be givin' kickbacks to anyone. *Compris?*"

"Why you wanna call it dat?" asked Gil. "The way it work is this: You get a job from us and den you charge a special consultin' fee. Alls you got to do is place what I call de 'sir-charge' on de bill, dat's jus our *consultin'* fee, y'see."

Bruce leaned back and thought for a long moment about how to handle this. He needed to buy some time, that was for certain. "Okay, I see. Jus' lemme t'ink it ovah."

"You had *enough* time to t'ink it ovah," barked René harshly.

Gil considered the situation. "One week, Vianney. You got one week. And den, as a show o' faith, we wanna see dat Garden District bid o' yours withdrawn. Don't you worry none 'bout work. If you withdraw your bid, we get you lined up with 'nother job right quick, *tout d'suite. Compris?*"

Bruce let the last little bit of bourbon swirl around the bottom of his glass. He watched the amber liquid turn in its tiny little whirlpool for a long moment, then he met Gil's eyes. "And . . . if I don't?"

"Well, now," said Gil, leaning back in his seat. "I 'spect you'd be makin' me t'ink on dat tresspassin' sign I tole you 'bout. And I 'spect my little brother here would likely begin persuading you *his* way, *oui,* Ren?"

A slow, malicious smile crawled across the length of René Vonderant's face, twisting his somewhat handsome features into an ugly mask.

"Go ahead, Gautreau," oozed René threateningly, "screw around with us. I'd jus' *love* to screw around with you—"

"Dat's enough, Ren," warned Gil.

"—or maybe I'll jus' start with dat fine-lookin' woman you been helpin' restore that run-down ol' mansion—"

That was as far as René got before Bruce launched himself from his chair and straight across the table.

"Jesus H.—!"

"What in hell?!"

Shouts came from the bar as the beer pitcher and glasses crashed to the floor and René found his whole body flying backward, the thick gold chains around his neck now tightened against his throat by Bruce Gautreau's enraged hands.

"You listen to me, you little piece of shithouse filth," bit out Bruce, his angry strength keeping René at bay. "What's between us, is between us. But if you ever, *ever,* go near that lady, I'll rip your throat out. *Have you got that?*"

René glared at Gautreau with sheer hatred as he was forced to *nod* yes because his voicebox had been paralyzed by his own chains. But as Bruce began to release his grip, he felt a sharp kick to his ribs from someone above him. The blow knocked him off René and onto the bar floor.

"Get up!" shouted the bar bouncer, or at least that's who Bruce figured him for. They guy was well over six four and looked about three hundred plus pounds. "Out o' here, now!"

Gilbert Vonderant was standing back from the scene, his arms crossed calmly over his chest as Bruce rose to his feet and began striding toward the door. But just before he made it out of the bar, René decided to get in a final lick or two. He jumped Bruce from behind and showered blow after blow to his face and body.

Bruising pain shot through Bruce, but he managed to return some blows in kind before the bouncer stepped in again, this time with Gil.

As Gil restrained his brother, the bouncer shoved Bruce forcefully out of the bar. He stumbled forward, and finally caught himself just before falling into the gutter. The world was suddenly spinning—either from the drinks or the beating, or both.

Bruce sat down on the curb to catch his breath. His eye and mouth were aching, and he reached up to touch them. When he brought his hand down, a trickle of blood was running along his fingers, hand, and arm. It hadn't just come from his face. Apparently, he'd rolled into the broken glass on the floor—he hadn't even felt it.

Wincing, he pried a small shard of glass from his palm.

Then he looked down and saw that both of his knees were bleeding through his pants.

Hell.

"T'ink about it, hey, Vianney?" came Gil's voice from the door of the bar. "I'm tellin' ya, plenty o' perks come with doin' bizness with us." With a quick nod to Charlie, Gil turned and disappeared back into the near-black darkness of Lafitte's.

The blonde stepped up to him and crouched down. "Well, come on then, honey. My place is real close, and I'll clean ya up good before we start havin' our fun."

Bruce looked up the shapely legs of the willing blonde and sighed. He was still hungry. Famished, in fact. And he still had an appetite for a woman tonight . . . but not *this* woman. In fact, not any woman . . . but one.

I'll be damned.

He could hardly believe it, but at that very moment, something inside Bruce Gautreau finally understood: somewhere along the line, a northern princess had actually gone and refined his palate.

"Thanks, darlin', but no, thanks. I got another appointment."

The hell if I'm not damned, at that.

Back inside Lafitte's Blacksmith Shop, at the very back of the dark bar, the flare of an eighteen-karat gold lighter illuminated the aristocratic features of a respected New Orleans businessman.

"What do you think, Gilbert?" said the man, pausing to take a drag off the expensive Cuban cigar—a smooth smoke that had been smuggled in just the previous morning. "Is the man persuaded?"

Gil laughed, sitting down at the table. "*Dat* man?" He laughed again, shaking his head. "I sincerely doubt it."

"You like him, don't you?"

Gil stopped laughing. "Business is business. We'll do what we got to do to protec' what's ours."

"Good," said the well-tailored man, letting a long puff of white smoke rise from his mouth. "Would you like one?"

Gil shook his head. "I'm not a cigar smoker, Franklin, don't you recall?"

"Forgot."

Gil couldn't say that he actually liked his cousin all that much. It didn't matter though; blood was thicker than water, and money was thicker than both.

Ever since the Vonderant brothers had teamed up with Franklin Morgan, they'd made the Big Easy cough up plenty of the Big Green. And they weren't about to start lettin' a man like Gautreau threaten the sovereignty of their little operation.

"Ask René Phillipe to come out here a moment," instructed Franklin, flicking an ash.

"Why?"

"Just *ask* him."

Gil knew his younger brother was hotheaded, but he didn't like Franklin nosing in on what Gil considered his end of the business. After all, Gil didn't tell Franklin how to get the fat-cat local leaders into his back pocket. Nor did Gil tell him which city sites to sabotage. *Non.* After Franklin pointed out the target sites, Gil took complete charge of inflicting "accidental" damage so's they'd be in need of expensive repairs. *That* was Gil and René's part of the business.

Jesus, thought Gil as he pushed through the door to the men's room and tapped his brother on the shoulder, Franklin didn't even know how to set a fire without the stupidest rookie in the N.O. Fire Department shoutin' arson.

"Your cousin wants a word with you."

"Franklin?" René was at the sink, washing the blood off his face.

"Yeah, jus' talk to him."

Gil walked to the bar and watched his younger brother sit down at Franklin's table. Gil knew René was a little afraid o' Franklin. Never did make much sense to Gil. That boy'd made sport of walking into the toughest joints in the Big

Easy and callin' out every man there, just to get some exercise. And yet, René absolutely dreaded dealing with his own cousin. Go figure.

"Sit down, René Phillipe," stated Franklin flatly.

René did.

"How are you, cousin?" asked Franklin in a tone that said he didn't really care all that much.

"Aw right. My face'll have a few new colors tomorrow, is all."

"Yes, well, anyway, I asked Gil to have you come ovah 'cause I'm a little concerned."

René swallowed. " 'Bout what?"

"I know you've got a temper, René Phillipe, but I'd like you to do somethin' for me. Are you listenin'?"

"Yeah."

"I want you to be *careful* with what you say and do. Especially now, understand me? I will not let anything jeopardize this casino deal I've gotten underway."

"But I was—"

"Shut up." A long silence ensued as Franklin took a drag on his cigar, studying his young cousin's reddening face. After a good minute Franklin spoke again. "There, y'see, René, you *can* control your temper if you need to."

René glared daggers at his cousin, but didn't utter a word.

"Now listen, René Phillipe, there are too many people sniffin' 'round our operation these days, and I want things handled *carefully*. You see, Gautreau has some friends in delicate places. He can make trouble for us, unless we're *careful*. And that threat you made tonight, it wasn't *careful*."

"But—"

"It wasn't"—with agitation, Franklin flicked a burning ash into a cheap plastic ashtray—"*careful*. Now, I'll tell you this once, and I don't want to tell you again: Let me and Gilbert do the thinking and the talking. You stick to doing exactly *what* we tell you, precisely *when* we tell you to do it. Have you got that?"

glass. God, she'd been blind tonight . . . at the very least to the glass, and at the very most to her own desires.

She wanted Bruce.

Or at least her body did. Maybe her heart was even starting to want him a little, too. It was her *mind* that had yet to be convinced. But that was a problem she didn't know how to solve—or even if she should.

Sighing, she moved to clean up the glass. Then, not knowing quite what to do with herself, she descended the stairs.

Now that her fiery anger had burned completely out, it felt like nothing was left inside her but the heavy weight of its leftover ashes. And, yet, strangely, this sad, weighty feeling felt somehow more than internal. She moved down from step to step, and it seemed as if the gloomy mood had somehow permeated the very air of the mansion.

Then, when her foot touched the last step on the staircase, she heard something odd—like voices whispering. She froze, listening intently. Then she turned sharply and scanned the steps and landing above.

She *had* heard the soft whispering of voices behind her. In fact, she could *still* hear them. . . . But she *saw* nothing.

"Who's there?" A frisson of apprehension rippled her soul as she suddenly cried out the question to thin air.

"What do you want?" she tried again. Then she stood another moment, listening for more whispers, or perhaps for an answer. But the next sound was the patter of kitten paws. Squealing mews followed as Bruce's two furry gifts came running, perhaps thinking they'd been summoned.

Shaking her head, Tori turned. She was being ridiculous. "I do *not* believe in ghosts," she muttered. "Do you hear that!" she finished, shouting angrily up the staircase.

Then she bent to pet the kittens, and they followed her down the hallway. When she noticed the old diary on a side table, she took the leather-bound book into her hands, hoping it would serve as an elixir for her distressed state. The kittens mewed and circled her legs, then they followed her back up the stairs and into the master bedroom.

Tori opened the windows and the French doors wide. The night was warm, and a rolling mist was now swirling about the thriving greenery that surrounded the house. Like her limbs and heart, the outside air felt thick and heavy. The sweet scent of blossoms floated in on the damp night, the moist air like a velvet kiss to her skin.

She kicked off her shoes and stretched out on the mattress. As the kittens played under her bed, she opened the diary, then stopped a moment. Closing her eyes, she remembered Bruce's calloused hands as they smoothed out the soft cool sheet now beneath her. She suddenly pictured the Cajun here, next to her, on this exquisite antique bed. She saw them making love in the thick, sultry air. . . .

But then the echo of a wandering street musician's jazzy sax flowed down the street and into her bedroom. Drifting in with it came a different image—Bruce making love to another woman.

Instantly Tori imagined it all again: that seedy apartment, the voluptuous, worldly-wise blues diva, the sweaty thrusts of two lust-crazed partners.

Quickly she opened her eyes.

Her mind needed an escape, and she knew exactly where it was going—to the world that existed one hundred years ago, a world that still existed for her. In the pages of this diary . . .

FEBRUARY 20, 1897

Terrible news to write today.

I have heard, finally, from Robert. The letter is dated January 20. He offers his profound apologies for not having written before and explains that back in October, not three days after he'd last written to me, he was badly injured.

He'd been so distraught at the sudden grave decline of his former professor's condition that he began crossing a busy thoroughfare blindly after leaving the hospital.

A delivery wagon struck him, and he was almost killed. The result of his injuries was a coma of over two months. In

*early January he awakened with fever and was hardly
strong enough to write. But now his fever is gone, and he is
recuperating. Sadly, his professor friend expired back in
October.*

*"At least," writes Robert, "I had the chance to visit with
him and perhaps offer some comfort before his passing."*

*Robert writes that he is growing stronger each day and
expects to come back to me soon. He finally confirms in
writing that we should set our wedding date for May.*

*It is a cruel irony. For my May wedding date is already
set—with another man.*

I am heartsick.

*I tried to show Robert's letter to my father, but he would
have none of it, saying I am now publicly promised to John
M—. Father's debts have been absolved, the wedding plans
made. He will not discuss breaking his promise of my hand,
and he will not allow me even to consider it.*

*I found it within me to argue, even to shout. It was the first
time that I had ever raised my voice to my father. A look of
shock crossed his face. Then one of hurt, and finally anger.*

*"If I must lock you in your room until your wedding day,
I will!" he threatened. "But I will not hear the name Robert
again in this house. It is done, Marina, and that is the end
of it!"*

*I do not cry. I have no more tears. But I have not given
up hope. With all my heart I love Robert, and will go on
loving him forever. . . .*

FEBRUARY 24, 1897

*Tonight I crept down to Libbe's room and knocked upon
the door. I have been distraught for four days now, and I
have finally thought of a solution to my terrible dilemma.*

*Libbe let me in and closed the door. As she sat in her
rocking chair, I paced the room, spilling the whole terrible
story out, along with my fears and my struggles.*

"I need your help, now, Libbe."

"My help? But chil', what can I do?"

"Years ago you spoke of strong Voodoo. I need that strong Voodoo now."

"What you want?"

"I want John M— to die."

Libbe shrank back in her rocking chair, her head shaking. "Chil'," she said in a whisper. "You speak of the dark way. Don't go down this road, I warn you. . . ."

"I want him to die," I said again, this time stronger.

"Shhh! Quiet yourself now, chil'."

"Oh, Libbe," I said, tears coming to my eyes as I sat by her feet. "I remember what you said years ago. You said that when you were a little girl, on the plantation, you saw Voodoo black magic used by one slave to kill another. Now that I know the truth about my blood, I feel as though I have a right to know the secrets of this black magic. I have a right to use its power."

Libbe was silent for a long time, rocking and thinking. "There be a way to do him harm . . . through Voodoo . . . but I beg you, chil', to think hard before goin' down dat road. Black magic is like de coal dust. You cannot throw it in de air without de wind bringin' some of it back on you. . . . It a dangerous bizness."

"But you'll show me, you'll teach me?"

Libbe nodded her head. "Oui."

According to Libbe, I must get a lock of John M—'s hair and attach it to a doll made of matchsticks. I will wait until twilight and perform a ritual by candlelight. When the ritual is through, I will light the match and watch the tiny doll burn.

Then it will be done.

John M— will die.

I am resolved. I will do what I must to protect my family . . . and be with my Robert again. . . .

Tori lifted her pen from the notebook, too disturbed to keep translating. Whether it was the turn of the diary's events, or that of her own life, she couldn't say. But she did feel too restless to go on just now . . . and too sad for this poor young woman named Marina.

After rising from the bed, she walked to the open French doors, fingering the fine lace curtains she'd found preserved in the cedar chest. Not for the first time, she wondered whether they were connected to the Creole girl—and whether she herself was somehow connected, too. . . .

The turn of carriage wheels on stone and the haunting moan of a Mississippi riverboat drifted in on the warm night air. The mist had grown a bit thicker, and, in the distance, she heard a strange sound.

Curious, Tori stepped out onto the gallery, her fingers curling around the rail as she leaned out to hear better.

Drums? Yes, she realized. There were drums beating in nearby Louis Armstrong Park. *Were they ritual Voodoo drums?* wondered Tori. *Like Marina's and Libbe's Voodoo?*

Strangely, the evening felt increasingly permeated by the echoes of the past. The room, the house, the sounds. Everything was starting to make Tori feel as if she had somehow fallen into those yellowed diary pages.

"The only thing missing now is the great love of my life," Tori murmured to herself in jest. She scoffed at the idea, but the smirk of disbelief slowly left her lips as she cast her eyes downward, toward the street corner.

A man was standing there.

His head was thick with golden hair that shined like a halo beneath the flickering flame of the gas lamp.

Robert?

No. That was crazy.

Still, Tori felt a dizzying sense of déjà vu. When the man's face turned up toward the house, Tori suddenly knew why.

My dreams, she realized. *He's the man from my dreams. . . .*

It was near midnight, and a rumbling of thunder sounded in the distance when Bruce Gautreau had passed under the corner streetlamp. An odd impulse had urged him to glance up at the magnificent Victorian; and when he had, a sudden, unexpected vision struck his gaze, instantly halting his fast-moving form.

Tori's long bare legs were standing on the second floor's gallery. The golden glow of Rosegate's interior lights silhouetted her womanly form, burnishing her auburn mane, and bathing her shapely legs in an aura of shimmering light.

A need settled inside of Bruce. The drizzle of rain began, dampening the thick hair on his head, but he barely noticed.

After that lovely little scene at Lafitte's, he'd restlessly walked the length of the Quarter, trying to tell himself— noble guy that he was—that he simply wanted to check on Tori's safety.

With René Vonderant's ugly threat, it was only natural. But Bruce knew very well there were other things concerning him that were only natural where that woman was concerned.

Looking at her now, from this perspective, Bruce felt overwhelmed. Bathed in the golden glow of the mansion's light, her mass of unbound hair lifting on the night's breeze, Tori Avalon looked almost ethereal, and Bruce felt an intangible longing within him. . . .

If he dared to climb to that balcony, would she truly be there for him? Or was Tori Avalon simply an apparition—a vision he could admire from afar yet never reach out and hold?

The questions disturbed him, and he decided it was probably better if he just turned and left. But then he saw something.

A flash of light.

Two floors *above* Tori, Rosegate's attic window was suddenly glowing with illumination. Tilting his head, Bruce stared at the window uneasily. Tori lived alone. Yet two floors above the gallery on which she now stood, a bright light was begging to differ. A disturbing chill settled into his limbs as he tried to get a fix on what it was.

Bruce doubted René would try something tonight. On the other hand, the Vonderants had been known to hire out their dirty work. Then, Bruce swore he saw a shadow move by the window. The menacing sight set his body in motion within seconds.

He sprinted through the night fog, not stopping until he'd reached the large front door of Rosegate, on which he frantically banged and banged and banged. . . .

After a few minutes it finally swung wide.

"Bruce?" Tori stood there in the entryway, her expression perplexed. "Is something wrong?"

"Are . . . you . . . all right?" asked Bruce, catching his breath.

"Yes. Of course. Why—" Tori stopped as he stepped forward and she caught sight of the drying blood on his face, arms, and white T-shirt. Then she looked down and gasped at the terrible sight of two wet, red patches staining his pants at his knees.

"Bruce, you're bleeding! My God, are *you* all right? Come in, come in!"

Bruce followed her inside, and she shut the heavy wooden door. "Tori—"

"Come up to the master bedroom's bath," said Tori in a flurry at the sight of his injuries. "It's the only one with towels and first aid. . . ."

Bruce followed her, about to speak again—to ask her if she was alone in the house—but as he reached the staircase, he stopped, his senses overcome, as if a thick soup of fog had enveloped him.

"Bruce?" Tori turned to see his brown eyes staring into the thin air. "Bruce?" she tried again.

"Something's wrong . . . in the house . . . I can *feel* it, Tori . . . a terrible heaviness . . ."

Tori swallowed uneasily. *No,* she thought, *not this psychic stuff again. Not now.* "Stop it, Bruce," she tried. "Just follow me, okay?"

"Wait," said Bruce, trying hard to shake free of the weighty paralysis. "Tori, listen to me, are you alone in the house?"

"What?" Tori scanned Bruce's face for a sign that he was

kidding her. But her attention was distracted by the angry red bruise by his right eye, the cut by the side of his mouth, and the line of blood that fell from his scalp and was now drying on his cheek. *Had this happened at his "appointment" tonight . . . ?*

"Tori? Answer me," demanded Bruce trying to read her thoughts, except that his own kept intruding. *Is there someone here or not?* It occurred to him that Tori might have company at that—like Franklin Morgan. He backed up a half-step at that prospect.

The sound of loud mewing suddenly startled them both. The two striped kittens were acting strangely on the second floor landing above them. Each of them turned quickly in a tight circle, then they looked up the steps and hissed at thin air.

"Tori?" asked Bruce again. "Is anyone—"

"No one is here," she answered quickly, now hearing the urgency in his tone. "I'm alone."

In the next moment Bruce was struggling against the terrible weight of the house's aura and moving forcefully up the staircase.

"Good," said Tori, seeing him moving toward the second floor. But when Bruce's heavy work boots continued climbing upward, toward the third floor, Tori shouted after him. "Hey! Bruce, I told you, we're using the bath on the *second* floor!"

"I know," he called down to her. "Wait down there."

"Damn . . . stubborn . . . crazy . . . man," she muttered as she climbed the steps after him. She had no intention of *waiting* anywhere!

Still, Tori disliked coming above the restored floors, especially after dark. As she passed the dulled wood, dingy wallpaper, and peeling paint, she was sadly reminded of the neglect the house had endured over the years. And she still couldn't shake the eerie sounds she often heard coming from the upper floors at night.

Bruce passed the darkened third floor but stopped about

halfway up the staircase, trying to collect his strength before pressing on to the attic.

The aura was growing thicker as he moved closer to what felt to him like the source. It left him a bit unsteady and out of breath—as if he were laboriously climbing a mountain into the clouds.

"Bruce!" called Tori, running to catch him on the staircase. She flipped a light switch and a bare bulb on the ceiling near the attic door went on, dispersing the shadows. "Please tell me what you're doing! Are you drunk? Or is this loss of blood?"

"I saw . . . a light . . . go on," he said, still breathless. "I was on the street corner . . . and I saw you on the gallery." A half-smile touched his bleeding mouth. "And quite a fetching . . . sight you were, too—"

"Bruce—"

"Above you, Tori, in the attic . . . a light went on . . . in the window two floors above you."

Tori's face paled. "A light in the attic? But it's just the wiring again, isn't it?"

"I saw the figure of a man," said Bruce, gaining his breath back. "It was in shadow, but it was clear enough."

Tori felt a sudden chill. Bruce's deep brown gaze was shining with an unnaturally strong brilliance. "Could it be an intruder?" she tried, wrapping her arms protectively around her.

Bruce turned his gaze away. "Go back downstairs."

"No."

Suddenly both Tori and Bruce were interrupted by a low, mournful sound. At the top of the stairs the attic door was slowly creaking open, all by itself. The deep whimper of its rusted hinges was sluggishly transposing into a rising pitch, and Tori was oddly reminded again of the sad cry of her violin strings, their tiny voices cut off by her fingers into higher and higher screeches, as if she were choking the very life out of them.

The door slowly opened to blackness—*but hadn't Bruce just said that he'd seen a light on?*

There was no sound. No sign of any human.

Then, strangely, as Tori stared up into the darkness, her mind was assailed by a vivid memory—one from her childhood. A violin was being smashed to bits against a wall. It hadn't been her violin—she had given that up for a tin ear after her furious father had fronted the money for two years of exclusive lessons.

No, this violin had been her *mother's* . . . but her mother didn't play the violin—

The bang of the attic door jolted Tori back to the present. As strangely as it swung open, the attic door just slammed shut again—all by itself.

"Bruce?" whispered Tori. Neither one of them had moved a muscle from their position halfway up the staircase.

Then, suddenly, she jumped.

A brisk jet stream of cold air whipped between them. Tori felt it pass along her bare legs like a gust of winter wind.

But how could a draft this strong come down a staircase *after* the door above it was slammed shut? Tori turned to Bruce to ask him when she stopped. The sight of Bruce's face startled her.

His skin was ashen and his eyes closed. Yet, somehow, he appeared to be alert, and intensely listening to something.

Tori felt the cold jet stream brush by her legs again, and Bruce stumbled back, grabbing frantically for the banister. Gautreau was a strong man, but now he appeared barely able to support himself. His eyes were still closed, and she was afraid he was going to faint.

"Bruce?" she whispered, nearly frantic. Seeing his lips begin to move, Tori went to him.

Suddenly the jet stream passed by them again, and this time a sharp pop sounded at the top of the steps followed by a drizzle of tinkling.

The lightbulb.

Tori felt her lungs still completely on the now-darkened staircase.

"Robert . . ."

Tori heard the whisper and nearly screamed out in alarm, thinking a stranger had joined them on the steps.

"Robert . . ."

It wasn't a stranger, Tori realized. It was Bruce, whispering the name beside her. But his voice sounded eerily strained. Something about it—the tone, the accent—was not his.

"Bruce? What did you say?" asked Tori. "Who is—"

"Robert," he whispered again, "they have returned. *Ça prendra combien de temps?*"

"How long will it take?" echoed Tori in English. This was too strange. Bruce had spoken in French, but not in his usual rough Cajun patois. This French was a very formal form, the tone of his voice still strained.

"How long will *what* take?" asked Tori. "And who is—" She suddenly stopped. "Robert?" she breathed in disbelief. Robert was the name of Marina's lover, the man who'd built Rosegate.

My God. For a moment Tori herself was feeling faint. But she regained hold of herself when she saw Bruce losing his grip on the banister, his body slumping into unconsciousness.

She moved quickly to help him, wrapping her arms around his torso and trying desperately to prevent his large body from sliding down the staircase.

"Bruce!" she called. "Bruce, wake up. Please—"

Within a minute Bruce's eyelids moved, and Tori was soon staring into his deep brown gaze. It appeared unfocused.

"My God," whispered Bruce.

"Are you all right? What happened?"

"Spirits, Tori," he said weakly, trying to shake his head clear. "I didn't want to tell you, because you don't believe . . . but there are spirits in this house. And they're highly disturbed."

Chapter
Fifteen

Spirits? Tori studied Bruce a long moment. Finally she let out a confused and exhausted sigh. "Come on," she whispered and began to help him down the stairs.

When they reached the second floor, she guided him into the master bedroom. "Sit on the bed," she commanded.

Bruce wasn't about to argue. He was none too steady and needed to gain his balance back—then again, once he did, lying on Tori Avalon's antique four-poster was just about where he'd wanted to be tonight anyway.

"Ohhhh, damn," he moaned as he set himself down. Thunder was rumbling across the fog-shrouded river, but this second it felt to Bruce as if it were emanating from inside his skull.

"What's the matter?" called Tori from the attached bathroom.

"Got any—"

"Aspirin? Sure." Tori walked out with a bottle and a glass of water.

"Now who's the mind reader?"

By the time Bruce downed the two pills and cool drink, Tori had returned with a damp cloth and a small bowl of water.

"Tori, you don't have to—"

"Shhhh . . ."

That was the last sound spoken for long minutes. Silently Bruce watched Tori work. She stepped between his legs and began to clean the blood from his face. When she dabbed at the skin near his bruised eye, he winced. Her simultaneous intake of breath gave the strange impression that she'd felt the pain, too.

Bruce didn't need to be a psychic to see that Tori was generally distressed at the sight of his wounds. But, because he *was* psychic, he could sense that her hands wanted to do much more than simply clean the blood. They wanted to take away his pain. They wanted to give him comfort. And tonight they wanted something even more. . . .

As a soft rain pattered outside and the lace curtains billowed languorously on a damp breeze, Tori's slender hands slowly continued to touch the moist white washcloth to the bright crimson trails.

She was so gentle, just lightly dabbing and pressing, lifting the evidence of injury with every touch. She squeezed the cloth into the bowl, staining the water red. Then she returned to the task again.

When she finished with his face and neck, she tugged gently at his shirtsleeve. "Take it off please," she said softly.

Bruce pulled the bloodstained T-shirt from his chest and dropped it to the floor. He closely watched her face. She blinked a moment when she found herself faced with a solid bare wall of masculine muscle, the powerful shoulders and arms, the strong chest, the tapering torso, and well-sculpted stomach.

With satisfaction Bruce took in her admiration of his body, and the deeply buried seeds of her arousal.

For her part, Tori tried her best to concentrate on the practical nursing. Her eyes followed the tracks of crimson. She tried to forget about his body and focus simply on the rivulets of blood that had found their way down it. Turning again to the small bowl of water, she wrung out the wet cloth, then began to gently touch Bruce's skin, tracing the pathways that the blood had taken.

Unfortunately for her, each pathway found its way across strong masculine ridges and through sculpted contours. Her fingers never actually made contact with his skin, and yet she couldn't help but feel the intimacy between them.

A part of Tori knew that she could have easily put the cloth into Bruce's hands. But deep inside of her lived an unsettled desire for physical contact. Cleansing the blood suddenly seemed little more than a mask for the play of her fingers across his magnificent chest; an excuse to begin making love to him. . . .

She fought against the powerful impulse, resisting the whispering voice that advised her to toss away this thin cloth barrier between them and allow her fingertips to feel for themselves the warm skin just beneath them.

Bruce could feel the need flare up in Tori as surely as he could feel a flame in a freshly kindled hearth. It lit her up inside, warming the cold corners, melting the icy walls. And he could feel his own body responding, his own need, the tight pressure building inside.

As she touched him, his gaze took in the beautiful outline of her face, the high cheekbones, the ivory skin, the luminous catlike green eyes and soft invitation of her full lips. He smelled a sweet scent of garden on her slender neck and bared shoulders. It wasn't a perfume, but softer than that, like a honeysuckle soap. It mingled with her own gentle scent—sweet and fresh, and inviting.

As she bent forward he could see that she was wearing a sheer bra beneath the tank top. How his fingers itched to reach out and draw her body close, to pull off her own shirt, then reach up to unfasten all the barriers between them.

What would her naked form look like? he wondered. He could only imagine the exquisite perfection that waited for him underneath the plain tank and worn, cutoff shorts.

But imagining wasn't such a good idea, especially with Tori's soft touches along his chest. The tight pressure in his lower body was now building to an uncomfortable level.

Tori put down the cloth. Her hands were suddenly a bit unsteady, but she managed to find the first-aid kid in the bathroom and return with some antibacterial ointment. She did not, however, manage to recover an ounce of composure by her moment's absence from this man sitting on her bed.

As she leaned in to apply the salve to a cut by his mouth, Bruce gently stilled her fussing hand. Tori's green eyes met Bruce's liquid brown gaze, and then he gave her a small smile. She could see what was there, what he wanted, needed. It was plain as day.

The ministering had created an intimate cocoon around them, making Tori feel as if she and this man were the only two people in the entire city, the entire world.

The prolonged wail of a riverboat horn drifted in from the nearby Mississippi. Its strangely hollow echo seemed to come from another time, and, for a moment, Tori felt as if some strange force had actually sent them back to a place where only the shadows of the past existed—and they were the only two beings who lived there.

Perhaps a few weeks ago, she could have pulled away from Bruce. But tonight, she couldn't. Instead, she let him pull her closer, until her mouth was a feather's width from his. She closed her eyes, feeling the warmth of his bare chest against her thin cotton top.

"How can I thank you," he whispered, the small movements of his lips barely brushing across her own.

"You'll think of a way," she whispered back.

Then she felt him smile against her mouth, felt his strong hand coaxing at the back of her head. His kiss was just as exquisite as she'd remembered from weeks ago. His lips were full and luxurious, warm and hungry, and yet tonight she felt something new.

Tenderness, she realized, and a kind of sweet patience.

But suddenly she herself didn't feel so patient. Her own hands curled around his neck, and she pressed more firmly against him, her own lips parting, her tongue wanting to taste him.

It took a moment for her to realize that Bruce wasn't responding. In fact, she felt him pulling away. Tori was a bit surprised and disappointed when the lovely kiss ended so quickly. She looked into Bruce's deep brown eyes then and saw that they looked a bit unsteady.

Perhaps it was his injuries . . . and perhaps, thought Tori, this was for the best.

"Bruce? Are you feeling—"

"I'm fine," he said quickly. Only he wasn't. *You're not in control, Gautreau.* The idea of it was unacceptable to him. For one thing, it had never happened to him before. Oh, he'd felt attraction for other lovers he'd had in his life, but he'd *always* been in control of his feelings, completely steady with his own emotional balance—as well as his readings of theirs.

Not like this.

Never like this . . .

Bruce placed his strong hands on Tori's shoulders and gently pushed. He saw the look of confusion cross her face, the question of why, after weeks of pursuit, he was now pushing her away.

"I need to try again," said Bruce hesitantly. "To check the attic, I mean. I made contact. Maybe I can again—"

Tori shook her head. "Not tonight. You're obviously in no shape—"

"I'm fine . . . or at least I will be. And I'm concerned that you're safe here—" *For more reasons than one.*

"I am," said Tori a little more forcefully than she'd intended. "I mean, let me make us some coffee. I want to talk to you—about the diary I've been reading," said Tori, turning to put away the first-aid kit. But she stopped suddenly, her eye catching sight of his bloodstained slacks.

"My God," she said, pointing at his pants. "Take those off."

Bruce's eyebrow quirked.

Tori caught the look and threw him a withering glare. "They're *stained*. And I need to clean your wounds," she asserted.

"Okay," said Bruce.

The hint of his smile pricked her as she watched him stand up and slowly unbuckle his belt. He obviously was amused by the flush on her face, but she'd show him. She was no prude. *He* was going to be the one embarrassed here.

Tori waited, her hands remaining propped on her hips, even as he stared her down. She returned his stare, unblinking as his fingers finally undid the top button of his slacks. Then his thumb touched the tongue of his metal zipper, and Tori found herself shifting her weight uneasily from one hip to the other—but she still refused to budge.

Bruce had mixed feelings about dropping his pants in front of Tori. He liked watching the pretty blush creep up her ivory cheeks. He liked watching the mask of aloof ennui slip enough to reveal an embarrassed schoolgirl. What he didn't like, however, was the idea that she was about to see in his body the hard evidence of her ministering touches.

With tonight's string of strange events, he no longer felt it was such a good idea that they make love. . . . *Especially when your feelings for her are obviously out of your control. . . .* accused a voice inside of him.

Bruce wasn't going to argue—with the voice, or with Tori. Instead, his steady brown gaze became unrelenting as it bore into Tori's increasingly uncomfortable green eyes. Slowly his fingers began to pull down his zipper, and Bruce was intensely relieved when she became the first one to break.

Spinning abruptly, Tori headed straight for the bathroom.

Something about the sound of those metal teeth slowly separating made her turn chicken. Or maybe it was the way Bruce was staring at her—as if they were about to cross some line in the sand, some point of no return, and he couldn't be held responsible for what would happen next.

She muttered angry curses at Gautreau as she jerked open the small closet door and grabbed for the top of a large white stack of bath towels. But the truth was, she was angry at her own weakness—as well as her own uncertainty.

"I should just get him out of here. . . ." she grumbled just under her breath. "If anything happens between us tonight, I just know I'm going to regret it. . . ."

Finally she walked back into the master bedroom. "Here," she snapped, carefully averting her eyes as her arm extended the thick white bath towel out to the pantless Bruce.

"Sure you don't want to peek, *chère*?"

"No."

"It's quite the sight."

"Take the towel!"

The sound of Bruce's low Cajun chuckle ruffled Tori's dignity. Clearly, he was enjoying every second of her discomfort. "Just wrap it around yourself, please."

Bruce did.

"And sit back down."

Tori turned her attention to his torn-up kneecaps. She crouched low and examined the ripped flesh. "My God, Bruce, what did you do tonight, genuflect in glass?"

"Something like that—"

"There are shards embedded—"

"Please don't give me a description, *chère*. Just pull them. Or would you rather have me—"

"I'll do it." After routing around in the first-aid kit, Tori found a pair of tweezers. She knelt on the floor in front of him and placed one hand behind his knee.

"This may hurt."

"Just do it. . . ."

Taking a deep breath, Tori began methodically removing the jagged splinters. Some of them were imbedded pretty far, and she found herself wincing as she pulled them out. It wasn't that she felt any *physical* discomfort, but it pained her intensely to know that he was suffering.

She moved to the other knee and continued to work, listening to his uneven breathing and his sharp intakes of breath. She felt the tension in his leg muscles and saw he was holding his body extremely rigid.

A few times, when she pulled out the thin daggers, trickles of fresh blood would be released, running down his muscular leg like tears of crimson. She had little awareness that with every red tear that fell down Bruce's leg, a translucent drop of her own would fall.

When she finally finished, she leaned back on her heels, ready to turn to the cleaning and dressing of the wounds. But before she moved, she felt a slight pressure underneath her chin. Bruce's hand tenderly tilted her face upward. His brown eyes curiously studied the damp tracks along her cheeks—the evidence of what she'd been feeling. Tenderly Bruce brushed at the salty trails with the pad of his thumb.

Tori gently turned away. With the edge of her tank top, she wiped at her eyes. "I . . . I don't know what's wrong with me tonight," she whispered, suddenly embarrassed by her emotions.

"Maybe it's the house," he whispered.

Tori rose to fetch a clean soapy cloth. She knelt again, ready to wash his wounds. "What did you say? About the house?"

"There's an overwhelming sense of sadness and longing here tonight. I felt the presence—"

The shooting pain in his knee made Bruce stop a moment. He knew Tori's hand was trying to be as delicate as possible as it cleaned his wounds, but the sting was still sharp.

"Two of them actually," continued Bruce through gritted teeth. "There are two spirits—and they're highly disturbed."

"And you think one of them is Robert?" asked Tori, aware of the pain that she was causing him and glad when she'd finished cleaning and medicating the wounds. She grabbed a roll of gauze and began to wind it around each knee.

"Robert?"

"That's the name you whispered. On the stairs. Before you blacked out."

Bruce nodded. "Then it must be the name of one of them."

"Robert is also the name in Marina's diary."

"Marina?"

"Don't you remember? Marina is the girl from a century ago, the one who kept the diary." Tori finished fastening the second dressing and rose from the floor, then she grabbed the diary off the bed and sat down beside Bruce.

"Look," she said, flipping through the yellowed pages. "The evidence is here. Marina loved Robert, and it's clear earlier in the diary that Robert built Rosegate."

"Tori, the spirits are extremely agitated. Was there anything in the diary that indicated trouble. Or danger?"

"Well, yes. Marina wanted to marry Robert, but her father promised her hand to a man she calls John M—. It seems the man discovered she was of mixed blood—"

"No big surprise there."

"Why? What do you mean?"

"Well, as good old Huey Long used to say, you might well feed all the pure white people of N'Awlins with one cup of beans and rice and still have some left over."

"That may be so, but Long was a politician in the 1920s. This diary was written before the turn of the century, *and* this young woman's father was trying to pass her as a white debutante among the upper French Creole circles."

"Yeah, I see. That would mean trouble."

"Yes. Besides which, this John M— doesn't sound like a very nice sort. He basically blackmailed her father into making the engagement. Marina was dead set against marrying this man. So she asked the family cook for a spell to see this John M— dead."

Bruce studied Tori. "Sounds like violence was in the making, all right. What happened?"

"I don't know yet. . . . It's clear in the diary that she loves Robert. But she's legally promised to John M—."

"So we know that Robert built the house," stated Bruce, ticking the facts off on his fingers, "and that Marina's diary was in the house—"

"Yes," put in Tori. "And that Marina and Robert loved each other."

"And we know that Robert is one of the spirits haunting Rosegate," said Bruce.

Tori said nothing. She took back the diary, shut it, and placed it on the nightstand. Then she rose and began to gather up the first-aid materials.

"What did I say?" asked Bruce.

"Nothing," said Tori, bringing the cloth and bowl into the bathroom.

"It was my mention of the haunting. You don't really want to believe that there are ghosts here, do you?"

"I didn't say that."

"No. You didn't have to."

Tori came back out to face Bruce. She held out a thick terry bathrobe for him. "Here, this will be more comfortable than the towel, I think."

"It's a man's size," noted Bruce, standing up and taking it from her.

"It was Edward's," said Tori. "We had identical robes, and I ended up packing his along with mine."

"I see. I suppose he's the kind of ghost you'd prefer to have haunting you?"

"Oh, please . . ."

"Tori, when I was traveling in the navy, I met a priest from Lima, Peru," said Bruce as he slipped the robe around his shoulders, then tied it at the waist, letting the towel that had circled his hips now drop to the floor. "It wasn't the first time I had talked to someone who'd seen a ghost—"

"The priest saw a ghost?"

"Yes, it had been haunting the crypt underneath his church."

"Uh-huh."

"The reason his story struck me was that he said the exact same thing about ghosts that my mother used to say."

"And what's that?"

"Ghosts have so much power that they move faster than thought."

Tori studied Bruce, wondering exactly what he was getting at. "Are you saying that's why human beings can't see them?"

"I'm saying that's why human beings can't see a lot of things that haunt them."

Tori sighed with skepticism as she stared at Bruce. Then she turned and headed for the bedroom door. "Would you like that coffee now?"

"*Oui,* sweet," said Bruce with a smile. "Lead the way."

Within fifteen minutes Tori and Bruce had settled into the mansion's kitchen, and Tori was pouring a pot of freshly made decaffeinated coffee. The pattering rain was still at it outside, the fog even thicker on the slick streets.

"So, if you don't believe in spirits," asked Bruce as Tori finished filling his cup, "then what do you think happened on the staircase up there?"

Tori poured her own coffee carefully. She also considered her answer carefully. She didn't want to offend the man. "Perhaps, up there, you were in pain. Confused."

"Loss of blood, huh?"

"Bruce, I *had* been reading the diary. Maybe you read the name Robert in my mind. Perhaps all this 'haunting' stuff is just a lot of my own pent-up anxiety or something." Tori placed the pot back on the burner and sat down at the table. "How did you get so bloodied tonight anyway?"

Now it was Bruce's turn to consider his words carefully. "I had a disagreement."

"Over what? Or should I say *whom*?"

Bruce studied her, then a smile lit his face. "Why, *chère,* you're jealous."

"I am not!"

"I can read it in you like the cover of the *Times-Picayune.* You think this fight was over some woman, don't you?"

"I—"

"Well, well . . . what do you know."

"You mean it wasn't?"

"It was over a woman all right—*you.*"

"What do you mean, *me?*"

What the hell. In for a penny . . . "I'm bein' squeezed by some men that you might call somewhat less than *genteel.* They've been after me for months to turn over a bad leaf, so to speak, and join a crooked contracting organization they've set up."

Tori considered his words as she studied him. She recalled the shady characters that had approached him at Café Du Monde all those weeks ago. "And . . . you're thinking of joining them?"

"*Bon Dieu,* woman, what in hell has given you such a bad impression of me?"

"I . . . I don't know," she said quietly after a moment's pause.

"Well, get this through your mistrusting ears, sweet, I'm no damn thug, and I'd rather be driven out of the city than go join a band of thieving pirates."

Driven out of the city. The words echoed in Tori's head as she recalled the colorful decals on his toolbox, each one a likely sign of some woman's heart broken wide open.

"So," said Tori, "what does this have to do with *me?*"

"A little punk named René Vonderant mentioned you in passing," said Bruce, calmly sipping his coffee. "And so I mentioned, in passing, that if he came near you, I'd rip his throat out."

Tori's green eyes widened.

"That's about when things got a *tad* uncivilized."

Tori took in a deep breath and expelled it. "Okay . . . so what are you going to do?"

"I don't know, but I've got one week to figure it out."

"Then what?"

"They'll play rough. Most likely with me and my jobs. I'm liable to see some vandalism and thefts on my current sites. It could get rougher."

"Bruce, you have to go to the police."

He just shook his head. "Not the Bayou way, *chère*. This is territorial. We swamp boys'll work things out."

"And if you don't?"

Bruce put down his coffee cup. "Then I'm off to see Seattle, or Savannah, or back to San Francisco."

Tori nodded unhappily. They sat like stones for long moments until finally Tori spoke up in a soft voice. "And . . . what do you think I should do about the other thing then?"

"Other thing?"

"The ghosts."

Bruces's brown eyes were shining with surprise when he gazed into her face. "Are you tellin' me that you're finally becoming a believer?"

Tori shrugged. "I'm willing to consider the possibility. And I suppose I should try to figure out how to deal with them, *if* they do exist."

Bruce nodded, figuring that was the best admission he'd get out of her tonight. "Keep translating the diary," he advised. "And next week I'll bring Serafine by. She's an old friend—and someone who'll be better able than me to read the spirits."

"Read?"

Bruce nodded. "This city's full of haunted houses, you know."

"So I've heard. Zoe said people call New Orleans the most haunted city in America. God knows why."

"Water," said Bruce.

"Water? That's right, Zoe told me to ask you about it . . . some theory?"

Bruce nodded. "Ever wondered why the proverbial dark and stormy night is the thing that turns up spooks?"

"I suppose . . ."

"It's the rain," explained Bruce. "You see, some para-psychologists believe water can trap emotions and events, like magnetic tape. It can also provide a kind of force field, trapping energy."

"And New Orleans is below sea level . . ."

"Yep. It's got Lake Pontchartrain on one end, the Mississippi on the other. And a body of land surrounded by water is more likely to trap spirits. England's pretty much a natural in that department, too. Spook Central over there all right."

"So, you know someone? This Serafine, can she talk to the ghosts?" Tori was still finding this all too much to believe, but she was willing, at least considering her present circumstances, to keep an open mind. If only because she had no other choice.

"Serafine is psychic, but on a different level than I. She's able to communicate with the dead, or at least read what's going on with them. And, Tori, not all spirits are benign. You should at least be aware of what you're dealing with."

Tori never really considered the possibility of spirits doing her any harm. Suddenly she wasn't so keen on Bruce Gautreau leaving. "What about tonight? I mean if they're especially *disturbed* tonight, as you say . . ."

Bruce's gaze met her eyes. He saw the worry there. "I'll stay if you'd like." He shrugged. "Beats walkin' down Bourbon in just a bathrobe—not that some haven't done it already."

Tori smiled. "I'll throw your clothes in the washer."

"Thanks."

Bruce eyed her cautiously as they finished their coffee. "Where shall I sleep?" he asked.

Tori didn't answer right away. She made a consuming business of bringing their cups to the sink and flipping off the warming burner under the pot.

"Tori?"

Finally she turned to face him, her green eyes shining with frank openness, and something else. "Wherever you want."

Bruce could feel the need within her. The desire. All he had to do was take a tiny step forward. *You're out of control, Gautreau.*

Suddenly Bruce's brown eyes dropped from her face. When they lifted again, he saw her staring vacantly at the robe. Bruce fingered the lapel of the luxuriously thick terry cloth.

"Nice robe," he said, his tone distant.

"Yes. I bought it for him. A gift. You can keep it, if you like. . . ."

A cynical smile touched Bruce's lips as he read her mixed emotions tied up with the memories of this robe— and of Edward. "You like doing that, don't you?"

"What?"

"Draping me with something that belongs to another man."

"I don't know what you're talking about—"

"Yes, you do."

Confused, Tori stared at Bruce, searching for a connection. But there was only a coldly bitter mistrust in his gaze. It shocked her, hurt her. She'd never seen mistrust in Bruce's eyes before—at least, not when it came to her.

"This is stupid." Tori tried to brush past Bruce, not wanting to argue with him, but he caught her arm.

"I'm not Edward."

"I *know* that!"

"Do you? I think maybe a part of you wants to cover me with his garb so you'll feel justified in assigning me his character."

"Bruce, I grant you I'd thought that of you before, but—"

"You listen to me, Victoria Avalon, I don't care whether you're looking for a way to screw your old lover again, or just screw the guy over, but I'm not about to conjure him for you to vent your lust or vengeance or whatever else you've got left over for him—"

"You're wrong," said Tori, furiously jerking her arm from his grip. *Why are you pushing me away?* thought Tori. *Why, after all these weeks of pursuit? Why, on the night when I'm finally ready!* "I don't want that man in my life again—to screw or screw over, or anything else! And if you were a real mind reader, Gautreau, then you'd know that!"

Bruce blinked in shock as Tori's words penetrated. She was telling the truth, he realized. The *truth* . . .

So, what in hell had come over him?

"I'll put you in one of the guest rooms tonight," snapped Tori as she headed for the stairs. "And you can burn that damn robe for all I care!"

Chapter Sixteen

An hour later, in Rosegate's master bedroom, Tori Avalon had tried three times to lie still underneath her bedcovers. But three times she had found a reason to get up.

First she wanted the French doors closed.

Then she wanted them open.

Then she'd heard a strange bumping noise under the bed.

She'd dropped her head over the side, her long auburn curls falling down to brush the floor, only to find the two striped kittens playing.

With an exasperated sigh, Tori sat upright. Why was she fighting it? She simply couldn't sleep. Not with a potently masculine body denting a mattress twenty feet away.

She wanted the Cajun.

Her whole body seemed to tingle with it. She closed her eyes and still felt the power of his rigid muscles beneath that damp cloth; still saw the burning sexual need in his dark eyes.

He'd pushed her away tonight. First physically, and then mentally. Even using the specter of her past lover to keep himself clear of her bed . . . but why?

Had he lost interest? Perhaps, finally, he had. And her resistance to him over the weeks had at last won out. *And that's what you wanted all along, isn't it?*

Tori flopped back onto her pillow and threw an arm over her eyes. It wasn't what she'd wanted *tonight!*

God. She was such a fraud. She'd wanted that man from the first moment she saw him.

Tori sighed and truly wondered if she and a man like Vianney Bruce Gautreau could actually make things work between them. It was a terribly self-defeating train of thought. Hadn't the man just mentioned his possible plan to leave New Orleans? And hadn't he stated to her, weeks ago, that he never stayed in long-term relationships?

Why are you analyzing the man, Tori! Just forget him. Concentrate on meeting other men. Think about Franklin.

But she couldn't.

And she knew she wouldn't. Not until Bruce Gautreau had packed his bags and moved out of the city. And her life.

"Don't worry," she whispered to herself, forcing her eyes to close. "That day will come. You can bet Rosegate on it."

Twenty feet down the hall Bruce's body was tossing and turning as his mind was trying to forget the warm, female form lying on the antique four-poster in Rosegate's master bedroom.

Closing his eyes, Bruce could still see the image of Tori as she made up this spare bed for him in one of the second floor's guest rooms. She'd changed from her tank top and cutoffs into a sheer white nightgown and matching robe, and he'd bet a million bucks that she normally slept in an oversize T-shirt.

"That woman probably dug out her best Victoria's Secret purchase just to torment me," grumbled Bruce.

The ghosts, his mind advised, *think of the ghosts.*

Trying to distract himself from the memory of Tori's tender ministrations, Bruce replayed the contact he'd made with the spirit earlier tonight.

At first he'd felt a tingling, then a chilly draft, and finally an array of dark emotions. There was so much pain, longing, and despair, he'd been overwhelmed, dragged down into a blackout.

He tried to better define the contact, but he just couldn't make any cognitive sense of it. He couldn't even identify who the spirit was that was speaking through him.

Bruce cursed himself for not having enough training to control this aspect of his ability. It was his own fault. For too long, he'd denied his ability completely; ignored it and his roots, running away to join the navy rather than face his own human condition—and the pain that it had caused him.

After reading of the adultery in his father, Bruce had spent years trying to shut out his ability. And for a long time he'd shut down his emotions with it. But the sad truth was, no matter whom he loved, he would be doomed to always see too much.

That's why, years ago, he'd been forced to make up three simple rules to live by:

1)　*Thou shalt not lose control.*
2)　*Thou shalt not fall in love.*
3)　*Thou shalt not stick around long enough to risk either of the above. . . .*

The truth could be painful. And if you loved someone, a hidden truth could devastate. Bruce never again wanted to feel the pain of betrayal. Long-term love was for the folks who could maintain masks—that was their protection; and those three easy-to-follow rules were his.

But you can pay a price for protection. . . .

Bruce tossed again underneath the thin cotton sheet. He felt a headache coming on and a chill in the room. He rubbed his tired eyes with thumb and forefinger as he pulled a blanket over his body. How he wished his mother were still alive. He had so many questions for her, so many questions . . .

Bruce felt a sadness overwhelm him; a loss and emptiness that paralleled the spiritual gloom that had descended over Rosegate. His eyelids were heavy and drifting shut. And it was then that he heard it. *Vianney . . .*

A voice was calling him. But was it in his mind? Or in the room? *Vianney . . . Vianney . . .*

Bruce sat up slightly in bed. . . .

Vianney, are you fretting again? The words were soft at first, but gradually he could almost hear her voice. Yes, it was his *mother's* voice. . . .

Love is like a sun within us, Vianney, existing above the daily vagaries of changing winds. Darkness comes, pain and disappointment come . . . and then we think like primitives, fearing in the night that the dawn has deserted us. . . .

I know you don't understand now, Vianney, but you will. . . .

Bruce blinked and settled back under the covers. He didn't really know whether he'd just heard an echo from inside his own memories or his own mother's spirit. He supposed it didn't matter. Maybe, in the end, the two were one and the same. . . .

"I'm in the dark now, *Maman*," he whispered into the shadows as his eyelids drifted closed. "But I'll try to find my way. . . ."

Do not fret, Vianney . . . it is not so complicated . . . because when love comes to you, it will bring the light.

"I cannot believe this!" exclaimed Robert.

"Neither can I!" agreed Marina.

Hovering near the ceiling in the second-floor hallway of Rosegate, the two apparitions were incensed by the present situation. They had been flowing back and forth between the master bedroom and the guest room for the last hour.

"They are tossing and turning," noted Robert. *"They both desperately* want *to make love—"*

"And yet there they lie, in separate *bedrooms! How utterly ridiculous!"*

Robert sighed. *"Not so ridiculous, my love, if you can recall the strictures of human society—"*

"The fear, *you mean. The living are consumed by it!"*

"I know," said Robert. *"But then I am not living, and yet I fear that I will never again be able to hold you. . . ."*

"There must be a way." Marina flowed toward the master bedroom, and Robert followed her. They looked down on the sleeping form of Tori Avalon. She rolled onto her side and then onto her back, the sheets twisting around her body.

"She wants him," said Marina. *"I can feel the need rising as strongly as the heat of her life."*

"Yes, and I felt the same from the man, and that means they are now both open to each other. . . ."

"What can we do? We tried to influence them earlier, and we failed."

"But we almost *succeeded,"* pointed out Robert.

"They were so resistant. But, of course, now that they are both asleep, their resistance is certainly lowered. . . ."

"We should try again, Marina."

"Yes, Robert."

"But what?"

"Loud noises?" Marina was always ready to flex her ghostly power to haunt. *"Perhaps that will frighten them together?"*

"No," said Robert.

"Temperature change? They may huddle close in the chill?"

"No."

"Then what, my dearest?"

"I think, perhaps, something more subtle. After all, this is the first time they've been asleep together under this roof."

"True." Marina drifted closer to Tori's sleeping form, her spiritual energy just brushing the living woman's soft warm cheek. *"We've never been in their bodies when they were asleep."*

"Shall we try, then?" asked Robert.

"Do you think it will work?"

"Well, reason is on our side, Marina. After all, when we've entered their waking forms, we exist at the back of their minds, do we not?"

"Yes."

"And when a living person sleeps, the back of his mind rules the front, does it not?"

"It's true."

"Then it is agreed," said Robert before flowing down the hall toward the tossing form of Bruce Gautreau. *"We shall try another experiment."*

Inside Tori's mind she could see the master bedroom lit up. Dozens of candles created an unworldly aura of flickering shadow and shimmering light.

Through the wide-open French doors, the sound of drums drifted in on the sultry night air. The rhythm seemed to throb through her veins in a compelling pattern, a driving pulse that lulled and entranced.

She was naked and her hands shamelessly touched her bare flesh, cupping her firm breasts, then snaking lower to feel the velvet of her skin and the silky triangle of curls at the apex of her thighs. The primal cadence tapped a deep well of sexual longing within her—a need beyond all others and a desire like no other she'd ever known. . . .

Moving from the elegant four-poster bed, her bare toes touched the smooth cool wood of the bedroom floor, then slid across the threshold that lead to the second-floor gallery.

It was night, the fog thick outside her window. She stepped outside, strangely uncaring that she was completely naked. She peered down at the street corner—yes, she'd done this before. Standing there, under the gas lamp, was the handsome lover she wanted in her bed. . . .

That's when she heard it. Suddenly. Violently. A thunderous burst behind her. A fateful explosion that brutally tore at her very soul!

She wheeled instantly and felt the terror assault her. Her

vision failed her and all went black just as a wrenchingly tragic scream filled her ears.

And then it was she who was screaming—

"Tori?"

And screaming—

"Tori!

And screaming—

"Tori, wake up!

Her green eyes fluttered open to find Bruce sitting on the mattress. He was leaning over her, his strong hands gently shaking her shoulders.

"Bruce?" Her breathing was fast and shallow, her skin damp with perspiration, her heartbeat quickened by fright.

"Tori, are you all right?"

The room was in shadow, but it wasn't dark. The moon was up tonight, cutting through the rainclouds and into the bedroom. Tori could see Bruce's handsome face so close to her own. The rugged contours, the strong, square chin. She could see the look in his shining brown eyes—the open caring, and beneath it, the need. . . .

The need for her, she realized.

Her breathing slowed, her heartbeat calming as she studied his face. Yes, this is how she wanted to see him. With this caring expression. Never again did she want to see the bitter, mistrusting look in his eyes that she'd seen downstairs in the kitchen.

Her hand went to his face, touching the shape of it, brushing back the thick rich gold of his hair. She watched his brown eyes close, as if her touch really did mean something to him. . . .

"Make love to me," she whispered.

She watched as his head tilted back a fraction and an almost painful smile of relief appeared on his lips.

"*Oui,*" he whispered, his voice raw, his eyes still closed.

And then his eyes were opening, and he was gazing into her own. Suddenly she realized she could still hear the echo of the drums from Congo Square—no, it was Louis Arm-

strong Park now. That was odd . . . why had she called it by
the old name?

And, now that she was awake, why was the sound of the
drums still faintly beating in her ears—as if it were a
dream?

That seemed odd, too.

But then Bruce's lips were lightly touching hers, and all
further thought was blotted out in a warm, luxurious bath of
sensation. He seemed to be sipping now, just sampling. His
lips brushed back and forth across her own, his tongue
slightly tasting.

She felt the gentleness in the kiss, the sweet persuasion—and yet she *needed* no further persuasion.

As he kissed her, she let her fingers curl into the luxurious thickness of his golden hair. Her body began to feel a
building tension as the sound of the drums grew slightly
louder. Bruce seemed to hear it, too—because his kiss became more demanding, his tongue pushing through her lips,
just as her own became eager to taste him, too.

She slipped into his mouth, relishing the warm, spicy flavor of his desire—pungent and deliciously addictive.

"Sweet chérie," he breathed into her ear when he'd finally come up for air. "I've wanted this for so long. . . ."

"I know. . . ." Then the wet warmth of his mouth was
sliding across her shoulders while his calloused hands were
pushing aside her sheer nightgown's straps.

"I want to see you," he whispered. His hands dragged
down the filmy material of the lingerie, slowly revealing
her to his intense dark gaze. "Mmmm, *oui* . . ."

With one palm Bruce felt the weight, the shape, the velvet smoothness of one near-perfect breast and then the
other. Then he paused for an excruciating moment, his gaze
steady on her face as he slowly brought the rough pad of
his thumb to his lips, then returned it to one of her breast's
dark pink tips.

With his gaze still holding hers, he slowly flicked it over
her nipple. Tori gasped softly at the sweet ache of his
touch. The sharp arousal rolled through her veins like liquid

heat, seeping into her muscles and kindling a smoldering fire low in her body.

Another flick. Another soft gasp. And still his steady gaze kept watching, clearly pleased by his creation of so intense a reaction from so tiny a movement.

"Vous êtes belle," he whispered.

You are beautiful. A small smile touched Tori's lips. She felt his words were sincere, yet she found it odd that he'd abandoned his Cajun at such a moment for the formal French.

Bruce's gaze was still burning into hers as he moved his rough thumb to her other breast and slowly aroused its pink tip. Then his lips followed where his thumb had been. He lathed tenderly with his tongue, and nipped teasingly with his teeth as his hand moved lower, stroking the length of her bared leg as he lifted the skirt of her sheer nightgown.

Finally his fingers traveled to the top of her thighs; and while his mouth remained busy at her breasts, his hand intimately touched and caressed, fondled and teased.

For the second time since she'd awakened, Tori's breathing came fast and shallow, her heartbeat quick; but this time it was not from fear. This time it was the hot-blooded response to an expert artisan's masterful skills.

Bruce's ardent caresses, his worshipful kisses were almost maddening to Tori, invoking an uncontrollable primal response. Inside her, she felt the growing need to make him just as insane with this driving hunger, and, eagerly, her hands sought him out.

With impatient fingertips, she explored the rugged outline of his muscular chest. Peeling back the open lapels of the white terry robe, she fanned her hands for a moment against the hot, strong contours. Then her hands moved lower.

The robe's belt was only loosely tied, and it didn't take much for her fingers to unfasten it and pull the robe from him. He moved to help her and then he was there, bending over her, perfectly masculine and fully aroused.

Tori's lungs took in a satisfied breath as she gazed upon

this man. But he was impatient now and cut short her admiration. His hands began to fumble with the sheer nightgown bunched around her waist. She let him pull it over her head and drop it to the floor, at last casting off the remaining barriers between them.

With extreme satisfaction, Tori sent her fingers to the place they'd been hours ago. This time, though, there was only skin against skin as she stroked the sculpted muscles of his broad, strong chest. She luxuriated in his power, his strength, even as he took pleasure in her softness and vulnerability.

Gently she pushed him onto his back, then bent over him, using her mouth to taste the salty warm flavor of his skin. As she moved her tongue over his masculine nipple, she heard a low moan escape his throat.

The sound made her even bolder, and she let her fingers move lower. Gently she captured his hard arousal in her soft palm. With pleasure, she watched his eyes close and his lips part as he enjoyed the sensation.

Now it was her turn to build the tension within him. She smiled as more sounds of pleasure escaped his throat. Again she let her mouth taste his flesh, moving over his body to sample the rich, warm spice of his neck and shoulder and chin.

And when her lips found his again, she felt something change within him. His strong fingers tangled impatiently in her thick auburn curls, and his hungry tongue was plundering her with a pirate's ferocity.

The sensual assault left her joyously breathless, and her fingers slipped from his manhood to catch her balance against his chest. Without a moment's pause he took control again, rolling her to her back and eagerly feasting on her flesh. His mouth was everywhere, her lips, her neck, her breasts, and his hands wanted all of her.

Then she felt his palm move down her torso, his fingers curl in her silken triangle. This time, though, they were much more demanding.

He teased and rubbed the soft folds at the top of her

thighs until his fingertips were drenched with her arousal. His lips again sought the tip of her breast; and as he suckled and stroked, tempted and tormented, the throbbing in Tori's ears became louder and louder, her need more acute than ever.

When two strong fingers pushed greedily into her, she cried out with the exquisitely welcomed invasion. In and out his fingers moved, but it wasn't enough for her. She had to have more . . . she had to have him.

"Bruce . . ." she whispered raggedly, her breathing fast and quick as he was bringing her closer and closer to a shattering release.

"Let go, *chère.*" The Cajun was back as he drawled low into her ear, and then he drove three fingers deeply into her and she was screaming and screaming . . . but not in terror . . . this time she was screaming with pure, joyful release.

She was so wet now. So very ready for him. And he was rock hard and pulsing as he moved over her, his bandaged knees coaxing her legs to part for him. She opened for him and he settled between her legs, his swelled manhood barely touching the soft wet curls glistening with need above her thighs.

"You do want me?" he asked softly. His dark brown gaze was shining with such frank need, such raw desire, that Tori felt a dampness touch her eyes, making them glitter as brightly as his.

"Yes," she said.

And then all of his power and strength was thrusting into her.

Tori let out a soft cry of pleasure at the feel of him filling her. And then, slowly, he began to move.

There was a rhythm in the air. And they both moved with it. His length stroked her, and Tori felt the tension within her building again. Now the drums seemed to be beating louder than ever in Tori's ears. They were almost deafening, but she didn't want to hear, only to feel.

Tori was far from a virgin. She had made love before,

and yet, never before had she experienced anything quite like this. The tension within her wound itself tighter and tighter, and something amazing began to happen to her senses.

Through heavy-lidded eyes, Tori felt that her awareness was somehow lifting out of her body. Shadows shifted before her like phantoms—and the room itself seemed somehow to be fracturing, dissolving in and out like the shimmering electrons on a static television screen.

And the throbbing in Tori's ears became like thunder. Louder and louder it pounded until she knew the beating was no longer in her mind, but in this very room. And strangely, as hot as her blood seemed to flow, Tori felt a chill circling her and Bruce, even as a sizzling energy tingled within her.

As the hard, powerful length of Bruce dipped in and out of her, she knew she was feeling a depth of desire she had never before felt. Experiencing a kind of passion and freedom she never knew existed.

And yet, a part of her felt strangely familiar with it all.

Although Tori Avalon's mind *knew* she had never before made love with Bruce Gautreau, her body *felt* as if she were coming home.

It seemed to her that his body had been made for her alone to enjoy—that his touches, kisses, and caresses had always been, and were always meant to be . . . hers.

"Don't stop, Bruce." His lips had dipped down for a moment to take a taste of her, but she didn't want the pace to slow, even for a moment.

"*Oui, chère,* you want more?"

"Yes . . . more and more."

"*Oui, de plus en plus.*"

Their bodies had become slick with sweat and their movements were now becoming more frenzied, more desperate, the strain on their faces more pronounced. They both needed release, urgently needed to find the apex of their passions.

Bruce's thrusts were now greedy, impatient. She felt him

penetrating farther and farther with every stroke, until, finally, one deep thrust touched off a chain-reaction within her and the tension inside of her began to slowly shatter.

Like a mirror cracking into a thousand shimmering points of reflection, Tori's climax shuddered through her in a spectacular array of sensations. Every molecule of her body was tingling with ice and fire as waves of blissful release flowed through her.

The long, high cry of ecstasy came unbidden from her throat. It joined Bruce's own shout of desperate release as his body arced deeply into hers one last time.

Bruce softly collapsed onto Tori, breathing hard. She enjoyed his sweet weight, her arms embracing him, holding him close, stroking the soft gold of his head. Her own lungs were still working to catch her breath as Bruce moved slightly off her. His head slid to the pillow beside her and his hand cupped her cheek.

No words were said. He just smiled. His eyes shining with tenderness. Tori had never seen such a look in a man's eyes. At least, not when they were looking at *her*.

She returned his smile, and then her eyelids felt very heavy . . . unnaturally heavy. Strangely, her awareness felt fractured again, as if her mind were lifting from her body and looking back at herself lying sated on the four-poster bed.

But then her vision went dark, her eyelids seeming to close of their own accord.

This was strange.

She never drifted off like this after lovemaking, and yet, here she was uncontrollably drifting off. . . .

She felt the bedsprings moving beside her. Felt her limbs being moved and silk material flowing down over her. Then came a soft peck to her cheek . . . and finally oblivion.

She didn't know how long the dark, deep sleep had ruled her, but it was still night when her eyes abruptly opened.

"Bruce?"

The room was in shadow. No lights were on, but a sharp

slice of moonlight was knifing through the French doors, draping the room in silver. Slowly she sat up and turned to the pillow beside her.

Bruce?

But no one was there.

She rubbed her eyes. Glancing at the bedside clock, she saw that it was a quarter past four in the morning.

Did I dream it?

She tipped her head down and found herself even more confused. She wasn't naked. Her nightgown was still on her.

But it seemed so real.

Her fingers went to her lips, her breasts. She could practically still feel his mouth, his hands . . .

How could it have been a dream?

Confused and yet curious, Tori pushed back the bedcovers and swung her legs off the high bed. She padded to the bedroom door and down the dark hallway. . . .

Chapter
Seventeen

When she got to the guest room where she'd put Bruce, Tori gently pushed open the door.

Bruce was there, sleeping in one of the guest beds—exactly as she'd left him before midnight. Well, not *exactly* as she'd left him. Last night, a brooding, unhappy look had darkened his face. Now his mouth was turned up into a smile of . . . well, satisfaction.

Tori liked the smile.

Just the sight of it produced an answering upturn of her own lips. Quietly she turned to go, hoping he was having as pleasant a dream as she'd apparently had.

But just as she'd moved through the door, she heard the squeak of bedsprings.

"Tori?"

She turned back. His eyes appeared heavy-lidded, and his elbows were bending to prop himself up.

"I'm sorry I woke you, Bruce," whispered Tori. "Go back to—"

"What did you dream, Tori?"

"Dream?"

Bruce nodded his head. Tori stepped closer. As he sat up, the sheet slipped down, revealing his strong shoulders and broad chest, its smooth muscles bronzed from the sun. Strangely, she felt intimately familiar with it—every line and contour, as if she'd just caressed him with her fingers, tasted him with her mouth and tongue.

But she couldn't have. It had all been a dream.

Or had it?

"Come closer," whispered Bruce.

"No," said Tori, suddenly aware of his nakedness under the sheet. "I should go back—" She started again for the door, her hand was closing on the knob.

"We made love."

The words stilled her movements. "Did we?" she whispered.

"In the dream. In *my* dream, anyway."

Tori's eyes closed. Her forehead rested itself on the smooth, cool wood of the door. "In mine, too," she managed, her voice a bit ragged.

"There was something strange about my dream. . . ."

Bruce again rubbed his eyes, then studied the lovely woman standing only a few feet away. Her back was to him and his gaze caressed the seductive curves just under the sheer white nightgown. The pink of her flesh, the scent of her skin, the luxurious fall of her untamed auburn curls were causing his body to waken fully, and respond.

"Strange?"

"It felt so . . . real."

"Yes."

"For you, too?"

"Yes."

"So, *chérie*, maybe we should *make* it real. . . ."

Tori hesitated a moment before stepping from the room. Bruce watched her go. *Hell and damn.* Two *yeses* in a row and then she'd gone and left him in the dark. He snapped off the covers, revealing his strong, naked form. Next he swung his legs off the edge of the bed and grabbed the white terrycloth robe.

He slipped it on quickly, tying it loosely around him as he walked through the half-open door and began striding purposefully down the hallway. He had made a decision and there was no going back. Whether he was going to get this woman out of his system for good, or into it forever, he was sick and tired of struggling with uncertainty. One way or another he meant to do something. And he was going to do it right now.

"Bruce? What are you doing in here?"

Tori hadn't gotten back into bed, but was standing near the French doors, her arms wrapped around herself. The sight of her reminded him of how she'd looked earlier that evening, when he'd spied her from the street and she'd been silhouetted in golden light while standing on the gallery.

She had looked like an ethereal creature then and she did now. This time, though, she was not bathed in gold, but silver. The shaft of shimmering moonlight pierced the veil of her sheer nightgown, revealing in the shifting shadows the beauty of her face and form.

Even as he felt the vision of her arousing a heat in his body, he noticed an oddly familiar tingling on the surface of his skin.

"Tori, you never answered me," he said softly, his hands slipping into the robe pockets.

"But I did . . . I left your room. . . ."

"I know you left," said Bruce, stepping closer, joining her at the open French doors.

"Well, didn't that give you a hint?"

Bruce shook his head. "I want to hear it. From your lips."

He watched her think it over, her attention shifting to stare out the French doors. The sweet scent of roses, magnolia, and night-blooming jasmine clung to the fresh temperate air that slipped through the doors and filled the bed-room.

But there was another kind of air in the room, a kind that did not come from the garden. Bruce felt the slightly chilly stream surround them both.

He ignored it and stepped closer to the gallery doors. The rain had stopped and the sky had cleared. The night was as warm as ever, yet he noticed Tori was strangely hugging herself, as if she felt the same chilly airstream that he had.

A dampness still clung to the night, and a sultry mist lingered on the streets below, though Bruce guessed it would likely burn off after the coming of dawn.

Dawn.

Yes, it would come, wouldn't it? And then what? Would his chance with Tori evaporate along with the mist?

Again he felt the cool draft surround him, felt the tingling in his limbs. It was just like his experience the evening before, when he'd made contact with the house's spirits. Except this time Bruce felt no dizziness or sense of dark foreboding. This time he felt only a clear, pure desire to make Tori his.

Suddenly Bruce couldn't wait any longer for her answer. Stepping toward her, his hands reached out to pull her close, persuade her any way he could. . . .

"Bruce," she breathed, slightly startled. "Wait—"

His soft kiss interrupted.

"Maybe we shouldn't—"

And interrupted again.

"Yes, maybe we shouldn't," he whispered after he was through with another tender taste of her. "Or maybe we already did."

"But how—"

Again his head descended, his lips brushing across hers. She didn't resist this time, but yielded, her eyes slightly closing with the press of his warm mouth, the feel of his strong arms holding her against his powerful body.

"I'll show you how, sweet," he drawled low into her ear, and then his hands were lifting the skirt of her nightgown as his body was dancing her backward, trapping her against the frame of the open French door.

Tori's arms curled around his neck, her lips finally releasing the pent-up hunger of her own. She nibbled his lower lip first, then used her tongue to taste him. Bruce moaned with the feel of her desire, the release of her tight inhibitions.

His rough hands relished the smooth pale velvet of her bare thighs, then reached behind to gently stroke her sweetly rounded derriere. He smiled when he heard her aroused sigh, and his hands moved higher beneath the nightgown, fanning along the contours of her lower back, moving up the gentle curve of her waist.

As her fingers tangled in his hair, he finally removed her nightgown, raising it over her head.

Then he stepped back.

The obscenely sheer silk dropped unnoticed from his hand, and for a long silent moment his arrested gaze drank in her beauty.

She was a work of art. A celestial creature, like a spirit . . . or a sea nymph. Standing there in the sliver of shining moonlight, Bruce felt for a moment as if he were back on his ship, watching a gull's white wings skim across the starlit waves.

She seemed to have risen from those silver-capped waters, her skin almost glimmering in the moonlight. Her untamed curls cascaded over her ivory shoulders, almost to her waist, and her full, firm breasts peeked out of the auburn veil, their tips hardening under his steady gaze, tempting him to taste their sweetness.

And so he did.

Moving close again, joining her in the ethereal kiss of the moon, his own golden hair was transmuted to silver as it bent over Tori's form. His calloused fingers cupped one delicate breast and lifted it to his mouth. The tip of his tongue barely touched it, and he heard her sharp intake of breath, felt her hands fly to his strong shoulders for support.

She was ready. So ready to be made love to. The slightest touch, slightest breath, was enough to undo her.

Bruce smiled with the power he now had. A power of persuasion that he would not take lightly. She was an exquisite sculpture to him, and was left almost blinded by his desire to possess her. So he closed his eyes, deciding to force blindness fully upon him and seek to explore her secrets through his other senses.

His hands started at the delicate curve of her slender neck, moved over the softly rounded shoulders and on to her curving torso. His calloused fingers caressed the peaking mounds of her full, soft breasts, passed the slight indentation of her belly, and stroked the gentle slope at the small of her back.

When his palms found the nicely rounded flesh of her bottom, they tenderly cupped and caressed. She let out a small gasp of excitement as he suddenly pulled her roughly against his solid form, pressing her lower body against him.

Now it was time for his tongue to know her. He moved to taste the salty velvet at the tip of her breast. His lips worked the hard pink bud, suckling and teasing until he'd drawn more sharp breaths from her lungs and a long, slow moan of wanting from her throat, proving to him that he was no longer the only one who wanted.

She wanted, too.

Her hands became eager, pushing impatiently at the terry robe still tied around him. She drew it from his shoulders, and he moved to undo the belt and remove it completely, letting it join her nightgown in a white pool on the wooden balcony floor.

Then her slender hands were eager to explore him. He kept his eyes closed as her delicate touches danced across the muscles of his chest, the sensations sending sharp pangs of need through him. Soon he was feeling the tight swelling tension in his lower body, the quivering pressure of his arousal.

In fact, he didn't realize just how aroused he now was. When her soft fingers finally curled around him, he was not

prepared for the violent response through his body. His arm
flew to the frame of the French door for support as his need
to take her lashed through him, completely shaking his control.

His *control*...

"Bruce?" Tori's hand on him stilled. Her green eyes
studied the strain on his face.

Bruce's breathing was ragged, as his body throbbed with
wanting her. "I... need... you," he managed to bite out, a
part of him shocked, even angry at himself for his loss of
control. "Now, *chère*."

"Yes..."

The affirmation was barely out of her mouth before
Bruce stepped forward, backing her completely against the
French doorframe. Impatiently his large rough hand
reached behind her right thigh, quickly pulling it above his
hips.

He wasted no time. With his muscular arm around her
waist, he lifted her slightly and pressed her hard against the
doorframe. Then he rapidly thrust into her.

Bruce watched her eyelids flutter, her lips part, her
breathing become shallow and rapid as he relentlessly
pushed his rigid length into her luxurious soft folds, unwill-
ing to stop until he'd filled her completely.

She was as warm and damp as the Louisiana air, and oh,
so exquisitely tight. *"C'est bon, chérie?"* whispered Bruce.

"Yes... mmmmmm... so good..." Her arms were
curled around his strong neck, her eyes half closed in ecstasy.

"Oui," he breathed, reveling in the feel of her velvety
flesh fully enveloping his own.

I have been here before.... he realized. He knew it un-
equivocally. And he also knew that he would be here again
and again, until the stars burned out and the moon went
black.

Yes, he had made love to many women. He had cared for
them, and slept with them, and even helped heal the pain in

some of them. But nothing, *nothing,* compared to this feeling. This passion.

This, he knew, was heaven.

And yet he feared that, for him, it could never last. . . .

He closed his eyes, not wanting to mar the moment. Instead, he focused on the feel of the woman he was now moving inside. He took pleasure in stroking her, taunting her, driving her, until she was moaning in ecstasy.

He smiled as he felt her shudder against him with one small orgasm and then another, her arms clinging to his strong form as he began to move even more urgently.

The tension within him was near breaking and he pushed deeper and deeper inside of her, almost desperate to force her to experience a peak of ecstasy she'd never before known.

This was how he'd have her forever.

Yes, this would be the moment that would eternally brand her memories. And *he* would be the one great lover who would haunt her for the rest of her life, the one to whom no other lover would ever compare.

This was how, realized Bruce. This was how he would make her his . . . no matter what happened to them. . . .

His movements were almost savage now, her cries of pleasure strong in his ears. And, strangely, Bruce became aware of that same odd tingling throughout his body.

The pressure inside him now was more than he could bear, and finally he was thrusting so far and so deep, that he felt Tori's own body tightly coaxing him to climax.

Finally the shattering release came at once, in a powerful assault to his senses. He shuddered violently against her, and felt her hands clawing his back as her own cry of release joined his, rising into the damp, dark morning mist.

And then his eyes went wide with surprise. The tingling chill. He felt it clearly now. It was an energy field, moving through his body independent of his own will. Now that his senses were clearing, he recognized the spirit flowing through him.

"Tori? Do you feel something?"

Her eyes were wide with wonder. "Yes—of course . . ."

Bruce considered telling her, but he thought it best not to. Why alarm her? There was no harm here . . . not for them. And not for the spirits.

"Forget it, sweet," he whispered. "Let's just enjoy each other."

The sky had lightened perceptibly. The sailor in him knew well the gradations of blue that escorted night into dawn. Glancing to the street below, he let a bittersweet smile touch his lips. The mist was still there. But he knew it wouldn't be for long. . . .

"Bruce? What are you doing—"

"Carrying you, sweet."

He enjoyed the happy surprise on her face as he lifted her into his arms and brought her to the antique bed.

No, there was no harm here, thought Bruce. Tonight, for the living—as well as the spirits of those who once lived, and had obviously loved—there would be only pleasure.

At least, for as long as fate would let it last.

"Morning, sweet."

Sunlight flooded Tori's squinting vision as she awakened. She was aware of a warmth beneath her cheek, the calm sound of a heartbeat in her ear, and a hand gently stroking her long hair.

"Bruce?" Tori yawned as she lifted her head from Bruce's bare chest. She twisted toward him and saw that his eyes were bright and focused, as if he'd been awake for a little while. But his features were tense, his expression pensive, as if he were worried about how she would react to his being there.

And how should *I react? How do I even feel?*

For a moment Tori wasn't sure. Perhaps, a few weeks ago, she would have been upset, instantly anxious about his intentions. Then she would have found a dozen ways of ruining the pleasure of the present with worries about the future.

But it wasn't weeks ago. It was today. *And today Bruce is here. So why not enjoy him—for as long as he's here. . . .*

Oh, well, thought Tori, maybe it was inevitable. After weeks of living in a town called the Big Easy, any neurotic Northerner was liable to feel differently about life—and love. Especially after the amazing night she'd just experienced.

And with that thought, Tori smiled.

Still studying her face, Bruce apparently liked what he saw, because he quickly returned her smile.

"Bruce?" asked Tori, settling her cheek back onto his chest.

"Mmmm . . ." His fingers resumed stroking her hair.

"How many times did we make love last night?"

Bruce's eyebrows rose. "What?"

"We *did* make love last night?" Suddenly Tori became a little disoriented. Oh, she remembered the exquisite sensations, the ecstasy of their coupling. But for a moment, she got the idea that it had all been in her dreams. . . .

"Yes, *chère*," he whispered, "we made love."

Tori sighed. "It was so perfect. So wonderful," she murmured. "It felt like . . . a dream."

"Yes, it did."

"And . . . you know, I had this strange feeling . . . I know it will sound odd, but I had this feeling that something was . . . well, inside of my body while we were making love."

"Hmmmm. Well, I should hope so."

Tori's head rose and she caught his wry smile. "Be serious," she said, lightly socking him in the arm.

"I am."

"What I mean is . . . something that wasn't you."

"Mmmmm."

"I don't know. It's so strange. Now that I think about it, some of last night *was* a dream. Wasn't it?"

Bruce wasn't sure how much he should tell her. Last night he'd made the decision to keep her in the dark. This morning the bright rays of sun were beating through the French doors, shedding light on everything. Everything but this . . .

"Bruce?"

"We made love three times," he said softly. "Once while we were dreaming, and twice while we were awake."

Tori rubbed her eyes, then placed her cheek back on Bruce's chest. "I remember the French doors. And I remember your carrying me to this bed, and making love a second time. But . . ."

"There was a time before the French doors," said Bruce softly, his hand returning to Tori's silky auburn hair.

"My dream?"

"Yes. And mine."

"And you're saying we both dreamed *exactly* the same dream?"

"Yes. And acted on it."

"That's crazy, Bruce. How could we—"

"The spirits, Tori. It was the spirits."

"What do you mean, the—"

"They used our bodies."

A long pause followed Bruce's remark, and he started to become worried about Tori's reaction, but he didn't push her. He just waited.

"You know, it's strange," said Tori finally, "but I don't think it bothers me all that much. . . . I mean, maybe I should be frightened, or upset or something, but, for some reason, I'm not."

"I think they started using us from the very first time we entered the house."

"You mean when we first kissed? Down in the dining room?"

"Yes."

"What do you think we should do?" asked Tori.

"Well, to tell you the truth, I'm not sure. Like I told you last night, I'll call my friend, Serafine, and see how soon she can do a reading here. Let's just wait and see what she has to say."

The jangling of the phone made both of them jump. Reluctantly Tori left her warm, comfortable place on Bruce's chest and reached over to pick up the receiver.

"Hello?"

"Hello, Tori Avalon?"

"Yes."

"It's Franklin. Franklin Morgan."

Tori's entire body tensed. "Oh, hello."

"I take it we're still on for this evening."

"Oh . . . ah . . ." *Timing is everything.* At this moment she knew she'd rather be with Bruce. *But how long will this moment last?*

Tori closed her eyes, cursing herself as a silent war waged within her. Her heart wanted Bruce. But, despite her resolve to cast off her customary worrying, her mind was warning her that if she clung to this man in any way, he'd run like the wind.

Bruce Gautreau was a phantom in the night, a lover for her dreams—not a man for her future.

"Say yes." The words were strong, almost harsh as they rasped from Bruce's throat.

Tori took the phone from her ear, covering the mouthpiece with her hands so she could say something to him, but by the time she looked across the bed, Bruce was already rising from it and grabbing up the bathrobe she'd given him last night—Edward's bathrobe, the one that had set him off so easily. The one that became a lame excuse to cruelly push her away.

"Tori?" Franklin called over the receiver. "Are you there?"

"Yes. I'm here, Franklin," said Tori as Bruce's tense form strode across the bedroom's floor. "And yes . . . we're still on for tonight."

"Good, good," said Franklin. "I couldn't hear you before."

Tori watched as Bruce walked purposefully into the master bedroom's bath; and then, with a sharp movement, firmly shut the door between them.

"Oh, well," said Tori, forcing her green gaze down—anywhere but on the closed door. "I guess we have a bad connection. . . ."

*   *   *

Two days later Bruce was taking a break from the restoration job on Esplanade Avenue. His small crew had been working hard and the exterior of the house was almost finished.

A few men made comments to him about his strange behavior. Bruce usually oversaw the outside work and then directed work on the inside. But today he'd climbed onto the scaffolding himself to take up the sanding and priming. And he was working in a frenzied silence, like some kind of madman.

"What got into dat boy, him?" kidded a fellow Cajun.

"He might just be possessed. . . ." answered another young worker.

"Dat true. And he be possessed by one o' two t'ings," guessed the Cajun.

"What's that?"

"Either de devil or de woman."

"Hey, Bruce, you got the devil in you?"

The rest of the men laughed heartily, but Bruce barely smiled. The crew had never seen their boss so sullen and quiet. After some kidding, the men tacitly decided to let the man be.

Bruce just kept working.

Work seemed to be the only thing he could do to shut out the memories of making love to Tori, and the realization that he'd made a terrible error: While he was so intent on making their night together something that would haunt Tori for the rest of her life, he had neglected to realize that it could also haunt him. . . .

How could he live like this? he railed to himself. *Just steer clear of her. . . .* he advised himself for the thousandth time over the last two days. *Don't make it any worse than it already is. . . .*

When lunchtime came around, Bruce sat alone on the front porch steps with his po-boy of fried oysters. He picked up the morning paper and began skimming the stories.

"Hey, Bruce, wanna Dixie?" called another man on his crew.

"Sure."

Bruce took the bottle the man had opened for him and raised it in thanks. The beer felt good sliding down his throat, but suddenly the Dixie froze in midair. Bruce's arm was locked into place as he spotted a young man in a T-shirt and gold chains watching him from across the street.

It was René Vonderant; he'd recognize that punk's vicious expression from a mile away. The guy was smoking a cigarette and loitering—obviously spying on him and his crew.

A terrible tension infected Bruce. As much as he wanted to flip him an obscene gesture, he knew that he had to play it cool. In exactly one week Bruce would know whether or not he had the restoration job for the Cemetery Library. He was counting on Zoe—and he knew that she was counting on him.

She'd already told him that the last thing she wanted was for the Vonderants to continue cornering the market on this kind of work. It was the worst thing that could happen to the city. And Bruce agreed. He wouldn't let her down. At least, he'd try not to. If he got whacked in this process, there wasn't much he could do.

Forcing his gaze back to the newspaper, Bruce thought he would get his mind off the Vonderants. But what he read next made his beer bottle drop from his hands and shatter into a hundred razor-sharp pieces.

"Bruce? Hey, what wrong?" The Cajun worker saw the shock in his boss's gaze, and he walked over to sit beside him.

"A girl I met two nights ago," said Bruce, his voice raw, "she's been . . . murdered."

The Cajun picked up the paper and began reading aloud. "'Charlene 'Charlie' Robins was found dead in her French Quarter apartment yesterday morning, the victim of multiple stab wounds . . . motive unclear . . . possible solicitation. . . .'" The Cajun looked at the picture of the pretty blond woman, then back up at Bruce. "She's a pro?"

Bruce nodded.

"Dis look bad fo' you. I mean, she was killed de night you was with her, yeah?"

Bruce shook his head. "I wasn't *with* her. I just *met* her. Briefly. Over at Lafitte's."

The Cajun studied Bruce a long moment. "You didn't leave dat bar with her, did ya?"

Bruce didn't answer. He was too busy standing, his eyes searching for René Vonderant.

But the punk had disappeared.

Chapter Eighteen

Mardi Gras is tomorrow. And another final grand ball. I can hardly believe it has been a year since I first met Robert. . . .

For weeks now I have been playing the role my father insists upon. John M— now wears the mask of gentleman fiancé. He has not overstepped the bounds of propriety; and I believe it is because he will not risk grounds for termination of our match.

Meanwhile, I have not yet performed the Voodoo ritual that will set in motion the demise of John M—. On the night I spoke to Libbe, I thought I was resolved. Yet her warning haunts me.

I am holding out hope that there is another way. Perhaps I will not be forced to go down that dark road. . . .

*   *   *

Tori turned the brittle yellow page of the diary, closed her eyes a moment, and took a deep breath. The sweet scents of the night garden were drifting in on a Mississippi breeze.

When she opened her eyes again, the billow of the white lace curtains drew her attention to the French doors. The sight sent sharp memories shivering through her—memories of Bruce, and their spectacular night of lovemaking nearly a week ago. Again she closed her eyes, conjuring the sight of his glorious body and the feel of all the wonderful things he'd done to her with it.

Since their lovemaking, Bruce Gautreau had been on Tori's mind every day—and especially every night. Oh, she'd gone to an elegant dinner with Franklin Morgan. He'd been the perfect gentleman—charming, amusing, considerate—and Tori had to admit that she'd enjoyed herself. Yet she still found herself wondering about Bruce and whether he was thinking of her.

She knew it was pointless. Ever since their night together, Bruce hadn't even bothered to call—he may as well have vanished into thin air. Unfortunately, it was *exactly* what she'd expected of him, so Tori hadn't wasted time picking up the phone herself.

What was the point? Bruce had warned her weeks ago that he was a phantom—here today, gone tomorrow. Tori knew she wasn't going to change the wandering Cajun into the settling kind just by wishing it. So why torture herself?

With a resolute sigh, she forced herself to swallow down her wishes and open her eyes. And when she did, her gaze found itself again reading the pages before her. . . .

MARCH 2, 1897

I can hardly believe it, but my Robert is finally back. . . .
  Mardis Gras evening began with the annual grand ball given by my father's krewe. I attended with my family and John M—. This year the ball did not require costumes, only

*masking. Mine was of violet and red feathers to match the
deep violet ball gown, a gift from John M—.*

*It was vulgar of him to give me a dress. Father and Step-
mother knew it, but they said nothing when it was delivered
to the house. Tante Camille was the only one who dared
say it was an indiscreet gesture for a man to buy clothing
for his intended.*

*"John M— is an American, not a Creole," was Father's
only response. "She will wear it."*

*I did, but I despised wearing it, knowing it was from him,
just as I hated the second crystal swan bottle of perfume—
the same cloying Parisian brand I had flung from my window a few months before. Like the man, I found it nothing
but a vile scent in a comely bottle.*

*I may have been forced to wear the gown, but I refused
to wear the perfume, and he commented rudely in my ear
that I smelled like a virgin—all soap and no wantonness.*

*"But do not despair, my girl," he whispered, careful that
no one else would hear. "I will teach you the latter." He
thought this amusing, laughing at my expense. But I
thought of the matchstick doll hidden in my bedroom and
secretly laughed at him.*

*After a few dances he went off to take a smoke with his
cousin and friends. I wandered out of the ballroom and
down the hall of the hotel, desperate to get away from the
press of people. And that's when I heard his voice.*

*"Excuse me, mademoiselle, but can you answer me a
question: What do you think the reason for the hanging
mirrors in the ballroom could be?"*

*My limbs went numb, my eyes closed, as if I had heard a
voice speaking out of thin air. I dared not turn, certain I
would find evidence that I had gone mad, my mind having
insanely conjured Robert's voice alone with no body attached.*

*"Or perhaps you can tell me where I might find the
fairest creature my eyes have had the good fortune to set
themselves on? She is known by the name Marina. . . ."*

It was him. It was!

Tears fell from my eyes as I stood there. "Robert . . . Robert . . . Robert . . ." I said over and over as he embraced me.

I removed my mask, and he quickly removed his. Then I cried upon the shoulder of his tuxedo jacket, and he did not care in the least, just held me as my tears fell. He petted me and whispered his love, and I saw tears in his own eyes.

"It is all right now, my love," he finally whispered as I tipped my head back to look into his strong, handsome face. Oh, how I loved his golden hair, his warm and kind brown eyes.

I reached up to touch him, but my hand was gloved. I instantly removed it and tried again, allowing my naked fingers to feel the warm curve of his cheek, the strength of his chin, the softness of his hair. Yes, he was real.

"Marina, my darling," he said, "how can I ever make my absence up to you?"

"Oh, Robert, are you well now?" I asked. "I cannot bear that I was not able to be by your side during your illness—"

"Hush now. It is over. I am well and I am here. I arrived just today in fact."

"Why didn't you come to the house?"

"I knew your family always attended this ball, so I thought I'd surprise you," said Robert with a smile. "Oh, Marina, I am so happy to be back with you . . . and now we have our whole life to be by each other—in sickness and in health . . ."

Tears filled my eyes again. But this time they were not tears of happiness. "Oh, Robert, how can I tell you . . . ?"

"Marina!"

I heard the sharp voice shouting from down the hall. It was like a dagger's point ripping at my heart. John M— had found us together, in each other's arms.

"Who is this?" asked Robert as the man came storming up.

"He is . . . my fiancé . . ." I said haltingly.

I shall never forget the look on Robert's face, how disbelief turned to agony as he watched John M— pull me forcibly away, handing me over to his two vile cousins. The men grabbed me and ushered me toward the hotel door as I watched harsh words exchanged between John M— and my Robert. I tried to cry out, but I could not overpower his two cousins.

The two men were always doing John's dirty work. They roughly stuffed me into John's covered carriage, standing guard over me until he came out. Finally John got in beside me; and, as the driver pulled away, I felt a hard blow to my stomach.

The words were ugly, threatening. He called me a colored whore and warned that he would ruin me if I did not at least act the part of the chaste and haughty Creole virgin that I had thus far maintained with him.

I bit out my hatred of him.

"On the contrary," he said with a laugh. He said I should learn how to feel affectionately toward him, either that or he would teach me how to mask my hate.

"It's up to you," he said, "but I must admit that I'll be all the more aroused by the latter."

Then his hands began to run roughshod over my body, his fingers harshly squeezing my breasts through my gown as his mouth went to my bare neck, his rough cheek scratching my tender skin. I tried to fight him off, but it was no use, he was too strong, the moving carriage a prison in this vile assault.

His mouth traveled down my neck to the tops of my breasts. His tongue snaked into my cleavage, and again he asserted that I should wear the imported perfume he had bought for me upon pain of a beating. He pulled at my neckline then, partially ripping the fine fabric until he had freed a breast.

"I bought it for you, I suppose I can rip it off you. . . ." he said, laughing at his obscene joke.

Again I tried to push him off, but he shoved me back hard against the seat, somehow determined to prove his power. It was as if he wanted to make clear that my body was not mine, and that no one could stop him from using it to his liking.

He fondled the bared ivory flesh, squeezing its fullness, playing with its tip. Then he ripped at my neckline again to free the other.

Once more I tried to push him, and again he shoved me back in the seat. "Be still, girl," he threatened. Then he again fondled me, and I closed my eyes, trying to block out the vile touch of his hands, the loathsome voice whispering disgusting adulations.

"So beautiful, so perfect," he murmured raggedly as he pillowed my breasts together. "Oh, what I'll enjoy doing with these. . . ." Then he rolled each nipple between his thumb and forefinger, taking obscene pleasure in watching them pebble in his hands. "Yes, girl, you see, this is the sign of your arousal. . . . Now let's have a taste. . . ."

"No!"

He laughed as my eyes flew open and my hand lifted to try striking his head away. I landed a mild blow, but his hands quickly caught my wrists and pinned them to my sides. Then his head descended again, and I was helpless to do anything more than close my eyes again and try to block out the feel of his mouth and tongue on such an intimate part of my body. But I could not. My helplessness made a rage boil up inside of me. . . .

"Mmmm," he murmured, lathing his tongue across the tip of my breast, his hands still fighting to force mine down. "How I love the sweetness of virgin flesh. . . ."

"I'll kill you," I murmured with loathing.

His head came up and he stared into my eyes. "You listen to me, colored whore," he said, "you're bought and paid for."

As he spoke, I felt one of his hands release my wrist and move below the seat. Before I knew what was happening, he was working to jerk my skirts upward.

I froze in terror that he was going to rape me then and there. His fingers ran up the length of my leg. Then he *pinched my thigh hard, meaning to cause pain, and shoved his hand shamelessly against my underthings.*

"There's where I'll be on our wedding night," he threatened coarsely, his hand lewdly fondling the soft folds. "And I'll be the first man there . . . or you'll pay a dear price."

With my free hand I reached up. Staring into his eyes, I grabbed hold of some of his hair and pulled with all my strength.

He howled in pain and I braced myself for another blow, but he did not hit me. He did back away, though, and I quickly covered myself, drawing up the ripped material of the bodice. I remembered the straight pins in my hair and reached up to retrieve one. Then I pinned the dress back in place and slipped the strands of his hair down my bodice.

My hairpins, I realized suddenly. I had something to defend myself with after all. Quickly I reached up to pull out another pin. I held it up. The metal glinted in the dim light of the carriage.

In that instant I knew I would shove it in the man's eye if he came near me again. He looked into my face and saw that I had finally found a way—and more to the point, the nerve and will—to defend myself. He slid farther away then, a look of anger in his eyes even as his lips carried a smirk of superior triumph.

We arrived at our family's home that moment. I was still numb with shame and rage. In a mockery of social graciousness, he showed me politely to the door.

When I arrived, I ran immediately to my room and was sick in the porcelain bowl. I could not rip off his purple ball gown fast enough. I could not wash and scrub where he had touched me hard enough. I could hardly believe I'd come so close to being raped.

I looked in my armoire mirror a long time after I was done bathing. I knew what it was I wanted that moment, and I knew what I had to do. . . . I opened the drawer that held my underthings. Hidden in a handkerchief at the bottom of the drawer was the matchstick doll.

It was time.

I was ready to go down whatever road I needed to.

Using the piece of hair I had pulled from John M—'s head, I performed the ritual that Libbe had shown me. At the end of it I struck the bottom match on the doll and watched it burn, swallowing John M—'s effigy in fiery flame.

I suppose my soul will be damned for this, but is that any worse than my body being damned as I live? I will make the trade. I'll suffer in purgatory, even in hell, but I'll make the trade.

I rose from the ritual, determined now. Everything was changed. Especially me.

Quickly I donned a plain day dress, then I threw my long black cape around my shoulders, I pulled the hood down low over my head. I knew the dark cape would help to hide me in the night, and on this reveling Mardi Gras evening, it was unlikely anyone would even look twice at me.

On foot, I sped to Robert's mansion. The beautiful house was lit up tonight, as if welcoming me, and I ran through the filigree gate and up to the front door, knocking hard. His housekeeper let me in and led me to the parlor, explaining that Robert was not yet home.

I waited twenty minutes, then grew impatient. I knew the housekeeper had retired for the night, so I quietly slipped up the stairs to the master bedroom.

I gasped when I saw the room. It was so beautiful. The four-poster bed was masterfully carved with roses and fleur-dy-lys, matching the beautiful cast-iron fence around the mansion. I knew that Robert had designed the fence and decided that he must have also designed this exquisite bedroom set. The other matching pieces, the mirrored armoire, the nightstand, the carved chest were just as stunning in their intricate design.

I went to the French doors and flung them open. I stepped out onto the gallery. The chilly night air was damp and I saw that mist and fog were rolling in. I could hear the sound of Mardi Gras revelers in the nearby streets . . . singing and laughing.

All of a sudden, I began to feel apprehension at coming here. What would Robert say to my story? Would he understand? Was it possible he would cast me out?

I wondered if I should simply return to my father's house. I was about to give up hope and go when an odd sound in the distance caught my ear . . . a sound like drums. It came from the direction of nearby Congo Square, and as I listened to their increasing volume, I knew instantly what they were, the drums of the Voodoo, or Vo-du, as Libbe sometimes calls it.

I closed my eyes, swaying with the rhythmic power of those drums. Before long I felt lifted from my fears, and I began to understand what Liberté had felt when she'd renamed herself and set out on the road away from the plantation. . . .

With renewed hope I opened my eyes again. And there, beneath the gas lamp on the corner, I saw a figure moving out of the mist. A head of golden hair glowed like the halo of an angel as it walked toward the house.

My Robert.

When he at last came up the stairs, I told him everything. And I told him why I had invaded the privacy of his bedroom.

"I would rather die before I allow a man as vile as John M— to forcibly take my virginity," I explained. "It is mine to give, not his to take. And this night I freely choose to give it to the man I truly love."

Robert listened silently as I continued. "Now that you know of my mixed blood, I do not expect that you will marry me. But I will live as your mistress, if you will have me."

Finally Robert spoke. "I will not have you as my mistress."

"You will not?" I could not believe it. His voice was firm, incensed. He did not wish even to consider it. At once I felt the despair overwhelm me. This was worse than I could have ever imagined. I had greatly misjudged this man. *My heart was near breaking, my eyes filling with tears at this terrible revelation.*

I was about to rise and go when I realized Robert was speaking. I remained seated only because I needed a few minutes to regain my strength so that I could leave with dignity.

"Marina, do you recall when we first met and I told you of my grandfather's relationship with a free woman of color?"

"The plesage *arrangement?" I said vacantly, my body numb.*

"Remember when you asked me if I knew what happened to their two illegitimate sons?"

I swiped at an escaping tear. "Yes . . . you said you were much too busy to concern yourself with lost relations. . . ."

"Back then, Marina, I didn't know you very well. I didn't know how'd you react to . . ." Robert left off for a moment.

"Robert? To what?"

"To the idea that . . . I am my own cousin."

"What?"

"You see, my grandfather was indeed a wealthy plantation owner, as I said. He kept his colored mistress here in New Orleans. He loved her very much, and, when he died, he willed her and their two sons this lot we now stand on, along with a great deal of money. . . ."

Robert began to pace the room as he spoke. He appeared agitated and his fingers flexed into and out of fists. "One son took his money and went off to find adventure while the other, Henri, passing for white, journeyed to Paris to study.

"When Henri returned after many years, his quadroon mother had died, so Henri decided to take up the guise of a legitimate heir to his white father. He established a successful business and married the widowed daughter of a white American banker. Eventually Henri sent his own son off to Paris for education. Do you see, Marina, what I'm saying?"

I was confused. My desire to be with Robert was so strong, my devastation at his rejection so harsh, I could barely follow him. "You are saying that your relatives have mixed blood—"

"No. I am saying that I do."

"You?"

"My father was Henri, you see. My grandmother was the free woman of color who owned this lot. That is why I own it now."

"But then, I don't understand." *Now I was not only confused, but stunned.* "Are you worried that your true lineage will somehow be found out? Are you saying that is why you do not want me as your mistress?"

"My love, you do not understand. I don't want you as my mistress . . . unless it is as mistress of this house. I mean to marry you, Marina. I want you as my wife."

The words produced a gasp of shock from my lips. "Robert?"

He smiled at me with such love in his eyes that I nearly broke down in sobs. "Together we will find happiness forever," *he said.* "I swear it."

We did not hesitate a moment longer. I went to him and he came to me, our arms opening to the promise of the future. There was such burning fire in Robert's eyes, it seemed to warm the very blood within my veins.

"I was only afraid that you wanted him," *he whispered, holding me close.*

"No," *I assured him.* "Never. It is you I want, you that I wish to wed."

"Then we shall, Marina," *whispered Robert.* "We shall."

He made love to me then so masterfully, so beautifully, that I could not have dreamed up such an experience. The power of our final union was overwhelming. As he thrust slowly into me, tenderly, sweetly, his eyes were filled with so much affection that tears slipped from my eyes.

"I am not hurting you, love?"

"No . . . it is wonderful . . . to be so close to you . . . to become a woman in your arms."

And then he and I were greedily moving against each

other, unable to stop touching and caressing, kissing and stroking. All night we made love until the rays of a beautiful, quiet dawn began to slip through the bedroom windows.

Before the streets could stir with morning traffic, I returned to the house on Esplanade Avenue. I slipped into my room and under the covers. Too excited to sleep, I began writing.

Now, I think, I am finally fatigued enough to rest. . . .

Tori closed the leather-bound book and finally settled under the covers, enchanted by the idea that the young Creoles had made love in this very bedroom a century ago, and Marina herself had lost—no, *given*—her virginity to Robert in this very bed.

A yawn overtook Tori, and she forced herself to close her eyes. Tomorrow was Rosegate's Halfway-Through party, and she knew she needed the rest.

"*Suitable* bachelors," Tori whispered to herself, trying to rally her spirits. Some wonderful new men would be coming by the mansion tomorrow, and so would Franklin Morgan. Tori was sure she had the whole thing set in her mind, when the chisel of fatigue began chipping at her wall of certainty.

Oh, how she hated herself, but the last thoughts that slipped through that wall, just before she drifted off, had to do with one other bachelor who might be dropping by the party—a decidedly *un*suitable bachelor, but who cared?

Tori sighed, knowing that a secret part of her still desperately wanted that cocky bayou bastard who was crazy enough to peer at a ruined wreck of a building and see the gorgeous mansion it once was; or stare into the eyes of a perfectly put-together woman and see the wounded child inside.

Yes, that was Gautreau, all right.

Tori moaned with longing as she again felt the touch of his lips on her neck, the feel of his hands at her breast. *Not again*, she thought as she pulled the sheet over her head.

But it was too late. Once again she'd lost the nightly battle of driving him from her mind.

Damn.

No matter what happened with Rosegate's spirits, Victoria Avalon knew that when it came to the cocky Cajun, she was doomed to be haunted for the rest of her life!

Chapter
Nineteen

In no other city in America did people enjoy a party like the citizens of New Orleans—it was simply in their blood.

For two centuries, while the sober Puritans were branding the U.S. citizenry with an austere work ethic, the old-line French Creoles were embellishing their little plot of land along the crescent bend in the Mississippi with a tradition of unrivaled festivity.

Mardi Gras was only one slice of that party pie. Tori knew well how much the Creoles loved to dance and sing and laugh the whole year round, throwing galas and balls and constantly attending the opera.

The old Creoles seldom held parties in their homes on weekends. Such a conventional choice was actually considered vulgar in the upper circles. Fashionable *soirées* were thrown during the week. And so, Tori supposed, it shouldn't have been much of a surprise that *Tante* Zoe, a doyenne from an old-line family, had suggested a Wednesday evening for Rosegate's first party in almost a decade.

With satisfaction Tori strolled through Rosegate's restored first floor and out onto the back of the large wraparound porch, weaving through laughing party guests as she went.

Near the back door a bartender from Duchamp's was pouring drinks next to a damask-covered table where a shucker was cutting open an endless supply of fresh oysters. A jazz trio was set up on one corner of the porch; and as Tori swayed to the mellow music, she admired, for the tenth time, the beautiful job that Zoe's "party elves"—as her aunt called them—had done with the newly landscaped garden.

Candle lanterns cast the whole area in a romantic glow, and strings of tiny white lights twinkled like diamonds around the trunk of a large oak, making the old tree appear to have snatched the starlight right out of the night sky.

"Well, sugar, we're more than halfway through our little Halfway-Through party," offered Zoe. "Looks like a hit to me."

Tori smiled. Her aunt looked wonderful tonight in an elegantly simple dress of blue lace. "I was just recalling what Uncle Richard used to say about not missing parties."

Zoe laughed. "I remember my own father, Adrien, would say the same thing. 'Finish the work *tomorrow,* but don't miss the party *tonight.*'"

"It looks like you've convinced a lot of heavy hitters in this town of that philosophy."

"Oh, my dear," said Zoe, placing a warm hand on her niece's shoulder. "When it comes to a party, New Orleans' folks don't *ever* need convincing."

It was true. Many of the movers and shakers of New Orleans had been by Rosegate tonight to laugh and talk. From the district attorney and the *Vieux Carré* Commission's historian to the director of the Historic Voodoo Museum, all had stopped by to enjoy some champagne with an array of unique delicacies prepared especially for the party by the famous Chef Pierre of Duchamp's.

"I think I've got some interest in the stained-glass window, too," whispered Tori. "I've had it set up in the parlor all evening, and three people said they thought it would look divine in their homes. Franklin Morgan even wants to buy it. Surely he'll offer me a good price."

"Have you gotten it appraised, dear?"

"No, I've been too busy—"

"Tori, you *must* get it appraised before you sell."

"Of course, of course . . ."

"But it is good news that you've gotten some interest," said Zoe encouragingly. "And now that *one* part of your party plan is an obvious success, what can you tell me about the *other* part?"

"Other part?"

"My dear," whispered Zoe, "what's your opinion of the local gentlemen you were so eager to meet? The *suitable* sort . . ."

"Oh, yes, of course." Tori smiled weakly. "They're very . . . ah . . . suitable. Very . . . nice."

"Mmmmmm," said her aunt. "But not as *nice* as one particular gentleman, maybe? One you've already met?"

Tori said nothing. She simply sipped from her flute of champagne and pulled gently at the short strand of pearls at her neck. Her mother had left them to her, and she cherished them, but sometimes the string felt a little too tight.

"Well, you know what they say," said Zoe, a strangely devilish smile touching her lips. "Perhaps what you're looking for is right behind you."

"What?"

"Bonsoir, chère."

The touch of Bruce Gautreau's low murmur to Tori's ear sent her back up quicker than a hissing cat.

"So, you came," she snapped, turning so quickly to face him that the crystal flute in her hand nearly sloshed champagne on the tailored bodice of her white silk halter dress.

Bruce quirked an eyebrow at her tone, even as his gaze

caught on the bare-shouldered cut of her elegantly simple dress and the upsweep of her auburn hair, a refined style that reminded him of the first day they'd met here in the garden. "Fashionably dressed people having fashionable conversations and eating fashionable cuisine . . . how could I miss it?"

Tori's gaze brushed over him. In his sharp blue Armani suit and signature tieless neck-fastened shirt, Bruce looked plenty "fashionable" himself. Actually, he looked good enough to eat. *Stop thinking about him like that—it will only drive you insane!*

"Good evening, Bruce," said Zoe, extending her hand.

Bruce smiled warmly at the sight of Zoe Duchamp. He squeezed the older woman's hand and leaned over to peck her cheek. "How's my favorite restauranteur?"

"Fine, sugar. How are you—and the *other things* in your life?"

"I'm okay, Zoe. So far there are no problems."

"Jack Pitot is here."

"Where?"

"I think he's going to find you."

Tori's brow wrinkled at this exchange. But before she could question them, her aunt was turning on her heel.

"I'm off to mingle. Tori, your guest is in need of some champagne. . . ." And then Zoe was gone.

"Follow me," Tori said softly, leading Bruce to the makeshift bar. She retrieved a three-quarters full flute of the bubbly from the bartender and turned to offer it to him. He accepted with a silent half-smile, then softly clinked his glass against hers.

Damn that pair of brown eyes. They were drinking her in as surely as his lips were savoring the champagne. It unnerved her, reminded her too much of their lovemaking a week ago. She blinked a moment, trying to regain her distance. *He never even called me. Not once . . .*

"I know," whispered Bruce, guiding her to a shadowy section of the porch. "And I'm sorry."

Tori's limbs froze. *How* could she forget the Cajun could read her mind! "Stop doing that," she ordered.

"Can't help it," he said.

"I'm sorry, Bruce," said Tori, turning from him, "but I have to mingle."

"It's been a complicated week," he said sincerely, his breath slightly brushing the top of her head.

"Has it?" Tori stopped moving. Part of her wanted to walk away, but another part froze her to the spot, forcing her to listen to him.

"I've had some . . . troubles."

"What kind?"

"I'm here now, *chère*. Isn't that what counts?"

"Maybe" was all Tori said. She didn't glance back. Couldn't. She just moved forward, off the porch, and into the rear grounds.

"There you are, Tori. I've been looking for you." With a genteel smile and a confident gait, Franklin Morgan approached.

Bruce watched from the porch, but said nothing, did nothing. His hand merely tightened dangerously on the crystal in his hand.

Tori was unaware that Bruce even noticed where she was going. She smiled up at Franklin as he took her hand and intimately wrapped it around his arm, gallantly guiding her toward the large oak strung with tiny white lights.

The dark-haired, blue-eyed financier had been charming Tori since the first hour of the party. To her, he seemed ever the dashing figure with a buttoned-down shirt, Windsor-knotted silk tie, and a custom-made British suit.

"Where are we going?" asked Tori.

"I wanted you to meet a business associate of mine who's just arrived from Chicago. You recall the casino I showed you last week?"

"The one just being built?"

"Yes. It's near completion, but there are a few financial problems—very small ones, you understand—but this particular finance lender is a bit on edge, so I thought I'd have him come around tonight and relax."

"Oh, that's a good idea."

"Won't you help me charm him?"

"Of course." Tori honestly liked Franklin. He was handsome and successful, and his confidence in her own abilities to fit into his jet-setting world made her feel a rare sense of satisfaction. In her mind's eyes, a part of her saw herself filling her own elegant mother's shoes, standing beside her handsome, successful father during the many New Orleans social occasions they'd attended.

Franklin introduced her to the older gentleman, a Mr. Laurence, who appeared quite happy to meet her. Tori smiled warmly, feeling self-assured with Franklin standing by her side, initiating a conversation about sightseeing in the city.

" . . . and, of course, there's the Mardi Gras museum, set up at the old U.S. Mint. Quite a nice display of memorabilia."

"And the NOMA, the New Orleans Museum of Art, has undergone an expansion," added Tori.

"Yes," put in Franklin. "Twenty-three million dollars."

"I believe there are four centuries of French paintings housed there," said Tori. "I've been so busy with Rosegate that I haven't yet had the chance, but I do adore the French Impressionists, especially Degas. Did you know Edgar Degas' mother was from New Orleans?"

Mr. Laurence tilted his head in fascination. "No. Really?"

"Oh, yes," continued Tori. "In the 1870s he visited his uncle's cotton office here and painted a scene from it."

"Fascinating, Ms. Avalon," said Mr. Laurence. "Will I see that painting in the New Orleans' museum?"

"No," said Tori. "It's housed in France."

"Mmmm. Pity it's not in *my* collection," said Mr. Laurence.

"You're a collector?" asked Tori.

Mr. Laurence smiled enigmatically. "You might say I

collect—and appreciate—the finer things in life. Isn't that right, Franklin?"

Franklin nodded. "Mr. Laurence has excellent taste."

"Well, I understand there is a record in his relatives' letters of his painting a New Orleans French Market scene for a friend's home here in the city. But if that painting exists, no one has discovered it. . . ."

"Pity," said Franklin. "That would be some find."

"Yes, wouldn't it," agreed Mr. Laurence. "Of course, there are many other beautiful things worth collecting . . . and enjoying, wouldn't you agree, Franklin?"

"Yes, indeed." An odd smile touched Franklin's lips, and the men seemed to exchange a meaningful look.

"Well, of course, I agree, too," put in Tori, then she turned, hearing Zoe call her name. "Won't you excuse me? It seems some guests are departing, and I'd like to see them off."

When Tori left, Franklin's eyes chilled to chips of blue ice as he turned them directly toward the older gentleman. "She's a beauty, isn't she?"

"Yes. Very nice." Calvin Laurence's gaze followed Tori's young, slender form as it sauntered across the lawn. Now that she was gone, he lifted his carefully wrought mask of civility and allowed himself to make a much cruder estimate of her worth.

"She's very agreeable these days, what with some debts and being on her own," explained Franklin.

"Mmmmm. You have some debts of your own, Morgan."

"Of course, of course. I just think that you and I should get started on the right foot. I mean, as I've assured you, my cousins are working on one avenue of monetary gain that will come through only tomorrow, and I myself have a nice sum coming in—"

"I'm getting tired of waiting."

"How about I arrange a nice little dinner this week, then. Between you and Ms. Avalon. I believe she'd be agreeable to sharing an evening with you."

Cal Laurence's eyes returned to the slender bare legs of the young woman standing across the garden. A lewd smile barely touched his lips. "Yes. All right. I suppose I can wait a little longer. . . ." Then the man's eyes turned on Franklin again. "But only a little while, do you understand?"

"Yes, yes. Of course . . ."

"And you say she'll be agreeable?"

"She'll join you happily, I'll see to that. But you and I both know your methods of 'persuasion' are up to you. You always liked a little drama as I recall? A little resistance always spices up the fun, don't you agree?"

"Mmmm . . . yes, I do at that. As long as you take care of any . . . mess."

"Don't I always?"

Cal Laurence laughed as Franklin excused himself. Immediately he sought out an acquaintance. "What we discussed earlier—two hundred thousand. You're sure?"

The acquaintance nodded. "If it's an authentic Tachant window, I myself can get a quarter million from a Japanese collector. As I said, I'll take fifty thousand as my broker's fee. But, Franklin, you'd better make sure it's authentic."

Franklin smiled as he started across the rear garden. When he saw the window standing in Tori's parlor, he knew immediately that he'd found a hidden treasure. He'd seen that window in an obscure book on New Orleans artists and recalled that, like the Degas painting, it was thought to have been lost over time.

What a find! The woman had no idea what she had in her home.

It was all too good. In one fell swoop he would solve his problem with Laurence *and* Gautreau, and he'd have a little fun at the end of it, too. Oh, yes, he thought, his ice-blue eyes raking Tori's fresh, innocent beauty as she turned toward him. *Just look at the trust in her eyes.* This one would be pure entertainment.

"Well, Tori," began Franklin. "How about that tour of Rosegate you promised me?"

"Watch me, Robert! Watch me!"

"What are you doing, my love?"

"I'm making myself appear solid. . . ."

Above Tori and Franklin, in Rosegate's master bedroom, the ghosts had been watching the colorful flow of people for the last two hours.

Earlier in the evening, when the *soirée* had first begun, Marina and Robert had drifted curiously through the array of arriving guests. But within an hour so much fiery life energy had poured into the house that they found themselves overwhelmed and retreated upstairs.

Still, after so much time spent in silent coldness, the spirits of Rosegate rejoiced with the heat and life that now pulsed through the air. A new level of power was flowing through Marina and Robert. Enough to make Marina want to try a new experiment with her spiritual form.

"Appear solid?" queried Robert.

"Yes, I wish to see myself again . . . as I was in life."

Sure enough, Marina focused this new amount of tremendous life energy and used it to pull her scattered particles together. Slowly a somewhat flickering image of herself began to appear.

Marina watched her form materialize in the full-length mirror of the bedroom's antique rosewood armoire. As in the moment of her death, she appeared naked, beautiful, and young, her long curls falling like a silky auburn veil past her waist.

"Oh, my love . . ." breathed Robert. *"Look at you."*

"Yes, this is what I had been." And it was true. When Marina looked in the mirror at her own flickering image, she was able to see again her life of so long ago—the many nights in Robert's arms, the moments of laughter and love.

"Robert, you must try now."

"I don't know—"

"Please, I wish to see you, again. To remember . . ."

Robert concentrated. He focused the tremendous life energy he'd skimmed from the many bodies below. Gradually his swiftly vibrating movement of his molecules began to slow, until they neared the same rate of speed found in light molecules. Soon his form began to coalesce as an image began to flicker. . . .

"You're doing it, Robert. Keep trying. . . ."

Robert gazed at himself in the mirror, the likeness of Marina's handsome young man with the golden hair. He was deeply pleased to see his essence materialize where it belonged—and would always rightfully belong—beside the woman whom he'd made his bride one hundred years ago.

"Oh, my love . . ." whispered Marina, overcome by emotion with the sight of her love's deep brown eyes looking into her own once more. Then suddenly she was thrown back a century in her memories and standing beside him at the altar in the twilight shadows of the cathedral. He was slipping the exquisite emerald-encrusted ring upon her finger, and the church candles were casting a glow upon his face, their flames reflecting the eternal fire of love in his shining eyes.

Robert could see Marina's face melt into memory, her eyes burn with a depth of feeling, of wanting. He reached out to touch her, to draw her to him, but his hand passed through her body like a light beam through a candle flame. The illusion of contact was there, but Robert and Marina both knew that no amount of superfluous energy could ever coalesce their spirits back into living beings again.

"Hell and damn," Robert softly cursed.

"I know, my love, but take heart," said Marina, trying to force herself to do just that. *"It was not long ago that we were able to lie together once again. It was so wonderful."*

"Yes, it was. It was. But it's been a week," said Robert, pacing the room in his flickering human form. *"Why hasn't Gautreau been back?"*

"He will," coaxed Marina gently.

"He'd better."

Marina was silent for a long moment. *"Victoria is speaking with a number of different men at the party. Did you notice?"*

Robert stopped his pacing. *"No. What are you getting at?"*

"Just that . . . well, perhaps, even if Bruce does not return . . . perhaps we will still be able to touch—"

"What are you saying? That the lady of the house will take up with another man?"

"She may." Marina moved over to the French doors to spy on the party. Tori was laughing and talking in the garden with a handsome well-tailored man with dark hair and blue eyes. *Franklin.* Yes, that was his name. She'd heard Tori speaking to him one night at the front door.

"Hell and damn . . ." Robert cursed again, looking over Marina's shoulder to spy on the house's mistress. Tori and Franklin were just leaving the garden together and coming into the house.

"What's wrong, Robert? I mean, does it matter who she ends up with? We'll be able to use their bodies just the same. . . ."

"I know," said Robert, beginning to pace again. *"I guess that I just . . . well, I liked this Gautreau. Something about him pleased me, made me feel"*—Robert shrugged—*"at home in his body."*

"Perhaps you will feel that way in the new man, too."

"Perhaps, but don't you think—"

"Robert, listen!"

The sound of voices approaching silenced the ghosts. Faster than the speed of living thought, their images vanished.

". . . and he just kept holding out for more money."

"What happened then, Franklin? Did he get his asking price?"

"Well, unfortunately, no. By the time he realized the generous offer was indeed worthwhile, he'd lost his chance. The collector had found another piece to set his sights on. One can never be too slow to accept a good offer."

"No . . . I guess not." Tori wrinkled her brow in thought as they entered the master bedroom.

"Oh, Victoria, *look* at this room."

Tori smiled with pride as she watched Franklin admiring the restored bedroom and newly polished antique furniture. "Isn't it wonderful?"

"It is," Franklin asserted as he examined the intricately carved posts of the large bed. "And you say that you found it in the attic?"

"Yes."

"Well, we'll just have to take a trip up there together and see what else we can find." Franklin took a sip from his champagne, but his blue eyes had shifted to admiring her openly.

Tori looked over Franklin's handsome face and bright blue eyes and smiled her own admiration back. "I do want to finish the restorations."

"Yes, you must. This house is a showplace—and the first and second floors you showed me have been restored magnificently."

"Well, Bruce Gautreau should get most of the credit, but I did work hard, too."

"Gautreau, yes. You know, Tori, I'd be careful of that man."

"What? What do you mean?"

"He's been linked—now I'm not saying he's guilty—but he's been *linked* to a murder in the Quarter."

"What!"

"Oh, yes. I understand the woman was, shall we say, a *professional* lady. Gautreau was seen at a bar drinking with her and the next morning she was found."

"Found? How?"

"Stabbed to death, poor girl. But the police have only questioned him so far. I suppose they'll need more evidence to charge him."

Tori managed to find her way over to the bed and sit down. "It can't be true," she whispered.

"What do I know. Perhaps the man had been drinking. Perhaps he had nothing to do with it," said Franklin carefully. "I just think you should be wary."

"Yes . . ." Tori mumbled, stunned by the news, and truly unable to believe it.

"But, Tori, you were saying? About finishing Rosegate?"

Tori had to take a deep breath to calm her nerves. She tried to concentrate on Rosegate. Clearly, Franklin wanted to be her friend. After all, he'd taken an interest in the house she loved. Tori's mind counseled her to stop thinking about Bruce, who was clearly the *wrong* kind of man, and start waking up to the good man who now stood before her, waiting for her answer.

"Yes, Rosegate. Well, you see, Franklin, I very much wish to see my mansion fully restored, but, well . . ." Tori turned and walked to the open French doors. The party was almost over, a few couples had begun to dance in the garden, to the jazz band's last song. She noticed Bruce in the garden, talking intensely to Zoe. What was going on with those two, anyway?

Stop it! Stop thinking about him. Put him out of your thoughts, for God's sake!

"What is it, Tori?" asked Franklin, walking up behind her.

"I'm in need of funds," said Tori, abruptly turning from the window to face Franklin.

"Oh, I see. Well, no need to be embarrassed, Tori, funds are a fact of life. Have you thought of selling these antiques?"

"I could," said Tori, hoping Franklin hadn't already lost interest in the window. "But I truly love the furniture. It seems to belong here. It's a perfect fit. . . ."

"Yes, that's true."

"And there is the, ah, window," said Tori hopefully. "You know, the stained glass. You saw it earlier downstairs."

"Yes, of course," said Franklin with a small smile. "I'd almost forgotten. You know, I'd love it if you let me help you with the house—if you'd let me buy that window from you."

"Really? Are you really interested?"

"Well, I'd say it's a matter of collecting. And that can be a rather precarious market."

"I suppose," said Tori, nodding. "Collectors can be fickle."

"Yes, my dear, but they can also be . . . *passionate*." Franklin stepped a little closer to Tori, his voice softening to a low, almost intimate tone. "Take that stained-glass window of yours. To a casual observer, that window looks as if it's just an interesting design, you know. Nothing so special—other than some fine workmanship of course, solid artisan crafting—"

"Yes, yes?"

As Franklin moved in a little closer, his hand casually reached out to finger a loose auburn curl that had fallen onto her bare shoulder. "But to somebody who has an instant . . . *connection* to the central image. Well, to that somebody, the window would seem priceless."

"And . . . what do you think, Mr. Morgan? In your professional opinion," asked Tori. She was growing a little breathless with Franklin's advances. "I mean, what do you think it's worth?"

He smiled, his blue eyes burning into hers. Then he moved his hand from her hair to brush the underside of her chin, coaxing her face to tilt toward his. "Priceless . . ."

Tori let her eyes slightly close. It was the first time Franklin had approached her physically like this, and Tori felt a little thrill sparkle like champagne through her veins, even as his lips came closer to her own.

"Robert, do you see?!"
"Yes, my love, they are going to kiss."
"I'm so happy we will have this chance tonight!"
"Quickly, my love, quickly—"

Marina wasted no time, she instantly flowed downward into Tori as Robert prepared to enter the dark-haired man named Franklin. . . .

Chapter
Twenty

As Franklin's lips connected to Tori's, she felt that now-familiar cool stream of air surrounding her and a tingling in her limbs. But, oddly, while the lips against her own were warm and pleasant, something felt very wrong.

Something was *missing*.

It wasn't a question of aggression. In another moment Franklin's hand came to her waist and she felt his mouth pressing harder, his lips parting to coax her own to part.

But still Tori felt *nothing*.

Strangely, she felt no sense of caring in the touch, no urgent feeling of deep passion, of need. Nothing even close to the way Bruce had held her, kissed her . . .

Tori closed her eyes completely, but it didn't help. All she could see was *Bruce's* face, all she could yearn for was his kiss.

This can't be happening! railed her good sense.

Tori wanted nothing more than to fall in love with

Franklin Morgan. This man was handsome and erudite. He was a respected, successful businessman, an obviously stable and dependable gentleman. Unlike Bruce, a man like Franklin would not offer her a finite affair. A man like Franklin would be looking for respectable stability, she was certain. Marriage, children . . .

Yet, as she tried again to kiss him, her body begged to differ. Something inside her was not so certain about this man.

"Non. Non! It cannot be!"

Robert cursed a blue streak in a simultaneous state of anger and panic. Marina had been able to enter the lady's body without any sort of problem, but Robert was blocked from flowing into the dark-haired man's form. The ghost's energy could swirl all around the living masculine body, but never *into* it!

Robert was helpless to do anything more than observe the living couple embracing and kissing more passionately. In another few moments Marina flowed out of the lady.

"Robert! What's the matter! I was waiting for you to—"

"I'm blocked. Completely blocked!"

"What!"

"It's this man. There's something wrong."

Marina tried to calm down and consider the situation. She allowed her awareness to flow around the man, observing, sensing, attempting to glean the problem. *"Oh, my God. Robert, my God . . ."*

"Marina, what is it?"

"Look at this man. Look. I thought I could sense a foulness to him when I was within the lady, a vague sense of familiar revulsion. This man, Robert, this man! His surname is Morgan."

"Good God, Marina, I see it now! He is the descendant of that bastard John Morgan—"

"Yes, I am recalling it now. John Morgan was the vile man who blackmailed my father. He purchased me as if I were a slave, then nearly raped me in a carriage—"

"And tried to ruin us at our own wedding dinner. . . ."

"Oh, no. Robert. Did he . . . was he the one who . . ."

"Two men *shot us, Marina. From what I recall of their faces, they looked vaguely familiar, but neither was John Morgan. And yet I am* certain *that he engineered our deaths."*

"His two cousins," said Marina with agonizing realization. *"I did* see *their faces. I did. And I remember now. We were shot by the two cousins who always did Morgan's dirty work. Oh, Robert, I cannot bear it! The blood of their blood is now kissing the mistress of our home, and in the bedroom we once shared!"*

"Yes, my love, I know. . . ."

"It is like an attempt of rape all over again! This shall not be!" In a burst of fierce anger Marina focused her energy in an arrow of force. It slammed wildly through the room and landed on a dressing table, where an array of Tori's perfume bottles suddenly found themselves shattering violently against the wall.

"What was that?" asked Tori, abruptly parting from Franklin.

"Whatever it was, forget it," said Franklin insistently, pulling Tori's slender arms back around his body.

"No." Tori broke away instead and turned to see three perfume bottles lying shattered on the ground. Expensive perfumes were now dripping down the wall near her recently purchased antique dressing table. "Franklin, *look* at this!"

"What's the matter? Did something slip off the table?"

"Franklin, these perfume bottles have been shattered, as if they'd been *thrown* against the wall. *Look* at the perfume dripping . . . but we were alone in here. How could it happen?"

Franklin shrugged as he stepped up to Tori and carefully snaked a hand around her waist, trying to pull her back into his embrace. "I felt a little draft around me. Perhaps—"

"No *draft* could have done this."

"Then what else?"

"Well . . . Bruce Gautreau thinks the place is haunted," said Tori, looking all around the room for evidence of ghosts.

"Haunted? That's ridiculous—"

"I'm not so sure, Franklin. I think he may be right."

"*Oui,*" came a voice from nearby. "He may be, at that."

Tori turned her head to see Bruce leaning against the bedroom doorway, one of Tori's kittens in his hands. Easily he stroked the kitten as he sauntered in. Tori didn't miss the intense possessiveness in Bruce's eyes as he looked at her—she didn't miss the anger, either.

Well, he had no right to either feeling. *Hear that, Gautreau!* After all, he'd virtually ignored her for a week after they'd made love. The man had no claims on her at all—*not one!*

Tori took a deep breath, deciding to *try* handling this civilly. "Franklin, you know Mr. Gautreau, I believe—"

"Oh, so we're back to *Mister,* are we?" interrupted Bruce, putting down the kitten. It scampered straight over to Franklin and began to sniff at his pant leg.

"Don't be rude," said Tori to Bruce.

"Right," said Franklin, holding out one hand while keeping his other firmly around Tori. "No need to upset the lady."

Bruce pointedly ignored Franklin Morgan's outstretched hand. "What's your game plan, Morgan?"

"Game plan, old boy?" he asked, his attention distracted a moment by the kitten's determination to spread fur along the pant leg of his custom suit. Franklin tried to kick the kitten away, but it was too quick for him.

Bruce watched Cleo hiss and swipe at the man's suit, snagging the expensive cloth before scampering under the bed. Bruce smiled in delight, silently promising the fur ball a spoonful of caviar.

"Yeah, Morgan, your game plan. What are you doing here? And what do you want with Tori?"

"Bruce, stop this—"

"Mr. Gautreau," said Franklin, "if you're going to use bayou-boy tactics with me, then why not slip into the whole act and use the accent, too?"

Tori's eyes widened at the fury that raced across Bruce's face. She was certain there was going to be a punch thrown any moment. Well, not in her bedroom, there wouldn't!

"Both of you, stop it!" exclaimed Tori.

"Yes, of course, Tori," said Franklin, eyeing Bruce cautiously. "Gautreau, I'll have to compliment you on the restoration work thus far on Rosegate."

Bruce folded his arms over his chest. "And? I'm sure this is leading to something?"

"And I'd like to know your estimate on what it would cost to finish the restorations."

"Why?"

"Bruce, please. Answer Franklin."

"No."

"Then *I* will. Some weeks back Bruce gave me an estimate for the entire place. It was sixty-thousand dollars. But that was before we finished the first and second floors. I'd say it would take around fifty to finish the rest of the house—including the kitchen, baths, and exterior—wouldn't you agree, Bruce?"

Bruce quirked an eyebrow. "Yes, I suppose."

"Well, then, Victoria darling, that's precisely my offer to you for that splendid stained-glass window. What do you say?"

"Oh, my goodness, Franklin, you can't be serious!"

For a moment Franklin's cool smile faltered, uncertain whether her surprise was over the amount being too much or too little. Then he saw the happy amazement dawning over Tori's face, and he quickly corrected the slight slip in his expression.

"I'm stunned," continued Tori. "I never expected to get that high an offer on the window." Immediately Tori extended her hand to Franklin, but then she withdrew it.

"What's the matter?" asked Franklin, suddenly worried.

"I can't, Franklin. It's just too much—"

"Tori—" tried Bruce. "Don't sell the window."

Tori ignored Bruce. "Franklin, you have to understand that I do want to sell it, but I don't want to take advantage of your kindness. Let me get it appraised, and then I'll just ask you for whatever its market value turns out to be."

A look of pure terror flashed across Franklin's face so quickly that no one but a mind reader could have picked up on it.

Lucky for Bruce Gautreau that he was.

Obviously Morgan was trying to swindle Tori. That was clear enough to Bruce. But what wasn't so clear was how, or what other motives were lurking in the back of this man's dark soul. The blocking and corruption were a high art with this one, Bruce thought. Franklin Morgan thoroughly believed every lie he told.

"Now, Tori, let me tell you how I really feel. I want that window because its central image resembles the most beautiful woman I've ever known. You, Tori. I want that window to hang in my Garden District mansion as soon as possible, so that I'll always be reminded of your exquisite face."

"What a load of *merde*."

"Bruce! Get out of here!" demanded Tori.

"No, Tori. The man's lying. I guarantee that if he's offering you fifty grand, it's worth at least two times that."

More like five, thought Franklin.

"I got that," warned Bruce, pointing a finger in Franklin's face. "Five times, Tori. That window's worth a quarter of a million bucks to somebody this joker knows."

"Gautreau, you're talking gibberish—" challenged Franklin. "And, as I warned Tori, I think you're unstable . . . even dangerous."

"*I'm* dangerous—"

"That's enough. Okay, *Everybody out!*" cried Tori, her hands going to her throbbing head. Between the shattered perfume bottles and the shattering insults, she just couldn't take it anymore! Not in her own bedroom.

The men simply stood there and stared at her, so she just

gave it up. "Fine, stay and kill each other for all I care—*I'll* leave!" And then she did.

After a few more juicy threats spoken between them, the men broke up and Franklin immediately searched out Tori. He caught up with her in the parlor, where the stained-glass window was set up on a wooden artist's easel. "Tori, please don't let that man ruin what's starting to happen between us. . . ."

"No. No, of course not," said Tori. "It's just that my head is spinning right now."

"Please, at least say you'll accept my offer. I promise you I'll put it in my mansion. The amount I'm offering is really nothing to me, and it's everything to Rosegate, so there's no need for you to feel that you're taking advantage of me. Don't you understand . . . it would give me so much pleasure to see you restore Rosegate . . . to see you happy."

Tori listened to Franklin's words and they sounded so sincere, so convincing. More than anything she *wanted* to believe. She turned slightly, her gaze touching the beautiful stained-glass window. A part of her did feel that taking it away from Rosegate was wrong, and yet the mansion needed the funds more than the window.

Well, she told herself, perhaps if something more permanent *did* happen between her and Franklin Morgan, then maybe the window would be back at Rosegate someday anyway.

"All right, Franklin," said Tori, extending her hand. "It's a deal, then."

At the base of the stairs Bruce watched silently as Tori shook hands with Morgan. Bruce felt torn. He wanted to go in and break them up again, yet he knew it would be a disaster. *Maybe I should just leave quietly . . . give her up. . . .*

"What's going on?" asked Zoe softly beside him.

"She's making a mistake."

Zoe looked past Bruce's broad shoulder to see her niece talking intimately with Franklin Morgan. "She needs you Bruce. Don't desert her now."

"Zoe . . ." He wanted to tell her the truth. *I need her, too.*

But somehow he couldn't get the words out. "I'll try," was all he could manage.

"Good," she said, putting her hand on his shoulder. "You're winning the bid on the Cemetery Library, you know. It will be announced tomorrow."

Bruce nodded. "I'll be ready."

"Will you?"

"If I'm not, then I'll be in big trouble."

Zoe's hand squeezed his shoulder. "Don't worry. The district attorney is counting on us."

"I know." Bruce took a deep breath. If they were going to nail the Vonderants, then he had to keep playing along. The DA's office had just about enough evidence to take them down, including the corrupt law-enforcement officials who'd been helping them. Now all they wanted was for Bruce to wear a wire one more time and testify against them—both of which he was more than willing to do. "I'm just worried about her."

"I know, sugar. I am, too, but for different reasons than you are."

"What do you mean?"

"Oh, I think you know," said Zoe.

But he didn't. He'd read Zoe but picked up nothing more than warm feelings toward him and vague thoughts about her late sister, Coco. "Who was—" Then it hit him. "Coco was Tori's mother, wasn't she?"

"Yes."

"You're afraid Tori will make the same mistake that her mother did. . . ."

"Coco thought marrying the 'right' sort would make her happy. And so she ended up miserable."

"And dead."

"Yes."

Bruce nodded. "I suppose Stanton Avalon was about as 'right' a sort as Morgan, eh?"

"Not quite so bad as Morgan, Bruce, but bad enough. And Tori is just like her mother—and me, I suppose—stubborn as a mule. If you pull her to the right, it's a sure bet she'll resist to the left, just because it's in her nature."

Zoe's gaze narrowed as she watched Franklin say good-bye to her niece, then step onto the wraparound porch through the parlor's door-size open window. "I'm afraid I hated Stanton from the beginning. I pushed and pulled Coco right into that bad marriage."

"Aren't you being a little too hard on yourself?"

Zoe shook her head. "There's more to the story. More than Tori even knows."

"Maybe she should hear all of it."

"No. When Tori was just a child, I promised her mother that I'd never tell her."

"But, Zoe, her mother isn't here to judge what a grown woman needs to hear. *You* are."

Zoe's brow wrinkled at those words, but she said nothing. Then, when she saw her niece heading in their direction, she quickly squeezed Bruce on the shoulder. "I'll think about it," she finally whispered to Bruce.

"Deserting me, Zoe?"

"Damn right," she said before vanishing.

As Bruce watched Tori striding up to him, a look of pure fury on her face, he felt an unsteadiness within him. Anger in general was never something Bruce retreated from, but pure fury arrowing straight at him from someone he cared for as much as Tori—that was enough to make a normal man flee, let alone a psychically sensitive one.

But Bruce didn't flee. Instead, he took a deep bracing breath. Maybe for the first time in his life, Bruce Gautreau was going to force himself to stay put and try to work things out with a woman he cared about.

"Are you through embarrassing me now?" snapped Tori angrily.

"I was not trying to embarrass you, Tori, just protect you."

"Protect me? *Protect* me! Is *that* what you call it? Listen, Gautreau, I can take care of myself just fine."

"Okay, Tori, I get it. I'll back off."

"Thank you."

Bruce could read the mixed feelings in Tori. Part of her really wanted to call it quits with him—maybe for good. But she had yet to walk away. She was still standing there, toe-to-toe with him, so maybe he still had a chance. . . .

"I'm sorry I didn't call you," said Bruce softly.

Tori swallowed uncomfortably. "Why apologize? It's your prerogative—"

"No. Not if I care about you. And I do, Tori. Very much."

Tori's green eyes stared into his face, trying to determine if his words were true. "Do you?"

"Yes," he whispered. "And how about you? How do you feel?"

"I don't know, Bruce. I'm very . . . confused right now."

"I understand." Bruce slowly allowed his hands to move to her bare shoulders. He wasn't sure if she'd pull away from his touch, and he released a pent-up breath when she didn't. He let his large calloused hands rest on her soft, warm skin and begin a light massage of her tense muscles. He could see her enjoy the touch as he himself enjoyed the luxurious feel of her velvety smooth flesh.

"Tori," he whispered. "How about we just give it a little more time, then?"

"How much time?" she said, her voice a bit raw. "You told me that you don't plan on staying around here very long."

"I know I did. But . . . that was before . . ."

"Before what, Bruce?"

"Before we made love."

The words pierced Tori deeply. She hadn't expected this. Not at all. She thought she'd had it all figured out—thought she'd had Bruce all figured out. . . .

Suddenly Franklin's words came back to her: *Gautreau was seen at a bar drinking with her . . . a professional . . . stabbed to death. . . .*

Tori broke from his touch and stepped back, her hand going to her head, which was starting to pound once more.

"Tori? What's wrong?" Bruce could feel her turmoil toward him, but he needed to hear her express it.

"Bruce, did you . . . were you . . . *questioned*? By the police?"

"Yes."

"Oh." Tori looked away.

"Tori, either you know and *trust* who I am by now, or you don't."

"I want to . . ." she whispered, and yet she'd trusted other people in her life, like Edward, and had found her trust had been misplaced.

"You know, my mother used to say that a good part of love is blind faith."

"Blind." Tori's brow wrinkled and she shook her head. "I don't know. I don't like being in the dark."

Bruce nodded. "Neither do I. But I guess that's where we're at for now, huh?"

Tori looked at him and nodded. Bruce could see that she was still confused, still torn between him and Franklin. But at this point, he knew it was something much deeper than a choice between two men: It was a choice between two ways of living, and of loving. It was something she would have to work out for herself.

"I have to go," he said softly.

Tori nodded and saw him out.

"Oh, by the way," he said before stepping onto the porch. "I have that friend ready to come by Rosegate and do a spirit reading for you."

Tori wrapped her arms around her, suddenly feeling a slight chill. "Yes," she said, recalling the frightening sound of her perfume bottles shattering. "Bring her by as soon as possible. Maybe she can figure out who these ghosts are—and what they want."

"Tomorrow night?"

"Yes. Tomorrow."

A few hours later Tori was ensconced in her four-poster bed. Her head was still spinning from the whirlwind of the party, but her real worries came from trying to make sense of the two men now in her life. She didn't want to think about a choice. Not tonight. So she decided to go back to her favorite distraction.

Marina's diary was now sitting on her lap, and Tori's fingers eagerly opened its pages to the place where she'd left off. . . .

MARCH 20, 1897

I went to another fitting today for my wedding dress.

Before Mardi Gras, I could not care less about the dress, but today I am only too happy to have such a fine silk and lace gown, because now I know it will be worn for my Robert!

Father does not yet know of our plans. Robert and I agreed to keep silent for a bit. Robert plans to settle back into his club here in New Orleans and set up his architectural business. He says that by mid-April, he will be ready to go to my father and explain that he intends to hold Father to the original promise of marriage.

Robert will use some of his inheritance to buy off John M— and absolve the debt my father incurred. Robert feels this will also make certain that the man stays quiet.

I know Father is still tangled up in business dealings with that base man; and it seems to be aging him by the day. Where once my father had salt-and-pepper hair, he now has a head of snow. Where once my father could smile at P'tit-Boy's games, he now simply sits and stares. And when he looks at me, there is a strain to his face, a sadness in his eyes. . . .

Robert tells me not to worry. "If your father is not too proud to accept money from me, then I will gladly offer it. The situation will be delicate, but I will see it through."

I outwardly agreed to Robert's plan, but secretly wait for the Voodoo to work. Perhaps the vile man will soon die, which will release me from the marriage—and my family of any shame or obligation.

In the meantime, I have been stealing away as much as three times a week to see Robert. I tell my family, "I am retiring early," then lock my door, take the key, and slip down the servants' staircase. Libbe knows my little route now. She lets me out through the French doors of her first-floor room, and I creep out to Esplanade Avenue.

I arrive at Robert's mansion at twilight, and wait for him there . . . usually in his beautiful master bedroom. And then we make love for hours and share the dreams for our future. . . .

It is like heaven when I am with him. He laughs and teases and when we are hungry, he fixes us a snack in his kitchen. When midnight has come and gone, he escorts me home again, and I slip through Libbe's French doors at the back of the house, back up the servants' staircase, and into my room.

No one has yet caught me, but I do not care if they do. I mean to marry Robert. The sooner this truth is told, the better.

APRIL 19, 1897

I am beside myself with grief . . . and guilt.

Father entered the hospital a week ago. Tonight, at twilight, he expired. The doctors said it was his heart.

I cannot fathom it. . . . I know the past months have been a strain, but he was not an old man. His own father and two uncles had all lived decades more.

I have tried to comfort Stepmother, but she is distraught, now locked in her room. I, myself, have cried for hours. I am aggrieved by this terrible blow, this awful loss to my family. But I am also guilt-ridden.

Libbe's warning has come back to haunt me. Her words turning over in my mind. "There be a way to do him harm . . . through Voodoo," she had told me, "but black

*magic is like de coal dust. You cannot throw it in de air
without de wind bringin' some o' it back on you. . . ."*

*During the Voodoo ritual I performed, I wished that my
father's promise of my hand to John M— be forever ended.
But in that ritual, I had wished John M— dead. And yet he
still lives . . . and my father now lies lifeless.*

Oh, what have I done!

Have I, by my own dark wish, killed my own father?!

APRIL 23, 1897

*Yesterday we buried my father, and today John M— paid a
visit to our family home.*

*Late last night Robert and I had already spoken with
Stepmother Zoe and Tante Camille. We waited until little
Adrian had gone to bed, and then he and I explained our
plan to marry and pay off John M—. Stepmother wrung her
hands but silently nodded her approval. After a glass of
anisette, Tante Camille agreed. . . .*

Tori stopped her reading a moment. Stepmother *Zoe*. It
was the first time she'd come across Marina's using her
Stepmother's name. And Marina's little brother—the one
she called by the nickname P'tit Boy—his real name was
Adrian.

Here it is . . . realized Tori. Here was the evidence that
Marina was her ancestor. Adrian was the name of Tori's
great-grandfather, the source of her own middle name Adrianne. And Aunt Zoe had said her name had come down in
the family as well. . . .

So if Marina was Adrian's sister, then she was also most
likely Tori's great-great aunt.

The only question now was how the family came to in-
herit Rosegate. Again Tori went to the pages of the
diary. . . .

*   *   *

*This afternoon the family stood united against John M—.
He came calling with cocky arrogance, thinking he was
paying a visit to a family that he now controlled. But he
found himself quickly reduced to panic and fury.*

*Robert did most of the talking, the rest of us looking on.
John M—'s face burned red with rage as he was forced to
comprehend our decision to break my engagement.*

*Robert offered money to cover the original debt that I
had been used as barter to pay, but John M— said he
would not take the money. He insisted upon my hand . . . or
else.*

*"Or else what?" asked Robert, impatient with the man's
petty threats.*

*"Or else the rest of your genteel friends shall learn what
breed of girl you mean to marry," threatened John M—.
"Or do you even know?" Suddenly John M—'s anger sub-
sided as he appeared to see his trump card. He turned to
me, a cruel smile on his lips. "I wager your fine, Paris-edu-
cated beau here doesn't know the truth about you, does
he?"*

*"You mean about Marina's mixed blood?" said Robert
calmly. "Please don't insult our intelligence with your
petty extortions. Times are changing, sir. We are nearly
through the door of a new century. Such a revelation is becoming less a stigma than it once was . . . at least in my circle of artisan friends and associates."*

*John M—'s eyes turned deadly cold as he realized he
was, perhaps for the first time, about to lose something that
he had set his sights on possessing. He stared at me with
such hatred, I almost stepped back, but then I caught myself
and held firm to my position.*

*"You have lost," I stated quite clearly. "And I want you
out of this house."*

*"No, Marina, it is I who will want you out of this house,
along with your pathetic family," returned John M— "for
your father's debts have weeks ago forced him to turn this
house's ownership over to me, and I will have you, your
stepmother, your aunt, and even little Adrian turned out on*

the street unless you honor his promise to me. You have one week!"

Then he slammed out the door in a rage.

Robert instantly turned to Stepmother. "Do not give it a second's worry, madame," he said, bowing formally. "I open my home to your household and invite you to live with Marina and me at Rosegate."

The relieved smiles on the faces of Stepmother and Tante Camille were more than enough answer for us. We all hugged each other and began our plan for a hasty move—and a hasty wedding!

MAY 12, 1897

Robert says not to worry, but I am worried.

Our wedding has been planned for the 26th. My dress is ready, the priest has been arranged, and the celebration dinner. But John M— was enraged by all of it and has made dire threats of revenge to Robert.

Robert laughs this off, but I am concerned. I hope his threats lie only in his tongue. I have found out just today that he has begun telling people of my mixed blood. Our dearest friends and family understand, but many acquaintances do not. People who I have known for years, families who have taken me into their homes are now crossing the street when they see me.

I now look about me with new eyes. I see that I have been a hypocrite, uncaring about unfairness until it affects me.

Today, I do care. It's true that I am a hypocrite, and yet, this new knowledge I have of myself, even of Robert, it does not frighten me. If people wish to treat me differently now, then they can go to the devil. I will not deny who I am!

Today I spoke with Robert. "It is strange to me that John M— would want so badly to take a wife whom he knew was a woman of color," I said. "I mean, he obviously feels so strongly against people of color."

"It is not so strange, my love. The man was not interested in a wife to love. Only one to own . . ."

Tori stopped reading abruptly. *Only one to own . . .*

For some reason, the phrase jarred a memory to the surface. Thoughts of her own mother came back to her, and with it that strange image of a violin being smashing against a wall. It was Tori's *father* who had smashed it, she realized suddenly. But what was her mother doing with a violin? Her mother didn't play the violin—or for that matter *any* instrument that Tori could recall.

The puzzle pieces floated around in Tori's head without a place to go. Perhaps tomorrow she would ask Aunt Zoe if her mother had ever played the violin.

Tori went back to the diary then, but saw that she was near the end of the writing.

MAY 24, 1897

Too busy to write more than this—the day is almost here!

MAY 26, 1897

The wedding was beautiful.

I will write more of it tomorrow, describing every blessed detail, every wonderful moment. My family was so happy, even young Adrian, in his little cutaway jacket, was part of the bridal party.

There was only one blemish to the day and that was John M—'s drunken appearance to cast insults to us both. But a tall, strong friend of Robert's, a man he has known for years, roughly ushered the man out.

Now I wait for our wedding night. I am still in my gown! Robert has excused himself for a short trip to a friend's home. He says his friend Monsieur Tachant has created something especially for Robert to give to me on our wedding night.

What could it be, I wonder? He has already given me so much. And tonight I will give him a gift as well, the news that I will have his baby in seven months! Oh, I am bursting with joy, for I know we are going to be so happy in this house!

But Robert will be here soon. I will write more tomorrow. . . .

Tori turned the page, but the next one was blank.

She turned another page, but it was blank, too . . . and the next one, and the next . . .

Slowly she shut the leather-bound book. "What happened to the newlyweds?" she murmured with curiosity.

A chill seemed to permeate the air around her as she flipped off the light, then nestled under the covers. No answers came to her mind as she drifted off in the darkness, just a strange sense of deep loss that so many pages of a promising life, *so very many,* had been left empty.

Chapter
Twenty-one

Tori's eyes opened to a strange sound, like a whimper.

The kittens?

Immediately she sat up. But it wasn't the kittens. They were at the foot of her bed, wide awake, their furry ears pointed backward in agitation as they listened to the same mewling.

Tori swung her legs off the bed. She pushed the French doors open and stepped onto the gallery. But the sound wasn't coming from outside. Suddenly a flash of light caught her attention, and she noticed a car parked across from Rosegate.

A man was sitting inside. He had just lit a cigarette.

A wariness enveloped Tori and she wrapped her arms around her. She didn't recognize the car or the man. Yet he was sitting there, watching Rosegate.

Puzzled, Tori stepped back inside. The sound of the

mewling was still there. No, not mewling. *Crying.* A woman was crying somewhere in the house.

This was crazy, thought Tori, glancing at the digital clock's 4:15 reading. The last of her guests had left hours ago.

Could someone have fallen asleep in one of the rooms? Perhaps that's what had happened. Maybe a woman had had too much champagne and was now having some sort of a nightmare.

Cautiously Tori left the master bedroom and entered the dark house. The crying seemed to be coming from downstairs, so she took to the shadowy staircase. As she descended, the sound did indeed become louder. And this was not the mere whimpering in a nightmare, realized Tori; this crying was a steady weeping.

Tori's heart went out to this mystery woman. Her sobs were wrenching—clearly she was in great pain. Whoever the woman was, she was obviously distraught, and truly suffering. Tori hoped she could help her.

Tiptoeing closer to the parlor's half-closed sliding door, Tori heard the weeping grow louder than ever. The woman had to be inside the parlor, so Tori stepped around the edge of the door. And what finally met her eyes left her gasping in total shock.

There, standing in the middle of the room, was the shimmering white image of a woman. . . .

She was beautiful, her long hair flowing well past her waist, veiling her nakedness in a curtain of auburn curls.

Tori's entire body went numb, and her mouth gaped as she stared. The woman was weeping violently over the stained-glass window set up on the artist's easel. Racking sobs shook her form as she buried her face in her hands. And then her weeping slowed, and she lifted her head.

Tori looked into the woman's face, so much like her own. The glowing white light surrounding the woman seemed to increase then, brightening the room, and Tori realized that the woman's face was an exact match for the one in the stained glass.

"Are you Marina?" Tori asked, her voice barely there.

But the woman's face simply stared. Her image started flickering in and out, and then it was gone. With a chilly rush of cool air, the room was plunged back into darkness.

Shaken, Tori stood there, her body trembling and numb.

Move, Tori . . . Do something!

Finally she did. After stumbling awkwardly to the hall phone, Tori began punching out a phone number.

It was not a number that came to her fingers consciously, but instinctively, because it was a number that her heart knew would connect her to the one man who would really understand, the one man who she truly trusted. . . .

"Hello?" came the groggy male voice.

"Bruce?"

"Tori? Are you all right?"

"No. I've just seen a ghost."

"*Bon Dieu.* I'll be right there."

Bruce made it to Rosegate in twelve minutes flat. She opened the front door to a breathless man in sweatpants, a light jacket, and sleep-tousled hair. Clearly he'd run all the way.

As Bruce stepped into the light, Tori noticed his face was injured again—there was a fresh red bruise near his eye and a cut near his lip. It looked to her as if he'd had another run-in with somebody last night. But she didn't say anything because he immediately started questioning her about the sighting.

She took him to the parlor and ran through the whole thing.

"Okay, Tori, and then what happened?"

"And then the woman just vanished. . . ."

"You said she was here, standing over the stained-glass window?" asked Bruce, moving to the exact spot the ghost had been.

"Yes."

Bruce closed his eyes. Tori watched his face go blank, his lungs steadily pull in air.

"What do you feel?" she whispered.

"A tingling in my limbs . . . a sense of pain, loss."

"Why was she crying, Bruce? What do you think is wrong?"

Bruce continued to concentrate, but he just couldn't extend himself to that realm with any kind of clarity. "I don't know, Tori. I'm sorry. I can tell you something else about the ghosts, though, something I didn't get a chance to tell you earlier."

"What?"

Bruce reached into his jacket pocket and brought out a piece of paper. Tori took it and quickly skimmed it.

"Do you know what this means?" she asked.

"Yes, it's a will of Robert Le Pelletier's. He was the original builder of this house and bequeathed it, upon his death, to his wife, Marina Duchamp Le Pelletier, and upon her death to the Duchamp family."

"This is Marina and Robert, then, the couple in the diary?"

"There's also a record of a Marina Duchamp and Robert Le Pelletier marrying on May 26, 1897."

Tori's brow wrinkled. Had she read this wrong? She looked again at the document. "But this says . . . my God, it *is* true. Marina and Robert both died on May 26, 1897. Bruce, they both died on their wedding night. . . ."

"Murdered. Look at the next clipping."

Tori read the photocopy of a newspaper item. It described the brutal shooting of the newlyweds in their own bedroom on their wedding night. The murderer or murderers were still at large at the time of the news item's printing. "Bruce, Marina and Robert *must* be the spirits haunting Rosegate."

"There's something else, Tori."

Tori looked through the papers but saw nothing else. Then she realized it was not in the papers. The room's silence left her feeling a bit unsteady. Slowly she lifted her gaze to meet Bruce's eyes. "What is it?"

"You know your mother's maiden name was Duchamp."

"Yes, of course."

"But what you don't know is that *my* mother, Angelique, had the maiden name of Le Pelletier. *Le Pelletier,* Tori, the same surname as Robert's."

"Oh, my God, Bruce. What are you saying?"

"My mother's grandfather had a brother named Robert; and if they're the same person, it would make the builder of this house my great-great uncle."

"And, Bruce, I'm almost positive from the diary that Marina was my great-grandfather's sister, which would make her my great-great aunt. They were our *ancestors. . . .*" breathed Tori, amazed.

"Yes. Of our blood."

"Is that why?"

"Why they're using our bodies to . . . connect?"

Tori nodded.

"I don't know. We're just going to have to wait for Serafine. I'll bring her by tonight."

"Who is she, exactly?"

"Serafine Beltremieux is a *Vo-du* priestess and a psychic. But she doesn't just read the living."

"What does she—?"

"She'll connect with the spirits. You'll see."

Tori nodded her head, then sat down heavily on the antique sofa. She'd just had it newly upholstered with a cheerful flower print. It perfectly complemented the dusty rose fabric wallpaper covering the parlor walls. Right now, though, all she cared was that it would support her weight. After all of this, she didn't think her legs could carry her any longer.

"Bruce, there was an incident earlier in the house. Maybe it's connected. I didn't get a chance to tell you. . . ."

Bruce sat down next to her. "There's something else I didn't get a chance to tell you, either, Tori. But you go first."

"I was in the master bedroom when I heard a crash. I was, uh, distracted, but when I looked up, I saw that three perfume bottles had been shattered against the wall, as if they'd been hurled by some force."

Bruce nodded. "What were you doing when it happened? You said you were distracted?"

Tori's gaze dropped. "I was . . . with Franklin Morgan."

"With him?"

"Kissing him."

"I see." Bruce rose from the sofa and walked over to the carved wooden mantelpiece. "And . . . did you enjoy it?"

Tori's emerald eyes studied him. His whole body was tense, one hand had curled into a ball. "Would it really matter to you if I did?"

A sharp laugh escaped Bruce's throat, and his hand covered his eyes. "It's hopeless, you know. We're hopeless, answering each other's questions with more questions."

"But what you just said wasn't a question. Was it?" teased Tori.

"No," he said softly, then walked over to the sofa again and sat down. "And the truth is, Tori, it *would* matter to me."

Tori's gaze brushed the fresh injuries she'd noticed when he'd first come in. Her hand tenderly touched his face. "And what's all this about?"

Bruce accepted her soft touch with an abrupt intake of breath. The chilly sense of pain and longing that still lingered from the ghost was now warmed by the contact with this living woman. He felt her passion for him, her tenderness, her caring . . . and more than anything, he felt her need to be with him.

He leaned closer, his burning gaze mesmerizing her as he felt his own need flaring up inside him—a need to be with her.

"Bruce?" she whispered. "Answer me. Were you fighting again?"

He nodded. "That's part of what I didn't get a chance to tell you. Last night there were still people milling around at the party, and I didn't want to—"

"Just tell me now, then."

"I was in danger, Tori. I didn't want to have any contact

with you because I didn't want you to get hurt. But now it looks like the danger's over."

"Danger?" Suddenly she remembered the man sitting in the car on the street outside. She quickly rose from the sofa and strode to the curtained window.

"Tori, what are you looking for?"

"I saw a man sitting in a car, watching Rosegate. I think he's still there."

Bruce smiled. "I hope he is."

"What?"

"He's a cop, Tori. He's assigned to keep an eye on you. I insisted."

Tori shook her head. "Bruce, *please* explain what's going on!"

"I went to the district attorney's office last week. When I saw that Charlie had been murdered—"

"Charlie?"

"Charlene. She was a prostitute the Vonderant brothers were trying to set me up with. When I refused to go home with her, it seems they killed her and tried to frame me with the crime. They were going to use it as blackmail to force me to work for them and keep my mouth shut about their corruption."

"Oh, my God, Bruce!"

"It seems the DA's office was already wise to the Vonderants, but they needed more evidence. I agreed to wear a wire and get it on tape for them. Tonight it got a little rough, since I refused to back out of a bidding war for your aunt's Cemetery Library restoration job.

"They came on strong and I claimed to want a better deal, got them to spill their whole operation, name names. They should both be arrested very soon. The DA's got some other witness reporting in this week on their connections in the New Orleans Police Department. After that, they'll be behind bars."

"For heaven's sake, Bruce, you could have been killed!"

Bruce shrugged. "I couldn't let Zoe down. She gave me

the chance on restoring Duchamp's when the Vonderants started squeezing her. Zoe knew she could trust me."

"She did?"

Bruce nodded. "Apparently, Zoe knew my mother. I'm not sure how, she just said their paths had crossed a few times in the city, and Angelique used to talk about me."

"Well . . . that explains a lot."

"It does?"

"Zoe's been pushing me toward you from the beginning . . . although she's backed off considerably since."

Bruce laughed softly, recalling Zoe's latest theory on the applied forces to stubborn Duchamp women.

"Why are you laughing?"

"Oh, I don't know. I suppose I'm relieved it's all over."

"And so . . . are you going to stay?"

"I told you I was last night."

"No," said Tori softly. "Not in the city. Are you going to stay *now*." Her emerald eyes met his. "With me."

Bruce's brown gaze became liquid as it understood her meaning. He leaned closer, a small smile touching his lips.

"That depends," he whispered.

"On what?" Her hand went to his cheek, and he closed his eyes again to thoroughly enjoy the feel of that soft touch, the connection to her deep feelings for him.

"On where you'd like to make love first. . . ."

She smiled. "How about here?"

"Here, *chère*," he drawled low, "and now?"

Tori nodded.

"*Oui*," he whispered. "I t'ink I can agree to dat. . . ." Turning his head slightly, Bruce pressed his mouth to the inside of her wrist. "Mmmmm, honeysuckle . . ." And then he was kissing her palm and the tips of her fingers, and finally he was pulling her into his arms and tasting her lips with his.

She didn't stop him. Not in the least. It was what she wanted, what she needed. Her hands went to his head, tangling in his hair, and then his kiss turned hungry, his tongue impatient as it pushed through her lips to sample a sweet feminine flavor he'd been starving for every second, every minute of the past week.

Tori felt the cool stream of air, the tingling in her body, and knew the spirits were with them again. But she didn't care, because now, in the arms of *this* man, she could finally feel the passion, the caring, and the burning hunger that had been missing in the kiss she had shared earlier with Franklin.

For some indefinable reason, Bruce Gautreau was able to release all of her self-imposed impediments and unlock her closed heart to the most splendid joy she had ever felt.

The feeling went deeper than concrete logic, and beyond any notion of obvious attributes or lists of characteristics her father would approve of. There was no intellect to this feeling . . . only a kind of invisible magic. It was knowing without seeing; and seeing without sight. It was what Bruce had told her last night was blind faith. A thing that was pure and basic, and a choice that was all hers.

But, asked a tiny skeptical voice inside, *is it love?*

Whatever it was, Tori could see that like the shimmering image of the beautiful spirit, the room seemed to brighten with its presence—and she was going to enjoy it.

Bruce felt her opening to him as she wrapped her arms around him and sighed with contentment. Slowly he laid her back, reclining with her on the sofa. Her hands began to fumble with his clothes and his hands worked on hers.

Then he touched her, and when he found her ready and waiting, he smiled, because tonight he didn't want to wait. Closing his eyes, he lay between her legs and thrust himself as close to her as he could, in a place as primal as the beginning of life itself.

Tori's emerald eyes were glistening with tears as he moved inside of her. She smiled, then laughed with the pleasure, the freedom in allowing herself, finally, to want him so much.

"Why are you laughing?" he whispered, his own smile betraying his joy.

"Because I don't care anymore. . . ."

"Don't care?" asked Bruce, his eyes opening abruptly to stare worriedly into hers. "About what?"

"Being afraid."

"Of what, Tori?"

"Of loving you."

Bruce closed his eyes with the words. Then he opened them, stilling his movements inside her as he stared into her emerald eyes. "Say it again."

"I love you, Vianney Bruce Gautreau."

Bruce's hands tangled in her hair, and he kissed her with as great a passion as he'd ever felt. "And I love you, Victoria Adrianne Avalon."

"How did you know my middle—" But she stopped herself as he just smiled his mind-reader's smile, and then he was moving again.

She joined him in the dance to a primal rhythm. Faster and faster, higher and higher they moved, their bodies feeding the mounting tension, the mounting need, until they both reached a place where release was inevitable. Finally Bruce thrust deep into her and they both cried out at the joy of the irrevocable connection.

They clung to each other as their bodies shuddered with wave after wave of pleasure, the very blood through their veins tingling with the bliss of their shared exertions. At last Bruce fell against Tori, and she wrapped her arms around him. For long silent minutes they were breathing hard, yet still kissing and caressing, still mesmerized by each other's nearness.

"So," whispered Tori, brushing back his silky golden hair, "I've always wanted to ask you about that unusual first name of yours."

Bruce laughed. "Vianney?"

"Mmmmmm. Where did it come from—some old Cajun uncle?"

"Non, chère. Vianney was the name of Maman's favorite saint."

"Saint?"

"Oui. I was born on his August feast day, so I got nailed with the name."

"I see. And what sort of saint was this Vianney?"

"Oh, you want the whole rundown?"

"Of course."

"Well"—he smiled—"you asked for it. . . . Jean-Baptiste Vianney was born near Lyons, France, in the late eighteenth century—Maman made me memorize this from her Book of Saints—"

Tori laughed, enjoying the playful smile on his lips, the slight lines at the corner of his brown eyes.

"—anyway, good ol' Saint Vianney supposedly excelled at counseling, both inside and outside confession, because his insights into personal difficulties, as the Book puts it, were helped by supernatural gifts of prophecy and reading the secrets of the heart—"

"Secrets of the heart?"

"Oui, mademoiselle, that's what the book says, cross my own heart."

"This biography sounds rather suspicious."

"Hey, why do you think I go by Bruce?"

"Do you really hate Vianney?"

"Not at all, but it was my mother's choice to name me Vianney and call me Bruce."

"I don't understand."

"I didn't at first, either. But now I think I do. She wanted me baptized with a name that would always remind me of my gift, yet she identified me with a name that allowed me some distance from it. I think she knew how hard life would be for me as a sensitive."

"Has it been so hard?"

Bruce sighed. "Sometimes. For a while I wanted nothing to do with the gift at all, but then I realized I was rejecting half of who I was—living half a life and half a lie. So I decided to keep looking for a way to make my life work, my whole life."

"I see," said Tori, still playing with his hair. "And . . . have you found a way?"

Bruce dipped his head enough to brush his lips across Tori's. "What I've found is enough light to show me the way."

"Is it going to be enough?" she asked softly.

"Mmmm. I don't know how easy it will be with me, Tori, but I'm willing to try if you are."

"What are you asking me, Bruce?"

"I'm asking you to try to make it work with me."

"Yes," she said softly. "I'm willing to try."

Chapter
Twenty-two

"So, Bruce, how do you know this ghost reader, exactly? You never told me," called Tori from the master bedroom's bath. She'd just stepped from her morning shower and was wrapping a towel around her naked torso. Bruce was still relaxing in the antique bed, his arms behind his head.

"My mother knew Serafine while she was growing up here."

"Your mother was from New Orleans?" asked Tori as she walked into the bedroom and began dressing. Bruce smiled, enjoying the sight of her long bare legs stepping into a lacy pair of underwear in the sunwashed room.

"Bruce?" She turned to see the look in his eyes. "Don't get distracted now." She smiled.

"Come over here and say that."

"No way, I've got a lot to do today. So tell me how your mother ended up leaving the city. . . ."

"Angelique met my father, Paul, when he was raising

hell here one Mardi Gras, and they fell in love. Well, as they tell it, it was quite clearly lust first and love later. His home was in Cajun country, so she followed him there."

"And you met Serafine through your mother?" asked Tori, slipping a sundress over her head.

"Yeah, *Maman* would visit the city regularly, and I tagged along. So, Tori, where are you rushing off to exactly?"

"Oh, to see my aunt and do another thing. . . ."

Bruce's gaze narrowed. "And *another thing* is seeing Franklin Morgan?"

"Stop reading my mind, Bruce."

"Can't help it."

Tori turned from putting in her earrings to glare at him. "Try."

"Why are you seeing Morgan, Tori?"

"I need to finalize the sale of the window."

Bruce sat up and rubbed his forehead. "Tori, please don't attempt to use subterfuge. It's not going to work with us if you aren't honest with me."

Tori sighed heavily as she began to towel and comb her damp hair in front of the armoire's full-length mirror. "Bruce, are you telling me our relationship is going to be based on one-hundred percent honesty one-hundred percent of the time?"

"Yes," he said, snapping the covers back from the bed, grabbing up his sweatpants, and stepping into them.

"That's not only unfair, but it's impossible."

"Why is it unfair?" he asked, placing his hands on her shoulders and spinning her to face him.

"Because only *one* of us can read minds!"

"Then I guess you'll just have to learn."

"Don't be ridiculous," she said, turning back to the mirror.

"I'm not being ridiculous," insisted Bruce, "and I still want to know why you're going to see Franklin?"

Tori shook her head, then she stared into Bruce's eyes. "You tell me?"

"It's *more* than the business with the stained-glass window. I can feel it."

"If it is, then you know more than I do."

"Ah, Tori, are you this fickle?"

"No, Bruce, I'm not. I do love you. It's just that I need to see Franklin again. I left things unresolved with him."

"So, what are you telling me?" snapped Bruce, his strong arms crossing his broad chest.

"I'm telling you to give me a little breathing room. I can see loving a mind reader isn't going to be easy. But as I told you, I'm willing to try." She stepped closer and placed her soft palm against his face, still rough from morning stubble. "I have to try. I love you. But, Bruce, you have to try, too. Try to trust me."

"Okay," he said, turning his lips to kiss her palm, but as he did, a dark vision was moving quickly through his mind. He saw Tori laughing, and Franklin Morgan's arm around her. Bruce knew instinctively that it was a moment in the near future, but he said nothing to Tori as she finished getting ready to go.

After she left the room, he closed his eyes and sat down heavily on the bed. Bruce finally realized something in that moment. He had always condemned his mother for remaining in love with a man who had been unfaithful to her. But now Bruce was beginning to understand something about both his mother and his father: They'd put together a life that had worked for them. It hadn't been perfect, but it had been the best they could do.

Bruce had always been angry with his father for taking a job that led him away from their bayou home—and his lovesick mother. And yet, for the first time, Bruce was beginning to understand how difficult it may have been for his father, how overwhelming loving a sensitive might be.

And if his mother loved Paul Gautreau as much as Bruce was beginning to love Tori, then he could also see how Angelique had grown to accept Paul's occasional straying. Loving her husband had been more important to Angelique than her pride. But, God, thought Bruce, it must have been a painful existence.

Bruce rubbed his tired eyes as his own credo of self-protection echoed cruelly in his ears. *1) Thou shalt not lose control. 2) Thou shalt not fall in love. 3) Thou shalt not stick around long enough to risk either of the above. . . .*

He'd violated every damn one.

Yeah, for the first time, Bruce was left wide open, without protection. He didn't like it. Not one bit. But over and above his own fear of emotional pain, Bruce feared taking the woman he loved down a path that would lead to her emotional agony.

"Oh, *Maman,*" breathed Bruce into the empty sun-washed room, "Have I made a terrible mistake?

Although the morning had dawned bright and sunny, the day gradually became overcast with thick, heavy clouds. A drizzle of warm rain began over the Quarter in the late afternoon, and as Tori made her way back to Rosegate at twilight, thunder began to roll in on the steady current of the Mississippi, bringing with it a layer of sultry mist.

Tori cursed softly when she looked at her watch. It was so late. Bruce was probably waiting for her. But what could she do? She'd missed Zoe entirely this morning, and when she'd dropped in on Franklin to finalize the window's sale, he'd insisted on taking her to lunch. She'd never expected to be eating it on a yacht docked in Lake Pontchartrain.

Cal Laurence had been there, also, and at one point during their afternoon, Franklin had taken Tori aside to tell her how much she'd impressed the Chicago businessman.

"Laurence is talking about offering you a little position based here," said Franklin. "This is quite an opportunity."

"Really? What sort of position?"

"Hospitality, after a fashion. You'll be a sort of hostess for him—and perhaps some of his friends—whenever he comes into town. A guide, so to speak, for the local attractions."

"Really? That sounds quite lucrative. I mean, Rosegate will be an operational Guest House by next year."

"Yes, of course."

"What should I do, Franklin?"

"Just humor him," he advised, curling an arm around her waist. "He does like you, Tori, and he's quite a powerful man. Let him take you to dinner Saturday evening. He'll discuss the particulars then."

Tori was only too happy to agree. It looked as if things were going just fine. But on her way home the more she thought about Rosegate finally being finished, the more worried she became about the ghosts.

If she was going to run a *reputable* lodging, she'd need to be certain that guests' perfume bottles weren't going to start flying off in all directions and that naked ghost women wouldn't start appearing in bedrooms, terrifying paying customers.

Tori entered the dark house and closed the heavy front door behind her. As she started for the staircase, she began brushing the rain from her damp hair. Her French twist was falling and she became irritated, struggling to keep it in place.

"So. Here you are."

Tori's movements stilled. The male voice had come from the dark shadows of the parlor. For a terrible split-second she thought it was the ghost of Robert Le Pelletier.

"I've been waiting for you. . . ."

"Bruce . . ." she breathed in relief. She walked to the parlor entrance and stared into the shadows. A small red glow floated in the air, and Tori saw that it belonged to the end of a cigar. The drapes were drawn across every tall window except one at the far end of the room, which was pulled wide open. Thunder sounded softly in the distance.

"You were with him," said the shadowy figure standing near the open window.

"Yes." Tori tried not to become defensive, even though his tone was unfairly accusatory.

"Why?"

"Because he's a good associate to have."

"He's a liar, and I don't trust him."

"Look . . ." Tori took a deep breath. "I think maybe your jealousy is clouding your ability to see the man clearly."

"Tori—"

"No, Bruce, I asked you to give me some breathing room. Now, listen to me, Franklin will help me find the *right* sort of guests for Rosegate. He's already gotten me a chance at a position working for a well-connected Chicago businessman. It could mean a good deal of income."

"And what about your teaching French at the girl's academy this fall? When we first met, you said it was a job you looked forward to—"

"It won't pay."

There was a long silence. "You said it would make you happy."

Tori swallowed uneasily. For a long moment she simply watched Bruce's shadowy form take a long drag on the cigar and then blow out a white cloud of smoke. Finally he spoke again: "I thought you said you were going to end things with Morgan."

"I don't see why I can't be his friend. I mean, the man didn't exactly chart out some kind of relationship with me, Bruce. I'd look ridiculously melodramatic telling him we had to *end* something that never even began. And as I said, he's a good connection to keep. You know, networking and all that . . ."

Bruce again took a drag on the cigar, the next smoke cloud joining the first one in an airy dance. It unnerved her a moment; the white haze seemed to take on a bizarre shape, reminding her of the spirit she'd seen in this very room.

"I've also been thinking about the ghosts," said Tori.

"What about them?"

"They'll have to go," she said shortly. "Are you going to bring your friend by?"

"She's here."

"Here? Now?"

"Yes, I've put her in one of the second-floor furnished guest rooms. She's about seventy years old, and she needs to rest before she attempts to work as an oracle."

"Oracle?"

Bruce nodded. "The ghosts of our ancestors will speak through her. She'll start at midnight."

"Fine. Then I'll take a rest, too. Maybe she can help to exorcise them or whatever. . . ."

"What's going on, Tori?" Bruce moved slowly across the room.

"What?"

"First you want to get rid of the stained-glass window—"

"I need the money, Bruce."

"And now you want to get rid of the ghosts—"

"It's practical!"

"And I get the feeling, Tori, that the next item on your list of Things To Get Rid Of—"

"Bruce, don't."

His form stepped out of the darkness to stand toe-to-toe with her. She could see his handsome face, the lines of worry, the eyes a bright, honest glare in the dark house. She felt his gaze doing its best to pierce her soul.

It was too much, too intense.

Tori released a sigh of agitation, then turned sharply, heading for the stairs. Part of her expected him to stop her. But he didn't. He just stood there, letting her walk away.

"I have to change," she called softly from the stairs.

Bruce felt something rip into him at her words. "Do you?" he whispered. "Or have you already?"

Hours later the three of them met near midnight in Rosegate's large front parlor. Tori didn't honestly know what she expected of a Voodoo priestess—someone weirdly off-the-wall maybe, a witchlike New Ager with eccentric clothes and a wild look in her eyes.

She felt thoroughly ashamed of her assumptions when, near midnight, Serafine Beltremieux descended Rosegate's stairs. The elegant, educated, and well-spoken mulatto woman was warm, gracious, and quite attractive.

Serafine did not look her age at all, but twenty years younger. Her caramel-colored skin was still supple, her figure, draped in a stylish ivory pantsuit, was full but still attractively curved, and her smile was infectious.

Tori immediately noticed her eyes. They were a darker brown than Bruce's—almost black—but, like his, were clear and bright as if twin candle flames were burning in their depths. There was also a kind of liquid shine to them, and Tori wondered if it was a shared characteristic of their gift of psychic sight.

"Serafine's been a *mam'bo* for over forty years," Bruce told Tori as he introduced them in the parlor.

"Pardon me," said Tori. "A what?"

Serafine laughed. "A *mam'bo* is like a mother," she explained, a soft Southern lilt to her melodious voice. "It's not unlike your calling a Catholic priest 'Father.'"

"Oh, yes, of course."

"But unlike a priest, we do not answer to Rome. Each *mam'bo,* or in the case of a man, each *houn'gan,* answers to his or her own connection to the spiritual powers of the invisible."

"I understand."

"Do you?" asked Bruce with a quirked eyebrow.

"Well, I'm trying. . . ."

"You see, Tori," said Serafine, sitting on the sofa. "One explanation of Voodoo might be in the etymology of the word itself. *Vo* means 'introspection' and *du* means 'into the unknown.'"

"So it's a mystical religion, then?"

"Religions, if they are worth anything," said Serafine, "are by nature mystical. We call it *faith* for a reason, my child. If we could see life's answers easily, then we would not need to have it."

"What about the charms and the black magic?" asked Tori.

Bruce brought out a small cloth pouch from his pocket. "You mean like this?"

"What's that?"

"My mother made this for me," explained Bruce. "It's a *gris-gris* bag."

"*Gris-gris?*" Tori's brow wrinkled.

"Yes, *gris* is French for 'gray,' " pointed out Bruce.

"I know, but what is it used for?"

Serafine smiled. "A *gris-gris* is a charm that can be made to ward off evil or aid any number of problems."

Bruce nodded. "Men wear *gris-gris* on their right side, women on their left—that's what my mother always told me, anyway. She made this one for me for overall protection."

"That's a common one," said Serafine. "I've made many in my day for many different purposes. Some for people addicted to gambling or alcohol, others for out-of-work people who wanted to find jobs, for young lovers who said they had broken hearts . . ."

"I'm not sure I get it," said Tori. "I mean, what exactly does the *gris-gris* do for these people?"

"Come here, Tori," said Serafine, patting the spot beside her on the sofa. "You see, child, you may think your hands are empty—" She took Tori's hands and held them palm up in her own. "Perhaps you are desiring money or power, control or love. And so you believe your hands are in need of these. They are wanting, desirous, desperately reaching out."

Tori's green eyes widened as she listened.

"So the *mam'bo* prepares a special *gris-gris* bag," said Serafine as she gestured to Bruce's bag. "Inside the bag are charms that give the power to fulfill these desires."

Tori nodded.

"The *mam'bo* takes these grasping, needing hands, the black void, the darkness. And into them she places the power to answer those needs, the white magic, the light." Serafine crooked a finger at Bruce and he leaned close. She then took Bruce's hand and placed it over Tori's.

Bruce's brown eyes studied Tori as the soft *gris-gris* bag dropped into her empty, upturned palms. Bruce lifted his hand, and Serafine helped close Tori's fingers tightly around the little worn, handmade bag.

"You see, my child, when you mix the white magic into the black void, what it is that you get?"

Tori's emerald eyes lifted from the soft bag in her hands to the dark, shining eyes of the *mam'bo*.

"Gray," she whispered.

"That's right," whispered Serafine. "It's a difficult idea for some. Voodoo doesn't separate good and evil, black and white. In that way it's like modern psychology—seeing the good and evil as part of a whole, two sides of the same coin."

"So," reasoned Tori, "you're saying that we have the power within us to fulfill our needs? And the spells and charms are just a way to—"

"To tap into our own unseen power. Yes, my child. You see, we are all part of the ebb and flow of life. It is easy, in our modern world, to believe we are disconnected from everything around us, that we are without meaning, without worth, and without power. But we are all spiritual beings, existing in a world of forces—some seen, others unseen. And the unseen can be the most powerful force we may ever know."

Tori nodded in understanding and fascination. She held on to the little bag in her hand, liking the warmth that still clung to it from living so long in Bruce's pocket.

She looked back into Serafine's eyes. "And what about the unseen in this house?"

"The spirits. Yes, Bruce tells me they are your ancestors?"

"We think so."

"Tori wants to get rid of them," said Bruce flatly.

"No!" said Tori suddenly, her gaze flying to Bruce's face.

"No?" asked Bruce. "But earlier you said—"

"I know what I said, but . . ." Tori looked to Serafine.

"I'd like to know more about them first. To know why they're here."

Serafine nodded and smiled. "Then we shall begin."

As Serafine prepared her materials, Tori moved toward Bruce. She didn't want to let go of the *gris-gris* bag, but she felt that it rightfully belonged to him. She held it out, and he looked at it for a long moment, hesitating to take it back. But then, silently, he did, quickly returning it to his pant's pocket without looking at her.

"It is time," said Serafine.

Tori watched in fascination as Serafine went to a large bag and began taking items out. She positioned a number of white candles in a circle around them and one in the center of the circle. Then she placed statuary out and lit the candles.

"White candles burn to protect the participants from evil," said Serafine. "The statue of the Virgin Mary brings added protection and sanctifies the space."

"Why a Catholic icon?" Tori whispered to Bruce.

"Voodoo is a mixture of African and Catholic faiths," whispered Bruce. "The West African slaves developed it as they were forced to adopt the faith of their European masters."

"Ah . . . I see . . . and the other icon?"

"This is Legba," said Serafine, hearing Tori's question. "He is an African god. The master of the crossroads. He opens the way for us to pass into the realm of the invisible."

She brought out a cigar and a bottle of rum. "Let's move the furniture back. We shall sit on the floor in a circle."

They did. And then Serafine began the ceremony. "Like all religion, Tori, Voodoo has its prayers. I will begin first with prayers, and then I will begin my meditation."

"I understand."

Serafine smiled. "Bruce, you may explain to her as we go."

"*Oui, madame,*" he said with a slight bow of his head.

Tori watched in fascination as Serafine placed a piece of

paper on the floor, then drew a design on it with flour. Tori was reminded of the crosshatch chalk she and Bruce had encountered weeks ago on the backporch.

Serafine then rose and blew the remainder of the flour in four directions. Then she crossed herself, mumbling words.

Next she lit a cigar and blew the smoke in four directions.

"She's cleansing the area," whispered Bruce. "East, west, north and south."

She then poured rum into a glass. She took a mouthful and again turned in all four directions, blowing the rum out through her teeth.

"Papa Legba, ouvri barrie pou nous passer...."

"She's asking the Voodoo god Legba to open the way for us to pass," whispered Bruce softly in Tori's ear.

Serafine then looked at them. "Please pray with me the Hail Mary."

They did and then Serafine asked them to sit down and join hands. She closed her eyes. "In the name of God the Father, God the Son, and God the Holy Ghost, in the name of Mary, in the name of Jesus, in the name of all the saints, and especially Saint Jean-Baptiste Vianney, and in the name of all the dead, grant us success in our undertaking, grant us the ear to hear what we must hear, the power to understand...."

Tori felt a chill envelop her as Serafine continued to pray. The room itself was becoming colder and colder, and a familiar tingling was spreading through Tori's body. She looked for reassurance to Bruce, but his eyes were closed, his face tilted up.

She felt alone all of a sudden, the only blind woman in a room of seers, alone and confused in her lack of awareness. To Tori, it seemed part of a darkness she felt had enveloped her all of her life. Suddenly she felt herself wanting nothing more than a chance, finally, to see ... to *really* see. . . .

The candles around them seemed to be flickering as if a draft were blowing through the room. But no windows were now opened, and there was no draft that she could feel.

Tori began to close her own eyes, and a strange blackness overcame her, darker than merely closing her eyes. Suddenly an image came to her mind. That same image that had been haunting her for days. A violin smashing violently against the wall, shattering, then splintering into many pieces.

The hands around the violin's neck, choking the neck, were the hands of her father. It was her mother's violin, realized Tori again. And Coco Duchamp Avalon was standing there in the room, watching the destruction, then placing her face in her hands and crying. . . .

"I hear crying," said Bruce softly.

Tori's eyes opened and the room was suddenly darker. Two corner lamps were outside of their circle of candles. One had gone dark and the other was flickering.

"I feel them," whispered Serafine.

A moment later the second lamp's bulb shattered. Now the room was only lit by candle flames. A draft was now present in the room; a cool stream of air flowed around them and across the candles, making their individual fires crackle and dance with low whispering flickers.

Thunder rumbled again in the distance, and rain began to beat down on the house. Tori couldn't believe it, but she could actually hear the distant sound of drums . . . just like her dreams.

"Do you hear the drums?" asked Tori.

Bruce squeezed her hand in answer.

"Good spirits," said Serafine aloud, "for I can feel that you are good and that you do not mean any harm . . . I have summoned you to ask about your purpose and your wishes. These good people with me would like to know: What is it that you want?"

Serafine's eyes remained tightly shut, her breathing seemed labored. She nodded her head silently. "The spirits say they wish to see their destiny fulfilled."

"Their destiny?" asked Bruce. "Ask them who they are. We need to make sure."

Serafine did. "They are Robert Le Pellitier and his bride Marina Duchamp Le Pellitier. They say they were murdered in this house . . . that the stained-glass window in this room was Robert's wedding gift to Marina."

Tori gasped in shock.

"What do they want?" asked Bruce. "Are they here for revenge?"

"No," said Serafine. "They do not seek revenge. They wish to cause no harm. They only seek fulfillment of their destiny."

"But what does that mean?" asked Tori.

Serafine continued to concentrate, but she said nothing more. The candle flames stopped flickering. Gradually the room began to warm again. The draft was gone.

Serafine opened her dark, shining eyes. "They have left us."

"Yes," said Bruce.

She turned to him. "Did you hear their voices, Bruce?"

Bruce shook his head. "I heard nothing."

"Not in your ears, Vianney, in your head, in your mind."

Bruce closed his eyes a moment. "Near the end, there was something."

"Try to recall," urged Serafine.

"It was a man's voice," said Bruce.

"What did it say?" asked Tori.

Bruce opened his eyes and looked at Tori. "I can't remember."

Tori knew at once. "You're lying."

Bruce blinked. *How can she know that?*

"I know," said Tori.

"Tori?" Bruce couldn't believe it. Was she reading *his* thoughts now?

Tori's emerald eyes looked at Bruce, then to Serafine. The older woman was smiling broadly.

"What's going on here?" asked Bruce.

"She is opening her mind," said Serafine. "And when we open our minds, all things are possible."

Chapter
Twenty-three

Within an hour the three ascended the stairs to retire for the night. As Tori said good night and headed for the master bedroom, Bruce walked Serafine to her room down the hall.

"Thank you again, Serafine, for coming."

"It was my pleasure, Vianney," she said. "Now that we are alone, I must tell you that I have gotten the sense that there is danger coming to this place."

Bruce nodded. "I can feel it, too."

"Won't you tell me what the ghost of Robert said to you?" she asked.

Bruce looked over his shoulder to make sure Tori had gone into the master bedroom. "I think we should keep it to ourselves, *madame*."

"As you wish, but he gave you the message in private. I did not hear."

"It was only two words," he said softly. *"Marry her."*

"Ah, I see. That is how they wish to fulfill their destinies, then, through you and Tori."

"Oui."

"And you do not wish to marry this lovely girl, Vianney?"

"I doubt we can make it work."

"Don't you love her?"

"Oui, I do. Very much."

"Then you must find answers through the love, not the fear."

When Serafine saw that he was unconvinced, she placed her hand on his shoulder. "Vianney Gautreau, I remember you in your youth. You were so full of righteousness, so full of anger. You could not readily see where the path before you led, and so you refused to start down it."

Bruce sighed, but Serafine merely gave him a wise smile. "Today, Vianney, I have seen that you at last are accepting the things that are beyond the human eye, beyond the wood and concrete that you have made your life's work. I'm so very pleased to see that you've accepted your gift—"

"Yes, but—"

"All your destiny requires is that you simply open your mind and stop running from the paths before you," said Serafine. Then her eyes peered sharply into his. "But you've not decided to stop running, have you?"

Bruce knew he was being read by this wise older woman, and he couldn't deny her vision. "No," he said, "I don't know if I've stopped running. I've been served well by moving on."

"Perhaps it is time for you to stay. To pursue a course even though you cannot see where it will lead."

Bruce shook his head. "What good is a seer who can't see what's in front of him? It's too overwhelming, Serafine. Please understand, I'm happy that I was able to help Tori grow stronger. But now I can see that she needs space to find her own path—and maybe I do, too. I'll make sure that any danger coming to Rosegate is past, but then I'm going to end it. Cut myself off from her. For my good as much as hers."

Serafine was not happy, but Bruce gave her a hug, thanked her once more, then turned to go. And as he shut the door to her guest room, he looked up to see Tori standing a few feet away in her white nightgown and robe.

She had heard it all, he realized. Her face was cool and controlled, but her green eyes were bright with fury. She looked as if she were about to say something, but then she stopped herself. In the next instant she was turning to flee.

Bruce strode after her, but she was moving too fast, racing down the stairs and out the back kitchen door. He didn't catch up with her until she reached the fresh-cut grass of the enclosed rear grounds.

"You son of a—"

"Tori, calm down."

"So you made the decision to end it all by yourself, right? Was I even going to get a good-bye, or were you just going to be gone one day when I stopped by your apartment?"

"I was going to say good-bye."

"Bastard!"

"Tori, please . . ."

"Why, Bruce? Why? I *love* you, don't you understand that?"

Bruce placed his hands on his hips and took a deep breath of warm, moist air. "I understand it," he said softly.

Tori felt her heart pounding hard in her chest. She was expecting it to break, and herself to break into a million pieces, just like she had with Edward. But this wasn't like Edward at all, she realized. Not at all . . .

She stared at Bruce and realized, really realized, that she never actually *loved* Edward. She had felt something, but it had been born out of vain wishes and a desperate need for approval. It hadn't been love. She knew that with certainty now, because she knew for certain that *this* was.

Tori didn't want to be with Bruce to meet her father's or even her mother's expectations; she didn't want to be with him to validate some missing or failed part of herself. Tori wanted to be with Bruce simply because she felt *alive* when she was with him. He reached some part of herself, deep inside, that she didn't even know was there—and whatever it was he'd found inside of her, it seemed to make her whole.

"Bruce," she whispered. "Do you want to leave because you don't really love me?"

"Ah, God . . ." Bruce put a hand to his forehead. He looked at Tori standing there in the moon's eternal reflection of the sun's brilliance, her eyes bright with expectation, with hope, her lovely face and form kissed by silver light. "Tori, don't you understand, I need to leave *because* I love you."

Tori stepped close to him, she placed her hands tenderly to the sides of his face. "Then just love me, Bruce. Why is that so complicated? Just love me. Right now . . ."

Bruce's arms wrapped around her and pulled her soft body against his hard, strong form. He dipped his golden head down, and Tori's mouth opened like a blossom drinking in rain.

Slowly Bruce brushed the petal-soft surface of her lips. When she flicked the tip of her tongue against him, it set off an instant chain reaction through his already-tense body.

In a sudden torrent of need, the floodgates opened up for them both. Tori's fingers went to his shirt, urgently undoing buttons. Then they flew to the snap of his jeans. Unlike a week ago, when she blushed at the sound of his descending zipper, Tori couldn't wait to reveal him. She was thrilled to unmask his most basic desire; free his deepest longing.

Her soft hands caressed him with an empowering feeling of mastery, glorying in knowing that at least for this brief moment, he could not refute his need for her.

Bruce's eyes closed at the exquisite torture that Tori was inflicting. He couldn't withstand it long, though, and within moments he took her beautiful body in his arms and leaned her back, laying her gently in the night shadows of the wet garden grass.

Now that the rain had stopped, the freshly washed garden was sweet with the perfume of white roses. He breathed in the sweet scent as his fingers fumbled with her robe belt. He wanted her so much that he could hardly keep his hands steady. Quickly he drew up the sheer fabric of the long nightgown beneath the robe, exposing her shapely bare legs to the sultry night air.

When his trembling fingers found her more than ready for him, he wasted no time. Kneeling between her legs, he thrust forward hard, his hands coming down on either side of her shoulders, his gaze burning into her eyes as he filled her with what she wanted, what she needed.

And he needed it, too. Oh, how he needed it!

Moving against her in the rain-washed grass, he felt their bodies becoming slick with moisture. He closed his eyes as they moved faster against each other. Their movements were frantic, almost savage, as they both desperately clung to the thing they most wanted, yet were both about to lose.

He didn't last long. After only a few short minutes, the tension was near bursting within him. Her sudden soft cry in his ear triggered his own desperate moan, an expression of the shattering release that mingled with her own in the night garden.

Bruce kissed Tori and immediately rolled onto his back, his eyes closing. When they opened, he found himself staring up at the cloudy night.

For a split second, Bruce seemed to spy a break in the haze. He could almost see the clear sky miles above, where the bright stars were shining. But the glimpse of clarity was only brief. The clouds quickly returned.

Bruce fastened his clothes back around him, then lifted Tori into his arms and carried her into the mansion and up the stairs. After softly kicking open the master bedroom door, he laid her gently in the center of the four-poster bed.

But Tori's initial joy was soon turning to panic. Bruce wasn't getting in beside her, He was turning to go!

"Bruce—"

"I can't stay," he said softly.

"If you're really going to leave me," she said, her words stopping him at the open bedroom door, "then let's do it *now*. I can't take the agony of waiting for *you* to decide when."

Bruce's back stiffened, but he didn't turn around. "Don't push me, Victoria," he said, his jaw tight.

"No," she said. "Up until last night, you always said you were going to leave. So if you're going to do it, then this is good-bye right here and now."

"And that's all right with you?"

"I thought you could read minds," she snapped, angry and hurt, and at the end of her rope with trying to reach him.

Bruce could feel her love for him, but he could also feel her hesitation, her fear of loving him completely, with all her heart and soul.

She was too afraid of being hurt to allow herself to let go. And Bruce knew in his heart that he felt the same.

There was just no way they could ever make their life work as long as they were both holding back—it would be a terrible life. A life of suspicion, of jealousy, of second-guessing. A life that would eventually tear down anything that they could ever build.

Bruce reached into his pocket. He turned and walked to the bed, then took her hand in his. "Good-bye then, Tori," he said, then placed his soft *gris-gris* bag in her palm.

As Tori watched him go, she was unprepared for the revelation that followed. Vianney Bruce Gautreau was actually leaving, and as that agonizing fact registered on Tori's numb mind, she felt something inside of her breaking.

But it wasn't her heart.

Miraculously, it was something else that she felt breaking—but not breaking exactly, more like breaking down. . . .

As Tori's fingers tightened around the small, worn *gris-gris* bag, her mind took hold of a realization: Now that she was losing this man, she was becoming aware of just how much she loved him.

It wasn't a love that tapped a mere part of herself—while another part remained safely hidden behind a wall of protection. No, this love was something she never even knew existed. It not only encompassed *all* of her heart, but every last particle of her soul.

Chapter
Twenty-four

"Aunt Zoe, I need to know something."

Tori had found her aunt the next morning. The older woman was busy readying Duchamp's for the luncheon crowd, but when she saw the look of distress on her niece's face, Zoe stopped working immediately. She brought Tori to a back office and poured her a cup of coffee.

"Okay," said Zoe. "I'm listening."

"Why did my mother own a violin?"

At Tori's question, Zoe's face turned chalk white, and for a terrible split second, Tori was worried she'd given her aunt a heart attack. "Aunt Zoe? Are you all right?"

"Y-yes . . . yes . . ." Zoe took a deep breath and then a sip of coffee. "Why are you asking me, Victoria?"

Tori had never heard this high-pitched tone of near panic in her aunt before. It shocked her.

"I had a sort of . . . well, a vision. Or maybe it's just a memory playing itself back. My father is smashing a violin against a wall. And I know the instrument belongs to my mother—but I also know she doesn't *play* the violin. And she's crying and crying, and I don't know why. . . ."

Zoe wrung her hands. "Tori, I'm going to tell you something now. It's a thing that Coco, your mother, asked me never to reveal."

"Then . . . are you sure you should?" asked Tori, shifting apprehensively.

Zoe nodded her head. "I've thought a lot about this. The other night, at the party, Bruce told me something that I can't get out of my mind—"

"What?"

"He pointed out to me that Coco didn't know *then* what you might need to know *now*. Sugar, I'm the one who must make the decision regarding what you need to know today, regardless of what I'd promised your mother years ago."

Tori leaned forward with interest. "And? What is it that I need to know?"

"It's Stanton Avalon."

"Yes?"

"He isn't your real father."

"What?!" Tori nearly dropped her coffee cup.

"It's true, dear," whispered Zoe. "I'm sorry."

Tori slammed her cup so hard onto its saucer that it cracked. Coffee seeped out onto the desk, staining some papers there, but neither woman cared a fig. "My God, Aunt Zoe, what are you saying?"

"Your mother fell in love with Stanton Avalon's facade, but she *never* should have married him." Zoe rose from her chair and began to pace the small office, wringing her hands. "I can't even say that the only good thing that came out of it was you—because you didn't."

Tori sighed in frustration. "But then how did—" She stopped a moment to try to steady her shaking voice. "What happened?"

The older woman was still pacing. "Coco always liked the idea of social climbing," she explained, "and I was always warning her to be careful. She hated that, accused me of being a hypocrite because I liked rubbing elbows at the best balls and with the best people as much as her. But, you see, Tori, I knew the difference between the pretense and the reality. I knew how to look behind the masks people wore. Coco didn't. She was so easily led, so easily fooled—"

"She was?"

"Yes. I'm sorry to speak ill of her. You must understand that I loved her dearly. Our mother died while she was still young and I felt responsible—maybe that's why she resisted me so, but I think a lot of it was simply in her nature. Anyway, Tori, I always knew that social acceptance couldn't hold a candle to real love. I tried to tell Coco. It's like comparing a match flame to a hearth—one goes out at the slightest puff, the other warms for a lifetime."

"Aunt Zoe, what in hell happened?"

"I came home one summer from studying in Paris, and I brought a half-dozen French friends with me. Pierre was one. He was nobody then . . . it took him years to become the renowned chef he is today. But back then he was still learning from established master chefs. He stayed for the summer and started working at one of the finer restaurants. That's when we first fell in love—"

"You and . . . Pierre?" asked Tori, surprised.

For the first time that morning, Zoe smiled. "Yes, Tori. He and I have been in love for years."

"But . . . why didn't you ever . . ."

"Get married?"

"Yes."

She shook her head. "Some loves are not cut out for traditional matrimony, my dear. But I assure you, our love has stood the test of time—not to mention the hellacious vagaries of food service!"

"Oh, Aunt," said Tori, a smile finally touching her lips as well. "I'm happy for you . . . but what about my mother?"

"Yes," said Zoe, her smile fading. "There was another young Frenchman who came to spend the summer as well. His name was Armand. He was a musician—"

"A *musician?*"

"Yes, he was terribly gifted."

"And he played—"

"—the violin. Armand was instantly smitten with Coco. They had a brief affair, and you were conceived. Armand left, not knowing he'd fathered a daughter, and Coco continued in her marriage, which by that time she knew had been a grave mistake."

Tori took a deep breath, trying to comprehend that her father, her flesh and blood, had been a gifted musician from France. Not a coldhearted lawyer living in New York City.

"Did Stanton know?" asked Tori finally.

"Not at first. He is listed on your birth certificate, and he did not shirk the legal responsibility when he discovered later that you were not his."

"How did he—"

"He suspected. He had tests done. Behind Coco's back."

"Why didn't mother leave him?"

"She wanted to, especially when she realized how bad it had become. But Stanton was determined to hold on to your mother. I think, in the end, his pride wanted to take some vengeance out on her, and I suppose in his business it was better to have the facade of a happy marriage. Divorce meant instability. He could always fool around on the side, you see, and he eventually did."

"Oh, Zoe . . ."

"Your mother mentioned divorce, but Stanton was a powerful attorney. He threatened to take you away, and Coco didn't fight him, even though I urged her to."

Tori's head was spinning. "But Stanton didn't threaten to take me because he *wanted* me?"

"No," said Zoe softly. "What he wanted was to control your mother. Punish her. And she wanted to protect you, so she went to New York, and she ended up drinking herself to death. She killed herself, Tori, not consciously in one stroke, but carelessly—out of despair."

Tori shook her head in silence for long minutes. Tears

welled up in her eyes as she realized how much heartache her mother had endured for so long.

"Stanton Avalon never wanted me because I wasn't his daughter," whispered Tori, her voice raw. "It had *nothing* to do with who I was. It had *nothing* to do with my *measuring up*. . . ."

"No," said Zoe softly. "I should have told you. I should have. But you seemed all right. Hestia and Richard insisted that you didn't have to know. That it would only disturb you, make it seem as though you were losing a father, too, after you'd already lost a mother."

"But what about my *real* father, what about Armand?"

"Tori, I'm so sorry, but he died in a motorcycle accident. Seven years after you were born. . . ."

"And the violin? Did Armand give my mother his violin?"

Zoe nodded.

"My God," breathed Tori. "Father—I mean *Stanton*—smashed it to bits when Mother brought it out. I was seven years old. I remember now. She must have been grieving for Armand's death and brought it out to remind herself. . . . Oh, Zoe . . ."

"If only Coco had tried harder to break away, to fight him for your custody. If only she had had your strength, Tori."

"*My* strength?"

"Yes, look at you. You're so strong, making your own life for yourself."

Tori never thought of herself as particularly strong before. She always felt as if she were ready to break into a million pieces. She always thought strength was something that everyone else possessed. . . .

"Stay strong, Tori, and don't give up on following your heart. It's easy to go along with what other people tell you to desire. It's much harder to discover for yourself what you truly want your life to be. You don't know how many times I wished that Coco had understood that. I *know* she would still be with us now if she had."

*   *   *

"Good day."

Tori Avalon opened Rosegate's front door that afternoon to find the perfect picture of a Southern gentleman. "Franklin. Won't you come in?"

"Thank you."

Tori led him into the parlor. "I'd like to talk with you."

"Of course," he said, smiling at her, that same pleasant smile he always had. He sat down on the sofa, and Tori sat in a nearby chair.

She noticed his hand going to the top of his hand-painted silk tie, the thumb and forefinger adjusting the already perfectly adjusted Windsor knot.

He's nervous, realized Tori. *Why?*

"Franklin, I realize that you're enamored of the window—"

"Oh, yes. I am," he said instantly, his gaze straying to the corner where the window was displayed on the artist's easel. "It's going to look quite stunning in my home."

"Well, that's what I need to speak with you about."

She noticed Franklin check his watch. "Are you in a hurry?"

"Actually, I am. There's an appointment I have, you see. Perhaps I'll just take the window now and we can talk more tomorrow night. We'll go to dinner, how's that?"

"But I was supposed to have dinner with Mr. Laurence tomorrow night. Don't you recall?"

"Oh, yes. Of course. I've just been so busy."

Tori noticed his smile again and realized that it didn't reach his ice-blue eyes. Perhaps, in retrospect, it never did. "It doesn't matter, Franklin. That's one of the things I wanted to tell you. I won't be meeting with Mr. Laurence after all."

"Good heavens, why not?"

"I'm so busy now with restoring Rosegate and then I'll be teaching French part-time at the girl's academy in the fall. I won't have time for another position."

"Teaching? At a girl's academy? You must be joking. Tori, there's no payoff in that—"

"It will make me happy."

"Don't be silly. I'll take the window now, and then I'll stop by tomorrow morning to help you get things straight in your mind—"

Straight in my mind, thought Tori, crossing her arms over her torso. Why, this man wasn't hearing her at all. She watched him rise abruptly from the sofa.

"I am sorry about rushing off," he said walking, toward the window in the corner. "But I do have another appointment. Now, the packing material?"

Tori left the room a moment to retrieve an item from the hall table. She returned to the parlor and held it out to him.

"What's this?" he asked.

"It's an envelope. Inside it you'll find your check for fifty thousand dollars."

"Tori?"

"I'm not selling the window to you, Franklin."

"What? You're joking. You can't be serious."

"I'm not, and I can." Tori shook her head. Finally it was registering. This man didn't give a damn what she wanted unless he could twist it to his own purposes.

"But, Tori, darling . . ." He stepped closer, his voice dropping low to affect a slow seductive drawl. "Don't you remember why it is I wanted to possess this window so much? It's so I can be reminded of your lovely visage," he purred, stepping even closer, his hand reaching out to softly stroke her cheek.

Had she actually fallen for this garbage?

"Tori, the auburn-haired goddess at the center of this window . . . she reminds me so much of your own innocent beauty . . ."

"My lord, Franklin, what a load of—what did Bruce Gautreau call it the other night?—*merde!*"

"Tori!"

Suddenly Franklin's hand at her cheek felt like insect

legs brushing her face. She recoiled, stepping out from under him.

"You'll just have to accept it, Franklin. The window stays at Rosegate."

"Is it the money?" he asked, his tone magically changing from seducer to haggler. "How about I throw in another ten thousand. That should help you with your little Guest House project."

"No."

"What is it? Have you found another buyer?"

"No. Franklin, please try to understand, I won't be selling this window at *any* price. Now maybe you'd better leave," she said, turning from him and walking to the front door.

"But, Tori, don't you need the money to restore Rosegate?"

"I'll figure something out." Tori opened the door and stood waiting.

"Just . . . sell me . . . the window." The words held a barely contained fury. And for the first time, Tori saw the hard ferocity that Franklin's ice-chipped eyes were capable of.

But she wasn't budging in the least!

"No," she said. "The ghosts would never forgive me if I sold their wedding gift."

"*Ghosts?* Are you crazy?"

"Please go, Franklin."

"You're certifiable, you know that!" cried Franklin, walking through the door. "What is it, PMS week?"

Tori slammed the door hard and took a deep breath. *Good girl,* said a little voice inside of her as she flipped the locks into place and started for the stairway.

And she *did* feel good. Surprisingly good. Tori knew that keeping the window was the absolute right thing to do. And doing the right thing seemed to restore her battered soul, infusing it with a renewed energy.

Well, she would make good use of it, because right now

she had no idea how she was going to come up with the money she desperately needed to repair Rosegate.

Franklin Morgan was never so enraged in his life.

Stupid, air-brained bitch!

As he peeled away from the curb next to Rosegate and steered his Jaguar toward his downtown office, he slammed his leather-lined steering wheel with the palm of his hand. A moment later he was reaching that same hand toward his cellular phone and dialing the number of his broker.

Thanks to that giddy female he was down two points. He'd have to put off the sale of the window another day, *and* he'd have to arrange another girl for Cal Laurence.

Well, his cousin Gilbert always had a dozen girls available for Saturday night. He'd give Gil a call and have him line up the classiest of the bunch.

It must have been Gautreau. He must have gotten to her.

Franklin didn't give a crap that Gautreau had told Gil that he'd now cooperate with their operation. Franklin didn't trust that smirking bayou ass, and he wanted to get him out of the way. René Phillipe would help him, thought Franklin. Perhaps he and René could work around Gil.

Yes, and that kind of maneuvering would work for his other problem as well. Franklin was going to pay another visit to Tori Avalon. Only this time he'd be bringing his vicious little cousin René with him.

Yes, I might just have some fun after all, decided Franklin Morgan. And for the first time that week, the man's smile actually reached his cold blue eyes.

Chapter
Twenty-five

"What do you mean, they haven't been *arrested* yet?"

That morning Bruce had woken up with a splitting headache and a sense of terrible dread. It was more than just saying good-bye to Tori—more than the sum total of a battered heart and bruised ego. He felt this gloomy foreboding was the prophecy of second sight, the warning of the *traiteur de pouvoir* inside him.

By the afternoon he was certain enough to talk at length with Serafine. She had much to say to him, yet he still couldn't define the exact nature of the turbulence, only the dark clouds on the horizon—as sure a sign of a violent storm as he'd ever seen at sea.

He'd restlessly walked by Rosegate a few times today, but everything seemed fine. And then, at eight o'clock this evening, he noticed that the unmarked police car was gone.

Bruce had raced back to his apartment and immediately dialed the home number of his contact in the district attorney's office. Jack Pitot tried to explain the situation, but Bruce was livid.

"Listen, Bruce, calm down. The Vonderants will be picked up soon, but right now we're waiting for some final evidence."

"What are you talking about? I thought this was all going to be wrapped up in less than twenty-four hours after my meeting with those lowlifes."

"No. There's something else. I just found out there's going to be a meeting in the next few days between a Chicago businessman and a contact of the Vonderants. Once that takes place, we'll have a connection to a major organized crime operation. The FBI's involved now, Bruce, and we've agreed not to jeopardize their surveillance. We can't move locally until they give us the go-ahead."

"I don't like it, Jack. I have a bad feeling. You've got to understand—"

"You're perfectly safe, Bruce. We've got enough bugs in place to make an exterminator's convention gag."

"A bug won't stop a bullet."

"But I'm telling you, you're not in danger. Gil Vonderant loves you. He's convinced you're going to join their operation. The man's even planning which buildings to vandalize in the next few months to get you some nice juicy jobs—"

"It's not *me* I'm worried about."

"Then who?"

"I already told you at the beginning of this call, Victoria Avalon."

"Victoria. Right, right, the girlfriend. Listen, as long as you're safe, she's safe. The threat was to use her to get to you. And they've got you on board. So relax."

"But what about the protection you promised me for her? The cop's gone, Jack."

"Sorry, Bruce, but it's Friday night in the Quarter. The department needs every body on patrol, and we couldn't justify the protection any longer. Believe me, we have witnesses in much worse positions right now than you and Ms. Avalon."

"This other stuff," said Bruce, still trying to get a handle on his feelings of coming danger. "The Chicago business-man. Who is he? And who is the Vonderant contact exactly?"

Bruce listened to a lot of hemming and hawing, but finally Jack admitted that he couldn't talk. "I'm just not authorized to release the information, Bruce. Understand?"

"Is this line bugged?"

"What do you think?"

"I think that I'm getting pretty raw. And when I'm raw, I like to go down to the *Acme Oyster House* for a few raw oysters. Understand *that?*"

"Yeah."

"Then I'm leaving. *Now.*"

Bruce slammed down the phone and grabbed his wallet. He hoped to hell the assistant district attorney was at the bar when he got there or he'd be hand-delivering a plate of raw oysters to the ADA's house—and making sure they ended up down the man's throat.

Shell and all.

For most of the evening Tori had been on the sofa reading back over Marina's diary. She felt the century-old chronicle should rightfully be donated to the Historic New Orleans Collection, but she was pretty sure she could sell the translation rights to a small press. It wouldn't be much money, but it would be enough to get started on the third floor.

Tori sighed, not knowing what she was going to do about the costly exterior restoration. That would be a major job, and she'd need the approval of the *Vieux Carré* Commission, as well.

For the twentieth time today Tori felt her acute need for Bruce Gautreau. Oh, she could always hire another contractor, but she knew that Bruce's work was special to Rosegate. It was obvious that he had a unique relationship with every building he worked on, as if each were a living thing.

Tori could just see him entering his next tattered, run-down structure, noting its unique characteristics, appreciating its strengths as well as its flaws, sensing the many lives it held within its walls for decades—or even centuries.

She recalled the first conversation they'd had in the backyard of this house, how he'd told her about *animism* and the spirits living in all things. She hadn't understood him then. But now she leaned back on the sofa and smiled, happy in knowing what lived here at Rosegate.

Tori reached into her left pocket and brought out a small cloth bag. *Men wear* gris-gris *on their right side, women on their left.* Something small and wet dampened her cheek as she turned the worn *gris-gris* bag around in her hands.

She would always cherish what Bruce had freely given her.

Maybe I'll take up the violin again, thought Tori with a smile as she brushed at a tear. Maybe she'd be good at it this time around, or maybe she wouldn't. But, somehow, she knew that this time around, she would find joy in it.

The sudden sound of the doorbell startled her.

It was just past nine o'clock and she wasn't expecting anyone. As she rose from the couch, a seed of hope stirred in her heart that Bruce would be on the other side of the door.

She cracked it open. And the hope died.

"Franklin."

"Good evening, Tori," he said, peeking across the chain on the partially opened door. "I'd like to speak with you."

"Aren't we finished speaking?"

"No, Tori. You owe me at least one more conversation."

"Franklin, I don't owe you a thing."

"Please, Tori. I thought we were friends."

Tori shook her head. She'd *never* get rid of him if she didn't really set him straight. *Don't do it, Tori. Don't let him in,* counseled a little voice inside of her. But she overruled the voice. Part of her wanted to finish this for good, and she wasn't going to hide behind a door chain to do it. She closed the door, slipped off the chain, and opened it to him.

"Fine, then, Franklin, come on in."

He came in and shut the door behind him, then took a few steps into the entryway, but Tori stopped him from going any farther. "Right here, Franklin. Talk to me here."

"I want you to see reason, Tori. That window is an important investment for me, I won't lie to you. I'll offer you seventy thousand dollars. Take it or leave it."

"Franklin, I'll tell you again. And I hope you hear me this time. The window belongs at Rosegate. It is *not* for sale. And neither am I, by the way, so please leave."

"Seventy-five."

"That's it! Franklin, this is borderline harassment, and if you don't leave, then I'll be forced to call the police."

"I see, Tori. I suppose, then, you give me no choice."

No choice. The words stayed with Tori even as she was beginning to feel a sense of triumph. After all, Franklin was finally turning to go. But then something registered. The words she'd just been rereading earlier in Marina's diary:

John M— did not sound happy, and though his words were that of acquiescence, it sounded to my ears more like a threat. . . . "I suppose, then, you give me no choice. . . ."

John M., thought Tori. *M.* As in *Morgan.*

The understanding came from deep inside as a shiver of dread registered in her body. Tori watched what happened next in a kind of paralyzed slow motion. Franklin slipped on a pair of black leather gloves, and then he opened the front door. But he wasn't leaving, he was gesturing in the darkness, as if he were inviting the black of night to step inside.

But something else entered instead. Or rather, someone else. A young man with a crew cut and a black T-shirt moved through the door, then closed and locked it behind him. His hands were wearing the same kind of black gloves as Franklin's.

The moment she understood, Tori turned and ran for the hall phone. She'd actually gotten two of the three emergency numbers pressed, but after the 9 and 1, she felt a blow to her body.

The young man had tackled her roughly, slamming her hard to the polished wood floor. Tori tried to struggle up again, but as she reached a sitting position, she felt a painful yank to her head. Her attacker had grabbed a fistful of hair to control her, his other arm was now clamped tightly around her arms and waist.

Another painful pull to her head forced her to look up at the man towering over her. Franklin was smiling as he unfolded a switchblade. Its cold metal reflected back her own panic as he took the phone cord in his hand and cut it in two.

Tori wasn't nearly as frightened by the severed cord as the fact that Franklin's smile, for the first time she'd known him, finally reached his eyes.

"You see, Tori, we could have avoided all this," he said as he demonstrated the razor-sharpness of the blade by running it along his own finger. The mere touch opened his flesh and a drop of bright crimson appeared. "But you went and forced me to make a mess."

Franklin licked the blood from his finger as the young man restraining her laughed. Why did he look familiar to her?

Think, Tori.

"I know who you are," she said abruptly. "You're that Vonderant punk—"

"Oh, now, did y'hear dat, cuz? She gone an' ID'd me. Whatcha gonna do, honey, tell the cops?" The young man laughed harshly as he brought her roughly to her feet.

Cuz, Tori realized. Franklin Morgan was the Vonderants' cousin? My God, why hadn't Bruce warned her? *He probably doesn't even know.* But he *had* warned her to steer clear of Franklin—and she'd been too blind to listen. Now it was too late. . . .

"Just take her in there, René," said Franklin.

Tori's head was swimming as René pulled her into the parlor. She tried to fight him, but he was too strong. He was also an obvious pro at this. He'd shoved her down in a high-backed chair and began binding her hands behind its back before she could even budge.

"All right, René, let's do this by the numbers," said Franklin. "Make it look like a break-in and"—he smiled at Tori—"assault."

"You wanna watch dat part, right, Franklin?"

"Don't I always? Now gag her and then get upstairs to find any pitiful jewelry or other valuables—"

"Franklin, I *know* de routine!"

"Good. Then get to it. I'll take a look at the kitchen stove and start something . . . cooking."

Cooking. What did that mean? *Fire* . . . Tori closed her eyes as they left her. There had to be some way to help herself and save Rosegate. *Think, Tori, think!*

She took a deep breath and concentrated, trying her best to open her mind. *Help me . . . please . . . I need your help. . . .*

Friday night in the Quarter meant that legs were faster than wheels. Bruce Gautreau was using the former now to move quickly through the drinkers and partiers spilling out onto Bourbon and Royal streets.

He had to get to Rosegate as quickly as humanly possible.

Ten minutes ago Jack Pitot had sat down with him at the Acme Oyster House. After some roundabout conversing, Bruce had found a few choice threats to get the ADA to spill what he knew about the Vonderants' operation. The second he heard Franklin Morgan's name, Bruce was on his feet.

"Jack, I'm gone. Victoria Avalon's in danger—"

"What? How do you know—"

"I just know. Now, listen to me, get a police car over to Rosegate. I'm going there now."

"But—"

"Do it!"

Bruce had run at top speed through the crowded streets

of the Quarter, and now that he was making the final turn that led to Rosegate, he found himself looking up at the place from beneath the glowing gas lamp on the corner.

Breathing hard, he saw that the mansion's lights were flickering violently on and off—first in the attic, then on the third floor, then on the second. It was as if the electricity in the house had gone haywire.

"The spirits," whispered Bruce, and he was running again, this time with the certain awareness that the two ghostly lovers were signaling for help.

"Hey, Franklin, knock it off with de lights!" called René near the top of the staircase.

"What?"

"De lights, dey goin' on an' off up here."

"I'm not doing a damn thing. It's probably just this dump's wiring. Now get to work."

A glimmer of hope penetrated Tori's terrified mind.

"Damn! One o' de hall lightbulbs jus' broke!"

That's when the hint of a smile touched Tori's gagged mouth.

It has to be them, thought Tori. *It has to!*

Chapter
Twenty-six

Marina and Robert had been resting in the attack when they'd heard Tori's weak call for help. At a speed faster than any living person could fathom, the spirits of Rosegate were awake, their raging energy wreaking havoc on the house's electrical system.

"*Robert, these men are daring to threaten our Victoria. And they're both of the same blood as John Morgan!*"

"*I know, my dearest.*"

"*And look!*" cried Marina. "*That one is invading the master bedroom—our bedroom!*"

"*I see,*" said Robert with a dangerously calm control. "*Let me take care of this one, Marina. I am only now beginning to realize my full power. . . .*"

René Vonderant had flipped on the light in the master bedroom only to watch it flicker wildly. He cursed as he went to the bed and yanked a pillowcase from one of Tori's

pillows. Swiftly he began to move through the room, opening drawers and shoving anything of value inside.

When he got to the mirrored armoire, he stopped cold.
Reflected in the glass was a tall, blond man. For a second
René thought it was Bruce Gautreau. With a smirk on his
face, the young man turned, ready to take care of the man.

What happened next tore a scream from René Vonderant's throat that sounded like all the terrors in a chamber
of horrors.

"What in hell?" Franklin Morgan came out of the kitchen
with his gun drawn. In another moment René was tumbling
down the staircase, blood dripping from his head and pouring over his face.

"René, who's up there?"

"A g-g-ghost. I saw a g-g-g-ghost. It attacked me!"

"What? Have you been drinking? How many times have
I told you not to drink before a job—"

"I saw a ghost!" he screamed. "And I'm getting out of
here!"

"Not before we finish the job, you're not," said Franklin,
pointing the gun at his cousin's head. "Got it?"

René blinked as he stared down the barrel of the gun.

"Now, get a hold of yourself," warned Franklin, putting
the gun back in his shoulder holster.

René nodded his acquiescence as he wiped his own
blood from his eyes.

"I've set the fire smoldering in the kitchen," said
Franklin, "so let's just finish this quickly, get the window,
and get out. And don't bleed on anything, for God's sake."

While Franklin was busy with René in the hallway, Tori
was busy concentrating again. *My ropes . . . cut my
ropes . . . free my hands . . .*

Miraculously she felt the ropes severed in one quick
slice. Her hands freed, Tori lunged for the phone tucked
away in the far corner of the parlor. She dialed 911 and was
able to shout fire and the address before she felt the blow to
her stomach.

She was knocked to the floor, and when she looked up again, she saw Franklin cutting his second phone cord of the night.

"Take care of her," he barked to René.

Tori was on her feet and running for the door in a heart-beat, but now René was flying at her, tackling her to the ground. She turned to see his black-fisted glove raised high above her head and ready to knock her unconscious. Tori closed her eyes, bracing for the blow. . . .

But none came.

She heard a hard clang, then a moan, and then felt the stone-cold weight of a body on top of hers.

When she opened her eyes, Tori saw a heavy cat-shaped brass vase lying next to René's bleeding, unconscious head. But that vase had been sitting on a table ten feet away in the entry hall. She'd put it there herself just last week, after rescuing it from the tarnish of years in the attic.

She looked over at Franklin. His mouth was agape, his face chalk white. "How did you do that?" he whispered. And then he brought his gun up. "Never mind. It doesn't matter now."

Tori tried to struggle out from under René's body, but the gun was already pointing straight at her and going off.

She expected to feel the bullet burning its way through some part of her body, but a moment later, the gun was no longer in Franklin's hand. An invisible force had knocked it loose and propelled it into a swift slide across the floor.

Tori pulled herself clear of René's body and lunged for the gun. But Franklin was lunging, too, and in another mo-ment he was on top of her.

"Oh, now, let's just do this the old-fashioned way." He reached for the heavy brass vase and lifted it high over her head.

"I'm looking forward to it!" came a voice from a tall window that had just opened across the room.

"What the—?" Suddenly the brass vase was plucked from Franklin's hand and, for the second time that night, levitating miraculously in the air as Bruce Gautreau launched himself at Franklin Morgan.

Tori rolled away from the pair as Bruce used his fists to land some good "old-fashioned" punches to Franklin's face and body, but it was that levitating antique cat-shaped vase that finally swung down by no visible hand to knock Morgan unconscious.

Smoke began to filter into the parlor, and Bruce realized the place was on fire.

"We have to get out of here," said Bruce.

"But the house!" cried Tori, turning to see if she could put out the fire herself.

"No, Tori, come on!" Taking her in his arms, Bruce began to forcefully guide her toward the door-size open window.

"Wait, the kittens!" Tori turned. "Cleo! Tony!"

At once the kittens came scampering down the staircase. Tori and Bruce each scooped a kitten into an arm.

"Okay," said Bruce, "now let's *go!*"

As Bruce and Tori got to the street, they heard the siren of the fire truck careening around the corner.

"What will happen to the spirits?" asked Tori in a whisper as she gazed at the smoke now billowing from the back of the house.

Bruce's own tense features reflected Tori's secret fear. "I don't know, *chère,* I don't know. . . ."

Two hours later the last of the New Orleans Fire Department emergency trucks finally pulled away from the curb of Rosegate.

Tori and Bruce walked through the miraculously undamaged front door and closed it behind them.

As it turned out, most of the house was saved. The kitchen and the den on the first floor were completely ruined. Some of the elegant wraparound porch had been destroyed as well, but Bruce had assured her that it could all be rebuilt.

"Well," said Tori, putting the kittens down on the floor.

"At least I had the satisfaction of watching René Vonderant and Franklin Morgan being taken away by the police."

"Yeah," said Bruce. "Now they can add attempted murder to their list of crimes."

Then he turned to face her, his hands brushing back the wild strands of auburn hair from her exhausted face. "Are you sure you're okay?" he whispered.

"I'm sure," said Tori.

Do you want me to stay with you tonight? The question lingered in Bruce's mind as he waited for the right moment to ask it.

"Bruce, I *do* want you to stay tonight, but I know it will only make it harder when you finally do move on. . . ."

Bruce blinked, then shook his head. *He hadn't asked that question out loud. How could she—*

"I can see it in your eyes," said Tori. "It's plain enough to me. Everything is now, unfortunately. . . ."

"What do you mean, 'unfortunately'?"

"I mean that I can see in you, feel in you, that you're convinced we'd be miserable in a life together. And I don't want you to be miserable. I love you with all my heart, all my soul, and that's exactly why I'm letting you go. I want, more than anything, to know that you're happy."

"Tori, I've never heard you talk like this—"

"Yeah, well, me, either. But I think I'm finally understanding something. I wanted love to be some neat, easy road, one guaranteed not to hold any heartache. But there are two paths a person can take in life as far as I can see— the path of the heart that holds great risk, great pain, and great happiness; or the path of protection that seems easy, but in the end holds the worst thing of all—"

"What's that?"

"Regret. You see, my mother chose the path of regret, and I feel sorry for her. But I swear I won't regret mine."

"And what about us, then? Do you regret us?"

"I don't regret loving you," she whispered, touching his cheek. "And I'll never forget you. You helped me, finally, to see so much . . . so much of what had been invisible to me."

Bruce nodded his head, a wisp of a smile on his lips. *You're sure of all this?* he asked silently.

"I'm sure."

Tori watched him go. She tried to keep the tears back as she closed the door, but they came anyway as she climbed the stairs, the kittens scampering after her as she headed straight for bed.

"Tori . . . Tori . . ."

She awakened on the ornate four-poster bed in the center of an ethereal room lit by a dozen flickering candle flames. A man's lips were softly touching her own, and when he raised his head, she was looking into the liquid brown eyes she had come to read so very well.

"Bruce . . . what are you doing here?" she whispered, not entirely certain that this wasn't a dream.

"I knew, *chère,* the moment you started reading my mind."

"Bruce?"

"I saw Serafine earlier today."

"You did?"

"She told me that when people love each other, they don't need to be psychic to read each other's minds."

"She did?"

"I didn't believe her—"

"But she's right," said Tori, rubbing her tired eyes. "Now that I think about it, Hestia and Richard were always finishing each other's sentences . . . coming up with answers to each other's questions."

"*Oui.* So answer this question, Tori: Will you marry me?"

"What?" Tori blinked. "Am I dreaming? I must be . . ."

"You aren't dreaming. This is real. And I would have asked you earlier, when I knew, but I needed to go back to my apartment to find something. You see, after all these years of searching, I wanted to do this right."

Taking her left hand in his, he slipped a beautiful emerald-encrusted band on her left ring finger. The carefully crafted golden circle glowed in the candlelight, the one-of-a-kind emerald design sparkling as brilliantly as her own eyes.

"My God, Bruce," whispered Tori, tears blurring her vision. "This ring is exquisite."

"It was a family heirloom, the Le Pellitier side. No matter how poor we got, my mother never parted with it. *Maman* left it to me in her will with a note that said I should give it only to the one I wish to be by my side through all eternity."

"And do you wish it, Bruce? Do you really wish it?"

"Oui, *chère*, I do."

"Then, my love, so do I."

Epilogue

The promise of springtime had once again come to New Orleans, and nowhere was it more evident than on the rear grounds of Rosegate.

Sweet smells of flower blossoms filled the air at the elegant Avalon-Gautreau garden wedding, along with the scents of some delectable French cooking, courtesy of Duchamp's gifted Chef Pierre.

Many guests commented how positively radiant both bride and groom looked as they stood under the white rose bower, exchanging vows of love. Other guests discussed the stunning restoration of the magnificent Victorian mansion. Still others commented on the newlyweds' good fortune at finding an Edgar Degas painting, perfectly preserved in the dusty depths of Rosegate's attic.

The Impressionist's lost masterwork of the New Orleans French Market brought a record amount at auction. The small fortune easily funded Rosegate's rebirth, with enough left over to establish the couple's foundation for historical restoration within the French Quarter.

But, for all there was to enjoy and discuss at this blessed wedding, the most curious was the whispering among a small group of girls—students of the bride, who taught them French at a nearby girls' academy.

At first the girls were vocally insisting that the faces of the radiant newlyweds were somehow being reflected in the French doors on the second floor. But when they looked again, they saw that it was not a reflection at all, but the now-famous ghosts of Rosegate.

Of course, few adults believed the girls. But the bride and groom had the strangest reaction when the little group loudly claimed that they had seen the ghosts appear just below the mansion's gorgeous stained-glass window.

"Of course you did," said the bride and groom. The pair raised their champagne glasses to the invisible couple, explaining to the girls that just because everyone doesn't see a thing, doesn't mean it isn't there.

Then a secret smile passed between the living couple. It was a smile of love, of joy, and of relief, because both Victoria and Vianney at last were certain that the spirits of Marina and Robert were seeing their destiny fulfilled—a fact that would finally help everybody at Rosegate rest in peace.

Up in the master bedroom the airy essence of Marina Duchamp was delightfully watching the newlyweds' toast. *"Are you watching, Robert? Isn't it wonderful—first, the house so beautifully restored and now this beautiful wedding!"*

"Yes, we were lucky they finally answered our nightly haunting in the attic and found Edgar's painting."

"What was lucky, Robert, was your father making you preserve the piece so well within glass."

"Well, after all, Father was a personal friend—and he had a hunch Edgar's work would stand the test of time."

"Are you at all disappointed that it had to be sold?"

"Of course not. It's much better off now that it will be on display. Edgar's work deserves to be widely appreciated."

"Well, I am relieved that they did not sell the stained glass. Your wedding gift to me belongs here at Rosegate. And it does look stunning in the master bedroom, all those rich deep colors backlit by the sun."

"As long as you are happy, my love."

"Oh, Robert, I am as happy as the newlyweds in the garden."

"And I am as happy as we were on our wedding day," seconded Robert. *"In fact, my darling Marina, I believe that we will be this happy always, as long as we are together."*

"Then we will be, my love. Through all eternity."